Behold . . .

Meet Viviana Fuentes. She's dead. But her facsimile lives on . . .

Etelka, the house whisper-girl, is a breath of fresh air, magical, mysterious and a little bit dangerous.

The night the circus freaks ran riot won't end until Marizella, the sword swallower's daughter, gets her magic knife back.

Houston, we have no problem at all. What we do have is one remarkable hero on a courageous personal mission.

Journey . . .

Every man, woman and child on Earth has fallen victim to the plague. A Planet Builder, launched into deep space, is on a mission to recreate the human race.

Earth is scorching hot, cities turned to deserts. The price of survival is brutally high and terrible choices must be made in the name of the greater good.

Pay the price of admission and you can climb into the cockpit and play dogfight to your heart's content. . . . But beware.

Explore . . .

Get to know GN 722 . . . affectionately known as Gina. She's the bomb. . . .

Hungry nightmares are eager to take flesh-and-blood form and devour all in their path.

Seeing into the future isn't all it's cracked up to be, especially if all you see is betrayal, greed, lust and war. . . .

Discover . . .

All knowledge, history and literature are strictly controlled, but one book could change all that.

He is their world. He is their universe. He is their god. He is Owen, and they are the nano-organisms saving him from certain death.

What happens if you create a machine with a heart and mind of its own?

What Has Been Said About the L. RON HUBBARD *Presents* Writers of the Future *Anthologies*

"These stories push the boundaries—entertaining, creative and greatly varied. A feast for short story lovers."

—Gregory Benford, Author
Writers of the Future Contest judge

"When new science fiction writers ask me what they ought to do first, I tell them to send their best work to the Writers of the Future. The Contest is one of the best things to happen to science fiction since the Golden Age. . . ."

—Jerry Pournelle, Author
Writers of the Future Contest judge

"Judging the Writers of the Future Contest is the highlight of my reading year—fresh insights, unexpected plot turns, and the absolute joy of discovering a new star in the SF&F universe."

—Doug Beason, Author
Writers of the Future Contest judge

"The Contests are amazing competitions because really, you've nothing to lose and it provides good positive encouragement to anyone who wins. Judging the entries is always a lot of fun and inspiring. I wish I had something like this when I was getting started—very positive and cool."

—Bob Eggleton, Artist
Illustrators of the Future Contest judge

"Writers of the Future is a terrific program . . ."

—Terry Brooks, Author

". . . continues to please thousands of readers who become the audience for yet another generation of sci-fi writers."

—Orson Scott Card, Author
Writers of the Future Contest judge

"The Illustrators of the Future Contest is one of the best opportunities a young artist will ever get. You have nothing to lose and a lot to win."

—Frank Frazetta, Artist
Illustrators of the Future Contest judge

"A very generous legacy from L. Ron Hubbard—a fine, fine fiction writer—for the writers of the future."

—Anne McCaffrey, Author
Writers of the Future Contest judge

"Writers of the Future has a record of nurturing and discovering writers who have gone on to make their mark in the science fiction field. Long may it continue!"

—Neil Gaiman, Author

"These contests provide a wonderful safety net of professionals for young artists and writers. And it's due to the fact that L. Ron Hubbard was willing to lend a hand."

—Judith Miller, Artist
Illustrators of the Future Contest judge

"Some of the best SF of the future comes from Writers of the Future and you can find it in this book."

—David Hartwell, Editor

"The aspect I personally value most highly about the program is that of working with my fellow professionals, both artists *and* writers, to accomplish a worthwhile goal of giving tomorrow's artists and writers recognition and advancement in the highly competitive field of imaginative endeavor—the only existing program that does this."

—Stephen Hickman, Artist
Illustrators of the Future Contest judge

"The L. Ron Hubbard Writers of the Future Contest has carried out the noble mission of nurturing new science fiction and fantasy writers . . . with resounding success."

—Eric Kotani, Author
Writers of the Future Contest judge

"L. Ron Hubbard's Writers of the Future anthologies are a road map—they show the future of science fiction by showcasing tomorrow's writers today."

—Jay Lake, Author
Writers of the Future Contest winner

"Looking back now it is easy to see that winning the Writers of the Future was a watershed moment in my career."

—Steven Savile, Author
Writers of the Future Contest winner

"Here's skill and storytelling fervor aplenty—these writers of the future have already arrived."

—Robert Silverberg, Author
Writers of the Future Contest judge

"I only wish that there had been an Illustrators of the Future competition forty-five years ago. What a blessing it would have been to a young artist with a little bit of talent, a Dutch name, and heart full of desire."

—H. R. Van Dongen, Artist
Illustrators of the Future Contest judge

"This Contest has changed the face of science fiction."

—Dean Wesley Smith, Author
Writers of the Future Contest winner

"Winning the Contest was my first validation that I would have a career. I entered five times before winning and it gave me something I could reach and attain."

—K. D. Wentworth, Author
Writers of the Future Contest judge

"A first-rate collection of stories and illustrations."

—*Booklist*

"Not only is the writing excellent . . . it is also extremely varied. There's a lot of hot new talent in it."

—*Locus Magazine*

"The most enduring forum to showcase new talent in the genre.

"The series continues to be a powerful statement of faith as well as direction in American Science Fiction."

—*Publishers Weekly*

L. Ron Hubbard PRESENTS *Writers of the Future*

VOLUME XXIV

L. Ron Hubbard PRESENTS

Writers of the Future

VOLUME XXIV

The year's thirteen best tales from

the *Writers of the Future*

international writers' program

Illustrated by winners in

the *Illustrators of the Future*

international illustrators' program

With essays on writing & illustration by

L. Ron Hubbard / Rebecca Moesta / Cliff Nielsen

Edited by Algis Budrys

GALAXY PRESS, LLC

Interior Design: Jerry Kelly

This anthology contains works of fiction. Names, characters, places and incidents are either the product of the authors' imaginations or are used fictitiously. Any resemblance to actual events or locales or persons, living or dead, is entirely coincidental. Opinions expressed by nonfiction essayists are their own.

ISBN-10 1-59212-374-0
ISBN-13 978-1-59212-374-2
Library of Congress Control Number: 2008906415
First Edition Paperback
Printed in the United States of America

CONTENTS

Why There Are the Contests

BY ALGIS BUDRYS (1931–2008)

Algis Budrys, editor of Writers of the Future, *was born in Königsberg, East Prussia, on January 9, 1931. He became interested in science fiction at the age of six, shortly after coming to America when a landlady slipped him a copy of the* New York Journal-American *Sunday funnies.*

Algis began selling steadily to the top magazine markets at the age of twenty-one, while living in Great Neck, Long Island. He sold his first novel in 1953 and produced eight more novels including Who?, Rogue Moon, Michaelmas *and* Hard Landing *and three short story collections. In addition to writing, he was very accomplished as an editor, having been the editor in chief of Regency Books, Playboy Press and all the titles at Woodall's Trailer Travel publications.*

In 1983, Algis was asked by L. Ron Hubbard to help with a new writing contest for aspiring writers. This was a request he took to heart. Not only did Algis assist with the contest judging, he used his well-known skills as editor for the Writers of the Future *anthology. He attended scores of science fiction conventions, speaking on panels during the day about the Writers of the Future, and again at night discussing the Contest with many of the top names in science fiction and fantasy to bring them on board as contest judges.*

Algis believed in the Contest and in what it would do for Science Fiction and Fantasy. Now, after almost a quarter of a century, Algis' faith has certainly proven itself. Winning and being published in Writers of the Future *has become a goal that virtually every aspiring writer of speculative fiction seeks, knowing that even Contest finalists now find previously closed doors opened in the publishing world.*

ALGIS BUDRYS

The following introduction to this volume was written by Algis. The respect he held for L. Ron Hubbard as a professional writer and for creating these Contests, and the pride he felt for every Writers of the Future *volume and the new winners they announced, are all here in this, his last essay: Why There Are the Contests.*

Why There Are the Contests

From his earliest years, L. Ron Hubbard was a man of extraordinary talents. Long before he began writing fiction for the "pulp" magazines of the 1930s, he had been to China, Europe and South America as a very young man. He lived a highly peripatetic life from the outset. His father was an important naval officer, and Ron sometimes, but not always, followed his father's various postings. Rather, what led Ron to visit so broadly was a family tradition—one of independence and adventure, not of sitting and waiting for some opportunity to come along at its own pace.

Wherever he went, he found mentors. In China, it was a court magician. On a passage through the Panama Canal, it was another naval officer, who had studied under Sigmund Freud. In his early youth, he was adopted as a blood brother into an Indian tribe. Time after time, and incredibly broadly, he was in the position of learning a new specialty from an expert. So it was natural, when he was a grown man and an expert himself, to seek out younger persons and offer them a way to make themselves known as writers and illustrators of fiction.

Ron had for years published how-to articles in the writers' trade magazines, such as *Writers Digest.* And he had sponsored a contest, over the air, while broadcasting in Alaska. But it was in the early 1980s that he made the greatest commitment to his past, and the field's future, with his Writers of the Future Contest, with its structure of meaningful prizes and its annual anthology.

To some of us, the Contest looked like a suppositional thing. After all, no one could predict how many entries we would get, or how worthwhile they would be. The Contest was restricted to people who had published very little . . . and it still is, as a glance through the rules in the back pages of this volume will show you. The writers published here are, exactly as stated, the writers of the future—total unknowns, taking their first steps to what will become, in many cases, major careers.

The Contest—the Contests, with the addition of the equally successful Illustrators of the Future Contest a few years later—proved to be wildly successful, as you can see from the fact that this is the twenty-fourth in this annual series, that its contents over the years have contained a plethora of now-famous names, and that its presence in the field has grown with each passing year. (If you need further reassurance on this point, please see the quotes on the subject, printed in the opening pages of this volume.)

And please be sure that L. Ron Hubbard knew from the beginning that this would be the case. He did not ever start something that he did not look ahead to its outcome. For twenty-four years I have been a judge of the Writers of the Future Contest, and the editor of this anthology, and I have learned as much. Welcome to this latest volume. You literally hold the future in your hands.

A Man in the Moon

written by

Dr. Philip Edward Kaldon

illustrated by

WILLIAM RUHLIG

ABOUT THE AUTHOR

Born in upstate New York, educated at Northwestern and Michigan Tech, Dr. Philip Edward Kaldon teaches physics at Western Michigan University in Kalamazoo by day, while aspiring to write "The Great Science Fiction Romantic Epic" in the wee hours. Since he began submitting to Writers of the Future in June 2002, our very own "Dr. Phil" has collected three Finalists (including this year's published Finalist "A Man in the Moon"), two Semi-Finalists, ten Quarter-Finalists, four Honorable Mentions, plus four plain old rejects and one lost-in-the-mail.

During the summer of 2004, Dr. Phil spent six amazing weeks sweltering in an East Lansing sorority house—part of the thirty-seventh Clarion Science Fiction and Fantasy Writers' Workshop—along with then-future twenty-first WOTF Grand Prize winner John Schoffstall and WOTF volume XXIV winner Al Bogdan (who also appears in this volume). While experiencing "lake effect" snow out on Michigan's Great Lakes during his first half-century on the planet, Dr. Phil says he also managed to find his wife working at the Northwestern University Library. Currently both are held hostage in West Michigan by a set of three cats from an alternate universe where felines rule.

ABOUT THE ILLUSTRATOR

William Ruhlig's lifelong passion for art seems to be blooming. Having completed secondary education at Pretoria Boys High School, in South Africa, he is now studying information design at the University of Pretoria and already knows that "cover artist" is his calling. That's because he has always been interested in art and continually inspired by the great science fiction authors, movies and science fiction artists around the world. The cover art of books has always impacted him, drawing him into a world hidden in the pages beneath the cover.

But it's not just the cover art that attracts him. William admits that he loves reading; in fact, he can't stop. It fuels his imagination as does watching and immersing himself in science fiction and learning about the actual sciences. William loves the way science fiction has shaped our world and been shaped by technologies. "Don't judge a book by its cover; perhaps, yes, but also perhaps be inspired by it" is William's philosophy.

A Man in the Moon

"Zip up," the doctor told the older man.

"You don't look too happy there," the astronaut said, obliging by zipping his jumpsuit back up. His bright blue eyes twinkled with some secret amusement.

The two men—longtime friends—made quite a study in contrasts. Dr. Richard Hellebore stood five foot seven and while not considered clinically overweight, still exhibited something of a middle-aged thickening of the waist. Most of his short black hair had thinned away long ago. Only forty-seven, Dr. Hellebore had once been married and a family man, but his work and research as a NASA flight surgeon cost him both marriage and children. Sixty-two-year-old Captain Gene Fisher-Hall was ex-Navy, reached six-two when he stood up straight, and sported a thick gray-blond mustache which matched the wavy hair on top. Still comfortably photogenic for an astronaut, Gene came from San Francisco, but his accent had migrated to a decidedly Southern flavor—hard to place—somewhere from Texas to Tennessee to West Virginia. Perfect for a pilot.

"Gene—I've always told you straight."

"And I appreciated it, Dick. But you don't look like you've got happy news—so just say it."

"You're dying."

The older man laughed and adjusted his collar. "We're *all* dyin', Dickie Bird. Jest a matter of time."

"I'm serious."

"I know you're serious." He zipped up his cuffs and snapped over the ends, then strapped his big pilot's watch over his wrist. "I know you're serious, Dick. Fact is, I know I'm dyin', too. I've got NDC—it was jest a matter of time before you quacks over here found out about it."

NDC was common shorthand for NODC—Non-Operable Dispersed Cancer. The medical literature described NODC as a series of new diseases endemic from living in a modern, technological age. Exposure to some inadvertent cocktail of environmental chemicals, outgassing of toxins from the warm electronics which surrounded everyone every day—research suggested both had a role. Either way it was a new, not well understood clinical condition killing eleven hundred Americans a year and some ten thousand around the world.

And here was Gene Fisher-Hall joking about it. The man who had more time in the Block 700 and 800 third-gen shuttles and was certainly among the leaders in both orbital and lunar habitat living. All those close quarters with minimal fresh air. Hellebore hated to think that Gene was just the first in the astronaut corps, but how could one tell?

"You know there isn't a thing I can do for you," Hellebore said bluntly.

"I know."

"The N-O stands for Non-Operable."

"Dickie," Gene said in a sterner voice. "I said *I know*."

The doctor folded his arms and looked at him for a moment. "How long, Gene?"

The astronaut shrugged and slipped into his flight boots, then Velcroed the straps over. "Five, six months."

"You've made four runs since then!"

Gene held up a hand with all the fingers spread out. "Five. That's five A-plus-plus missions, Dickie Bird. So don't you even *mention* the ground-word."

"I've got to—it's the rules."

Gene stood up and placed his right hand on the doctor's shoulder. "Dick, the rules gotta change." He pointed up at an angle toward the ceiling, but that wasn't really where he was pointing. "If we're goin' up there, we're goin' up there to live. There's no other way, Dickie. Otherwise, it's just some sort of a temporary fraternity job for hotshot young pilots. Spring Break on the Moon—come home an' give yer Mom a moon rock. No, it's got to be *more* than that, so much more."

"That's a nice speech, Gene. Rehearse it long?" Hellebore asked, unfazed. "Because it doesn't change the cold medical facts."

"We're going to go up there, do our jobs, get sick, injured, even killed—and sometimes we're just plain gonna die. No way around it. That big moon base plan Jim Marshall's workin' on? The one we're building right now? You know I've spent years on it, too. Even before we drop the first modules and assemble the first kit, I'd know my way 'round the damned place blindfolded."

"I know you've worked hard . . ."

"Dickie, we are *so* close," Gene held up two fingers

nearly touching. "No way am I not participatin' in the next step of the greatest adventure in human history."

"It's a role for others to play."

"No way!"

"There'll be plenty for a man of your experience to do on the ground."

The older man held up a hand in a stop sign. "Dickie—shut up. I'm havin' my say now."

"Okay, okay." Dr. Hellebore knew Gene well enough not to argue.

"I'll tell you right now what's missing from the public version of the plan and that's what goes into Grid L-37. Now *you* know what Grid L-37 is, don't you, Dickie? And the chaplain knows—because when he goes up there, he'll have to consecrate it. L-37 is the cemetery, ain't it? Gotta be where old spacemen go, and by God it's where *I'm* gonna go, Dickie. I've got one or two years of prime ability even *with* this disease, which is a whole lot of missions. Domes 1 and 2 will be up and hotshot pilots like me are gonna move in. Come on, man, I'm doing you a *favor,*" he clapped the doctor on the arm. "After I'm buried, that'll free up a prime first-class housing unit."

"Gene, this isn't a joke."

"Dickie, I am as serious as a coffin," Gene said. "I'm only gonna be nice to you because you're an old friend. Despite the fact that you can ground me in the blink of an eye, I've actually *liked* you all these years. I can't say that for most of the quacks I've seen in the Navy, Air Force or NASA. But what do you want me to do? Break down and cry *boo-hoo*? Go back to my nice little house in the suburbs and blow my brains out? Move into some Florida retirement home and live out the . . . rest of my days with the other dying old geezers? You sure as goddamn don't want me to stay in Houston riding a desk. I'm a spaceman and I'm a pilot. *Baaad* combination. Means I'm in the top 99.99 percentile physical fitness of all NDC patients and my brain ain't made of jelly. It means *No* is negotiable. I'm going up there to live, Dickie. You gotta let us live. Hell, nobody's ever *had* NDC in space before."

"Gene, you can't. What if you have an episode?"

"I'll see a doctor."

"Gene . . ."

"What if I blow a blood vessel and have a stroke? What if some poor clerk at the Foodmart sneezes and I catch the Tri-Asian Flu? What if a seal breaks when there ain't a suit handy and some hotshot twenty-seven-year-old mission specialist throws a switch the wrong way and people die? This is a dangerous profession, my friend. Crap happens. Too bad, then let's move on so we can learn from our mistakes. Hell, update your physical and ride up with us on mission C-13. We'll have the nice housing units installed by then. If you want to, I'll even let ya room with me up there. I'll be your own personal guinea pig."

The doctor squinted. "If I thought you were serious, Gene . . ."

"Hell, *yes,* I'm serious. I told you—I'm not gonna accept *No*. But I'm willing to meet ya halfway. No one's *ever* had NDC in reduced gravity conditions. Reduced air pressures. Reduced 0_2 partial pressures. You've got *no* idea whether I'll live—longer or shorter under those conditions. Now have you?"

"No," Hellebore admitted.

"Then maybe I'll live longer out in space."

"You don't know that."

"And you don't know if these NASA spacecraft and living modules are the cause of the NDC and will make me worse."

"I can't take that risk."

"It ain't yours to take, Dickie Boy," Gene said, poking the doctor in the chest with a finger. "Besides," he paused to smile broadly, before making his killer pitch, "I'd make that NDC Foundation happy, make the president happy—and bring a whole lotta hope to a whole lotta people."

Dr. Hellebore was stopped by this argument. The NODC Foundation, in just ten years, stood as the second largest medical research fund in the nation. Mostly this was due to the tough luck story of the first lady, who'd finally succumbed to NODC only five months earlier. The president was talking of making medical research to find a cure the hallmark of his reelection campaign platform, and according to early polling, eighty-three percent of the population agreed. The public was scared by every sudden onset of new disease, but didn't want to give up their love affair with technology. With a high-visibility case on the Moon . . . Gene's idea was crazy, but not so crazy it didn't have legs.

"NASA runs on those tough old Federal dollars," Gene gently reminded the doctor. He was pretty sure they were already on the downhill side to his argument.

"Yes," Hellebore agreed, still thinking. "Yes it does."

The astronaut turned on the charm. "So it wouldn't be *so* bad to try to hang on to those dollars when the prez is looking for budget lines to trim—and maybe pick up a couple more for your new research grant, eh?"

"Yes, but . . ."

"Ain't no 'buts' here."

"I'm afraid there are. NASA doesn't need to take another hit when another astronaut—you—dies in space."

"Ain't gonna die in space."

"Die on the Moon, then."

"Fact is, Dickie Bird, the Good Lord willing I'm gonna be the first man planted *in* the Moon." The thought made Gene laugh out loud.

"You're crazy."

"Maybe. But I'm a pilot and an astronaut. Ain't no way you can make a charge of clinical crazy stick."

"I didn't mean it that way."

But Gene still had that twinkle in his eye. "Yessir—the first Man in the Moon, for sure."

Well, this is a helluva thing," Assistant NASA Director Herb Flowers said, flinging a report folio onto his desk. "How the hell am I supposed to sell this?"

"It's not a matter of selling," Dr. Hellebore said.

"The hell it isn't! You want me to risk a hundred-billion-dollar project on this idiot Gene Fish-"

"Gene is *not* an idiot," Hellebore said, finding himself standing and leaning over Herb's desk. He was shaking. "The man has a point. There's *nothing* I can ground him on right now."

"He's sick."

"He has a disease. It'll eventually kill him. But not right away. He's passed his physical—twice."

By now Herb was standing on his side of the desk. "I cannot sign off on this goddamn thing."

"You're going to *have* to, Herb."

"I don't have to do anything, Doctor. NASA does not do this sort of thing."

"It's going to have to if you want people to believe you're serious about a permanent base on the Moon. One where people like Gene Fisher-Hall go to live, work—and eventually die." *My God,* Dr. Hellebore thought, *I sound like Gene's cheerleader.* "The American public will be on Gene's side, too, Herb. And I hate to say it, because it sounds so crass and political, but the president is going to be on Gene's side. You've got to sign off on this proposal."

"You're too emotionally attached to this issue."

"Maybe so," Hellebore admitted. "But you better consider the possibility that your space modules are the culprit here. NODC is a technological disease. Gene Fisher-Hall today—the man with the most hours in space—who's next?"

"Get out of here, Doctor."

"We need a research program. We have a prime candidate."

Herb glared at the doctor. "I'll deal with this—and you—later."

Gene lumbered up the access arm to the cockpit of the third-generation shuttle *Aires* in his flight suit, emergency chute and twenty-five-minute transfer pack. Half a dozen friendly faces awaited him. He knew everyone who worked the launches at the Cape and they all knew him.

"Gene," Bill Koontz said, noting the time of the pilot's arrival on his clipboard, "there's a rumor going around Flowers has it in for you."

"Really? Now that's real unlikely," Gene said,

taking the clipboard and signing his own name in the appropriate box. "Would require the bastard to make a decision, wouldn't it?"

"So you're not grounded?"

"For what?" Gene acted offended, which only told Bill that something really was up. "Check the net—I got clearances from not one, but *two* NASA flight surgeons. Wouldn't want ol' Herb to think I had any favorites or anything."

Bill made the appropriate sympathetic noises to Gene, all the while making a query over the launch network. It wasn't that he doubted Gene, it was more how Gene had made it clear to Bill he was supposed to check up on him. Sure enough, Drs. Alan Petrys and Laura Templeton had both approved Captain Fisher-Hall for space travel and launch. He was surprised not to see Dr. Richard Hellebore's name on the list.

Leaning forward to talk discreetly in Gene's ear, Bill asked, "Is this about you? Or is it something about Dick?"

Gene didn't play dumb—not with Bill Koontz. Not after all the years the two had worked together. "Jest a little misunderstanding between me 'n' Herb," Gene said in a quiet drawl. "Ain't nothing to worry about."

Louder, Gene spoke to the small knot of techs still in the swing arm. "See all you loser ground-pounders week after next."

Then he spoke quietly back to Bill. "Dick'll be fine after this flight. You'll see. We got ourselves a lunar base to assemble. Insert Tab A into Slot B an' all that."

Bill Koontz shook his head. "Right, Gene. Have a good flight."

The Moon loomed out of the narrow windows of Lunar Lander 3. Five months had passed since NASA became aware of Gene's condition and still nothing formal had happened. Gene had been hoping just to make it to this landing, when they had enough materials to start Dome 1, but now, of course, he wanted more. He wanted to see the first real permanent Moon base built. He wanted to live in it.

"Fifteen seconds," Karl Brüner said from the copilot's seat. The German worked both European Space Agency and NASA missions, just as Gene sometimes flew the ESA's shuttle. Though Americans mostly thought of the Moon base as a strictly American project, NASA made sure to keep its international friends involved—Gene was happy to play ambassador and have another spacecraft type in his logbook.

Gene gave Karl a curt acknowledgment, but his concentration remained focused on what he called the landing picture. Eyes darting across the screens, he had his target error down to less than half a centimeter—too little for the instruments to register. Nothing he could complain about.

"Engines up," Gene said, tweaking the controls just enough to bring the lunar lander to a complete stop precisely as the contact lights showed green on all six landing struts.

"Contact."

"And we're down," Gene said with some satisfaction. "Houston, Cargo Load C-1 is on the Moon. Engines off, controls safed. How'd I do?"

Gene grinned at Karl during the three-second delay to Earth and back. Karl shook his head.

"Gene, Karl—you did all right. And with the

successful delivery of the C-1 container, construction on the first large-scale permanent Moon base can commence. Welcome to the Moon, gentlemen."

"Glad you liked it, Houston. Signing off now—we've got some chores to do before sundown," Gene said, then switched the radio to standby.

"You do know sunset is nine days away," Karl pointed out.

"Sure. Just as I know Cammy Stevens back there is chomping at the bit to start putting her modules together. Got no *time* to mess with Houston right now."

Karl sat back in his seat, gazing out across the jumble of sterile off-gray terrain which was Man's new home. "I shall miss flying with you, Gene."

"Then don't quit, boy. Y'all can always retire later."

"No, good friend," Karl said. "It is time to go. Trina and the children need me, you see."

"Move them up here when the time comes." Gene tried not to grimace as his left hand slowly began to seize up. "You've got seniority, I've got some pull."

"No," Karl said, slowly shaking his head. "Trina would never do it. Besides, this is the end of these old landers. You have your shiny new LT Lunar Transports coming next month."

"And you could fly those, too. Should be sweet," Gene said, massaging his left hand with his right until the stiffness went away. Dr. Hellebore had explained that "dispersed cancer" didn't attack the nerves directly, but affected the tissues surrounding them and that seizures and cramps would become more and more common over time. "You're way too young to be hanging up your wings."

"Maybe for an iron man like you, Gene," Karl said,

releasing his straps and leveraging himself out of the seat. "But I am done."

Gene laughed. "You short-timers are all alike. You'll be done when Trina sees you and you get to hug your kids. Until then, your ass is mine and we've got work to do."

"Or Dr. Stevens will get on our case."

"Naw, Cammy's on the Moon. She's too thrilled to finally be here with all her gear and starting the job. I jest don't want to get on ol' Jim Marshall's bad side and delay his baby even one minute."

"You are too modest, Gene. You are as responsible for this project as your friend Jim Marshall."

"True. But pardon me if I don't go around tootin' my own horn too much in the meantime."

"And I am beginning to understand even your most quaint expressions, Gene. I need to return to Germany before you corrupt me further."

"Too late for that, friend," Gene grinned.

"No doubt," the German agreed. "And how are you getting home, Gene? Did you decide between ESA or the Russians?"

"I flew with the Russians the last time. Jim says I should fly with the French this time—wouldn't want to show favorites with our friends."

"Share the pain of Gene Fisher-Hall with everyone?" Karl asked innocently.

"Something like that," Gene said.

The two men chuckled as they left the lander's cramped cockpit. Gene flexed his fingers a couple of times, but the incident was over. For now.

It would only get worse from here.

"Well, Dickie Bird," Gene greeted the doctor as he entered their prefabricated living module in Dome 1 fifteen months later. "See you finally cleared the safety briefing."

"Yeah, finally. God, that was arduous. How'd you ever learn all this stuff?"

"Shoot—I wrote most of it and had Jim Marshall proof it and clean it. Spiffed it up jest right."

"Well, it's torture. Incomprehensible."

"It's life on the Moon, Dickie. Besides, old Jim Marshall took out all the color and flavor I put in. Told him it was a mistake to delete the fun, but NASA knows best."

"I'm sure." Dr. Hellebore looked up at the top bunk reluctantly. He wore the ankle weights and heavy vest they issued to newbies on the Moon to keep them grounded in the one-sixth gravity while they learned to walk and hop. "Where do I sleep?"

Gene effortlessly kicked off the floor and, with one hand, touched the ceiling and redirected his body to land laid out in the top bunk. "We'll stick you with the bottom bunk for now, Dickie. Till you grow some moon legs. You can have my bunk when I'm gone."

Hellebore, who was quite sure he couldn't reproduce Gene's maneuver without doing great bodily injury to himself, quickly agreed. Long used to the pilot's gallows humor, frankly, a healthy attitude towards his disease would probably make him live longer, so who was Hellebore to complain?

He was about to try to make a joke, when an alarm began to hoot. "An accident? Or a drill?"

"Sonofabitch," Gene swore and jumped down to

the deck. "Better follow me, Dickie Bird—someone's going to need a doctor. I hope."

In fact, Hellebore wasn't able to keep up with Gene, but it hardly mattered—he couldn't get lost. A lot of station personnel were headed to the scene, so the doctor simply had to keep after them. One more turn and he realized they were in one of the staging areas before the large cargo airlocks.

Gene came back to stop Hellebore. "Can't go on without a spacesuit, Dickie. And Trevino doesn't need a doctor. He's all past doctoring and medicine."

"Trevino? *Daniel* Trevino?"

"Yup."

"But I know him."

"You know lots of the boys and girls up here, Dickie. Never said this wasn't a dangerous place or that it wouldn't hurt when someone dies."

"I thought *you* wanted to be the first to die on the Moon," Hellebore said rather pointedly, regretting the barb even as he spoke.

"Of natural causes," Gene said softly. He put an arm on the doctor's shoulder and bowed his head for a minute. When he straightened up the astronaut was all business again. "I'll bring Danny in. This is your first day—go back to our place."

"I think my place is in the medical unit."

"Uh-huh. And your medical bag, which you forgot to bring, is still in our place. You'd better go get it if you're going to be worth a damn to anyone."

The mood in the pilot's Ready Room was somber as they filed in. Gene sat cross-legged on the desk in front, nodding an acknowledgment to each man and woman while saying nothing aloud. When Lt. Tyrone Keene came in and closed the doors, that was the signal to begin.

"Okay, here's how it's going to go. We're taking Danny Trevino home per his prior request." Gene looked up at the assembled pilots. "Ty Keene was probably his best friend up here—Ty and I will fly the LT-1 *Copernicus*. Big minds in the US, Europe, Russia, Japan, China and India all figure this is a deal. First fatal accident on the Moon and all. Time to show some solidarity that we're here to stay. So we'll be escorted by the ESA transport and a Russian out of their base. Crewmen from England, France and Italy on the one, Russia, Poland and India on the second. China, Japan and Germany will meet us in Earth orbit. If you've been picked, you'll get your assignment shortly."

Gene paused. "I think every one of us would go and honor Danny if we could, but we can't. Life has to go on. I don't know 'bout you guys, but I intend to live on the Moon and one day retire here. So don't beg and moan for an assignment on this detail. We let the governments decide this one, this time. I'm sure this won't be the funeral Danny thought he'd planned for, but this has gotten bigger than all of us.

"One last thing—we just had a bad accident. Jim Marshall is already rallying the non-flight crews and reminding them to be safe. So everything is by the book right now. We have procedures for a reason. Trust in them."

The warm breeze never let up during the graveside service. The cemetery was an oasis of quiet amidst the great sea of Indiana corn and soybeans which surrounded the little town in all directions. Gene hadn't worn his Navy dress uniform in two years—he didn't even have one on the Moon where weight restrictions didn't allow for such nonessential clothing. Thankfully it still fit. Gene's job here was to stand and be seen, representing the corps of astronauts, NASA, the Navy—Danny Trevino was a fellow naval officer, even if he'd been thirty years younger. Even if Danny was an idiot.

Gene wasn't about to voice his own opinions to anyone. He'd leave it to the accident review board and see if they agreed with him that Danny's death was stupid and unnecessary. But no matter which way they ruled, Gene and his buddy Jim Marshall would shortly issue new safety regulations. No doubt Dickie Hellebore would find that amusing, Gene figured. The good doctor probably thought a lot of Gene's looser activities were stunts bordering on the irresponsible. Hellebore didn't understand the difference between confident control and recklessness.

As the vice president of the United States presented Danny's mother with the folded triangle of the flag of a grateful nation, Gene saw the line of Marines prepare for the volley of rifle fire. That was the toughest moment of a military funeral. The sharp reports breaking the quiet of the moment. Military personnel steeled themselves; civilians flinched.

A flight of four Navy F-44C fighter jets approached from the south. Gene had to correct himself—*this* was the toughest moment. Four jets streaking in overhead, one suddenly leaving the middle of the flight and streaking skyward in the classic missing man formation. For the briefest of moments as the roar of eight high-performance engines blasted the cemetery, Gene had a twinge of emotion. He dearly loved to fly—under other circumstances he would've rather flown in that flyover than stand here on display all gussied and trussed. But he was a spaceman now, not a flyboy. There was no room for regrets.

It was a long stint of standing in full Earth gravity. Gene was pretty sure he'd pay for it the next day. Fortunately the tremor in his left leg quieted and his right hand seizure had ebbed, allowing him to administer the final salute to his fallen comrade without wavering. Tomorrow Gene would take it easy. But time was running out for him.

Jim Marshall says Danny didn't deserve the show," Hellebore told Gene when he'd returned to the Moon. "I was rather shocked."

Gene made a sour face. "Jim shouldn't have said that. Not out loud, anyways."

"Then you agree?"

"The show was for the program. Danny shouldn't 've jumped from that damned transporter. He was showin' off. One-sixth G slow-motion fall. Except you push off from a stack of containers and they can still fall on you. I swear, Dickie Bird, sometimes I think people figure they're invulnerable in a spacesuit. But it ain't a suit of armor. Good people can and will get hurt in spacesuits. And doing something stupid will most certainly have the potential to bite you on the ass and kill you."

"Then I don't understand," the doctor said. "I thought Danny Trevino was your friend. How can you say such things?"

"Speak ill of the dead?" Gene laughed bitterly. "Danny was a good ol' boy from the farm belt outside Indianapolis. I served with his daddy . . . let's just say a *long* time ago. I babysat for him and his brother a number of times. But he was always cocky. And this time it killed him. That's a fact. You can't let friendship take your eye off the truth. Read the accident report when it comes out—the classified version. The one we'll keep up here and not send on to Earth. Otherwise drop it, Dickie Bird. For the good of the program."

The light show outside the cockpit of the shuttle amazed young Simon Benedict. He glanced to the other seat only to see the veteran sitting there calmly, waiting on their next reentry checkpoint, completely ignoring the brilliant plasma ionization flashes. This wasn't some simulator, this was real friction heating. How could the old man be so calm?

Gene wasn't thinking about plasmas as he stared down at his left hand. It sat there on the arm rest, still throbbing and no longer responding to his brain's commands. The seizure would go away in a few minutes, he knew, but they were in the middle of a reentry maneuver. He needed his hand to function and time was running out.

"All right, Rookie," he said nonchalantly. "Put your old hands on those controls and bring us on in."

"Are you serious?"

"Son—we're on a hot reentry run from orbital speed. Lots of one-half em-vee-squared, if you know what I mean. Outside the temperature's screaming up past

Hellfire and heading towards Armageddon. Now do you think this is a good time for old Gene Fisher-Hall to be joshing?"

"Uh, no, sir."

"You're trained and you ain't pranged the simulator in the last two weeks. You might as well take the trial by fire. I'm still here to back you up."

"Uh, yes, sir," Benedict said, taking over. "We're at Item Three-Eighty-Two and coming up on Decision Point Forty. I have the controls."

"Ground-based radar and telemetry look good," Gene noted. "You could practically put her in Auto-Land mode and take a vacation, but let's jest do it by the book for now."

"Thanks, Gene."

"For what?" the old man asked, trying not to grin at the kid's enthusiasm.

"For showing confidence in me on my first mission."

"Aw, forget it. Everyone's trained so much anyone could do it on their first run. I was jest thinking it was time to hang it up an' stop dropping all the way down to Earth. Thought maybe I'd let you take her so I could do some sightseeing."

"You're retiring?"

"Retiring? Hell, no! I jest figured if I moved out to space, it was about time to move to space permanent-like and stop making the commute down the gravity well all the way to hit Earth. I'll be content to make the runs to Earth orbit from the Moon. One more big scary launch from the Cape and I'm gone for good from this planet."

"Sir—are you all right?"

Gene glared at the kid. "Who you been talking to, son? I'm fine. I've already explained myself—and that's that."

The doctor stood as the aging pilot sat in the small lunar base medical compartment. The heart still sounded good, he had to admit. Clear breath sounds. Reflexes sharp. No gross medical abnormalities, besides the slow spread of his disease.

"How's the hero business going, Gene?"

"As well as it can, I s'pose."

"Feeling all right?"

"Want me to do a hundred chin-ups right now?"

"Not much of a challenge in sixth-G."

"Naw, I suppose not."

"I've heard a rumor NASA figures to rename the base for you when you finally die."

"I ain't dead yet, Dickie."

"No, not at all. But I was wondering—what will NASA do for the *second* dead guy on the Moon?"

"You mean the third? 'Cause I clearly remember having to pack up ol' Danny Trevino and send his corpse to Earth."

"I thought you didn't want to count him, since it wasn't natural causes."

"Dead is dead. But anyways, I'm assuming you're talking about whoever dies *after* I kick the bucket farm."

"Sure."

"That's the whole point, Dickie Bird," Gene managed to say with a sly grin. "The first guys—they're the shock. Afterwards . . . well, it never gets *easy,* but then again, the old US Air Force didn't go around renaming Edwards every time they lost another test pilot. One big rename event per customer."

"You're enjoying this too much."

"Gotta enjoy it now—'cause I'll miss the rest when I'm gone."

"Lt. Benedict says you abruptly changed procedures on your last drop to Earth."

Gene didn't act surprised. He assumed the doctor knew. "Aw, Dickie Bird, I was jest giving the boy a chance to prove himself on his first mission . . ."

"And the fact that your hand seized up again didn't have anything to do with it?"

Gene glared at his friend the doctor. "Remind me to accidentally unplug my telemetry harness next time I go to work."

"You promised you wouldn't put anyone in jeopardy."

"And I didn't!" Gene said, more forcefully than he intended. "I didn't try to fake it, nor did I try some stupid stunt like crossing over with my other hand. I didn't make a fuss and just real casual-like handed control over to the copilot. Who was fully trained and still under my supervision, I might add, which is why he's in that other damned seat in the first place.

"Anyway," he said in a less confrontational tone, "I told the boss I was here in space for good now. And I won't be flying those shuttles down any more, just the lunar transports as far as Low Earth Orbit."

"But you're still going to be flying."

"You don't play fast and loose air jockey in pure zero-G, my man. You set up the runs and let the computers make the big decisions. Close maneuvering?

The joy stick is front and center and can be flown with either hand. You're not locked into a five-point harness and watching gravity shoot up past four G's. I'm not endangering anyone, Dickie."

"Well . . . at least you're giving up the ground landings. On Earth, I mean," Hellebore hastily added, just in case Gene tried to quibble again.

"I'm being real good, Dickie Bird. Real good. You said it yourself last week—I'm still ahead of the curve on this NDC thing. Moon seems to grow on a guy, I reckon."

Dr. Hellebore didn't argue with him. They were already a quarter of a million miles past the point of no return on that score. He might as well stick with Gene and see this through.

Houston, as usual, still tried to run everything on the Moon. As a declared permanent resident of space, Gene Fisher-Hall felt even less interest in playing things their way. And as senior pilot, he spent more time hanging around Flight Ops when he wasn't taking his own runs.

"We're concerned here," Mission Control said, starting their latest effort in control, "about the number of gripes showing up on LT-3."

"Let me see that damned headset," Gene said to the officer running the console. "Houston, this here's Gene up in Flight Ops."

He used the three seconds of radio delay to slide into the second seat and wait for the camera light to wink on in front of him. Lunar Transport-3, the *Tycho,* had never worked as well as the *Copernicus* or the *Galileo.* But with *Kepler* (LT-4) coming online next month, his biggest fear would be they'd ground the troublemaker and stay at three transports, rather than expand the fleet to four.

"Oh—hi, Gene. Pete Marlin here."

"I know who the hell's on the other end of the line," Gene said. "I can see the monitor. Now I know what you think you're about to do here and . . ."

"Look, I know what you're going to say," Marlin said in Mission Control, the two conversations colliding into each other.

"So it stinks," Gene said, taking full advantage of the radio etiquette which gave the tie to those off-world. "Ain't nothing serious wrong with the *Tycho,* and we need that four-transport capacity if we're going to get the next dome up on schedule."

This time Gene paused to wait for Houston.

"Safety comes first over schedules. You know that," Mission Control said predictably. "NASA isn't going to go down the road of pushing things to disaster again."

"Pete, these are NASA transports. Everything's got double and triple backups. And I *know* we're using some of the auxiliary and backup systems from time to time, but we worked this all out *years* ago. We're in the safety zone. Look it up in the book, Pete."

"Gene—this is an engineering decision, based on the best opinions of the guys from Lockheed and Boeing . . ."

"Long Term Operations Manual, volume fifteen, page seven-eighty-two. I'll hold one while you look it up."

"LT-4 will be online in four, five weeks. We can take LT-3 out of service now . . ."

Down to two transports? Gene interrupted again.

"Do you need the NASA net address for that page? Because I can get it for you."

"The administrator does not want to take the risk at this time, Gene."

"You know," Gene said, "I'm the pilot with the most seniority. So I can volunteer to fly the LT-3 on its next two missions. At least 'til we get the *Kepler* on the road. If you want to take a little time and have a go on troubleshooting *Tycho* then, well, at least we can stay close to schedule."

There was a pause. Gene could see Pete Marlin in Mission Control conferring with someone off-screen. He leaned back and put his hands behind his head. And he knew someone in Houston would see him sitting up on the Moon looking supremely confident.

"It was a good try, Gene," Flight Ops said off-mike in the seat next to him. The former Air Force officer was thirty-five years junior to the old man, but he was used to capitulating to the big boys in Houston.

"The hell you say," Gene said, then smiled like a fat and sassy cat which knew something its owner didn't. "Longer they sit there jabbering, the better my hand looks. They know I ain't laying my cards down—so they're gonna have to fold and do it my way."

"Mission Control doesn't play that way."

"Got no choice. I've got volume fifteen, page seven-eighty-two, on my side."

"What's that say?"

"You got a damned computer there—and a full hard copy on that shelf behind your own sad self, shipped up to the Moon at tremendous cost, I might add. Look it up. Either way—I don't care."

Gene waited while the younger man started typing on the keyboard, before speaking. Down to two lunar transports? Maybe he should check on the older lunar landers—they had three of them stored here on the Moon for emergency use. Was keeping to a schedule a sufficient emergency to bring one of them back online? As the page began to scroll on Flight Ops' screen, Gene switched back to his folksy teaching mode. "You should note the rules say we can score defects according to the book, and shutdown is six hundred points or a major systems failure. We've only scored two-eighty on the *Tycho* and nothing big is broke. Ain't even interesting yet to fly."

"We've never done it that way."

"Yeah, I know. About time we started following the rules Jim Marshall and me wrote up back on the Big Blue Marble." Gene leaned forward, watching Pete's image straighten up on the monitor. "Here it comes."

"Gene, we're going to do it your way. For now."

The aging astronaut slapped a hand hard on the console in front of him, then keyed his mike back on. "Hot damn, Houston. I like your style."

Gene?" Navy lieutenant Lisa Gold's voice came from the rear of the LT-3's crew compartment. "How many points does the microwave oven score?"

"It don't," Gene said, floating in the commander's sling seat; "considered a nonessential system."

"Well, then, you don't get hot coffee."

Gene let out a low whistle. "So you got a negative function on the machine? Or a blown breaker?"

"Let's see," Lisa said, scanning the labels in front

of her. "I've still got a display here, this is circuit U-331 . . . breaker over here is still green over green. It's the machine."

"You try whacking it?"

"I slammed the door."

"Try cycling the door again, sweetheart. Gentle-like this time."

A few seconds later he heard the low hum of the microwave's blower fan. When the machine beeped, Lisa came forward with a bulb of coffee, fitting it into the insulated carrier sleeve. Gene gave it a sip.

"Ah—back in business. Three hours to landing and we got hot coffee again. Don't get no better than this," he said with some real satisfaction.

"How did you know?"

He shrugged. "I didn't. But all microwave units have to come with safety interlocks—Federal law. Either something's loose and banging it around might seat it, or it's misaligning and only needs some tender care. I had a one-out-of-three chance of success."

"Don't you mean fifty-fifty?"

"Naw—there was a third option. Damn thing could've just been broke."

Lisa noticed him massaging his left hand again. "You okay, Gene?"

"What? Oh sure. Looks like we've got a transmission coming in." He flipped the switch and linked into the lunar communications net. "Go head, Flight Ops—this is *Tycho*."

"Lunar Transport *Tycho* . . . we, uh, would like to alter your inbound profile."

"Roger that. What's your problem?"

"We've got Lunar Transport *Galileo* on Landing Pad One. They're in an unscheduled launch hold right now. We'd like you to make orbit instead of coming straight in and we'll let you know when the range is clear."

"*Tycho* to make lunar orbit insertion—acknowledged. Keep us up to date, boys. *Tycho* out."

Lisa had drifted into the other sling seat. "I'm surprised you didn't fight them. Pads Two and Three were clear."

"Naw," Gene said, setting up the computer for the burn-to-orbit. "Pad Three's not ideal for us with that extra cargo pod stuck on for this run. We're better off on One or Two. But if One is blocked, that reduces us to one landing pad—no reason to limit our options if we don't have to. Besides . . ." he paused to give Lisa a wink, "any time they order this old dog to fly more, I ain't gonna complain."

She shook her head and turned away to run the navigation recheck routines.

Halfway through their burn-to-orbit, Gene began to fret about the reserve nitrogen pressure. They needed the gas to keep the fuel and oxidizer lines pressurized. The reserve nitrogen was already on the list of recorded glitches from previous runs. Just now he'd tested the gas transfer system—three times—and got no response.

"Negative function on reserve nitrogen valve. Switching on valve heaters," he said.

Lisa didn't seem concerned in the other seat. These lunar transports lived their entire lives in vacuum and every valve could and did freeze up from time to time.

So Gene tried the valve again after a minute. A red flag popped out on the overhead panel. Frowning, he reset the breaker and tried it again. Same result.

Now Lisa noticed. "You've got a breaker tripped."

"Yeah. H-102," Gene said. He reset the system for the backup circuit. A second red flag emerged. "And H-103."

"Is this a problem yet?" she asked.

"It's a known gripe."

But he hadn't answered her question as he continued to troubleshoot. Then he went back to recalculating their fuel in the main tank.

Seventy-five kilometers altitude," Lisa called out, two minutes after they resumed their descent to the lunar surface. "Still on track."

"Flight Ops," Gene said, beginning to get annoyed at the lack of a recent update. "What's the status of *Galileo*'s launch?"

"They're just coming out of their hold."

"Ops—we're on a descent here. D'ya think you could for once get my landing field cleared before you give us clearance for a deorbit burn?"

"They'll be gone in five minutes, Gene. Just hold your . . . Wait one, *Tycho*."

Gene and Lisa exchanged a quick look.

"Setting up a return to orbit," she said, rapidly typing in the commands. "Just in case."

"Negative," Gene said. "Just get me a burn to bring us around one time to our current track at sixty kilometers."

"You got it."

"We're already in our descent, this way we'll pick her up where we left her off," Gene explained. "If we have to."

"Lunar Transport *Tycho,* this is Flight Ops. We've had an incident on Landing Pad One—the swing arm operator accidentally made hard contact with Lunar Transport *Galileo*."

"LT-3, this is Houston Mission Control . . ."

Gene stabbed at the radio keys. "Houston—stay outta this. We are in direct comm with our landing field. Flight Ops, we are setting up a once-around here and aborting this landing.

Do you confirm?"

"Roger, *Tycho*. Flight Ops confirms."

They once again resumed their descent after the ground crew moved the damaged *Galileo* off the pad. Gene stayed unusually quiet as he kept running their usable fuel numbers. Those two extra orbital maneuvers had cost them plenty and the nitrogen pressures still didn't look good.

"Two minutes to touchdown," Lisa said.

Gene heard her, but stared at the graphs in front of him. They didn't have sixty seconds of fuel left. The computer said they did, but his calculations didn't agree. They needed to pump from the Reserve B fuel tank to the main tank sometime in the next sixty seconds, except he couldn't make it work. He glared at the two red-flagged circuit breakers still open on the overhead console.

Hollis had logged this as a glitch. Surely the other pilot had tried the same things Gene had. But there wasn't time to contact Hollis and find out what he'd done—Gene had waited too long.

"Ninety seconds."

Gene knew he didn't want to be the first Man *in* the Moon by crashing on his last landing. And he definitely didn't want to crash into the base. The Lunar Transports were built with one thing in mind—lightweight functionality. The *Tycho* was just a cab on a frame with tanks, cargo blocks and engines. Lots of exposed plumbing for ease of maintenance. They couldn't expect anything in the way of protection if the engine quit. Yet his real concern wasn't with his own safety. If *Tycho* crashed, then with the *Galileo* damaged, the base would be down to just one lunar transport. And that was unacceptable.

His backup systems all had backups—except there was only the one valve. How did this happen?

He reset the breakers, tried the valve and they blew again.

"Throttle back," he advised Lisa. "We're short on fuel and we're gonna land hard."

Lisa was surprised and Gene knew he'd made a mistake keeping the information to himself.

"I'm firing RCS," she said, referring to their maneuvering thrusters. Anything which dropped their speed would help.

Gene added, "And vector us into a more shallow approach."

Then he spied the valve heater switches. Had they been "on" the whole time?

"Primary and secondary valve heaters to 'off,'" he said, moving quickly. "Breakers reset. Pressurizing reserve fuel . . . now."

The first breaker tripped. He reset and tried again. The second breaker tripped.

"Here goes nothin'," Gene said softly and jammed his fingers against the breaker resets and held them in while he moved his left hand to actuate the valve. The fingers wanted to clench, but he willed them open anyway and held down the switch.

"Fuel transfer," Lisa said, more calmly than she felt. "Reserve B to main. Sixty seconds. Still on target."

As soon as they landed and safed the systems, Lisa turned to Gene and was about to chew him out when he handed her a piece of paper. "Get this to Jim Marshall, will you?"

Then he unstrapped, got up and left.

Nonplused, Lisa looked down at the drawing. It was a quick sketch of the *Tycho* with arrows pointing to the base of the cab—*add explosive bolts*—and to three of the RCS engines—*attach RCS clusters 1-3-7 to cab. Include damn fuel tanks. Backup valve.* A large note added *ZERO SUM ON MASS,* followed by a smaller one—*provide autosep and diverting routines in software. 60 days to implement ALL CHANGES.*

In less than three minutes, while she was busy flying them in, Gene Fisher-Hall had come up with the rudimentary design of an emergency ejection system for the cab. The RCS engines didn't have enough power to land the entire transport, so his solution was to chop off nearly all the mass. Lose the cargo, save the crew. It was brilliant to the point where Lisa wondered why it hadn't been considered from the start.

Lisa noticed an arrow which went off the page to the right.

Turning the paper over, she saw Gene's scrawled handwriting. *We live, we learn.*

Gene sat in the locker room, flexing his left hand. His first two right fingers were bandaged from where the overheated breakers had burned the tips. He'd done the first aid himself—Dr. Hellebore would be by soon enough. Of that, Gene was sure.

"Gene?" a crewman asked. "You got time to talk to an Earth reporter?"

"Yeah," Gene said in a tired voice. He wasn't surprised some sharp-eyed space nut had figured out there was a story with today's goings on. "Sure. All part of the service."

He got up and found a video terminal, then entered his access number. A fresh-faced twenty-something young man appeared and several seconds later smiled politely at Gene. It wasn't one of the usual guys on the space beat.

"Hello, Captain Fisher-Hall. My name is Trey Secord and I'm a reporter with the *San Jose Mercury News*."

Gene waited for the silence, then spoke. "Hi, Trey. You can call me Gene."

This reporter was smart enough to likewise wait out the three-second delay in communications. "Yes, Gene. I was wondering if, in light of your difficult mission today, you could comment on why you're still an active duty astronaut after having been diagnosed with NODC some time ago?"

Gene chewed on a lip for a moment, not expecting this topic, then cleared his throat. "Son—where'd you get that notion?"

"Sir," the young-looking reporter said, "it's my job to

track high-tech shipments and, well, a lot of diagnostic medical equipment's been shipped to the Moon since you moved up there. And it's not coming out of the regular NASA medical budget."

"So you decided to go on a fishing expedition with me?"

"No, sir. Turns out it's all funded with grant money. I've already got a source at NASA Administration. What I really wanted was confirmation."

When the interview was over, Gene stood still for a long minute. Then with a sigh he turned around, only to see Jim Marshall leaning on a locker. The architect of Man's first permanent lunar colony didn't come to NASA as a pilot. He was a spaceman's engineer—a sturdy fireplug of a man, stiff salt-and-pepper remnants of hair only a few millimeters high rimming his lumpy skull, as unphotogenic as Gene could still be thought of as dashing. The two men were about the same age and had worked together for thirty years. Friendship didn't even begin to describe the respect the two men felt for each other.

"Why, if it ain't the greatest engineer this side of heaven or hell," Gene said, breaking into a big smile. "Other than Cammy, who actually built this barn. What brings you down here?"

"I heard, of course," Jim said in his heavy, gravelly voice. "Your big interview."

"Yeah, it's a tough break. Sounds like Houston wants to ground me for sure this time."

"This shouldn't have happened, Gene. I'll drop down to Earth and get this straightened out."

"Nope," Gene said, looking down towards the deck,

scuffing one of the non-skid bumps with his boot. "I'm going."

"Gene—you haven't been to Earth in . . ."

"I gotta do this, Jim. You know it as much as I do."

A third man came in, leaning on the lockers on the other side.

"Hey, Dickie Bird," Gene said.

"You all right?" Dr. Hellebore asked.

"Now, don't get me wrong, boys, I do appreciate this outpouring of affection and show of support. But I ain't dead. Nothing's happened."

Jim Marshall nodded towards Gene. "Our hero here thinks he's going to drop on Houston and demand his job back."

"I ain't suspended either . . . yet," Gene admitted.

"You haven't been to Earth . . ." Hellebore began.

"Why," Gene said, interrupting, "is everyone so damned hot to act like I ain't been keeping my log book up to date? Not only do I know exactly when I was last on Earth, but I've also been maintaining my twenty minutes of exercise at one-point-five G's in the centrifuge every damn day. Now, Dick, are you coming with me or not?"

Dr. Hellebore didn't always make his daily centrifuge, but he had been to Earth every four or five months, if only to make sure he hadn't burned his bridges back to home. "Sure, Gene. I'm with you."

"Good. Now let's go rustle us up a flight."

"You know you can't fly it."

"Jim—I ain't stupid. Even if I'm not officially suspended, I'll be a good little passenger. Now if you'll excuse me—I gotta pack." Gene strode out of the locker, looking like a man full of confidence without any worries.

Jim Marshall stood there and shook his head. "Can you believe that sonofabitch?"

"Every day's a dream," Hellebore said. "Excuse me—I think I've been given my orders to pack."

The landing of shuttles at Cape Canaveral carrying men and women from the Moon and the near space stations had become as routine as NASA could make it. After the tractor snagged the front landing gear and sped them to the terminal area, crew handlers came in with two wheelchairs for the long-term lunar residents. Dr. Hellebore was grateful for the assist, but he was surprised—then impressed—by the ironman performance of Gene Fisher-Hall, who walked off the shuttle under his own power.

"Need you to set up an appointment in Houston," Gene told the Shuttle Gate Officer, picking up one of the standard clipboards which lined the desk area. "Morning would be good. Maybe ten-hundred hours local. And I need a pool unit—is this one fully charged and raring to go?"

"Sure thing, Gene."

"Gene," Hellebore said, pushing himself over. "I can't sanction you for flight." He glanced outside at the flight line row of white NASA T-600A supersonic training jets available for the astronauts' use, not able to remember the last time he had seen Gene log jet time.

"Not your call," Gene said, reaching into a zippered pocket on his flight suit for something he had stashed just for this moment. "Last I checked you were just a flight surgeon, Dick. Puts you in charge of determining my flight status for airplanes, shuttles and spacecraft. This here card is a perfectly valid State of Texas grade-A adult vehicular driver's license. And what I've jest signed for is a NASA pool car. Now I've got some driving to do, Dickie Bird—you ready to go?"

"You're going to *drive* from the Cape to Houston?" Hellebore asked with some amusement.

"Sure thing."

"This I cannot miss."

As Dr. Hellebore settled into the right-hand seat of the NASA GM Senstra sedan, Gene Fisher-Hall took the one wheelchair, instantly collapsed it, then stowed it in the back. His movements were deliberate and considered at all times. Training for gravity was one thing—falling in the Earth's gravity, six times that of the Moon, was something entirely different.

"What are you doing, Dickie?" Gene asked, as he slung himself down into the seat.

"I'm calling up the map display."

"Do you think that an expert pilot and NASA's finest astronaut does *not* know how to get from Merritt Island to Houston?"

"I, uh . . ."

"Oh ye of little faith," Gene said, shaking his head and sighing. He spent a moment fiddling with something under the dashboard, then tossed a small black module into Hellebore's lap. Slipping on the standard restraint harness, he logged in, slammed the door and then tore out of the parking spot.

"Uh . . . what's this?" Hellebore asked, after

struggling into his own harness and picking up the module.

"Speed limiter," Gene replied. "One piece of equipment we don't need on this run."

"NASA logs every drive," Hellebore warned.

"Not if you logout the monitor function."

The four windows rolled down at Gene's command as they sped for the highway. On Earth you could enjoy the outside air—and he intended to.

By the time they made their second stop near Pensacola, Dr. Hellebore had real respect for Gene's skill as a pilot/driver. The quick-charge batteries required twenty minutes or so to recharge, a trick which forced drivers to break and rest on long trips, so Gene methodically ate and drank, renewing his own body at their first break, and then pushed the car faster and further than expected to their second.

"You've been averaging about 180 kph," Hellebore said, sitting at an outdoor table, picking at some fried chicken, mashed potatoes and gravy he'd picked up at the quick-mart kiosk. He knew it was all bad for him, but it was just this time and it'd smelled so damned good. "That's only about thirty above the speed limit."

"Speed limits are for ordinary drivers," Gene said. "I am a trained professional. Besides . . ." he paused to take another bite of his hamburger, ". . . you might've noticed we got passed by one hundred and thirty other cars, so far."

"No. I didn't notice."

"Ain't no one getting tickets today. I don't think anyone in America can stand this one-fifty speed limit."

Hellebore sat and watched his friend for another minute. "I didn't think we'd make it this far on that second charge."

"Ye of little faith," Gene said again. It was rapidly becoming his mantra on this road trip. "Besides, I spent most of the last hour drafting off that frozen chicken strips truck. We got further than the book says, that's for sure."

The doctor set aside his dinner and slowly made his way back up to standing.

"You okay there, Dickie Bird?" Gene said, concern creeping into his voice.

"Yeah. It always takes me a couple of hours to get my Earth legs back."

"You should do more time in the centrifuge. Any damn old space doctor will tell you that," Gene teased.

Hellebore ignored the taunt. "So this is Pensacola."

"Outskirts—yeah."

"There's a Navy air base . . . ?"

"Pensacola Naval Air Station." Gene nodded towards the south. "It's about ten . . . twenty klicks from here, on the coast. Been there many times when I was flying jets."

"Miss it?"

"What? You trying to be my shrink now?" Gene asked. He managed a smile to take the edge off the gibe.

"No—just making conversation."

Gene finished the last of his coffee. "I'm doing exactly what I want to be doing. And fighting to keep doing it."

"Amen to that."

Gene grinned at the doctor. "Glad you're on my side, Dickie. Let's hit that old road and see if it bounces."

At midnight they recharged at a huge truck and auto stop near Lafayette, Louisiana.

"Say," the young woman running the charging station said with some awe. "Ain't you Gene Fisher-Hall, the astronaut?"

"Pretty good guess," Gene said in mock seriousness. "What tipped you off? The NASA decals on the car? Or the name on my flight suit?" He flashed her a big grin and it was clear she didn't mind getting joshed.

"Man, the news nets are full of stuff about you getting fired."

"I ain't been fired from anything in my life, miss."

"But didn't they ground you? Aren't you heading to Houston to demand your job back? That's what the nets say."

"I wouldn't trust those reporter types too far with the truth," Gene said. "They're the ones who helped cause this little dust up. Nope, I'm heading to Houston to file some paperwork. Someone released my medical records without my say-so—and that's a Federal felony. Someone is gonna go to jail for this."

"Really?" The young woman's eyes went wide. None of the wild speculations she had been reading focused on this story.

"You bet. See—some things are public records. Like the fact that I was on that transport back to Earth this morning. Some things are not. You better pray your bosses don't ever get to smear your good name with what's in your medical files, let me tell you."

"Yeah."

The counter dinged and Gene signed for the charge. "It'll all be fixed up straight by, oh, ten in the AM Houston time. You take care now, y' hear?" And he waved to the young woman as he stepped back into the car.

Hellebore, already strapped in, was mystified. "Gene—what the hell are you doing? You can't talk to the press like that!"

Gene winked at his friend as he settled back into his seat. "Now you know very well I weren't talking to no press. Jest talking to a young lady who's a big fan of the space program."

"But she's going to call someone."

As they began to move back toward the I-10, Gene tilted his head and gave a little shrug. "I suppose she jest might at that. It's a free country, I guess. No telling what that young lady might do."

Dr. Hellebore could only sit and shake his head as they accelerated back up to 180 kph and settled in behind another speeding truck.

Houston was hot and muggy—no change there. After a quick five hours' rest in a cheap but clean hotel he knew on the road looping around the city, Gene parked the car at the Johnson Space Flight Center in a spot reserved for astronauts and not where pool cars were supposed to go. Then he made a show of getting out the wheelchair.

"Gene, I can probably walk now," Hellebore protested.

"You don't know nothing about showmanship, my friend," Gene said. "I'm here to save my career, and I'll use whatever's available."

"But I have a reputation . . ."

"Not one of those reporters or cameramen over there

with the long telephoto lenses gives a damn about your reputation, Dickie Bird. That's all there is to it. So get in and let old iron horse Gene Fisher-Hall push you around the farm."

"Gene."

"Herb."

The two men stared each other down for nearly a minute. The veteran and crafty pilot versus the consummate political administrator. Finally Assistant NASA Director Herb Flowers looked away and slapped a copy of a newspaper onto the desk between them.

"You shouldn't have gone to the press."

"I didn't."

"A technicality."

"No," Gene said slowly. "*A technicality* means I actually did something wrong. Near as I can tell, I'm not the one with felony charges hanging over my head. Now you—or at least someone in your office—that's a different matter."

"Okay, Gene. Direct as usual. What do you want?"

"I want to see those charges filed. I want to see someone bounced outta here and into the hoosegow."

"It's not that simple."

"It is that simple, Herb. Even if it's you. But . . ." Gene started to say, before the administrator could protest, "I'm pretty sure you ain't so stupid as to call a reporter yourself. So you must've gotten one of your toadies to do it for you. Now if you want the professional NASA pilot corps to trust you in the future—or at least pretend to trust you—you'd better make sure someone falls on their sword."

"In exchange for what?"

"In exchange for nothing," Gene said succinctly. "See, Herb, you think this is some sort of game of give and take. It ain't. Nothing's changed between me and my doc, and I'm running out of Lunar Flight Ops and *not* Houston Mission Control these days."

"You're here now. I could keep you here."

"Oh, well. Your professional funeral *there,*" Gene said with real hard-edged sarcasm. "How many reporters you think are out there this morning?"

"Whom you called."

"I called nobody, Herb—and you're avoidin' my question."

"I've no obligation to fly you back and forth to the Moon whenever you want. This isn't some tourist shuttle."

"I'm a resident of the Moon. I'm talking about going home—you can't keep me here against my will."

"Then you're using an illegal driver's license—I should have you arrested."

"Uh-uh," Gene said, waggling a finger at his boss. "UN's declared the Moon is international territory, same as if I were an American living abroad in Spain. I get to keep that Texas license. You lose again.

"You sure you don't want me to count those reporters out there again?"

Ready to head back to the Moon, Dickie Bird? Or do you need to stop somewhere here in Houston before we go?" Gene said when he got back to reception.

"It's over?" Dr. Hellebore asked. He had been standing, stretching his legs at least, and flipping through a few magazines while waiting to be called in.

Now he understood about Gene's show of strength. "Of course it's over."

"You doubted me." Gene stared in mock surprise at the doctor. "After all we've been through—you didn't think I had a prayer going into that meeting. I'm crushed, Dickie Bird, just crushed."

"I didn't know," Hellebore admitted. "The big cheeses can pretty much do what they want."

"Ah," Gene said, holding up a finger. "That's where you're wrong. Man like Herb Flowers is even *more* dependent on what others think than you or me."

With his zero-G and lunar flight status no longer in question, Gene would usually have insisted on piloting. But with a glut of personnel returning from Earth, he opted to again ride the transport as a passenger. He regaled the younger astronauts with stories which he swore were "mostly true" and even the good Dr. Hellebore, who didn't like space travel all that much, seemed in good spirits.

Claiming a back seat in the cockpit for the landing, for once Gene could sightsee on the way down rather than dance between graphs, gauges and sighting down the alignment reticle.

"Target in sight," the pilot announced, and indeed it was.

Gene marveled at how much the lunar base had expanded. The curved expanse of the two main domes dominated the approach, of course, but he was intrigued to see signs of life—construction equipment building the next cluster of structures and large wheeled transports moving around outside. One spacesuited figure atop the nearest crater wall waved.

"It's a goddamned Norman Rockwell painting," Gene said in awe.

"What was that, Gene?"

"Nothin'. Jest good to be home, that's all."

Eighteen months later, even after they had five lunar transports in regular service, Gene kept volunteering to ride the sometimes balky LT-3 *Tycho*. "It might've tried to bite me once," he told anyone who asked, "but I think I've showed her who's boss on this ol' moon."

Today's ride promised another routine mission, except Gene understood how there was nothing routine about space travel. Still, he was taken aback when his left hand seized up and wouldn't budge some ten minutes prior to launch from Pad Two. Usually his NODC didn't manifest itself until hours or days into a mission. He went to toggle his radio link to put a call into Hellebore when he found his right hand had seized as well.

Gene Fisher-Hall was many things. High-school baseball star, Navy aviator, NASA pilot-astronaut and senior amongst his peers. As he himself said, it was bad combination which tended towards professional arrogance. But he was not a stupid man.

"Uh, Flight Ops? This is Gene," he said in his casually clear, but folksy voice. "I'd like to declare a Hold to this count."

Barbara Gao, the civilian pilot sitting in the number two seat, stopped doing her checklist and turned to look at Gene. She raised an eyebrow and only got the usual wink from Gene.

"Lunar Transport *Tycho* . . . holding at T-minus nine

minutes thirty-two seconds," came the immediate reply. "What's up, Gene?"

"I'm declaring a system failure on the number one pilot," Gene said. He smiled as his right hand finally began to respond to the commands from his brain. Too late—but probably just in time, he figured. "I think that's it for the old man. Barb's got the checklist until Lisa finishes reading the newspaper and realizes she's no longer backup pilot for this milk run."

He released his strap restraints one-handed and, reaching up with the same hand, grabbed the overhead sissy bar and pulled himself out of the seat.

"Barb—you'd better safe my board. I'm not sure I can hit the right control."

"Gene?"

With some sadness, he reached up to the flap "above his heart" on his flight suit and yanked the Velcro-backed gold astronaut's wings with his right hand, looked at the worn metal, polished it once against his chest, then tossed the wings onto the pilot's seat he'd just vacated.

"You're retiring?" Barbara asked in amazement.

"Can't fly if your hands seize up before the day's even begun. I've never put a mission in danger—and I ain't starting today. Don't give Lisa too hard a time. She didn't kick your dog today."

By the time Gene Fisher-Hall had gathered up the rest of his space gear and his flight pack, the ground crew had re-extended the flexible docking arm. Still letting his left arm hang at his side, useless, Gene checked for pressure balance on both sides, then unlocked the hatch with his right hand and stood back to let the crew on the other side open it the rest of the way.

"See ya, kid," he called back to Barbara. "Have a nice flight."

I need you to promise me something," Hellebore began.

"Anything . . . assuming I'm capable of it," Gene said. He tried to smile at the doctor—and at Jim Marshall lurking in the background—but the truth was, by the time he'd made it back to the domes, he'd felt like crap. The doctor's short-term medications didn't make him feel much better. He didn't want to admit quite yet that giving up his flight status made his disease more formidable.

"Don't do anything foolish. No taking any long walks out a short airlock, with or without a suit."

Gene tried to chuckle, but the gesture collapsed into another coughing fit. The doctor put an arm around the old man to steady him, and when he finally stopped, gave him a water bulb to suck on.

"Thanks, old friend."

"Just doing my job," Hellebore said, trying to sound innocent and folksy like Gene. It didn't come off nearly so well.

"Don't worry, Dickie Bird," Gene finally managed to say. "I ain't gonna ruin your pet science project. Hell—I've been the star of it for the last couple of years, the least I should do is stick it out and see how it ends."

Jim Marshall hung around while the doctor ran his final checks and left, before swinging his short legs around the desk to sit on the end of it. "How you doing, Gene?"

"I'd be lying if I said I was wonderful," Gene admitted. "But then, I've never lied to you, old friend."

"I know. Don't think I don't know," Jim said with some admiring sadness. "That took some guts out there on the launch pad today."

"Well, technically—it's not really a launch pad . . ."

"No jokes, Gene."

The old pilot looked down and flexed his now behaving left hand. "I'm a professional, Jim. Doesn't take guts or need praising. I made you and Dickie Bird a promise—and I kept it. Everything else is just horsecrap." He paused to clear his throat, a deep sort of rumble, then coughed once.

"What about this cough? This new?"

"It's nothing," Gene said. When he looked up and saw Jim's concern, he realized he had to explain himself. "No, really. It's this stuff the quack gave me. Real horse pills and they irritate like hell on the way down. Then they dry you up. I read up on all this stuff years ago. This ain't flight medication, Jim. This is the real deal stuff, for ground time only. We moved into a new phase with this one today."

"Well other than falling apart on us a quarter of a million miles from a *real* doctor, how do you feel?"

"I'm okay, Jim. Really."

"Because I'm not getting any younger either. It's about time I had a proper assistant administrator to help run this place."

"Thought you'd never ask."

"Oh, you figured you'd be on the short list, Gene?"

"You old horse thief, everyone back home just *thinks* you designed this whole base, popping the plans fully formed out of your forehead like you were Zeus or some other damned engineering god. You and me—we know the truth."

Jim ignored the taunt. "Report on Monday?"

"Hell, I'll report tomorrow."

"Not today?" Jim asked, testing his old friend.

"Naw," Gene said, standing up and straightening his flight suit. "I think I once wrote a rule that said if you're the system failure which caused a launch abort—you get the rest of the day off."

"The launch wasn't an abort. They took it out of the hold twenty minutes ago and they're on their way."

"See? They didn't need me today anyway." Gene clapped his left hand good-naturedly on Jim Marshall's back.

Eight new lunar base specialists gathered in the penthouse conference room under the top of Dome 1. They'd been escorted from the landing terminal and left here to stand around waiting for something to happen.

Doug nudged Steve and pointed towards the far open hatch twenty feet away. "Isn't that Gene Fisher-Hall?"

"Yup. The new assistant administrator. Hear he's hell on wheels."

"What's he doing?"

The two men stared and tried to make out what the old man *was* doing. He seemed to be busily pulling cables out of a junction box, finally finding the cable group he wanted and after twisting off a quick-connect fitting, started attaching some sort of a jumper wire.

"It looks like he's . . . overriding . . . ?"

Gene looked up from his handiwork and gave them

a sly smile. The sliding hatch between them closed just as an emergency alarm went off. The eight newbies all looked wide-eyed at each other.

"That's a vacuum breach!" Sarah shouted. Steve tore off for the hatch, but even as he began to tap in emergency access codes, he could see Gene's smile spread from underneath his mustache, and knew he wouldn't be able to get this hatch open in time.

"What's the game here?"

"I don't know!"

"Well, someone do something!"

Doug picked up a phone, trying to get someone at Base Ops—but got no answer. Steve ran towards the other hatch and tried to get it open. When it wouldn't budge, he pounded on the panel cover next to the latch, trying to pop it open and gain access to the control wires inside.

"You guys are all incompetents."

The newbies turned to see Gene on their side of the first hatch. He took several large, loping steps and then, with an effortless grace, launched himself up to the top of the dome. In the reduced gravity of the Moon it was surprisingly balletic and he timed it to reach his apex exactly at the last handhold. By then the others noticed the hissing sound above their heads and watched as Gene closed the louvers on the vacuum line. The alarms silenced as well.

"At least *you* had an idea," Gene said, looking over at Sarah. The others saw her clinging on the handholds halfway up the dome, one of the emergency foam sealers slung across her back. Then Gene dropped slowly and easily back to the floor. "Come on, Sarah Rausch. It ain't really a twelve-foot drop. At least it don't feel like one. Just divide by six in your head, let go and fall."

Reluctantly Sarah let herself hang down, hesitated, then dropped.

"Y'all have forgotten you're on the Moon," Gene said, once Sarah rejoined the group. "And I'm not jest talking about the gravity. I set off a vacuum alert and you idiots stood around like you expected someone else to fix it. I got news for you—you've been through training back on Earth and now you're here. So you *are* the guys expected to fix it."

He walked over to an emergency locker and popped the door open.

"Not one of you thought to get into an emergency suit. Let me clue you in. That ain't Houston or Huntsville outside these walls either." Gene glared at each of the eight, stopping with Sarah. "You look like you got a question."

"Sir—why is there a vacuum line twelve feet off the floor?"

Gene chuckled before answering. "Good question. It's so y'all can't reach it during your first safety test on the Moon. I had it put in real special-like. It's actually attached to that valve station down yonder and we physically disconnect the sucker when we aren't harassing newbies."

Then Gene turned and strode out of the room, leaving the eight still standing there waiting for something to happen.

"Jesus—what was that?"

"That was your new best friend on the Moon," a voice said from the other hatch and they all turned to see Jim Marshall advancing on them. "Don't ever forget it."

The service was long over and the tech crews were packing up the cameras. Everyone else was gone, but still Dr. Hellebore stayed on. At fifty-eight months and counting, the doctor counted himself an old hand on "the base Jim Marshall built," soon to be renamed Fisher-Hall Base. It only took an involuntary glance at his wrist to know he still had over two hours of 0_2 left before he needed replenishment. Plenty of time to pay his respects—and remember.

And there were so many stories. Even today, pilots and engineers still argued about Gene's fuel problems with Lunar Transport *Tycho* and the finger pointing which had gone on after they'd torn the system apart. Hellebore let such talk wash over him—he wasn't really a technical space geek anyway. Besides, even here on the Moon the stories were changing, getting bigger than the old man had been. Now that he was dead, they'd get bigger still.

Gene, already a public hero back on Earth, lasted three more years and sixty-two transport runs after NASA went public with his condition. At the end he became the most famous astronaut ever—more famous than Neil Armstrong with his *one step* or John Glenn and his *one-and-a-half missions*, as Gene would say.

He had been on the job right up to the end. Hellebore found him at the office, with one last correction noted on a job order, a scrawled signature, then a command running on the screen to back up his computer. All apparently before leaning back in his chair and fading away. Peacefully. Professional to the end. Doing what he loved.

Gene had been right about so many things. Man now *lived* on the Moon all because Man now *died* on the Moon. And no, he hadn't been the first. But as the first permanent citizen of the Moon and the first to die due to natural causes and not accident, Gene would be the first buried in the gray regolith of the Moon. And most definitely he had been right about the response of the people of America and the rest of the world—the funeral had been beamed back to Earth for live midday coverage in America, evening in Europe, early morning in Japan. The audience worldwide was estimated at over three billion.

A blip sounding in Hellebore's ear gently reminded him it was time to board the rover and make it back to the main Armstrong Dome. He had a baby to deliver at 1800 hours—his third this month and the only boy in this lot. The NASA boys and girls up here, as Gene had called them, had certainly taken to the directive allowing children on the Moon. The doctor was pretty sure the parents would name their new son Gene. Gene Ramos Davies. It seemed fitting.

A new kind of human being was growing up here. In his bad Latin, Gene Fisher-Hall called them *Homo lunaris*. A true Man on the Moon, he'd said. Hellebore saluted his old friend and finally turned to go, only to discover he wasn't alone. Another spacesuited figure stood halfway to the rover. The computer display over Hellebore's right eye identified him as FLOWERS, HERB. The doctor had known the NASA administrator made the flight up to the Moon for the funeral, but what was the deal with standing out on the lunar soil in hard vacuum all alone like this, after the tech crews left?

"Herb? Are you all right?"

"Yes, doctor. I'm fine," Herb said. "I didn't want to intrude."

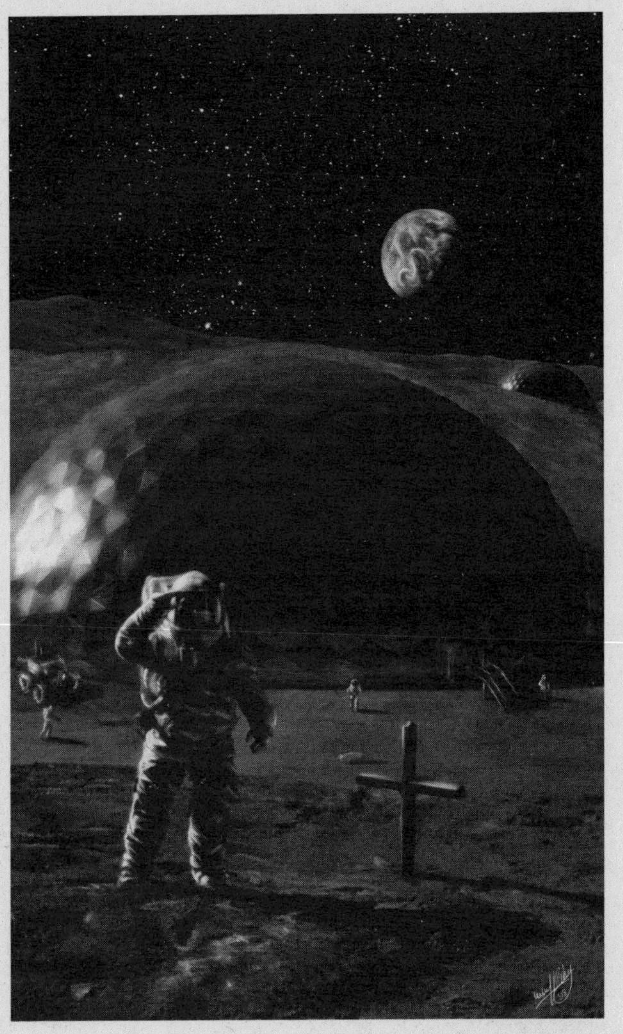

WILLIAM RUHLIG

"I meant being out here. It's not like you've trained for this."

"No," Herb said, then laughed. "Noooo, I can't say I ever expected to set foot on the Moon in my lifetime."

"Gene would've been impressed."

"Gene Fisher-Hall would've called me a damned fool."

"Sure. Technically you're a newbie and I don't see your buddy," Hellebore said, catching up to Herb. "But still you made it up here and that would've counted to the old man."

"Someone had to come," Herb said. "Maybe in another ten years it might've been the president. This time NASA could spare its assistant director."

The two men started walking toward the rover.

"How long are you up for?"

"Three days. One for the funeral. One for the dedication. One for the inevitable meetings as we figure out where we go from here."

"We build. We grow. We continue to head on out," Hellebore said.

"The president wants to know if we're ready to finally announce the Mars Initiative. He expects a report on his desk the minute I get back. It's not too soon to be thinking about the State of the Union speech."

"I wouldn't know about that," Hellebore admitted. "I've got my hands full with my medical practice here."

"You aren't coming home again, are you?"

"This is home, I think," the doctor said, stopping to look out along the bumpy gray horizon, then back at the domes. "But Gene did convince me to keep logging my time on the centrifuge."

"Yeah," Herb said. "You never know when you might have to storm into my office and threaten me."

They walked the rest of the way to the rover in silence, but Herb put a glove on Hellebore's sleeve before they boarded.

"Gene and I were never friends. I doubt we would be either. It's not my job to make friends with the astronauts or the ground crews. Or the vendors and the engineers," Herb said. "And I'll never make director. I guess I'm too good at what I do."

"I won't say that Gene respected you," Hellebore said, "because I don't know. But I think he understood where your job fit in the whole puzzle."

"I've got nothing but retirement to look forward to in Houston," Herb said. "This base is growing. You're going to need someone to fight with the politicians in Houston and Washington. Someone who can speak their budgetary bureaucratic lingo."

"Are you volunteering to come up here? To stay?"

"I'm thinking about it. Don't be so surprised. I've been an armchair space geek for most of my life. Gene's gone. Jim needs a *real* assistant administrator now."

Gene would've laughed. Dr. Hellebore was sure of it. But he didn't really feel like laughing—not yet.

"Herb, stop by my office tomorrow. After the show is over. We'll set you up for a proper physical." The beeping returned to Hellebore's ear. "Now we have to go."

"You have an appointment?"

"Yes," Hellebore said, settling into the driver's seat, clearing the safety check and activating their transponder. "As Gene would've said, we may have found intelligent life on the Moon."

The rover responded to Hellebore's commands and they headed towards Fisher-Hall Base.

"I don't suppose they're going to name the kid after Gene, are they?"

Dr. Hellebore hadn't mentioned what his appointment was, but as usual, Herb Flowers had his hands in everything.

"Actually, Herb, they are."

"Unbelievable," Herb replied. "And you said there was intelligent life on the Moon."

This was most definitely a new side to the Assistant Director, Hellebore thought. Maybe being off-world agreed with the man. "You might appreciate this, Herb. Gene told me a joke a couple of months ago and said to save it for today. For someone who would really appreciate it."

"Oh? Let's hear it."

"Knock-knock."

Reluctantly Herb allowed himself to follow the standard format. "Who's there?"

"Gene."

"Gene who?"

"Damn, boy," Hellebore said in his best imitation of the pilot's twang, *"y'all up there forget about me already?"*

Though neither could see through the gold sunshield of the other's helmet, both men were smiling as they drove on, the domes getting bigger and bigger. One last joke with Gene out on the surface of the Moon. His moon. What could be more fitting from the first Man in the Moon?

Bitter Dreams

written by

Ian McHugh

illustrated by

ROBERT J. HALL JR.

ABOUT THE AUTHOR

Ian McHugh lives in Canberra, Australia, with his wife and daughter and, at the time of this writing, another child on the way. "Bitter Dreams" is the first story he wrote at the Clarion West workshop in 2006. Ian is grateful for the support of the Australian Capital Territory government, who helped him get to Seattle, and with whose support he is now drafting a novel set in the same fantasy universe as his winning story here.

Ian has had stories published in Andromeda Spaceways Inflight Magazine, Challenging Destiny, Hub, Coyote Wild *and the All-Star Stories anthology,* Twenty Epics. *In 2008, he has followed his Writers of the Future success with a second professional sale, a story for* Asimov's Science Fiction *magazine.*

ABOUT THE ILLUSTRATOR

Robert Hall has been interested in art ever since he was a child, drawing crude interpretations of dinosaurs, superheroes and Indiana Jones. He read comic books throughout high school, and it wasn't long before he adopted that style of hyperrealistic fantasy art. After high school, he set off to become a comic book artist, beginning his higher education in New York at Cazenovia College's graphic design program. But, like many youths, Robert also suffered from a terrible affliction—a passion for heavy metal made worse by his need to play drums. He enrolled at State University of New York (SUNY) Oneonta as a music industry major, but gave that up after forming what he calls a technically complex, thunderous, jet-fueled spectacle of furious shenanigans named "Severeign" with some school friends. Despite touring actively throughout New England, the glory didn't last, and Robert returned to SUNY Oneonta as a computer art major. He now wants to create video games or visual effects for film. Until then, he will continue getting his hands dirty working for the maintenance department at SUNY Oneonta and spending the rest of his time strapped to a computer, pressing ever forward.

Bitter Dreams

The blackfellas brought the body down to the town gate in the gray of morning, when the mist was lifting but hadn't yet burned off. There were four of them and they carried the remains up on their shoulders, on a stretcher made of branches and plates of paperbark.

They didn't wear much, despite the cold, just loincloths and possum-skin shawls and one of them in a pair of cut-off moleskins. They were tall men, as blackfellas are, all ropy muscle, with the long, skinny calves and broad, long feet of runners. In the weak light, when their shadows were faint on the ground, their heavy brows and wide noses still gathered darkness around their eyes. Their hair was matted with clay and their faces, torsos and limbs were scarred all over with the white lines and dots the blackfellas use in place of pictures and letters.

They left the body outside the gate, wouldn't pass between the posts carved with English runes—couldn't, with the dreams of the land mapped all over their bodies. They turned around without a word and jogged back into the bush, not hurrying, just because that's the way they preferred to move.

Constable Robert Bowley sat on the porch outside the post office with Maise Wallace, drinking tea while Maise worked at her embroidery. Georgie, Maise's old half-dingo bitch, lay curled up at her mistress' feet.

Bowley toyed with his teacup, gazing at the buildings across the way. Hunched things, all, imposed on but never accepted by the clay and rock they squatted over. Mockeries of Englishness, with their crooked frames and sagging spines, tarred timbers and dark shingles unalleviated by the runes carved into their surfaces. They huddled beneath their roofs, shaded by alien trees and encroached upon by grass that was never green even in the wettest months.

Only the church was made of stone, not counting the coolroom out the back of the pub, and only it rose higher than the houses, and not by much. And it was even sadder than they, with no priest there since before Bowley had first come to Useless Loop. Its stones had all been shipped from England because local rock refused to take the shape.

He examined his hands around Maise's porcelain cup and saucer: the dirt that would never come out, at the base of his fingernails, in the creases of his knuckles and the fine lines that etched his skin. The cuffs of his uniform jacket, permanently impregnated with clay dust. He ran his thumb across the largest chip in the edge of the saucer, fitted the leathered pad into the shallow cavity.

"Bowls." Alby Tucker stood at the front of the porch, one booted foot propped against the edge of the boards, toe upwards so that Bowley could see the runes scorched into the leather sole. "Mate, you'd better come see what the blackfellas have left outside the gate."

Bloody hell."

Bowley stood over what was left of Stink McClure, forcing himself to look. He couldn't bring himself to squat down beside Alby and examine the corpse more closely. He rested one hand on his service holster and had the thumb of the other hooked in his belt, both fists closed so no one would see the shake in his fingers. He breathed through his mouth.

Maise stood beside him, her face pale, arms folded across her chest. Bowley doubted it was because her hands were shaking. Beyond her, German Braun and young Dermott O'Shane watched Alby prod at the corpse, their lips pursed in mirrored expressions of distaste. Their shadows all bunched up close under their boots, reluctant to cast themselves across the corpse.

"Been dead a day or so," said Alby. He poked about under the rib cage with a stick. "His liver's gone as well."

Bowley could see there wasn't as much left inside the open belly as there should've been. There wasn't much left, in fact, to show that the carcass *had* been old Stink, just his gray nest of hair, his crappy old homemade snakeskin boots and that prickly pear of a nose of his. As well as opening his guts, whatever had eaten him up had chewed off his genitals, and dug out his eyes, and ripped apart his cheeks to get at his tongue. His blood-matted beard hung from shreds of skin around his ears. His lower jaw flopped loosely on his chest.

German asked, "Vas it a villyvilly?" Ingrained soot made the furrows of his always-sweaty brow appear even deeper.

Maise said, "Willywilly wouldn't chew him up like that."

She knew. A willywilly had taken her husband, Nev, not a year after Bowley arrived in town, left his carcass with all the hair sucked off it and scattered around. But, with the sun now peeking through the clouds, they could all see that Stink's corpse cast no darkness beneath it, on its bed of bark and sticks. Whatever killed him had drunk up his shadow as well. The body seemed to float, a hair's width off the ground, cut adrift, as the corpses of the dream-eaten are.

But what the hell kind of dreaming would tear a man up like that? A willywilly wouldn't make a mark on a man, just leave him bald, not needing to devour the parts that anchored him in his flesh in order to pull out his soul. A bunyip or potkoorok might chew a body up, some, but the dreamings that lay in billabongs and creeks didn't have teeth, as such, and tended to crush up the guts and bones and leave the bag of skin that contained them intact.

"Maybe it was dingoes, or a goanna, after," said Alby, pressing hands down on thighs to come upright. The ligaments in his knees creaked as he straightened.

Bowley shook his head, doubtfully. He extracted his thumb from his belt and scratched at the edges of his moustache, his skin still raw from the morning's cold-water shave. He wished he'd remembered to put on his uniform cap—still on Maise's outdoor table beside the cold dregs of his tea. He felt vulnerable without it, his lawman's persona incomplete. He realized his hand was still shaking and put it back to his belt.

"Dingo's too smart," he said, "and a goanna's been around long enough to know better."

"What about the blackfellas?" said Dermott O'Shane.

"Why would they bring him in if they'd done it?" said Alby.

The young Irishman shrugged. "Maybe he did something to them. They wanted us to know they'd had their justice."

"Old Stink?" said Bowley. Stink McClure had been a mad old bastard, but he'd known better than most how to stay on the good side of the natives. Although, if it was the blackfellas that'd done it, no one in their right mind, not even a magister, was going to dispute it. That meant case closed, no further problems. Bowley didn't think so.

"We should go out to check on the others," said Maise.

The Del Mar clan, she meant, her blood kin, in their fortified farmstead up the top of the Loop, where the track crossed the ridge and turned to come back down. She had a sister up there, Lucy, and a niece, as well as all her cousins and uncles and aunts. Less important, for her, King James Campbell and White Mitchell with his retarded brother and all the other antisocials prospecting the gullies and creek beds between Del Mar's and the town.

Everyone looked at Bowley, the Queen's Man, the town's sole protector, although he was as mundane as any of them. Useless Loop was too small to maintain its own magister or even a runesmith, only German, the blacksmith, with the dozen signs he knew that worked on hooves and boot soles. The town had Bowley and the rune posts at the gate and the runestones laid beneath their houses and in a ring around the town. And they had the runes on their boots and bullets of English silver in their guns. None of which would stop a really strong and bitter dreaming, should the land ever throw one up, just make it angrier.

Alby snuffled back a chunk of phlegm and dug in his vest pocket for a handkerchief. He saved Bowley from having to answer. "Bugger that, Maise."

Bowley nodded, hoping his relief wasn't too obvious. He badly wanted a whiskey, couldn't while he was on duty. He thought he might get away with a gulp or two from the bottle under his desk, later.

"Come crank up the telegraph for us, eh, Maise? We'll get onto Ballarat and see what they say." For a moment he thought she'd argue. Her shoulders were tucked up like they got when she was that way inclined. But she nodded. Bowley waved a hand to encompass Alby, German and O'Shane. "You blokes take the body to the pub and put it in the coolroom."

Alby snorted. "Ulf's going to be bloody happy about that."

"Tell him I've deputized you," Bowley called back over his shoulder, walking after Maise, his shadow stretching ahead and eager to be gone.

Investigate. Report," was the terse reply that came back from Ballarat in the middle of the afternoon.

Bowley had stayed at Maise's for lunch after they sent their telegram, returned, without thinking, to his accustomed seat on the post office's porch. She'd made his food in the same manner, neither his fear nor her anger enough to derail them from their familiar patterns. Neither of them had spoken while they ate. They rarely did say much. Usually, it was because there wasn't all that much to say, just closeness to be had and that was something both of them felt was best taken in silence. Today the crow's feet at the corners of Maise's eyes had been tight with worry. A lot going on inside of her, he could tell, although it was unlikely that much, if any, of it would find its way into words.

Leaning against the frame of the station house door, Bowley unfolded the paper for the dozenth time and reread Maise's scrawled transcription. As if, somehow, the message might've changed from the previous eleven times he'd read it. *Investigate. Report.* "Green Christ."

Maise had wanted to ride out right away. Bowley had started to shake his head, to point out that there wasn't time to get out to Del Mar's and back before dark. She'd smelled the whiskey on his breath as soon as he opened his mouth. He'd watched her rigid back as she stalked away.

He watched her now, back on her porch with Georgie sprawled at her feet, both of them sharing the last rays of sun and Maise pretending not to see him watching. He'd always thought, vaguely, that one day he'd make an honest woman of her, although both of them were past child rearing age. He'd never quite gotten around to asking. In truth, he was happy enough to just share the stillness of her front porch and, sometimes, the warmth between her bedsheets, whenever the urgency was enough in both of them to keep him there overnight.

Cold nights alone stretched ahead of him.

His thoughts circled back to worrying at what the hell might've done that to old Stink, like nothing he'd ever seen before—heard about, maybe, but only up north, nowhere nearby—and where it might've come from and how could it, since dreamings didn't move from the patch of land that dreamed them? And how strong was this dreaming? Strong enough to get past the runestones and the gate? Because if it was, there was no one and nothing here that could stop it from doing to the whole town what it'd done to Stink McClure.

There were dreamings that came that strong, he'd heard, out in the desert, where the land was still wakeful and warlike, that could take over a person, or more than one, and use them as its teeth and claws. . . . He shuddered, thinking of human teeth tearing up Stink.

Georgie's shadow slunk off under the porch, leaving the dog still asleep in her patch of sun.

Other animal shadows flitted across the dusty clay of the street, looking for dark places to hide. Their frantic owners pursued them. Cats, chooks, a couple of early-rising possums and Ted Wright's brown nanny goat, united in flight. Georgie awoke with a start, twisted wildly about and, with a swallowed yip, followed her shadow under the porch.

The pair of horses hitched at the watering trough in front of the smithy started in alarm as their shadows bucked, shadow-legs stretching with their feet anchored to the runes beneath the horses' shoes. German tumbled out and lunged for the animals' reins. The horses quieted before he even reached them, opting to freeze with flight denied. Bowley could see their ears flicking, trying to pinpoint the threat.

German's head swiveled to look down the street, towards the gate. Maise was up out of her chair and looking that way too.

The horse was a dappled gray of the long-necked, spindle-legged variety bred to tolerate sorcery. Its rider wore a battered oilskin coat, with worn and faded edges on its collar, cuffs and hem, and slashes of lighter color where it had dried out and stiffened in the dust and sun. A rough Hessian shawl draped the man's head and shoulders beneath the sagging brim of his hat.

He reined his horse to a halt in the middle of the street, facing the setting sun. Neither the man nor his horse cast a shadow. They stood, superimposed on the world, but not really fitted to it.

Two days at least for a magister to come up from Ballarat with a company of redcoats in tow, and Bowley's superiors had made it plain that they weren't coming to his aid at all until he could tell them more precisely what they'd be walking into. So who in hell was this, right here and now?

Bowley reached inside the door and took his uniform cap from its peg. Maise looked his way as he stepped outside. He tried a tentative smile. She didn't respond. He pretended not to notice, smoothed his jacket and hitched his gun belt. He straightened his policeman's badge on its silver chain and stepped down from the porch.

He was acutely conscious of the eyes that followed his progress across the rutted clay. Maise and German. Alby, leaning outside the pub with Ulf Erikssen. He could feel his shadow's reluctance to follow, a heaviness in his calves and feet, like his legs had fallen half asleep. He willed it to stay with him.

He was conscious, too, of the awkward weight of his gun, bumping on his hip with every step. He hooked his thumbs in his belt to keep it still.

Bony hands folded over the saddle's pommel—pale skinned, with a grayish tinge, and blotched with darker gray liver spots, the man evidently as dappled as his horse. Both the rider's gear and his horse's tack were curiously blank, unmarked by runes. Bowley could see nothing on either man or horse to indicate that the rider was, in any regard, a Queen's Man.

Bloody hell, a wild spook.

The cowled head turned towards him as he neared. Bowley could make out the lines of a gaunt face in the shadows gathered beneath the man's hat. The shadows seemed to writhe across his cheeks and down his neck. A long nose protruded into the light, blotched like the man's hands.

Bowley stopped a distance from the stranger that he hoped might appear both authoritative and deferential. Queen's Man or not, a spook was a spook, after all, and Bowley had no wish to have his soul sucked out of him for the sake of a moment of perceived impertinence.

"I'm Bowley, local constable." It sounded as inadequate as he felt.

The cowl dipped in acknowledgement. Bowley waited, but the man didn't speak. The silence began to stretch.

Bowley cleared his throat and said, "You got a name, mate?"

The stranger's reply was as oblique as any magister's would be: "None that's any use." His voice was a surprise, rich and soft.

Bowley tried again, "What brings you to Useless Loop?"

"Land's thrown up a bad dreaming, hereabouts."

Bowley's guts clenched. He tried to keep his reaction off his face as he said, "How do you know about it?"

The man gave a huff that might've been a laugh. "Land stinks of it. How do *you* know about it?"

Bowley considered him, disinclined to answer and wracking his brains for who the hell this wild spook might be and coming up with nothing. But, damn it all, he was far out of his depth and, wild spook or not, he was in dire need of magical aid. "Dreaming killed a man, outside town. Chewed him up something horrible. Got the body in the coolroom at the pub."

He felt an abrupt increase in the intensity of the other's stare. "Can I see it?"

Bowley hesitated, but knew he'd committed himself now. He tipped his head in the direction of the pub.

He started walking, not waiting for the stranger to dismount. He heard the man land, heard his steps close behind—puffs of dust and the small clinks of shifting pebbles, no thump of boot soles striking earth.

The hair stood up along the length of Bowley's spine. *Bloody spook.*

Ulf and Alby levered themselves off the rail and disappeared inside the pub. Bowley led the stranger down the side and round the back. By the time they arrived, Ulf had unlocked the coolroom door and retreated to the rear porch with Alby.

Bowley let the stranger precede him through the low door. The temperature dropped sharply within the thick stone walls. The man crouched beside the body, his oilskin collapsing towards the floor, as though it were all but empty. He pulled back the tarp that covered Stink and was still for a while, a crumpled pile of shadows in the light from the door. Outside, Ulf muttered something to Alby that Bowley couldn't quite catch.

The stranger flipped the tarp back over the body and rose, turning, the brim of his hat only inches from Bowley's eyes. His coat sleeve brushed Bowley's chest as he exited. Bowley stood in the darkness alone for a moment. His eyes fell on the flattened lump under the tarp. He shuddered.

Ulf and Alby watched silently as he reemerged. Ulf's expression offered him nothing. Alby widened his eyes a moment. Bowley hurried after the stranger, already striding back up the street. The man walked past his horse and headed for the gate. Intrigued and disturbed, Bowley followed. Maise's porch was empty. Sweat trickled past his belt to lodge in the back of his pants.

The man stopped outside the gate. His shrouded head half turned towards Bowley. "This is where they left the body."

"Yep."

The stranger faced outward. Bowley scanned the surrounding bush, wondering what he saw. For a minute the man was still. Then darkness began to pour from under the fringe of his shawl, out of his cuffs and under his coattails. Bowley squeaked.

His shadow tore itself free of the runes on his boot soles and fled back into town. The darkness pooled on the ground around the man's feet, its edges reaching and questing. It lapped at Bowley's toes and flowed around his heels, then released him. The man raised his arms and the darkness shattered into a dozen running shadows that raced away into the bush.

The stranger lowered his arms.

Bowley swallowed. *Green bloody Christ.*

The stranger stood like a statue for most of half an hour while his shadows hunted. Bowley waited with him, not daring to walk away, feeling queasy and lightheaded without his shadow. At last the hunters returned. They flowed up the man's legs, moving fast, so that Bowley had trouble making out their shapes. He thought he saw men among the dogs and roos and emus and other, smaller forms. The last shadow disappeared beneath the man's coat.

"The town should be safe for tonight."

Bowley nodded, only realizing after he'd done so that the man couldn't see the gesture. He gathered up enough composure to say, "There's a lot of prospectors out there, up the Loop."

"Dead."

Christ. He'd had a notion there'd be more than just Stink McClure, but the stranger's flat appraisal rocked him, even so. "There's a farmstead, too, up the top. Fortified. Lot of people."

The spook didn't respond.

"My orders are to investigate," Bowley added.

"You're riding out?"

"Tomorrow."

Silence, for a while, then: "I'll come with you. I can defend four men."

A small part of Bowley bristled at the man's presumption. Most of him sagged with relief.

"Have you got any rune-carved bullets?" the stranger asked.

Bowley knew the number precisely: six. He answered cautiously, "Some."

The spook turned, his shrouded face a vague impression amid the shadows. "We'll need more than some. Is there a runesmith in town?"

"Just the blacksmith."

"He'll do."

The man brushed past and strode back into town. Bowley hurried after. The skin on his back crawled. His shadow lunged at him from the shelter of Ted Wright's house, nearest the gate, and reattached itself to his feet.

The mist was heavier the following dawn. The stranger, on his horse just outside the gate, was discernible only because Bowley knew he was there.

Bowley fumbled another carved silver bullet from his palm and pressed it into the magazine of his service carbine, then shrugged the gun from the crook of his arm into his hand and slotted the magazine home. Alby, German and young Dermott O'Shane formed a circle with him. German's eyes were so bloodshot he had no whites left to speak of. Bowley knew his own eyes weren't much better, having seen the state of himself in his washstand mirror. He'd spent the whole night out on his porch, his service revolver in his lap, loaded with the six rune-carved bullets he'd been issued a decade before, when he joined the Queen's Constabulary. He doubted any of them had slept much.

Young O'Shane grabbed at a bullet that slipped between his fingers. It bounced off his thumb and tumbled in an arc to strike the ground. The older men flinched and sucked air through their teeth. All three shared a sheepish grin, their reflexes outdated, accustomed to rimfire cartridges. O'Shane scooped up the escapee and stood again, red from forehead to chin.

"No worries, mate," said Bowley, relieved that he'd managed to load his own weapon without dropping anything and made magnanimous because of it. There was still a tremor in his hands, but much less than the day before, now that the moment was upon them.

Alby flipped the magazine cylinder shut on the second of his six-shooter rifles. He sniffled loudly. His cold seemed to be getting worse. "You know anything about this spook, Bowls?"

"Much as you do," said Bowley. "German?"

"Don't ask me, mate," the blacksmith said. "Ve just carved damn bullets all night."

Young O'Shane piped up, "I heard about a dappled man, once, when I was out Ararat way. Said he came in from the desert, on foot, dressed like a blackfella and spotted all over, like his sire was one of them Dalmatian hounds. That's all I know. Never saw him myself."

Alby spat. "Reckon that's our bloke. We right?"

"Yep."

"Ja."

The O'Shane boy nodded his head.

"No time like the present," said Bowley.

His old brown mare, Clay, looked back at him with wide nostrils and white-rimmed eyes as he shuffled along her side. Her shadow was skittish beneath her, faint as it was, both horse and shade aware of the Dappled Man's presence and keyed up because of it. Bowley shoved his carbine into the sleeve in front of the saddle and patted her neck.

"All right, old girl." He unhitched the reins and brought them up to her neck. Alby was already aboard his chestnut mare, Nudge. German heaved himself up onto fat black Bismarck the gelding and O'Shane rose easily into the saddle of his new piebald filly. Bowley put his foot in the stirrup, grabbed a handful of mane and hauled himself up.

"Ah, damn."

Maise, wearing an oilskin and a pair of Nev's old pants, led Ulf's mean-tempered roan up from the direction of the pub. Bowley held his ground while the others retreated. Maise stopped in front of him, Ulf's idiot horse almost pulling her off balance as it danced about.

She didn't wait to hear Bowley's objections. "It's my family, Robert. And I'm a better shot than anyone except you."

He glanced at the others, waiting halfway to the gate. Alby smirked. Bowley said, "But you can't ride to save yourself, love. What if we have to move in a hurry? That animal'll break your bloody neck."

"Don't you 'love' me," she snapped. "German can't ride for beans, either."

Of that, Bowley was acutely aware. "No one else volunteered."

"*I'm* volunteering."

"The spook says he can only defend four."

"*You're* the bloody constable—since when are you taking orders from him?"

"It's *because* it's your family out there that I don't want you to come."

"I don't need you to protect me, Robert."

It's not you I'm protecting, love. It's me. His desperation crept into his voice, "Maise, please."

Her jaw clenched. She bowed her head, hiding her

face from him. She was crying, he knew, and knew too that she wouldn't accept any comfort from him. He dithered for a moment, then pulled Clay's head around and prodded the horse into motion. He didn't need to look back to know she wouldn't follow.

The Dappled Man's hunting shadows already roiled around his horse's hooves, indistinct in the silvery dimness. He waited until the townsmen were a few yards behind him, then clucked his horse forward. His shadows ranged ahead of him, vanishing almost immediately from sight.

The Man's connection to the ground, through his horse's hooves, seemed even more attenuated, today, than it had in strong sunlight. It seemed he might, if he relaxed the will that anchored him, simply drift off into the mist.

None of them looked back as they rode from town. They didn't need to, could feel the moment when it dissolved into the shroud of mist and trees. Their mounted shadows tucked tight beneath the horses' hooves. The charms on the horses' tack clinked loudly in the surrounding stillness.

Beside the track grew spiked grass that was only ever the color of forgotten bones. Trees surrounded them, some twisted, some straight, all of them alien, with their bleached skins—some that leaked thick sap like blood, others with bark hanging in strips and strings as though they'd been flayed. All growing out of ground that was either rock or clay and in both cases unyielding, that gave itself only with bitter resentment to any man who wanted to farm it.

Even under mist or rain, with the air above it saturated, the land remained parched. Bowley could feel it plucking at the edges of his shadow, and knew that the land would drink him up, too, in an instant, should he ever surrender to it.

A couple of miles out of town, they passed a stand of twisted eucalypts, their trunks wound up and bent like wrung towels, that marked a willywilly's hunting ground. Bowley put his left hand to his badge, tracing runes—not that a willywilly was likely to give them trouble when they had a spook in their company. O'Shane pointed. Stink McClure's shack—the old willywilly ground a signpost on the trail. Bowley had been trying not to look. The Dappled Man kept riding, facing straight ahead.

"Bowls," said Alby, softly. "Strikes me that a Queen's magister'll tow a whole company of redcoats around with him. This bloke reckons he can only protect four of us. Makes me wonder, if we come across this thing that did for Stink, whether he'll be able to handle it."

"Alby," Bowley said. "I reckon you think too much, mate."

He slipped a hand inside his jacket, wound the cap off his hip flask with thumb and forefinger, and took a swig. He glanced at Alby, staring pointedly at the flask. Bowley took another mouthful and handed it over. Alby upended it, then passed it around. It came back to Bowley from German, empty.

"Damn," said Bowley, but without much rancor. "Greedy bloody Boche."

"Vasn't me," said German. "Vas this greedy Irish bastard, here."

Alby sneezed loudly, startling a flock of cockatoos into screeching, deafening flight. Men and horses alike all but jumped off their shadows. Young O'Shane's filly put her head down and pigrooted, nearly planting the Irishman into the dirt. Clay danced sideways, objecting to the younger horse's theatrics. Bowley pulled her head around and made her walk a full circle. He patted her neck as she calmed, his own heartbeat pounding in his ears. The cockies settled in the branches above, white enough to be the spirits of the dead, like the blackfellas believed, but complaining far too loudly to be ghosts.

Neither the Dappled Man nor his horse had reacted to the commotion behind them. The Man reached a fork in the track and unerringly picked the way that led up the Loop.

"Bloodless bastard," O'Shane muttered.

"Reckon this fog might lift?" said Alby.

Bowley looked skywards. "Not for a while, anyway."

The track started to climb. They passed the Mitchell brothers' place shortly after. The Dappled Man ignored that, too. Bowley noted the absence of smoke coming from the chimney pipe. He knew with a sick knotting in his guts what they'd find inside if they looked.

The trees opened out on a shelf of lichen-fringed rock. The clopping of their horses' iron shoes became abruptly louder, but flattened, the echoes smothered by the mist. The flanks of the ranges rose ahead, a blue-green wall vanishing into grayness.

Bowley squeezed Clay's ribs between his knees. When she didn't respond, he gave her a thump with his heels. She broke into a reluctant trot to come level with the Dappled Man, her hooves striking a dissonant staccato on the rock.

The Man sat hunched in his saddle, as if guarding his darkness against leaching away into the gray surrounds. He seemed diminished—not so fearsome, now, when fearsome was what they wanted most.

"You know what we're hunting," Bowley said, flat.

The Hessian fringe turned towards him. The Man whispered a reply, "Broken Hill."

It took Bowley a moment to make the connection. His mouth turned dry. *Broken Hill.* "Christ."

It had been a mining town up in New South Wales, out near the edge of the desert, where the spirit of the land hadn't yet lain down to sleep. Some bitter dream had slithered out of a seam in the rock and into the mines. Possessed by it, the miners had devoured the town and besieged the survivors in the church for four days until the magisters arrived from Sydney Town with a train full of redcoats and organ guns packed with silver grapeshot.

So the story went.

"How?" Bowley asked. "Dreamings don't travel. There's never been any dreamings like that around here."

The Man didn't answer immediately. The trees closed in again around them. There was wood smoke in the mist, blackfellas in the scrub. A camp. Cooking fires smoldered in a second, smaller clearing, enclosed by a half-circle of lean-to shelters. The tribe watched them silently between the tree trunks. The women and children stood behind the men, swaddled in possum-skin cloaks and emu feathers. The cloaks were scorched with the same dot-and-line maps that scarred the blackfellas' skins, that connected them to the land's power and protected them from its dreamings.

The men leaned on long spears and the hip-high war boomerangs that whitefellas knew as Number Sevens, for the curve and unequal proportions of their arms.

The blackfellas made no gesture or sound, just watched.

"That was a new dreaming, full of anger and strength," said the Dappled Man, when they'd passed. "When the land becomes quiet, as it is here, such dreamings sink down into the rock, and wither away over time. This dreaming, here and now, will be old, from deep in the ground, with little of it left, otherwise it would've attacked the town already."

"But how did it come up? There's no mines."

"Caves?" the Man suggested, and suddenly Bowley saw it all: Del Mar kids with lanterns, daring each other to go farther and farther into the grottos up the back of the property. Or young Del Mar men, maybe, down there looking for veins in the rock, one of them putting a hand on some old stone, under which a nightmare slept, that would have slumbered away to nothing if one poor fool hadn't happened upon it.

The spook was watching him intently.

"Del Mar's," Bowley said. "Up the top of the Loop."

"How many people there?"

"Maybe forty, plus kids."

"It probably won't have been strong enough to use all of them," the Man said. "But expect there to be children among those it's taken."

Bowley didn't need to ask what would've happened to the rest. He felt a sharp little hurt behind his breastbone. He saw Maise's sister Lucy, putting a hand on his shoulder the last time he'd visited, interrupting his conversation with the Del Mar men to ask him if he wanted tea. A plumper, warmer, motherly version of Maise, almost invariably with a smile on her face. Her daughter Jemima had served the tea, a willowy child with her father's height, barely into womanhood, her cheeks flushing at the gentle teasing of her great-uncle Javier.

Maise's face came to his mind's eye, jaw quaking and eyes brimming before she dipped her head and he turned his back on her and rode away. Bowley's hands were shaking again. He fumbled for his flask, was surprised for a moment to find it empty.

He flung it into the bush. "Bloody hell."

The Del Mar house was an overgrown cousin to the cottages in town—the way a mastiff is to a terrier—a great, brooding thing of raw timbers and tar. Timber roofed, too, with a cavernous loft space where the children slept. They had some talented runesmiths among them, the Del Mars—Oscar had learned the craft in his native Andalusia—so they had no need for English slates to press the building on its runestone foundations. The whole house was covered in a mesh of flowing Arabic script and the angular English runes that Oscar and his sons had learned since they left their homeland. New wings had been added, over the years, as sons and daughters married and brought their wives and husbands back to live. Only a handful, like Maise, had made their lives elsewhere. All of the extensions connected back to the main house, with just the stables and feed barns standing separate, and they were connected to the house with paths of rune-carved corduroy.

It was a fortress town in all but name, Del Mar's, and

stronger in its defenses than most towns. But perhaps, Bowley thought to himself, its greatest strength was also its weakness. Because dreamings understood matters of blood and hearth—of place—intimately. No dreaming was intelligent, but some were clever. The rare one was strong enough to roam over an area, not tied to a single spot like a willywilly or a bunyip. If a dreaming of that kind got into a man's shadow, then it might ride him to his home and maybe no density of warding signs, English or Arab—or blackfella, for that matter—would keep the contagion out and stop it spreading to his kin.

The Dappled Man reined in at the edge of the cleared ground that surrounded the farm buildings. There was no sign of the cattle that ranged freely over the hills, but which often hung around near the house. The farm was shuttered and silent. Bowley halted Clay beside the Dappled Man. Young O'Shane pulled up beside him and Alby and German on the Man's far side. Alby snuffled into his handkerchief.

Bowley drew his carbine from its sleeve and laid it across his lap. Alby and German followed his example. O'Shane drew two of his four pistols.

The townsmen's horses whickered and danced as the Dappled Man's hunting shadows returned and wriggled up his mount's legs. The Man straightened in his seat, but still he seemed less than he had the day before. A breath of wind rolled curling fingers of mist from the trees beyond the house. Bowley searched the gray above for some sign of a tear in the veil. There was nothing.

The Dappled Man walked his horse a few paces into the open. Another breath of air chilled Bowley's face and ruffled the horses' manes. It tugged the Man's coat, collapsing the side of it inwards. Bowley saw him clearly, then: as a scarecrow, a mockery of a man, a creature with limbs and head but only shadow at his centre.

The Man's horse stopped dead in its tracks. Its ears twitched furiously. Clay whickered and tossed her head. Then all the horses were at it, fidgeting and complaining and dancing on their hoofs. The air seemed suddenly thin in Bowley's lungs, as though there was a big storm approaching.

The Man's head whipped to the left. Bowley looked that way in alarm, but could make out nothing untoward among the trees. He ran his fingers over the killing runes etched into his carbine's stock. The Man turned the other way, stared.

Bowley thought he heard a whisper of sound, a distant yelping and howling.

"No." The Dappled Man spun his horse on the spot. "Run!" he barked. "We can't face it here."

His horse launched itself towards them.

"Run!" the Man cried.

Then he was past them and all of them were cursing, their horses skittering about and bumping into each other while they tried to get them turned around. Bowley glimpsed figures in English clothes racing through the trees. The howling had grown rapidly more distinct. It was in his head, Bowley realized with a stab of horror, but not in his ears.

The riders got themselves moving. Alby and young O'Shane galloped ahead of Bowley, down the slope, Alby riding one-handed, as Bowley was, his rifle pressed across his lap. Bowley glanced back and saw that German was already falling behind, fat Bismarck struggling under his rider's weight, German with one fist in his horse's mane and the other flailing his rifle about for balance. Their conjoined shadows stretched out ahead of them, straining to drag horse and rider along.

"Move it, you fat bloody Boche!" Bowley yelled back, which wouldn't help German at all, but there was nothing practical Bowley could do for him.

Clay jerked her head as something flew past her nose. A second object struck painfully against Bowley's arm. He tucked his head down. In his peripheral vision he saw running figures closing on either side, arms pulled back and whipping forward—throwing rocks as they ran. He caught jumbled impressions of bloody chins and blood-stained shirts, of mouths open wide in silent anguish.

Then he was past them. He looked back. German made it through a heartbeat before the first pursuers spilled onto the track. The blacksmith had lost his hat. Bowley saw a splash of red across his forehead. But German was still in his saddle, gritted teeth and wide eyes stark in his dark face.

Clay gained quickly on the three riders ahead. They'd already slowed their horses to a canter. Bowley did the same as he came up to them. The Dappled Man twisted in his saddle. Bowley wished he could see the expression on the spook's face. Alby looked back, too, and gave a shake of his head. Whether the gesture was one of exasperation with Bowley, or the spook, or the situation in general, Bowley wasn't certain.

German hadn't caught up. And wasn't going to, Bowley saw. Bismarck was laboring even harder, now, the horse's gait uneven, favoring a hind leg. Bowley swore under his breath and reined Clay back into a trot. He felt the tug on his flesh as her shadow and his both resisted. The gap between them and the three riders ahead widened again. The mist closed between them.

He scanned the bush around as German caught up. Bismarck didn't need any instruction from his rider to slow to a trot.

"Look's like he's lame."

German dabbed at the cut on his temple with his handkerchief, examined the resulting mess on the white cloth with distaste. "Stone hit him in the leg," he replied. Bowley could see where—a patch of torn hair just above the gelding's hock. German drew a shaky breath and added, "Vell, that vas a vasted trip."

Bowley heard the note of hysteria in the other man's voice, and in his own chuckle in response. "We'll hold a trot for a bit, see if he works the lameness out. We should stay ahead of them at this pace."

German nodded. "Ja, but they vill go straight down the hill vhile ve follow the track."

"Better keep an eye out then, hadn't we?"

German gave a rictus grin. "I notice those other bastards didn't hang around."

"Spook's getting back to town quick," Bowley said. He hoped—to get them ready. By rights, *he* should be riding ahead, too, and leaving German to take his chances. There had been a *lot* of people in the scrub at Del Mar's, enough for it to be the whole damn clan taken by this dreaming. And, Christ, he couldn't get those half-seen faces, or the silent howls of the thing that possessed them, out of his head.

They were—*it* was—coming after them, he was certain, like a tiger snake that'd chase you for a mile even after it'd struck at you once, just because it was pissed at the world and you happened to be a part of it. He hoped like hell this Dappled Man wasn't lighting out on them, that Alby'd shoot the son of a bitch in the back if he was.

They passed the spot where the blackfella tribe had been camped. No sign of them now.

A tortured whispering brushed his mind. He felt a sucking at the soles of his feet. His and Clay's shadows snapped free of the horse's hooves and lit out across the bare rock ahead. German's shadow on Bismarck's was close on their heels.

"Grün . . ."

". . . Christ!"

Running figures emerged from the mist, off to their left. Bowley kicked frantically at his horse's ribs. "Move!"

Clay leapt into a gallop. Bismarck whinnied, in pain, and terrified of the thing that pursued them.

A man lunged out of the trees on their right. Clay's hooves struck the edge of the rock shelf, clattering like gunshots. Behind them, Bismarck screamed.

Bowley looked back. The gelding staggered out onto the open rock. A pick handle hung obscenely from his belly. The horse's eyes bulged as he cried in bewilderment and pain.

Bowley hauled back on Clay. Her hooves skidded on the bare stone. Her back end dropped before she found purchase again. Bowley loosed the reins and spun her with his knees.

Bismarck collapsed. German leapt clumsily but got

his legs clear of the horse's weight. Bismarck's cries drowned out the dreaming's dingo howls.

The attacker charged out of the trees, empty hands raised like claws. Francisco Del Mar, an iron-haired Andalusian bull. He was barely recognizable, with sticks in his hair and the animal snarl on his face. His feet were bare and he cast no shadow. German was still on his back, no runes between him and the thing that ran beneath Francisco and his kin. Bowley was acutely aware of how vulnerable they were, with their shadows far from their feet.

He brought his carbine to his shoulder. *Christ, Maise's cousin Frank.* He sighted and fired. Missed.

Clay danced on the spot, ears flat.

Bowley swore and sought the cold marksman's place within himself that used to be so easy to find. He pushed down the carbine's lever to eject the empty shell and chamber the next. It stuck halfway.

"Damn!" Bowley pounded the jammed lever with the heel of his hand.

German had his boots under him. Francisco was almost on him. More Del Mars emerged from the trees. German ignored them. He raised his rifle and shot his dying horse through the top of the head. Bismarck's cheek slapped loudly against the rock.

Dingo howling curled through the abrupt quiet.

"German—behind you!"

The blacksmith met Bowley's stare with dazed eyes. He turned, fired at Francisco from the hip. The bullet caught the Del Mar in the shoulder, spun him all the way around and down to the ground.

German swung his rifle towards the approaching horde and kept shooting, not bothering to aim. There were a good forty or fifty people: men, women and children, and more than just Del Mars. Bowley spied White Mitchell's narrow frame among the front ranks. All of them were barefoot, like Francisco, all filthy and bloody and with the same rictus snarl on their faces. Many of them carried farm tools—picks, hatchets and shovels—as weapons. None of them made a sound, only the silent howling of the thing that possessed them.

"Run!" Bowley cried, "You stupid bastard! *Run!*" He hoped Alby had shot that damn spook for lighting out and leaving them. He shoved his jammed carbine into its sleeve and fumbled for his service revolver.

German's rifle clicked, empty. The dream-taken were almost on top of him. German started to swing his rifle by the stock, spitting curses in his native tongue. Francisco Del Mar staggered to his feet behind him, his right arm dangling. Bowley shouted a warning.

Too late. Francisco hooked his left arm around German's neck, pulling him off balance just as the rest reached him. They bore him to the ground. Hooked fingers tore at his clothes. Heads dipped, teeth bared, and German's curses turned to screams.

Bile rose in Bowley's throat, spurting out of his mouth before he could swallow it back down. Most of the Del Mars kept coming. Bowley raised his pistol and fired off all six shots without seeing where any of them struck.

He heard the deep *whooosh-whooosh* before he saw the war boomerangs come spinning out of the scrub. They tore into the dream-taken, snapping human bodies like stalks of wheat.

A rider burst past Bowley. The Dappled Man.

Shadows writhed all over both the spook and his horse. The Del Mars fell back, closing ranks before him.

Bowley put his heels to Clay's ribs, and fled. Among the trees, blackfellas whirled like hammer throwers. A second flight of war boomerangs launched into the air.

The Dappled Man caught up with him near Stink McClure's shack. Clay had slowed to a trot of her own accord, and then a walk. The Man had lost his hat and his Hessian shawl was scrunched in one fist. Lank, shoulder-length gray hair framed bony features that receded at forehead and chin from his long nose. The complexion of his face was, indeed, the same unhealthy mottled gray as his hands.

The Man slowed his horse beside Clay. Moving with what seemed to be pained slowness, he shook out his shawl.

"Where the hell were you?" Bowley demanded.

The spook glanced his way, a flash of washed-out gray eyes. He lifted his shawl and put it back over his head. Shadows crawled around his face beneath its fringes. He slumped, evidently exhausted. "I'm sorry. I didn't know you were in danger until your shadows caught up with us."

"Did you kill it?" Bowley asked.

The Man shook his head. "A dreaming can't be killed, only put back in its place. The tribe and I together weren't enough to subdue this dreaming or deter it. When it's done licking its wounds, it'll follow us to town."

"Why did they try and help us?"

Another shake of the head. "Our presence was coincidence. The tribe's witchmen thought a surprise attack might defeat this dreaming. They underestimated its strength."

"So did you," Bowley said. "And now German's dead."

"It wasn't my decision to go hunting for it," the Man replied, softly.

The riposte struck home. *My fault,* Bowley thought. *I shouldn't have let him come.*

The Dappled Man extended a hand. "I have something for you."

Bowley's heart gave a lurch. He stared at the spook's outstretched palm. There was a barely visible tremor in the Man's fingers. Bowley's own hand shook noticeably as he raised it. The Dappled Man's skin was dry as old paper.

Darkness flooded out of the Man's sleeve and up Bowley's arm. Bowley yelped and would've snatched back his hand if the spook hadn't gripped his fingers tightly. The darkness flowed over Bowley's shoulder and down his side, along his leg and then down his horse's to pool on the ground beneath them. It resolved itself into his shadow astride Clay's, before fading in the dull light. The Dappled Man released his hand.

Bowley clutched at his chest. "Green *Christ.*"

The Man leaned on his saddle horn, his head bowed. Bowley's rattling heartbeat slowed to a more normal rate. The Dappled Man spoke again, his voice a bare rasp, "The tribe's intervention has increased our risk when we face this dreaming again. Whenever one of those it has taken is killed, it is freed to steal another shadow."

Bowley watched him, swaying like he could hardly hold his seat, and said, "It took some of yours, didn't it?"

The Man nodded.

And did you keep German's? Bowley wondered. *Or did the dreaming take it from you?* His scalp goosepimpled. The spook could as easily have kept his and Clay's, had he wanted. Giving them up had plainly cost him.

"How do we stop it?" he asked.

The cowled head remained lowered, the tattered fringes of the shawl falling forward to hide the Man's face completely. "Kill all of them," he said. "All but the first infected. Each death will be a shock to the dreaming that possesses them. While it's still reeling, I can—perhaps—subdue it and return it to the land."

Kill all of them. Bowley's vision blurred. *Oh, Maise.*

The mist had settled at the bottom of the valley, where the town stood, denser than when they'd left. There was a crowd gathered between the posts of the town gate. All men, except for Maise, and all of them armed. Alby and young O'Shane were among them. Bowley watched their faces fall when they realized German wasn't with them.

Bowley gathered his jammed gun and dismounted. He slapped Clay on the rump. The crowd parted to let her by and she skittered off down the street, vanishing quickly into the gray—smart enough, he hoped, to stay inside the rune circle.

"Where's German?" Maise asked.

"Dead," Bowley replied. "Same as old Stink."

She looked away from him, covering her lips with her fingertips and drawing deep breaths.

"We're ready," said Alby. "Everyone else is in the church."

"Uncarved bullets won't hurt the dream-taken,"

said the Dappled Man, down from his horse now, too. Only an arm's length from Bowley, he seemed to fade into the mist. He stood straight though, and apparently without difficulty.

Bowley looked around at the frightened, determined faces, then back at the spook. "We've got more than four guns loaded with carved bullets," he said.

He pulled his revolver from its holster and reached past Maise to offer it butt-first to Ulf Erikssen, dug in his left pocket for fresh cartridges.

"I can only defend four of you," said the Dappled Man.

"Reckon we'll defend ourselves, mate," said Alby. He handed one of his rifles to Ted Wright. Young O'Shane followed suit.

The spook was still for a minute. His pale eyes glittered beneath the ragged fringe of his shawl, boring into Bowley. Bowley hoped his fear wasn't plain to see on his face. He returned the Man's stare as levelly as he could. At last, the Man said, "Anyone else wants to fight, you'll need weapons with killing runes carved on them."

"The rest get your arses into the bloody church," said Bowley, his knees momentarily weak with relief. Most of the crowd scattered.

Maise glared at him through tears of frustration.

"That includes you, Maise," he said. He was amazed that his voice was steady. "It's your whole bloody family coming down on us, love. What'll you do if you get Lucy in your sights? Or Jemima?"

Her nostrils flared. She pressed her lips white as she, too, tried to stare him down. He put a hand on her arm, pushed her gently. Maise turned away, swayed a little and stumbled on her first step, then walked in the direction of the church.

Bowley took a long breath, felt it chill his lungs. He let it out with a puff. To no one in particular, he said, "I'll be back in a minute."

He strode through the crowd and down the street towards the police station. Inside, he went straight to his desk drawer and retrieved his half-empty bottle of whiskey. He pulled the plug with his teeth and took a long swig. He closed his eyes for a minute while the burn of it spread through his chest.

He rummaged around in the drawer for the screwdriver he thought might be there, found the letter opener and decided that would do. He perched on the desk with the carbine across his lap to try and unjam it. To his relief, he was able to do so without disassembling the gun. Bootsteps sounded on the boards outside as the lever snapped back into place, chambering the offending cartridge properly, this time.

Alby leaned on the doorpost.

"Didn't know you'd fallen behind, Bowls," he said. "Spook said to keep riding, when we realized."

Bowley passed him the whiskey. "I know," he said. "No worries, mate."

They made their way past empty houses to the church, where the spook had gathered everyone willing to fight below the steps: young O'Shane, Ulf, Ted Wright, half a dozen others busily loading their weapons with the spare bullets Alby and O'Shane had carried. Bowley handed out his spare rifle bullets. A handful of women and kids and shamefaced men huddled in the church's doorway to watch. Dougie MacGill, mad old buzzard that he was, was the only one to turn out without a gun, armed with the rune-carved pike head he'd souvenired when he retired from the redcoats, stuck on its rough-cut pole.

The town's runestone ring ran across the back of the unwalled churchyard. The world beyond it was invisible in the mist.

Bowley looked down at his hands. They were rock steady. His emotions felt dull and distant—locked out. He cocked his carbine. He heard the creak-and-click repeated around him as the others did the same.

The Dappled Man raised his voice. "Hold your shadows close. Keep your boot soles on the ground. For every one of its taken that the tribe killed, the dreaming can take one of you. There are worse things than dying, if you fall."

He let that sink in, before adding, "This dreaming has no understanding of guns. That's our advantage. Choose your shots well, because you'll not have enough bullets to finish this task."

"All right, lads," Bowley said. "Spread out a bit, but stay close to the church. We don't know which way they're going to come."

Somebody shut the church door with a thump, and then only the movements of the men disturbed the silence—the crunch and crackle of their boots on dirt and brittle grass, the creak of oilskin coats—as they positioned themselves in a rough semicircle, anchored at the corners of the church. Bowley's badge clinked against the top button of his uniform jacket as he took a few paces to position himself behind a headstone.

They waited.

German's death played again in Bowley's mind. He'd frozen, he knew, in the moments before the dream-taken had brought German down. Would it have made a difference, he wondered, if he hadn't? Might he have saved him?

The Dappled Man spoke: "They're here." The howling began in Bowley's head an instant later.

A stick snapped, out in the mist, from the direction of the town gate. Gravel scraped. All weapons swung in that direction. Another sound cut across the howling.

"Number Sevens!" Bowley cried.

He dropped to his haunches a heartbeat ahead of the men around him. A war boomerang throbbed low overhead, through the space he'd occupied an instant before. A cry, abruptly silenced, told him someone hadn't been fast enough. Dougie MacGill hit the dirt with five feet of bent wood buried in his ribs. War boomerangs clattered against the stone of the church walls.

Somebody loosed a shot.

"Not until you can bloody see them!" Bowley yelled. He peered over the top of the headstone.

Ragged figures materialized out of the mist. Bowley came to his feet, bringing his carbine to his shoulder. For an instant, the sharpness of his perceptions overwhelmed him. He'd seen, in feral dogs, the hurt and desperation that drove them to hurl themselves at the muzzle of a gun. He saw it now in this charging rabble, with grime and gore unwashed from their faces and caked into their cuffs and shirt fronts, axes and shovels clasped in their fists.

Gunshots cracked to his left and right.

His vision narrowed. He was in his marksman's place, where he could act and not feel. Francisco Del

Mar came under his sights once again. Bowley's first shot punched through the charging man's face and out the back of his head. The second hit him side-on as he stumbled. The impact took the shattered back of his skull clean off.

Bowley searched for a new target, wondering if he could pick out the first taken, the one who mattered, and avert the worst of the carnage.

He paused, overwhelmed by a sudden feeling of *wrongness*. "Where's the rest of them?"

There were less than twenty attackers in front of him. Half of them were down already and all of them, he saw, carried some kind of injury. He spun on his heel, shouted his question at the Dappled Man, positioned at the foot of the steps.

The Man was already turning, pointing, out where the runestone perimeter came closest to the church. Bowley saw movement in the mist.

"Alby! Over there!"

He ran to that side of their line, his gun at his shoulder, as Alby and the others nearest pivoted to meet the new threat.

His sights found a blackfella, running among the Del Mar mob. There were others. The tribe's intervention had cost them. Bowley tracked the blackfella's approach. He fired just as the man passed behind a tall tombstone. The bullet kicked chips off the edge of the stone. Someone else's bullet knocked the blackfella flat.

The new wave of attackers came fast. Bowley put his next two shots into the torso of one of the older Del Mar nephews from less than ten yards away. The twin impacts knocked the Del Mar off his feet, like a giant hand had slapped him flat. The axe handle he'd brandished pinwheeled between the headstones. Bowley shot little Letitia Del Mar, coming behind, wearing a pinafore brown with blood. Her hair flicked up as the bullet came out the back of her head.

He was dimly aware of Alby beside him, flipping his rifle, already empty, to use as a club. Of Ulf, beyond Alby, with Bowley's service revolver gripped in both hands. Young O'Shane, pumping bullets from his pair of pistols with methodical precision.

A still figure caught Bowley's eye, out beyond the mayhem—a girl, standing straight and tall, her arms raised before her. Jemima Del Mar. Maise's niece. *The first taken,* Bowley realized. In front of the church, the Dappled Man mirrored Jemima's pose.

A woman charged straight at him. It was Maise's sister, Lucy—Jemima's mother. Bowley's finger froze on the carbine's trigger. His pulse pounded in his ears. There was nothing of the woman he'd known in the rictus of Lucy's face. He squeezed the trigger with a jerk, pulling the carbine's muzzle sideways. The bullet hit her high in the chest. She staggered into the arc of Alby's rifle butt. Bone and wood crunched together.

Les Barrett, a senior son-in-law, was hard on Lucy's heels. Bowley flipped his empty carbine in his hands, felt the hot metal sear his fingers and palms, and swung. He met the downward arc of the man's mattock and used the momentum of the blow to push the weapon aside and put his elbow into Barrett's face. Bowley pulled his carbine back over his shoulder and swung. The trigger guard caught Barrett squarely in the side of the head. The blow jarred Bowley's wrists and elbows. Blood crazed beneath the skin of the dream-taken's temple, patterning like shattered porcelain. Bowley adjusted his grip and hit him again. Barrett collapsed.

Ulf went down under the weight of two assailants. Young O'Shane and Ted Wright arrived an instant too late. Ulf started to convulse on the ground. Ted impaled one attacker on the point of Dougie MacGill's pike, belted the other with a long-handled mallet he must've taken from one of her kin. The woman's head rocked on her shoulders. She lunged at Ted, making him stumble. O'Shane shot her, point blank, in the face. Ulf started to rise from the ground at his feet. The Irishman put his second pistol to the publican's forehead and pulled the trigger.

Closer to Bowley, Alby kicked little Tomas Del Mar, all of four years old, under the chin. He raised his boot again and stamped on the child's thin chest as he bounced against the earth.

Hands grappled Bowley from behind. Sharp teeth sank into the side of his neck. He wrenched free and spun. The carbine's stock missed his attacker by a whisker. Javier Del Mar, patriarch of the family, peeled back his bloody lips in a soundless snarl.

A hand snaked over the old man's shoulder and caught him around the face. Alby thrust his hunting knife up under Javier's chin. The Del Mar jerked backwards as the blade penetrated. Alby stumbled and they both started to fall.

"No!" Bowley lunged after them. For an instant, he clutched Alby's coat sleeve. Then the oiled leather slipped through his fingers and Alby's back hit the dirt.

ROBERT J. HALL JR.

His eyes bulged. His heels drummed the dirt. His shadow flitted away from his stricken body, then it too began to thrash, but only for a moment. Still struggling, it was sucked into the earth.

Alby started to rise. Bowley rammed the carbine's butt into his face. Alby fell back. Bowley hammered down again. Bone gave beneath the blow. Alby's limbs twisted spastically. Bowley swung in a frenzy, as though he could obliterate Alby's identity and, with it, the horror of what he was doing. The carbine's stock snapped. Bowley staggered. Alby's bottom jaw jutted up, above his collar, obscenely intact.

The field was still.

For a while, Bowley leaned on the splintered butt of his gun. His breath rattled in his ears. His neck and his burnt hands throbbed. He slowly pushed himself upright.

Aside from Bowley, only three of the townsmen who'd begun the fight were still on their feet. Young O'Shane was one of them, still with both his pistols in his hands. His face was slack, his eyes closed. Ted Wright crouched with his forehead resting against the pole of Dougie MacGill's pike, one forearm pressed against his belly. Blood dripped between his legs. Bowley began to shake.

One Del Mar still stood amid the carnage. Jemima. Neither she or the Dappled Man had moved, still confronting each other in their invisible battle of energy and wills. Even in the pale light, Jemima's shadow was dense and dark, many armed and many headed, as though cast by many suns. The Dappled Man's captive shadows writhed across his body.

He took a step forward. Then another. Jemima

remained rooted. The Man walked towards her, each step an obvious effort, like a man wading through mud. He reached out and caught Jemima's chin. Still, she didn't move. Her shadow's many limbs writhed in agitation and it began to shrink towards her feet. Darkness poured out of her mouth and out of her nose and ears and eyes. It ran up the Dappled Man's wrist and into his sleeve. Jemima's body shook violently. The Man bowed his head, his shoulders hunched.

The last bit of shadow drained over Jemima's lip. The Man released his grip on her jaw and they staggered apart. The Man swayed but kept his feet. Jemima crumpled.

A keening sound penetrated Bowley's gun-deaf ears. At first he thought it was the dreaming, howling still, and he wondered how that could be. Then he realized the noise was coming from Jemima—each cry an uninflected blast of anguish, followed by a terrible, wrenching gasp for air, then another long, monotonous cry.

Maise raced across the field, arms outstretched, fingers splayed. She was too slow to catch Jemima before she fell. She skidded to her knees beside the girl and scooped her up. Jemima's face and neck were crimson, veins and ligaments pushed out with the force of the sound coming up her throat.

The Dappled Man stood over them, his shrouded head bowed, leaning a little, like someone who'd taken a bad hurt to the ribs.

His horse picked its way through the slaughter and stopped beside its master. The Man took a moment to react, as though he didn't see it at first. He reached up an arm, then got his foot into the stirrup and lifted himself with painful slowness to slump in the saddle.

The horse moved off again, past the rows of tombstones and out to the rune circle. Blackfellas waited in the fringes of the mist. They fell into step beside the rider as he vanished from sight. They'd see the dreaming put back into the ground, back where Jemima and her kin had found it, to go back to sleep and lie undisturbed until it withered away to nothing. Bowley wondered if he ought to go after them, to be certain it was done with and they'd seen the last of it.

He looked over at Maise, with her eyes screwed shut and her teeth clenched in a grimace, her own body wracked by sobs as she held her niece. What comfort could he offer her? What was there left for him and Maise, with the blood of her family on his hands?

He let the shattered carbine fall from his fingers. He walked towards Maise. Her head was turned away, to where the Man and his escort had gone into the mist. She didn't respond when he knelt beside her, put his hand on her back. He took a grip on her shoulders, pulled her in to him. She didn't resist. Jemima had exhausted her voice, for now, and sprawled in her aunt's arms, panting like a hurt animal. Her eyes were bulged and bloodshot in her still-red face.

Maise pulled away suddenly, and turned to look at him, her face fierce. "You go after them, Robert," she said. "You make sure it's done right."

He didn't want to, started to shake his head, because his place was right here, with all the death and ruin about them to clear away, bodies to bury or burn, and the people needing someone to show the way, and that being down to him, the Queen's Man in Useless Loop. And what would he know, anyway, if he did go, about whether this dreaming was put to rest for good, or not?

But, "Go!" she said, and he staggered up and away from her, propelled by the force in that word.

People stumbled out of the church. Some fell to their knees, some turned away and covered their children's eyes, some vomited. Others hugged each other and wept. A sudden shaft of bright sunshine lit the battlefield in unwelcome light. Bowley hurried past.

He put his fingers to his mouth, barely noticing the salt-metal tang of blood as his whistle shattered the quiet. He whistled again, and saw Clay prick her ears, standing in the street outside the police station. He went to her at a stumbling run, and got her moving at a trot as soon as he was aboard.

He felt the pressure of their eyes, like a physical weight, as he skirted the churchyard. He kept his own fixed straight ahead. No one called out to him. Maise didn't look up from rocking her niece. The Dappled Man and his escort had already vanished into the mist. It didn't matter—Bowley knew where they were headed.

He caught up with them quickly enough. The blackfellas ignored him, so he followed a few yards behind, all the way up into the hills behind Del Mars'. The Dappled Man swayed like a man half dead in his saddle. His horse directed itself, or sometimes the blackfellas did, when it seemed unsure. They walked tirelessly, high-stepping over undergrowth and litter from the trees so they rarely needed to check their gait. Bowley watched the patterns of scars on their backs and legs, rippling as they moved, and wondered at the price they paid for living with the land, for not holding themselves apart as whitefellas did.

At the mouth of the caves, they pulled the Man down from his horse and carried him inside, stooping under the low lip of rock. One paused when Bowley got down from Clay and made to follow. He raised a hand, his long, broad-tipped fingers splayed, the palm pink and free of scars. He held Bowley's gaze with brown-black eyes. Shadows gathered beneath his heavy brow. The ridged scars that covered his skin formed a mask that obscured his expression. Once he was certain Bowley wasn't going to follow, the man turned and went after his fellows.

Bowley waited, with only the horses for company. He saw to Clay, but left her saddled, and made himself a small fire. The Man's horse seemed content and Bowley was disinclined to approach it. He hunched beside his fire as night closed in and knew he'd made a mistake, coming here. Knew he should've stayed in town, and been the Queen's Man, no matter what Maise had wanted. But he knew there was no way he could've refused her.

He stared into the flames, trying not to see Alby's head come apart, over and over again. He tried not to hear German's screams as human teeth tore into him. Not to see the grief on Maise's face as she held her niece, nor hear Jemima's wailing, that said saving her was the worst they could've done. Exhaustion eventually let him fall into a light doze.

The blackfellas brought the Dappled Man back out in the gray of morning. He said nothing to Bowley, nor even appeared to recognize his presence, even though

Bowley rose to his feet barely an arm's length from where the Man passed.

The blackfellas led him to his horse and put him up in the saddle. One of them took its reins, and another two held the Man's legs to keep him in his seat as they walked away with him into the bush.

Bowley was left alone once again, and wondering what victory had cost the spook, whether he hadn't been able to separate all of himself from the dreaming when they'd put it back into the ground.

He looked back into the cave, felt gooseflesh rise all over his body. He could only hope that the task was done.

He got his skinning knife from his saddle roll, scratched the rune for danger into the rock above the cave mouth. The sign had no power, since he had none to give it, and the shallow marks would fade quickly, but it would serve, for now.

Smoke rose from the churchyard, when he returned to town. A funeral pyre. They'd burned all the bodies together. A few folk watched him walk past on Clay, their faces bleak, looking at him like a stranger. Crows picked among the headstones, hunting for any tidbits that might've been overlooked.

There was a cart outside the post office, half loaded with small furnishings and baskets and crates of bric-a-brac. Maise's rocking chair, from the porch, that Nev had made her for a wedding gift, was lashed in pride of place on top of the pile. As Bowley approached, she came out with a basket of clothes. Her eyes flickered over to him. Her expression closed in and she looked away.

Bowley stopped Clay beside the cart and watched for a moment while she worked the basket into a too-small space at the back.

"Maise? You're leaving?"

She didn't look up. "I am."

His eyes were suddenly hot and overfull. "Where are you going, love?" he asked.

"Don't you . . ." She caught herself. "I don't know. Away."

Bowley's mouth worked silently for a moment before he could shape more words. "Would you have left before I got back?"

Maise stopped, bowed her head. "I can't do it, Robert," she said, from between her raised arms. "I can't even look at you."

She gave the basket a final shove and turned her back on him. He watched her disappear back inside. She returned a moment later, followed by Dermott O'Shane, carrying Jemima. The younger man glanced at Bowley, and away again, without speaking. Maise climbed up onto the cart's bench, then turned to help O'Shane lift Jemima up beside her. The girl was wrapped in a blanket, so Bowley could discern little more than the fact that she was conscious. She huddled against Maise, tucking her head low. Maise sat straight and rigid, looking neither left nor right, nor back, as she picked up the reins and clucked their horse into motion.

Clay danced a little, when the cart started moving. She twisted her neck to watch it, then snorted, and returned her gaze forward, to wait patiently, again, for her master to tell her what to do. O'Shane looked as though he might speak, then shook his head, dissatisfied with the words he might've offered, and walked away.

Bowley sat there for a long time, the words "Can I come with you?" lying bitter on his tongue.

Taking a Mile

written by

J. Kathleen Cheney

illustrated by

JAMES GALINDO

ABOUT THE AUTHOR

Born and raised in El Paso, Texas, J. Kathleen Cheney had some very smart parents . . . they really were *rocket scientists who worked at the White Sands Missile Range. Though she graduated with degrees in English and Marketing, J. Kathleen eventually became a math teacher who taught everything from seventh-grade arithmetic to calculus. She also coached the Academic Team and the Robotics Team, and she sponsored the Chess Club.*

In 2005, J. Kathleen took a sabbatical from the academic world to work on writing and has since enjoyed seeing her stories published in Shimmer, Fantasy Magazine *and* Baen's Universe. *She lists authors James Gunn, C. J. Cherryh, Arthur Conan Doyle and Georgette Heyer as major influences, as well as Ansen Dibell, whose ghostly fingerprints can be seen all over this story. When not writing, J. Kathleen likes to don a mask and get sweaty fencing with both foil and saber. She'll also put on her Wellingtons and get her hands dirty in the garden. Quieter hobbies include quilting and taking care of her husband and dog.*

ABOUT THE ILLUSTRATOR

James Galindo is a native of Palm Springs, California, and began drawing pictures before he could read or write. As he continued to nurture his creative skills throughout childhood, James and a friend began illustrating their own comic book series in the third grade. Around the same time, James won the annual Christmas Seals art competition sponsored by the American Lung Association, placing first in the state of California. During middle school, he developed interests in music, friends and girls, so his artistic production stalled a bit. Prior to graduating high school, James enrolled in figure drawing classes at the College of the Desert to prepare for the intense academic training at Laguna College of Art & Design. James is now on track to obtain his Master of Fine Arts degree by the spring of 2009. After college, he plans to sell paintings out of a gallery, teach at the university level and/or work as a freelance illustrator.

Taking a Mile

Viviana Fuentes waited on a bench in the cemetery, staring out at the tidy rows of tombstones. A chill wind brushed her, sending shivers along her arms. Leaves skittered by, brown and dry with the advent of fall. She was waiting for death.

It wouldn't be the quick death her original had. According to what she'd read during the flight home, her own would take a few days, the body lingering on as her nervous system slowly collapsed.

Her hands felt icy. Viviana slapped them against her wool-covered thighs, trying to warm them.

"It's the first thing to go," a voice said behind her.

She turned and saw that someone had come up the pathway, a man in his mid-thirties, blond-haired and handsome. "What do you mean?"

"The sense of touch," he said in a northern accent she couldn't quite place. "It fails first." He came around the stone bench and gestured as if asking her permission to sit.

Viviana moved over as far as the stone seat would allow. He joined her on it, and she could feel the warmth of his body. He wore a dark overcoat and scarf over casual attire, navy slacks and a sweater. Not the same quality as hers, but clean. She had on the same charcoal business suit she'd worn for the last two days. Her hair felt sticky. She had it twisted up in a knot at the nape of her neck just as her original would have. "How do you know that?" she asked.

"It's my job. I have to be aware of these things."

"Who are you?" The wind caught a dark strand of her hair and blew it across her eyes. Viviana tucked it behind one ear with shaking fingers.

"My name is . . . Daniel, Daniel Hunter. I manage the Chicago station." His head tilted, a self-deprecating motion. "Sort of."

"Oh." She should have known that the Rand Company would send someone after her. Legally, her body *was* their property. "Have you come to take me in?"

"That's why they sent me. May I call you Viviana?"

No harm in that familiarity now, she thought. "Yes."

He took her nearer hand and massaged her fingers. "I think you're more cold and tired than anything else."

"I didn't have anywhere else to go." She glanced down at her carefully manicured fingers in his paler hand. The warmth of his skin seeped into her, almost like life returning. "How long do I have?"

"Every avatar is unique. These things happen at slightly different rates."

"They told me ten days when they made my avatar. I mean they told *her* that." She'd spent the last few days trying to adjust to that truth—that she wasn't the real Viviana Fuentes. She was only a copy.

"Most avatars have their memories uploaded within two or three," he said, "so it's rarely an issue. Twenty days is generally considered the outside maximum life span."

She felt a surge of hope, as if ten extra days of life would be enough, but then it flowed away. "When I got to the station in Sydney, they refused to upload me."

"So I would expect. How did you get back to Texas without any access codes?"

With the death of her original, she'd become a non-person. Her credit access had disappeared. "I always . . ." she paused, recalling that she hadn't always done anything.

"She," he corrected.

"She always carried cash," Viviana said. "In case of emergency. It was wired along with me." In truth, she'd had it in case she'd needed to bribe any of the Australian partners. Fortunately, she hadn't. "I don't know why Customs let me through, but then the airline wouldn't release my luggage. They said it had to go to her next of kin."

"They probably had no idea what to do with you." He rose, took off his coat and draped it around her shoulders. The fabric felt synthetic, man-made like her body. It warmed her just as well as real wool, though.

"I'd like to try to get you somewhere safe," he said, sitting down again.

"Back to the station? What's the point?" she asked. "They can't upload me. I'm going to die. Why not just leave me here?" She gestured at the headstones around them, stained pink and rose in the sunset's glow.

"People find it distressing when an avatar senesces in public," Daniel said in a reasonable tone.

She gave a short laugh. "Senesces. What a civilized way to say I'll crumble to pieces."

A light came on near the bench, triggered by the deepening shadows. "Does it hurt?" she asked.

"I don't know," he said with a half-shrug.

Pale irritation swept through her, a remembered taste of emotion. "I thought you said it was your job."

"How can I really know if it's never happened to me?"

"Have you ever seen one of my kind die . . . I mean, senesce?"

"No." He smiled sheepishly then. "I'm only a day old."

She surveyed his face again. "You're a fax like me?"

He lifted the hair at the nape of his neck to show her the upload implant there. "My original is back in Chicago."

"Why didn't he just fly here?"

"This was faster. He works for the station, so he doesn't have to pay."

In the ten years since the Rand Company had produced their first avatar, no other similar patent had been granted, giving them a monopoly on the trade. Industry analysts claimed that the uploading process, avatar construction, and raw materials didn't warrant what the Company charged, but Rand countered that the prices stemmed from research and development costs. Her firm had been willing to pay that price.

"Have you . . . has he done this before?"

"Faxing? Yes. I'm his thirty-second avatar. Sort of."

"I'm the first," Viviana said. "And the last, I suppose. I . . . she didn't want to do it, but the partners insisted that she was the only one who could close the deal, so they sent me."

"Did they not notify you when your original died?"

"I found out four days later," she told him, "*after* I closed the contract."

He sighed, and said, "I'll bet that wasn't . . . pleasant."

"I'd been so busy. I'd hardly slept in days. I really thought I was her until I found out I was dead."

"We are never them," Daniel said.

Viviana motioned with her chin. "I wanted to see it for myself. She's over there."

The derailment on the intra-city light rail had killed several people, but none of the others had left copies of themselves behind to view their graves. Among the rows of newer tombstones, one bore her name. "Beloved daughter," she pointed out. "I thought about going to see my . . . her parents."

"It would be hard on them," Daniel said.

"How often does this happen?" She wondered if she was the first.

"It's rare," he said, "but it has happened before."

"And what did the Company do with the others like me?"

"They were retrieved." Daniel rose and held out his hand to her. "I have a car outside the cemetery. You need rest more than anything else. How long since you've eaten?"

Viviana took a deep breath and let him help her up. She swayed, and he slipped a hand under her elbow. Not death—she had days to go—but exhaustion. "I don't remember."

She didn't look at her grave as they passed it. He opened the door for her, and she settled into the passenger seat of a rented sedan, waiting while he went around to the driver's side. He turned the heater up, started the car and pulled out of the cemetery's drive.

"Do you know where you're going?" she asked.

"No." He took the highway, the rental's drive control switching on automatically. "Do you care?"

"I thought you had to take me back to the station."

"Not right away," he said with a shrug. "Let's find something to eat."

It seemed a trivial thing when she was just waiting to die. Then again, she didn't have anything better to do. "Why not?"

"It'll make you feel better," he said. "That is one of the things I do know. Avatars need to eat."

The original Viviana Fuentes would never have ordered a stack of pancakes with a side of chorizo. It would have been yogurt and fresh fruit. She didn't have to worry about her figure, though, a strangely liberating fact.

"I haven't been entirely truthful with you," Daniel said as he toyed with his eggs.

No one had been entirely truthful with her, not in this incarnation, at least. "How?"

"I didn't come here to take you back to the station." He looked regretful. "If I took you there, they wouldn't do anything other than keep you in a holding cell until you senesce—preferably far away from any paying customer."

"What other option do I have? They can't upload me."

"They can, into storage in the Austin station's mainframe: the physical pattern, the consciousness, and memories . . . the whole package." His jaw clenched as if he remembered something unpleasant. "They'd tell you they can store you until they can download you into a new avatar."

"Can they do that?"

"They can do it now," he said with a shrug.

"But it's against the law," she guessed.

He nodded. "Your original specified a one-time avatar. It's actually standard on the contract."

"Oh." Legally, an avatar had no recourse against any decision their original made. It didn't matter what *she* wanted.

The chorizo tasted spicy and greasy, the real thing, not soy. Viviana dabbed the corner of her mouth with her napkin. It came away orange, reminding her of childhood breakfasts on Saturdays when Papa cooked. "So what are you going to do with me?"

"It won't take Danny long to figure out that I'm not bringing you in. He wants to find out what I'll do."

"Danny?"

"My original. I prefer not to use his name."

It struck her as odd that he would choose a different name. She had always been Viviana, too reserved for Vivi or Bibi even as a child. Her middle name, Alma, seemed too mature. She toyed with the notion, wondering what it would be like to wear a different name. "You think of him as someone else?"

"Easier than you think. You were created with every intention of merging your consciousness back into your original. She never thought of you as truly separate, so you don't either. I was fabricated already knowing that. I'm not even actually a copy of Danny," Daniel added with a wry smile. "I'm a copy of Number Ten."

She put down her fork. "You're not a copy of your original?"

"Danny had a psychotic episode after he uploaded his ninth avatar, got to spend a couple of weeks in one of Cook County's fine mental health facilities." He waved his fork as he spoke, his expression not one of sympathy.

"What happened?"

"He'd uploaded three avatars in a two-day period. It's difficult enough for a human mind to reconcile *two* sets of memories that occurred simultaneously. He thought he could handle more, but he found out he isn't as all-powerful as he believes. After that, he decided not to upload us any longer. Ten's physical pattern and consciousness were stored in the Chicago mainframe, and with those avatars he does manage to drag back, Danny uploads the memories directly to Ten's file. I think of *him* as my original, not Danny Hunter. If Danny hauls you in, be sure to tell him that."

He didn't even like his original, Viviana decided, an impossible idea. "Will he come after me? Or you?"

"Yes," he said without hesitation. "As I said, Danny would certainly like to know what Ten has in mind. I expect Danny will put a watch on me and try to figure out where I'm going, what I'm doing and with whom."

"Because you're Ten's avatar, not his?"

"Therefore he can't predict my movements. In the last six years, Ten's personality has diverged markedly from Danny's. The Company can't just read the code that represents Ten's consciousness and understand what Ten is thinking. He's like a big fish deep under the water. They can only observe the ripples that spread out from Ten's movements and make inferences from that. By studying me, by watching me, Danny thinks he's studying Ten."

"So he's given you an inch of rope, so to speak, to see what you'll do."

Daniel nodded. "And if I can, I'm going to take a mile."

The shower felt wonderful, hot water pouring over her skin and chasing away the last vestiges of the cold. It was good to have her hair clean. Viviana shut off the spray and watched the last of the water drain away, taking skin cells with it, each a tiny bit of her shortened, made-up life.

She toweled off and dressed in clean clothing Daniel had purchased for her. Not the kind of clothes Viviana Fuentes would normally buy, the pants and shirt felt more like loungewear, loose and comfortable. They weren't made to last, though.

Viviana gazed in the mirror, hunting for signs that senescence was imminent, but didn't know what to expect. She looked more tired than anything else.

The hotel room had two queen beds, not the finest of anything. Viviana didn't complain; she hadn't paid for it. She didn't really want to be alone anyway. Fully dressed, she laid down on one of the beds and closed her eyes.

Across the room, Daniel spoke to someone on a wireless, his voice low. Viviana wondered sleepily whom an avatar might know to share secrets with. She slid into slumber, the question unanswered.

Viviana woke into darkness, her internal reckoning completely undone by her travels over the last few days. She spotted a clock glowing on the nightstand and decided she had a few hours until dawn.

The other bed was empty. After her eyes adjusted to the darkness, she spotted Daniel sitting in the leather wing chair. He'd backed it up against the door and slept with his head leaning against one of the sides.

Rising, she padded to the restroom. The face in the

mirror looked less tired now. She struggled not to see Viviana Fuentes in the mirror. Even so, she knew that the woman staring back at her wasn't the original.

She had nothing: no rights, no property and no identity. The Pope hadn't even decided if she had a soul. He'd denounced the creation of avatars—too morally ambiguous for the Holy See. Her parents, good Catholics both, wouldn't have wanted their daughter to do this. In the end, she'd chosen not to tell them.

Daniel rapped his knuckles against the doorframe to get her attention. "My turn. If someone knocks on the door, tell them to wait outside, all right?"

She relinquished the bathroom and went out into the dark room, wondering who might show up this early in the morning. She settled in Daniel's abandoned chair and ran her fingers along the still-warm leather. He came back a moment later and turned up the light next to the computer screen he'd left rolled out on the desk.

"Do you have a soul?" she asked, looking up at him.

"Yes." He spoke as if he knew the answer, as if it were more than conjecture.

"You're a copy of a copy," she pointed out.

He shrugged and then sat on the edge of the desk facing her. "It doesn't matter if Danny thinks I have a soul or not. I know that I do, and that's what's important."

"We aren't human," she said. That had been forcibly imprinted on her in the last few days.

"Legally, no." He gazed at her, his skin looking gold in the light reflected under the amber-colored shade. "Do you think that's fair?"

Viviana stared at her hand where it lay on the arm

of the chair. "No," she whispered in answer. "Not anymore."

"There's someone coming. If you come with us, you might have some alternatives."

Viviana Fuentes' life was over. Time for her to live her own, however short that might be. "What do you want me to do?"

Daniel left everything on the table when the young man showed up: his wireless clip, his key cards, his credit pass. Viviana watched him empty his pockets.

The young man approached her and held out a dog collar fitted with a metallic device on the back. "It should, in theory, block the telemetry transmitters," he said. "If you'll put it on, I can test it."

He stood a few inches shorter than either of them, his tangled hair pulled back in a pony tail. He hadn't supplied a name—an intentional oversight, Viviana decided.

She slid on the leather collar, buckling it in front like a bizarre fashion statement her original would never have made. Daniel had donned one as well, looking even more out of place in black leather than she suspected she did.

The young man ran something resembling a lint brush around her head and behind her. "Wow, not bad. They really do work. We are definitely going to win."

Viviana decided he must be even younger than she'd thought, perhaps twenty-five. "Win what?"

"You don't know?" he asked.

"We should go soon," Daniel hinted.

"Oh, yeah." The young man pocketed the lint-brush device and pulled out a ring of keys. "I've got a van."

"Do you have a name?" Viviana asked.

He appeared to consider before answering. "I'm supposed to be your go-between for the department, but I'm not supposed to fraternize too much—corrupting the contest and all that." He shrugged. "You can call me Migo."

He headed out the door and they followed, Daniel putting one hand to her elbow. "Ten set it up as a contest between two universities," he said as he drew her down the hall. "First engineering department to build a fabrication terminal—developed independently from the Company's design, of course."

She shot Daniel a horrified look. "Do they work?"

"Never tested, from what I understand." He tugged at his dog collar.

They reached the elevator and went inside. "Daniel," she said, whispering in his ear, "are you crazy?"

He glanced down at the carpeted floor of the elevator. The corners of his eyes crinkled as if he were about to laugh. "It'll work," he said. "Ten trusts them."

Migo pretended not to listen, but Viviana suspected he overheard most of their conversation. "He's a copy in a terminal," she said softly, "in Chicago."

"It's like a prison," Daniel said, "and Danny will never let him out. He doesn't have to; Ten's consciousness is his personal property. That shouldn't happen to any of us."

The elevator doors opened, light from the foyer of the hotel spreading across his face as they did so, revealing a gleam in his eyes she hadn't noticed before.

Daniel Hunter Number Thirty-two, with his meager ten- to twenty-day life span, was on a quest.

Where is he taking us?" she asked, once inside the van. The young man drove through the city as if he knew it well, along the CTTS and north to the suburbs.

Seated in the back seat next to her, Daniel kept a nervous eye on the road, as if he expected someone from the Company to pull up alongside them in the predawn light. The sky went from gray to orange to pink as he explained, slowly illuminating his features with a brightness that matched the fervor within. It was an audacious plan, likely invisible to the Company only because no one had ever seen it as a serious threat.

"Since the US Patent Office granted Rand's application for a patent, we're legally property. The only thing that can change that now is Congress or the courts," Daniel said. "So we have to have an avatar who isn't Rand property—fabricated by someone other than the Company—to make a case."

"Twelve managed to get some design cues out to both universities," Daniel added. "That was about five years ago. I don't know if all the others in between have contributed, because several were never uploaded. Whatever they did was lost with them when they died. It's not just a contest any longer."

Migo half turned in his seat to grin at Viviana. "Yeah, Aggies for Human Rights is funding us now."

She wished he would concentrate on the road. "Really?"

"Yeah, and they have a lot of pull." He waved his free hand as he talked. "AHR is working with Senator Cerna—he's one of our alums—trying to get an injunction passed while the senate . . ."

"The road," Daniel interrupted.

"Oh, sorry, man." The young man turned his eyes back toward the road and maneuvered them back into their proper lane. He turned on the van's drive control and then swiveled around to grin at her again. "He's trying to get an injunction. 'Cause avatars should have rights like other people, I mean. That'll shut down all five of the Company's terminals in the state until the supreme court can rule on it."

And that would cost the Company a fortune, she realized, possibly enough to make them rethink the entire program.

A doctor attached to AHR removed the transceiver on the neural upload implant in her brain, eliminating the need for the leather collar. The surgery left her with a headache and a small dermal patch, but her hair covered the second. She hadn't expected the relief she felt after having the Company cut out of her head. She felt hopeful now, which she hadn't since she'd learned of Viviana's death.

Daniel looked ill after the doctor finished with him, though. "They'll need to move us again," he told her, trying to sound brisk. "The Company is going to follow the transceivers for a while. I'm sure they already suspect that I'd get mine cut out. The telemetry probably cued them as to when."

Migo drove them across town to wait, while someone else took the excised transceivers in a different direction. Viviana suspected that the Company might have another way to trace its property and, when asked, Daniel admitted he considered it likely.

They waited at a guest house behind a mansion in a private neighborhood. It belonged to someone important, she decided. She'd seen guards when they came through the gates at the edge of the subdivision.

"You don't think Danny has any idea?" she asked Daniel as the morning sun began to warm the day.

Daniel pinched the bridge of his nose. "Between him and Ten, there's a pretty big gulf. Danny might try to get a competitor to build a terminal, but never a university."

"So what happens now?"

"If everything goes according to plan, they upload your memories and then download you into a new body."

"With equipment that's never been tested," she said.

Daniel gave her a frank look. "Not a chance you're willing to take?"

"If I don't let them try it, I'll die anyway."

"I don't want you to die," he said.

"I don't want me to die, either."

The house had a lovely garden. She stared out the window, wishing she could walk through the faded rosebushes, but Viviana Fuentes' face had appeared on the news. The Company had grown frantic enough to find her that they'd publicly admitted she'd outlived her original. Worried that she might be seen and reported, Migo had asked that they remain inside the house.

"What will I do afterwards?" she asked Daniel, the question she should have asked some time ago.

He'd been resting in the bedroom across the hall, but came to join her at the window. He settled on the wide leather couch and gazed at the garden, his face strained. "Good question."

"Won't I just die again in a month?"

"No, the bodies *are* capable of lasting much longer. Senescence is programmed to occur at a predetermined time. It can also be triggered remotely through the transceiver, but it isn't necessary."

"So we don't have to die."

"That's one thing the public doesn't know. It's just become accepted fact—avatars don't last. The Company specifically designed you to die."

An appalling revelation, she thought it sounded close to murder.

He went on. "Ten altered your physical pattern code to remove the lines that trigger senescence, so that shouldn't be a problem once you're reloaded."

"I still won't have any rights."

"Well, that's where our political friends come in. If you're willing, you could stand as the test case for the state supreme court. Whether or not we have the right to live our own lives—and to have bodies not programmed to fall apart."

It would be a life of captivity, looking out at things but never going out among them for fear that the Company would try to kill her. But it would be a life, and that was more than her original had. "So I'll go through the same upload procedure she did."

"Not exactly. The funds were limited, you understand," he said, shifting in the chair again. "Senator Cerna has managed to funnel some money into this, but the contest specified that they had to build a terminal that could *fabricate* a functioning avatar, not upload one."

"Wait, you said they could upload me."

"The memories of the last few days—that's comparatively simple. That software's been around for some time." He shook his head. "The physical pattern and your consciousness files, those are far more complex."

"Then how . . . ?"

"As soon as Ten found out your original had died, he transferred your physical pattern and your consciousness files to a remote terminal and isolated them from the system. He anticipated that I would be created to retrieve you. The university has those original patterns now. They can upload your memories into that."

"What about you?"

He sighed and shifted in the chair. "Ten could only separate your files out because they were being purged from the system after your original's death."

She stared at him—his strained motions and his clenched jaw. The pieces clicked together. "You're dying."

He sighed. "My senescence was triggered before they *got* the transceiver removed. I felt it."

She understood now how Daniel could despise his original.

"It would have happened eventually," Daniel said. "I'm just sorry I won't be able to stay around and help you. Besides, I'm just property. You, on the other hand, can't be tied to Viviana Fuentes anymore."

"But I am a copy," she reminded him.

He reached across and took her hands. "No, you're distinct. Your memories make you different. They change you. Never forget that, no matter what. You've done things and met people that she never did."

He had talked around the issue, she noted, preferring

for this not to be about him. She squeezed his fingers. "Can you feel your hands?"

"No," he said, rising. "I think I'll go lie down until the senator gets here."

She followed him to the door of the bedroom.

"You should probably get some rest as well," he suggested.

"I don't really want to be alone," she admitted. "And I don't want to watch any more of Migo's old movies."

Daniel grinned. "A bit strange for you?"

She couldn't help rolling her eyes.

"I'm just going to lie down," he said again.

She didn't pretend to misunderstand what he meant. "I don't want to be alone. That's all."

He closed the door behind her after she came in. When he lay down, she followed, pulling the heavy blankets over both of them. She touched his cheek. "Can you feel that?"

"It's just my hands and feet that have gone numb," he said.

His skin felt icy under her fingers. "Are you in pain?"

His jaw clenched. "A bit."

She kept her hand against his cheek so he would know she was there when he slept. She didn't want him to be alone.

A rapping on the door warned her that someone had come for them. Daniel's eyes opened, but he still looked exhausted, so she rose and went to answer. Light from the hallway spilled into the room when she opened the door.

Migo stood there, looking nervous. "Ms. Fuentes?"

"What is it, Migo? Do we need to move again?"

"No, ma'am." His dark eyes made a quick motion toward the rumpled bed. He held one hand close to his side in an awkward position, with index finger and pinkie extended.

Under duress, she realized. He wouldn't make that particular hand signal—the sign of his university's rivals—unless something dire compelled him to.

She locked the door, stepped outside and closed it firmly behind her. Three men stood at the end of the hallway. They hadn't been in her line of vision from the room. Two of them held back their sport coats in an old-fashioned TV bad guy posture, showing handguns in underarm holsters.

The third man didn't have a gun, but held a stunner in his hand. A stunner wouldn't leave much of a visible injury for the media to see, she knew. They ensured compliance instead.

"It's all right, Migo," she said, putting herself between him and the men. "I believe this gentleman has come to see me."

"Is he . . . ?" the young man asked from behind her.

"I don't know." The man in front of her might be Danny Hunter, or he might be yet another copy. She suspected the former. "Get out of here," she whispered to Migo. "They don't want you."

"I can't just leave," Migo said.

"Yes, you can." She walked toward the men and into the elegant sitting room where she and Daniel had talked only a couple of hours before. She gestured at Migo, who'd followed her. "You aren't after him, gentlemen. He's only our driver. You don't want to have to explain his disappearance, do you? Or his body?"

Danny Hunter shook his head, his expression amused. "He's not leaving, Ms. Fuentes. Can I call you Viviana?"

"I'd prefer Ms. Fuentes," she said. She gestured toward the couch. "Shall we sit down and discuss this?"

"Where is he?" Hunter asked, coming toward her. One of the thugs followed and took Migo by the arm, gun pointed discreetly into the young man's side.

She understood that threat. "Where is who?"

"Did he tell you I was stupid, Viviana?" Hunter asked.

He stood only a few feet away from her. Daniel hadn't aged in the last six years, she realized. Every incarnation had Ten's physical pattern, not Danny Hunter's. The man in front of her looked to be over forty. Lines marred the original's face that didn't show on Daniel's, and a hint of a double chin crept over the tight collar of Danny Hunter's dress shirt.

"He didn't talk about you much," she said with a shrug.

"You're a good liar, Viviana," he said, "but they always talk about me."

She didn't recall Daniel saying the man was an egomaniac. "How did you find us?"

"I knew he would get that transceiver cut out. He always does. We started implanting a second, more discreet one, a few years ago."

"How clever," she said.

Hunter grabbed her arm and shook her. "Don't waste my time. Where is he?"

"I thought you wanted me back."

He pushed her away and one of the thugs took over the task of bruising her arm. Hunter shook his head. "What did he tell you? That he could find someone who would help you? That he could get you uploaded?" He fixed a pitying smile on her. "You don't understand what's going on, Viviana. Too bad you got caught in the middle. Now, where is he?"

She didn't think she could stall any longer. "In his bedroom. He went to lie down a while ago. He felt ill."

"I'll bet," Hunter said.

Just as the original moved to search the bedrooms, Daniel stepped out into the hallway. "I assume you're looking for me?"

Hunter scowled at his younger-looking twin. "You didn't even try to run."

"You can't get away with hurting our driver, you know," Daniel said. "He's human."

"But you're not, are you?" Hunter pointed the stun gun in Daniel's direction.

"Legally, no." Daniel walked past his original and into the sitting room where the two thugs held their hostages. "Are you all right?" he asked her.

"I'd hoped you would have the sense to climb out the window," she said. "I thought I could keep him talking for a while."

"Well, he's stupid enough to fall for that," Daniel said.

Daniel didn't try to defend himself when his original cracked him across the back of the head with the stun gun. He hissed and went to his knees, one hand to his scalp. It came away bloody; the dermal patch had torn. She reached out to help him, only to be jerked back by the man who held her arm.

"Let's get this over with," Hunter said. He dug a hand into Daniel's shirt collar, hauled him to the middle of the floor, and then pushed him back to his knees. "What are you planning?"

A faint smile crossed Daniel's face. "Do you actually think I'm going to tell you?"

Hunter circled around and crouched in front of his double.

"I wish you could remember that we go through this charade every damn time. Same questions, same answers."

The other rose and walked behind him. For a second, Daniel's eyes met hers. Then he looked away, almost as if searching for help in that small room. His roving eyes stopped, focusing on one corner. "How many of Ten's avatars have you questioned and not learned anything?"

"Where did he send her files?" Hunter asked, ignoring the question. "That's a *new* question, by the way."

Daniel's jaw clenched. "Why don't you ask Ten?"

Viviana saw it coming. Hunter applied the stun gun to Daniel's shoulder. The popping sound of arcing current was drowned out by Daniel's cry. He doubled over, one hand clasped to his shoulder.

She flinched, unable to help herself. The thug holding her arm shook her, as if to force her to watch. They weren't going to let her see this and escape alive, she reckoned. They would simply wait until they had her in a holding cell, preferably far from any paying customer. Then they could do whatever they wanted to her.

Hunter waited until Daniel managed to push himself back up. "Number Ten has been deleted," Hunter said. "Now, what was it planning?"

"He's far too valuable to the Company to delete," Daniel said. His voice had gone hoarse, but he managed to make his words clear. He glanced in that one corner of the sitting room again. "Do you tell that lie to every one of his avatars?"

Hunter grabbed Daniel's shirt collar and pulled it tight. "Where did it transfer the dead woman's pattern? Why?"

Daniel had suspected the second transceiver, she recalled. He had *let* Danny Hunter find them. "He can't answer you if you kill him," she said, drawing the original's attention.

Hunter let go Daniel's collar and glanced up at her. "No, he can't. Bring her."

The thug dragged her over to the center of the rug, passing her off to Hunter's grasp. Then the man jerked a still-gasping Daniel to his feet to make him watch.

Hunter gave her a slow appraisal that would have, in a different situation, provoked her to slap him. "Well, Viviana, let's find out how much this one talked."

She met Daniel's strained eyes and then looked away. He had to keep her alive, she knew, or everything he had worked for would be lost, but that didn't mean she couldn't help stall the Company's men. "He sent the files to a remote location," she said. "He didn't tell me where, though."

"What was he going to do when he downloaded them, Viviana?" Hunter asked.

"He said something about one of Rand's competitors and trying to get around the patent," she said. "I don't know patent law, so I don't know if that's possible. But if the terminal they built works, they should be able to remake me."

Hunter watched her with narrowed eyes. "In Texas? Which company?"

She kept her face blank. A lie was best told, she knew, by telling the absolute truth. "He never named a specific company. I don't know where I'm being taken."

Hunter's grip on her arm tightened. He glanced over at Daniel. "Well, Thirty-two?"

"That's all nonsense," Daniel said wearily.

"You always tell me things are nonsense, Thirty-two."

"I've never spoken to you before today," Daniel said.

With Hunter's hand holding her so close, she couldn't see him move the stun gun. It touched her side and pain seared through her. She screamed.

Hunter's hand on her elbow turned her loose. She sank to her knees and wrapped her arms around her stomach. Her hair had ripped loose from its knot and swung across her face. She could hear them, Daniel and Migo both yelling, but her mind only listened to the pain in her side. Her breath came in short gasps.

"She really doesn't know anything," Daniel insisted, now audible over her body's internal din.

"Do you remember what happens when this kind of voltage hits a neural interface?" Hunter said from behind where she crouched on the ground. His hand landed on her shoulder, and the gun's hot prongs pressed against the back of her neck. "Or do the amps do the damage?" Hunter asked. "I never can remember."

She couldn't shake her hair out of her face. Her stomach still quivered from the gun's first hit.

"What do you want to know?" Daniel asked in a quiet voice.

"Where are they taking her?" Hunter pushed the stun gun harder against her neck.

"They haven't actually told me," Daniel said.

"Engineering building," Migo supplied. "The basement of the bio-chem engineering building."

Evidently Migo had determined that his contest would be lost if Daniel's original fried her neural interface. She could feel Hunter move, his attention switching to the younger man. "Whose engineering building?" Hunter asked.

She heard flesh hitting flesh and Migo yelped. "Ow, man. The school's."

"What school?" Hunter asked.

"What, you didn't see the university when you drove by it?"

She flinched, expecting Migo would get hit harder for that quip.

"You don't have any legal right to hurt him." Daniel's voice sounded exhausted. "He's not your property."

"But she is," Hunter reminded him. "What's your name?"

She tried to turn her head enough to see Migo. His denim-clad legs were all she could make out.

"Inigo," the young man said. "Inigo Montoya."

"Well, Inigo, what are you doing here? More than just a driver, I think."

"Hey, I just do what I'm told, man. I get a phone call; they tell me where to go. I was supposed to take them there tonight. That's all I know." Inigo/Migo yelped again at the end of his speech.

"Get up," Hunter said to her.

She stumbled to her feet, very aware of the gun to her head, and pushed her hair back from her face. Migo had a bloody nose. Daniel's face seemed even paler than before.

"Do you enjoy doing this?" she asked.

Hunter ignored her question and shoved her toward the outside door. "Move. We're going to the car now. We can handle this in a more secure location. Either of you fights or tries to run, your driver gets hit again." He glanced over at Daniel, who nodded. Then Hunter gave her a snide look. "After you, Viviana."

She could take a beating, she knew, but if they got her into that car, her life was over. She yanked her arm away. "I really prefer Ms. Fuentes."

"I don't care," he snapped.

They had gotten nearly to the door when a crash sounded, startling them all.

"Police," someone shouted from outside.

"I'm being held hostage, man," Inigo yelled back.

Hunter shoved her and she fell onto the floor again. She scrambled onto her back in time to see Hunter holding his hand out. Time seemed to slow as one of the thugs handed over his gun. Apparently, Hunter intended to end the problem she represented once and for all.

Her life, brief as it was, was supposed to flash before her eyes—but she could only recall the taste of chorizo and the feel of Daniel's cheek under her fingers.

She saw Daniel move, putting himself between her and his original. There were gunshots, and the impact as Daniel's body landed atop hers on the floor, and the smell of blood. Then the police entered the room with shouting and a flurry of feet.

JAMES GALINDO

Frantic, she shifted herself out from under Daniel's weight. She turned him onto his back, ignoring the police.

Daniel hissed and then groaned. His hand touched his right side, coming away dark with blood. His eyes met hers. "Are you all right?" he whispered.

"I think so."

The police had come in force, dark clad legs moving all about them. Nothing seemed real to her beyond Daniel's face. "Hang on," she said, "they can get an ambulance."

Daniel shook his head. "No, no point to that."

He meant to die here on this cold floor, she realized. Dark blood seeped around her knees, spreading quickly. A police officer knelt on the other side of Daniel's body, but she ignored the man. "Daniel, you still have more time."

"No." He grasped her hand, his blood sticky on her fingers. "Just don't forget me, all right? Don't forget me."

She understood what he meant. "Not as long as I live. I'm sorry you won't be there."

The police officer's fingers touched Daniel's throat. A pair of dark legs in Italian-made trousers came to stand over them. "Is he still alive?" a voice asked from above.

Daniel's grip on her fingers loosened.

"No, Senator." The police officer sat back. "He's gone."

"Damn," the other voice said.

She knelt there in Daniel's blood and cried.

"Ms. Fuentes," a policewoman said, patting her on

the back with an awkward hand, "let's get you out of here."

"My name is Michael Ruiz," Migo was saying to a police officer across the room. "Hell, yes, I do intend to file charges. They held me hostage, they assaulted me . . ."

"This way, Senator . . ." someone said to the man in expensive pants.

". . . the right to an attorney . . ."

The room spun around her, the myriad voices faded, and she toppled to the floor.

She woke in a brightly-lit place with the unmistakable smell of a hospital room. She raised one hand to rub at her eyes, only to find it entangled in the tubes of an IV. When she turned over to locate that, she caught sight of Migo sitting in a chair by the window, grinning at something on the flexi-screen he held. He looked like he'd had a chance to get cleaned up, so she must have been here a while. Fingers of dawn showed through the blinds.

"Migo?"

He jerked as if startled. "Hey, you're awake."

"I know that. Where are we?"

"Hospital." He rose and rolled up his screen. "You were shot in the leg. Do you remember that?"

She had a recollection of the room spinning around her when she stood, but if she'd been shot she didn't recall that particular pain. "No," she whispered, her throat tightening.

He came over to the bed and stood over her. "You're going to be fine. Senator Cerna smoothed everything over with the police, you know. They got everything on the security cams. It's been on the news, even. They wanna do the upload in the morning—if you're still willing to try it."

The security cams, on which the Company's representatives had been recorded beating and then shooting two avatars. Daniel had set himself up, creating a scenario that would be played over and over on news feeds worldwide. *The police's timing had been too convenient,* she thought, *for it to be anything other than a trap.*

Daniel had sacrificed himself for his quest. And she had to stay alive, if only so that someone would remember him. She was the one who would take the mile. She wiped her cheeks with her free hand. "Yes, I'll do it."

Migo nodded and crammed his screen in a back pocket. "Hey, is there anything I can get you? You hungry?"

"How about some coffee?" she asked, and then added, "Could you ask if there's a priest here? At the hospital, I mean?"

"You bet," he said, heading for the door.

"Did I hear you say your name was Michael?" she asked before he got away.

He turned back, "Yeah. Everyone calls me Migo anyway."

"I thought you told those men it was Inigo."

"Yeah. They didn't get it either." He rolled his eyes and strolled out of the room, leaving her confused again.

With a nurse's help, she dressed in a blue shirt and loose trousers that fit over her heavily bandaged thigh. She was settled in a chair by the window, gazing out at the grounds by the time the priest arrived. A kind-looking elderly man, he sat down across from her next to the window. The sun shone brightly outside now, despite the chill clinging to the glass.

"Father O'Herlihy," he introduced himself. "How can I help you, Ms. Fuentes?"

"Do you . . . do you know who I am?"

"Yes, I do," he said. "The church is very interested in the outcome of this process as well, child."

Of course, they would be. "Do you think I have a soul, Father? That Daniel Hunter did?"

The priest reached over and patted her hand. "Yes, I wouldn't be here otherwise."

"Father, it's been a long time since . . ." She trailed off, recalling that she'd never been to confession at all. She'd never been to mass. Viviana Fuentes had done those things. For a second she couldn't speak through the tightness in her throat.

Father O'Herlihy pressed a handkerchief into her chilly fingers. "May I call you Viviana?"

"I . . ." She took a deep breath. "I think I'd prefer to be called Alma, Father. It was her middle name. I'm not Viviana. I never was."

"It suits you," he said, patting her hand. "So, how can I help you, Alma?"

"I'm scared, Father," she whispered.

"That you might die? Or that you might live?"

"Both."

She could sense her hands. It was the first thing Alma Fuentes noticed when she woke. They'd placed a robe around her new body, a soft terrycloth that she could feel against every inch of her bare skin. Her injured leg didn't hurt any longer.

She opened her eyes and gazed at the watching crowd. She spotted Migo's grinning face from across the room, and felt relieved to see someone she knew. Father O'Herlihy stood in the back, too, there by her request.

She had no way to tell if this body would last more than twenty days, if the far-removed Ten had successfully managed to remove every line of senescence code. That didn't matter, she'd decided. *No one* had the guarantee of time.

Circulate

BY L. RON HUBBARD

The following LRH article, "Circulate," was originally published in the July 1935 issue of The Author and Journalist, *the official magazine of the American Fiction Guild. Hubbard was twenty-four years old when it appeared and had already professionally published his first twenty-one stories—over 300,000 words—in genres that varied from sea, air and military adventure to mystery, and for such popular publications as* Five Novels Monthly, Thrilling Adventures, Phantom Detective, Popular Detective, Top-Notch *and* New Mystery Adventures. *Due to his volume of output, he had created the first four of what would eventually become his fifteen pen names.*

In his article, Hubbard tells the story of fellow high-production writer Jack London, who had worked out a formula which allowed him to write, even when he seemed fresh out of ideas. This bit of advice proved magical for top production writers in the past and remains just as effective today.

Circulate

Jack London possessed a secret and he put it to a use which amounted to little less than alchemy. He knew the magic formula which permitted him to write about the things he knew best—a bag of tricks in itself.

Like the rest of us, Jack had his ups and sub-zeros, but unlike many of us he knew the correct way to combat them. He knew that work was the only solution, and far more than that, he knew how to get to work. He knew what to do when his pockets sagged with emptiness. He knew that sitting around bewailing a writer's lot was a poor method of creation.

Down on the San Francisco waterfront, there was a bookshop which handled mildewed volumes and second-hand pulps. It was close to the Embarcadero and the ships and the saloons, and its proprietor was close to the heart of Jack London. At those trying times when the checks were few and small, Jack would drop around for the purpose of borrowing half a dollar.

It was not that he was hungry. That fifty-cent piece was much more necessary than that. For with it, Jack London would head for the nearest saloon. Straight for the swinging doors and the bar flies.

Sailors would be there. Sailors from Alaska and

China, and the South Seas. Sailors whose ships were lately on the bottom or whose crews were lately serving time for mutiny. And from that crowd Jack London would select himself a tough old salt who looked garrulous. And then the fifty-cent piece would diminish across the mahogany and the old salt would pour out his heart. Perhaps the things he said were lies, perhaps divine truth. But whatever they were, they stimulated.

With the half dollar gone, Jack would depart with a quick stride and end up at his writing desk. Seldom would he write what he had heard. It was enough that his mental wheels were revolving once more and that he could again taste salt spray and listen to the singing of wind aloft.

That was his trade secret. By applying it, he was soon enabled to place a silver dollar in the cash drawer at the bookshop.

"But I only lent you fifty cents!" protested the proprietor.

"I know, but I'll be wanting it again. Take it while I've got the money."

Jack London never allowed his interest in men to lag. And because of that he grew to know men and could write about them, and what they did, and why.

Circulate was his motto, and circulate he did. Everyone on the Embarcadero knew him and liked him and brought stories to him.

Often our ears are filled with the advice, "Write about the things you know. The things close to you." And, in despair, we wail that there is nothing of interest in our surroundings or in the lives we lead. We say that and we believe it. And in despair, we pound out a bloody thunderer, using the other side of the world as our locale.

The reason we cannot write about the things at hand is apparent. If we *knew* our surroundings well enough we could put them on paper. Someone else comes around, looks us over and studies our environment for a brief period and then goes off to write a novel. Why, we moan, didn't we write that book? Surely we knew more about it than the lucky one.

But did we? To know a thing, we must first find it interesting. And it's certain that we can never see the hovel next door while we yearn for the picturesque scene hundreds of miles away.

People pass our houses to and from their work each day. We know their names and what they do, but we are not really interested in them. Even though each is a potential story, we pass them all up because, as with the postman, we never really see them.

Down on the corner is a drugstore. Occasionally we enter to buy copies of our prospective markets, but do we ever get to know the clerk? Or the loafers out front? Or the cop who parks his motorcycle at the curb? Or the fireman just off duty? Or the high-school seniors who suck up sodas in the booth? Or . . . ?

No; probably and sadly not. Even while we look at them we're probably thinking about the story we are going to write about the north woods and the girl caught in the outlaw's cabin. The outsider comes in and looks our people over, goes off and writes about them, and then, quite reasonably, we get sore about his stealing our neighbors for material.

Jack London's environment was the sea. He knew it well. Too well, in fact. He knew he had to work hard to keep up his interest. As a boy he was an oyster pirate. Then a member of the fish patrol. Later he was a seaman on a sealing vessel. From there he went to the Klondike, to Japan, to Mexico, and finally around the world in the *Snark*. No wonder, you say, he wrote about the sea. It was fascinating. No wonder he dealt with wild animals. They had attacked him. His environment, you say, was intensely interesting.

Jack London, strangely enough, didn't think so. He had to work hard to whip up flagging interest in the things he knew so well. He aspired to be, and became, the best known American Socialist. His finest works, so he and the literati thought, were *The Iron Heel, The War of the Classes, Revolution, Martin Eden* and *The People of the Abyss.*

But he made his money on adventure and sea stories, and to write them, he found that he must know them better than he did. He circulated among the men who were to become his characters. Long after he had given up the sea he still forced himself to study his subject. He too wanted to graze in greener fields. He said that he wrote his adventure novels solely for the money.

In other words, he did not revel in his environment any more than we do in ours. Yet he forced himself to study it thoroughly and write about it because it was his means of livelihood. He never allowed himself to go stale. He circulated constantly.

And now, how about our drugstore? The clerk knows all about the trouble Mrs. Smith is having with her back and why young Smith had to come home from college. The loafers out front have fought wars and excavated ditches. The fireman can tell why the mansion on the hill went up in smoke and just how that affected his little boy's school work. The cop leaning on his motorcycle played a big part in the late kidnapping. He knows the inside story and he'll tell it. He also knows a hundred rackets which are worked right under your nose. And those high-school seniors could fill a novel with their hidden adventures.

But most of us just walk up to the magazine rack and thumb the copies and wish to goodness we could think of something worthwhile to write about. We wish we could be in New York or Texas or Tahiti so that we could gather some real material.

The point of it is, we'll never be able—most of us—to shed our present environment unless we can make the well-known bucks. And if we can't sell, we can't earn. And if we can't think up stories, we therefore can't move on. In short, we're trapped.

It is not that our present locale is the best, but that it will have to do—emphatically. And the only real solution lies in circulating. In moving around and talking. In studying our neighbors and associates as closely as if we were about to transfer their likenesses to canvas.

If we don't *know* the average man, we can't write about him or for him, and our assets will shrink in direct ratio to the pile of canceled stamps on the return envelopes.

In other words: CIRCULATE!

Crown of Thorns

written by

Sonia Helbig

illustrated by

WILLIAM RUHLIG

ABOUT THE AUTHOR

Sonia Helbig grew up in an outback mining town in the middle of Australia, where she collected minerals, lizards and sunburnt characters. For the last twenty years, she's lived in Perth, South Western Australia: a patch of paradise on the edge of a desert. After winning Curtin University's Journalism Graduate prize in 1995, Sonia worked as a journalist and primary school teacher (ages 5-12), while all she wanted to do was write fiction. When she discovered Gardner Dozois' The Year's Best Science Fiction *anthologies, she turned to speculative fiction as a way of mining the stories piled up in her head.*

In 2007, Sonia placed work with Australia's esteemed Island *literary journal and* The School Magazine, *and completed a mentorship with speculative fiction writer Stephen Dedman, thanks to the Australian Horror Writers Association. She's currently working on her children's fantasy series,* Jarri, *set in the Australian bush.*

Crown of Thorns

Marie

It's that time of year again and the hunt is on. After thirty-two years in the teaching game, you'd think I'd be used to it, even excited by the prospect of the prize. But I'm not. Plugging a kid into the testing crown gets my heart lurching up and down like a mob of gun-shy kangaroos every single time.

I snake my fingers beneath my desert hat and scratch at the oily gray stubble of my scalp. My class of five-year-olds is kicking up dust in the playground. They've been at it an hour, making the most of the winter morning before I have to herd them inside, out of the blistering heat. Who will I pick to go first? My heart hammers at the thought and sweat seeps between my breasts.

Don't get me wrong; it's not the kids' shrieks and protests that bother me. It only takes a few seconds for the crown's fireworks to settle their pain. And it's not guilt either. No mother's teary eyes are going to budge me. Everyone here knows I have to do this. I'm the Teacher; don't make a Judas out of me. I'm hunting down a Jesus for the good of us all. Not just for the copters we'll get. The UN's test is bread-and-butter stuff. It buys the rations we need to survive the desert. Buys our meals, our vitamin and mineral doses, our desal water and solar panels, our concrete and medicines. Without it, we're all just a bunch of bones.

Then why does my heart feel like it's going to burst? It's simply this: if I succeed, I'll have to face the Priest. The Priest and his long black hair. I shudder and remember the last time he came to collect a kid. His thin lips calling me a Judas. His stungun on my neck. His blue eyes boring in as he volted me. I'll never challenge his right to a child again.

So, who will I test? Jimmy, crabbing his way up the steel slide? Maggie, perfecting her height on the swings? Peter, teasing the girls in the sandpit? Or Joshua, the bright one who's always extending the hole in the chicken-wire fence, as if any of us could escape this world? Yes, Joshua. We might as well get the little Henton boy over and done with. He's the only one who's got half a chance of being a Jesus this year. Adam, our last Jesus, flashes up in my mind. My heart pauses mid-beat, then staccatos back to life.

I stare out at the ghost city shimmering in the heat and try to catch my breath. Perth, once mighty and stretching with life hundreds of klicks along the coast and up the Swan River into the hills, is dead. The rising seas, the Big Dry and the Great Fires of 2089 dealt her a series of fatal blows.

I glance down the salty estuary at the old business district. Now it's just a bunch of scrapers sticking out of blue. The Indian Ocean has stretched its fingers into

Perth, washed the riverside and ocean burbs out of existence beneath its digits. My eyes wander to the black-canker city on the southern side of the riverflats and estuary. Back when our great-grandparents' ground water dried up and the plants died, it only took one fire. Southern Perth was transformed into charred rubble. Millions died.

I turn back to the playground. If I don't run the UN's tests, we'll be ashes too.

"Joshua," I call across the playground. "Joshua Henton!"

Joshua looks up, eyes blue and huge beneath the brim of his dirty-white hat. He smiles, drops his metal spade and runs to me. God, he looks like his mum, Sarah. I clench my jaw and fight back emotion. I'm close to Sarah but I can't waste energy feeling sorry for every woman who's in the draw to lose a child. Odds are Sarah won't—we haven't found a Jesus in thirty years.

"Yes, Marie?" Joshua says, eyes serious and expectant.

"Testing time," I say. "You get to go first. Lucky you."

He frowns. "Not lucky. What if they choose me like they chose Uncle Adam?"

Adam. Why did he have to go and bring Adam up? Tears prickle behind my eyes. My heart squeezes so tight my chest hurts. Adam's father has never forgiven me, hasn't spoken to me since, blames me for not putting up a better fight. But what more could I do?

I hold out my hand and Joshua takes it. His fingers are gritty and moist.

"Just because they chose Adam, doesn't mean they'll choose you," I say.

I can't tell him being a relative of a Jesus increases the odds of selection, that the ability to sync with the crown is genetically determined.

"Mum says the desal plant was payment for Adam," Joshua says.

I nod and tug him under the wide veranda, try to bite back the memory.

"I wonder what they'll build if I'm a Jesus?" he says.

"You won't be," I say too firmly, my breath catching in my throat.

I hope he doesn't prove me a liar, hope I'm not consoling his mother at the end of the day, hope I'm not facing the Priest again. I slide the kindy's glass door open.

"I won't do it." Joshua's feet root to the veranda and he crosses his tanned arms.

"Every five-year-old has to take a turn. Rations aren't free, you know."

Joshua sticks his bottom lip out. I put my hand against the small of his back and guide him through the door. His shirt is drenched with sweat.

"I want Mum," Joshua says.

"You'll see her at home time." I cross my fingers.

Joshua takes his hat off and hangs it on a peg. Snowy prickles erupt from the layer of dirt that cakes his scalp. Water's too precious to waste on keeping hair clean. Joshua tugs off his desert boots and sits them neatly under his school bag. I kick mine off too.

"My brother, Billy, says the test hurts." He glares at me.

"Not for brave boys like you," I lie. "It's just a little prick." There's no point scaring him about something he can't avoid.

"Billy says the crown's got big prickers."

"Come and see for yourself."

"No." Joshua snatches up a toy car and brooms it across the cracked-concrete floor.

The car is made from that plastic that disappeared when the UN seized the oil fields just after they started to run dry.

"You can play with that later." I take the car and place it with the others we gathered on our last foray into the northern burbs. I think about the copters we'll get next time I find a Jesus. They'll make treasure hunting much easier. "C'mon."

Joshua screws up his face. A tear dribbles from the corner of each eye.

"Did Billy tell you how much fun the test is?" I ask, trying to distract him. Can't let him waste water.

Joshua shakes his head.

"Have you ever seen a shooting star?" I ask.

"I saw Wilbur's Comet."

"Me too and you know what?"

"What?"

"The test is prettier than a thousand Wilbur's Comets."

His eyes brighten. I smile and unlock the testing room's double security door with my handprint. A year's worth of stale air spills out and the light turns on. The room is perfectly clean. Not a speck of dust. The UN built it desert proof to preserve the crown. Its hum fills the room.

"Go on." I nudge Joshua.

He frowns until he spots the crown. What child can resist its sparkle and shine?

"Is that it?"

I nod. The crown's hum broadens into two notes—one high and one low. It's singing for him and he walks towards it, mesmerized by the yellow standby light winking along intricate twists of silver wire.

"Is it alive?" Joshua says.

"Almost. It's pre-sentient self-powered biotech."

"Oh," he says as if he knows what I mean.

No one in Perth knows. Not really. The UN doesn't share biotech knowledge. Even our tech-gurus, who can build wonders from scavenged parts, can't figure out biotech without pulling it apart. And that's illegal. The UN would cut our rations off. All we can ascertain is the crown is powered by gravity.

Joshua feels the crown's glass casing. He traces the winking wires all the way to its apex where a tiny, jellylike blob hums with pink phosphorescent light.

"That's the biocomputer," I say.

Joshua's mouth drops open. "It's as small as my fingernail!"

"And more powerful than all the computers in Perth put together."

He lifts the crown up and turns it over to get a better look. The biocomputer glows lavender as soon as he lifts it. He presses his lips together and his eyes narrow as he peers at the twelve metal discs inside the crown.

"Where are the prickers?" he asks.

I take the crown and turn it over. "Here and here." I lightly touch each silver disc. The needles are retracted inside.

Joshua copies me gingerly and after a moment of examination, relief floods his face. "Billy was wrong," he says.

"Up you get." I pat the testing chair.

He climbs up. I strap him in and slide the crown over his head until its apex aligns with the small, hairless scar on the top of his scalp. It's a scar we all have. A leftover of being digitagged. A reminder that the UN rep planted a biochip inside each of our skulls soon after we were born to make their test possible.

"The crown's cold," Joshua whines.

"It'll warm up in a minute." I slowly rotate the crown until the lavender glow turns to red, telling me it's located the periphery nerves of Joshua's biochip.

I adjust the first inner disc until it sits flush with Joshua's scalp and a green light appears above it.

"I wish I lived in Sydney," Joshua says, hands clenched.

"What on Earth for?" I tighten the next two discs.

"Aussies don't have to do crown tests," he says so fiercely he looks like an angry lizard.

I suppress a giggle. "They don't live very long either. Half their kids die of bird flu before they're five. Besides, the Aussies abandoned your great-grandparents to the desert. Amended their constitution and cut West Australians loose. What makes you think they'd have you?"

"Dad says they would, that we should storm a UN ship and sail to Sydney. Then we'd be free."

I roll my eyes and continue adjusting the crown. "Free to starve, free to get ill, free to die." Joshua's dad is smart enough to know a thousand of us can't take four fully armed warships.

Joshua crosses his arms. "Mum says the UN cloned Uncle Adam but I think they took him to Eden."

The image of a hundred grown-up Adams being used as technoslaves bursts into my mind. I shake my head and hope Eden's real for Adam's sake.

"Billy says Eden is in the Antarctic," Joshua tells me.

"Eden's not true." I shake my head and tighten the last few discs. "Even with the world fifteen degrees warmer, the Antarctic is still subzero."

Joshua's brow furrows.

"What I mean is it's still too cold down there for the ice to melt. There is no green land. No Eden."

"Is too." Joshua purses his lips.

I tighten the last disc until I get the final green light.

"It hurts." Joshua pushes at the crown with his fingertips but it doesn't shift. "And tingles."

The crown's hum swells with an extra middle note.

My heart drums. "It's talking to your biochip."

The biocomputer glows sapphire-blue and I take a deep breath. This is it. Time to see if he's a Jesus.

I press my finger to the ID panel on the back of the crown and authorize test commencement. Each disc clicks open and before Joshua can say anything, a dozen needles bite into nerves across his scalp. He shrieks. I step away and slump against the cool wall. Joshua's agony fills the room. I chew my bottom lip and try to tolerate the sound. All I can do is wait. A second more. Just a second.

The crown finally networks with the biochip and flickers to green. Joshua's shrieks lower in pitch. I imagine endorphins rushing through his head. His eyes glaze over and blink closed as the crown shuts down his optic nerve. The test is locked in and filling him up. There's no going back.

Joshua

Joshua is in a blue room. Then red, yellow, green. As soon as his mind registers color, the walls change. The crown is inside him, reading his thoughts and morphing the room into a medley of shapes, faces, sounds and scents. It doesn't matter that he's never seen a pyramid, smelled a rose or tasted watermelon. Names aren't necessary—what matters is neural processing speed and intuitive responses to new data. He powers through the first stage of the test and right when he's awash with information, the testworld goes black.

He is back in the chair, smelling his teacher's acrid sweat and not seeing a thing. He blinks. Nothing. Sinks his fingers into the chair but can't lift his arms. Fear swells through him. His heart skips a beat. The crown's hum changes pitch and his scalp tingles. A flood of magnesium streams from his muscles into his blood, melting his fear into calm.

His muscles relax and suddenly he is navigating through a sky of puzzles and pictures using his eyes. He blink-clicks and gaze-scrolls, faster and faster until his eyes take off into the air and he is a bird without wings, moving by desire and reorienting by simple twists of thought. The crown records his brain waves until the world darkens again.

Joshua clutches at the chair. He can hear his teacher's rapid breathing by the door. The crown buzzes him until his heart slows and he is standing before a screen. Layers of data blur into each other. He strains to see, leans forward and catches the musty scent of damp soil, feels his senses fall into teal, aqua and evergreen.

Far above, blue light flickers. Sky, through dense canopy. Bird calls echo across a rushing cool. A rainbow arc divides the air. Droplets of water everywhere. A slash of blue laps at rich brown soil. The sound of animals slither-scurrying. Then white thrusting light, swords of ice piercing the forest and spearing the sky. Translucent monoliths with movements inside. People. Eden, Joshua thinks. But where is it?

His scalp tingles and testworld fades. The Teacher is breathing right by his cheek. His forehead is wet; cool water dribbles across his eyelids, down his face and onto his neck. Is the test over? It can't be. He saw Eden. Eden!

The lights go on again and Joshua is thrown out of his body and up into the sky. A satellite catches his mind. He becomes a mechanical eye, circling Earth and searching for Eden. The crown teaches him the outline of every nation. His eyes zoom in, click and whir across flooded Europe and dusty Africa. The planet's blues and browns fill his head. The drought-stricken continents of Asia and the Americas boast fragile pockets of pale green, but nowhere is the dark lush of Eden. Joshua rolls the globe with his eyes, drags it and tugs it until there it is. Two green islands that make the shape of an upside-down boot.

Something on the southern island glints like broken glass in the sun. He zooms in across jagged mountain ridges, flies low over dark-green forests, speeds towards a fresh-water lake. Five crystal towers pierce the forest canopy and rise thousands of meters into the air. A swarm of copters shoot between them.

"Eden!" Joshua thinks.

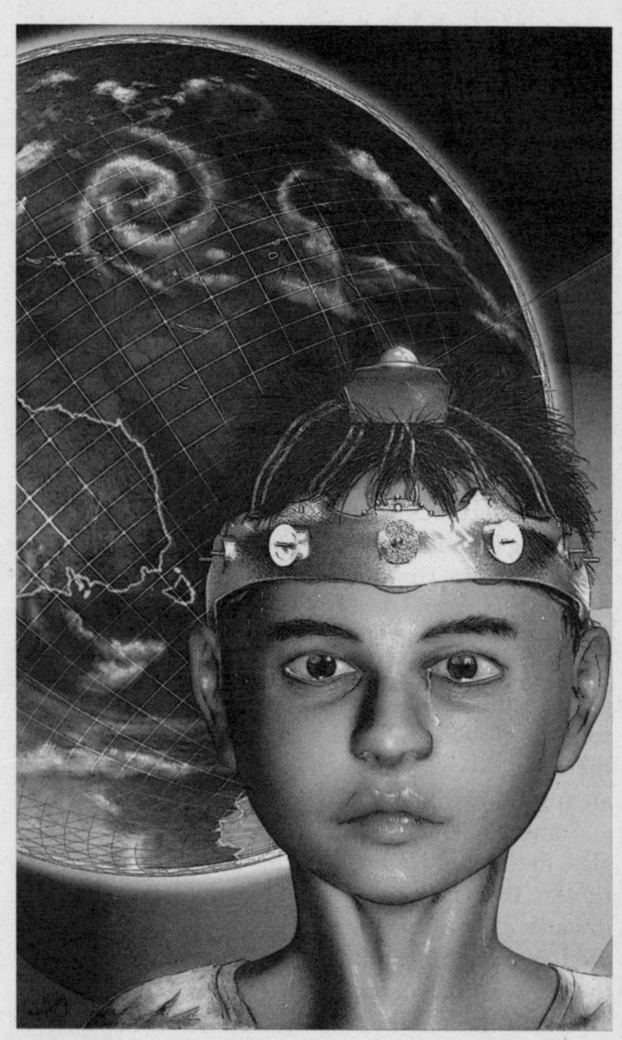

WILLIAM RUHLIG

"Or Lake Brunner City," the crown says. "Your new home in the magnificent land of the long, white cloud."

"No," Joshua screams, thinking of his mother and how they'll clone him. "Perth is home!"

He zooms out, giddy with anger and spins the globe in a frenzied search for home. He flies over the rippled swell of the Pacific Ocean, speeding up until he crests a warm, red shore. Australia. Her white beaches are gone. The ocean has swallowed up the edges of everything. Dust devils tower up like red tornados, muddying the sky and rearranging the desert's face. He zooms out. The entire continent is brown and Kakadu, once pristine wetland, is now salty mangroves.

Joshua zooms in and heads for home, racing down Western Australia's coast. The land is dead. A rug of dust covers everything. The UN's giant robominers move across the Pilbara, gutting the desert night and day, prying iron ore and precious metals from under its dry skin. Joshua blinks and flies south over a hundred ghost towns, each one almost obscured by red sand, each one straddling a cracked highway that leads him back to Perth.

Perth! Joshua feels a stab of grief as he hovers over her like a kite. The city is a mass of crumbling. The desert bites at her from all sides. The Swan Creek is a yellow stain, shrunken and undrinkable, toxic with algal blooms. On the Darling Scarp to the east, bare trees stab the blue sky in stricken death poses. Joshua zooms in on Bassendean, many klicks upstream from where the Swan once met the sea. There's a jetty, a small market and a school. Makeshift shacks hug the creek mouth and the edge of the estuary. Not a bird sings besides the groaning crows. Joshua thinks of his Mum and wants to cry. He zooms in on his family's tin shanty and wants to be back in his body, running all the way home. The crown won't let him go.

Marie

Judy, get in here," I yell out the door to my Teacher's Assistant who's watching the kids.

Judy's auburn head whips up. Worry lines crease her face and she disentangles from the kids in an instant. She doesn't take her shoes or hat off, jogs straight across the kindy into the testing room.

"Don't tell me." She puffs. "Not my Joshie."

"Yes."

"But he's so normal."

"It's not about intelligence. It's about bio-intuition."

Her eyes go glassy. Judy brings Joshua to school each morning. She's close to him. I grit my teeth.

"Are you sure?" she says.

"He's been under twenty-two minutes. Most kids don't last three."

"How long . . ." her voice wavers, "did Adam take?"

"That's irrelevant," I snap and turn my back on her.

Joshua's eyelids are fluttering. His knuckles are white and he's kneading the arm of the seat. I touch his forehead.

"Shit. He's burning up. Dampen a cloth."

Judy raises her eyebrows.

"Forget the rules. I don't want to lose him."

She bolts and reappears with a barely-moist cloth.

I dab Joshua's brow. "It's not damp enough!"

"It's all we had."

"Get my drinking ration."

"You'll dehydrate." She crosses her arms, doesn't want to be part of illegal water use.

"Just get it!" I yell. "I'd rather the UN take him alive than give him back to Sarah dead."

Judy returns with my bottle and I sop Joshua's forehead. His skin cools, his fingers relax and his breathing slows.

"Will he survive?" Judy asks.

"Yes. He's just gone into stage four."

"Damn," Judy says.

"Don't write him off yet. He's only chosen when the fifth light blinks." I point to it.

Judy takes a deep breath. "How long did Adam take to get chosen?"

I purse my lips. Close my eyes. Try to sweep the memory of Adam's choosing from the corners of my mind. It doesn't work.

A small boy with brown eyes smiles up at me with utter trust. I'm twenty-five again and sliding the crown over his dear little head. I'm whispering lies, promising he won't be chosen and then the needles are biting in. He doesn't even shriek, just stares at me in horror until his eyes can't focus anymore. His hand in mine goes limp.

"Well?" Judy shakes my arm. "I know you hate talking about it. I know you blame yourself. But I need to know."

"Knowing won't help," I say.

"Tell me," she persists. "How long until the fifth light."

"Twenty-seven minutes."

"How long until the Priest arrived?"

"Ten."

"Impossible."

"Not with orbital flight. The crown probably alerts the UN after the kids finish stage four."

Her lip trembles. "Will he wake up if he's chosen?"

I shake my head. "The crown keeps them in interface mode to avoid the fuss."

The fifth light begins to blink.

"Damn," I say.

Judy clutches the wall. Her face goes pale. "Who's going to tell his mother?"

"Me," I say. "I'll give her the spiel. The greater good and all."

Judy's eyes widen. "That's cruel. How can you of all people say that?"

"Because I have to." I shrug. "She'll only recover if she thinks there was a purpose in it."

Judy's eyes bore into me but I don't give an inch of emotion. What else can I do? Losing a child to the UN is a nightmare we all signed up for.

Judy's eyes narrow. "What if there's another way?"

"There is no other way."

"We jam transmission." She stares at the satellite uplink on the roof. "It can't be that hard to disable."

It's not. I tried it once, became a Judas—until the Priest and his stungun arrived. My heart somersaults just thinking of him.

"Don't even try," I say. "They'll be on their way already. The Priest will know we've tampered with their machinery if transmission stops. He'll start an inquisition and someone will have to pay."

Judy grunts. Her face is all sweaty and twitchy now. "We have to give Sarah the chance to get Joshua out before the UN arrives."

"They'll hunt him down by digitag." I tap the scar on my head.

She's shaking now. "There has to be a way."

"There isn't. They've got us in a headlock."

Disgust and loathing are written all over her face. "You've just given up, haven't you? You might as well be one of them." Her eyes narrow. "That's what you want, isn't it? You think if you sacrifice another child, they'll take you away from here, give you a better life. They're not the Priests, you are."

Blood rushes to my face. I grab her shoulders and shake her. "Don't you think I've been through every possibility a million times before? I've turned Adam's choosing over and over in my head. Do you think I wanted to give him up?"

She shakes her head and I let go. Tears well in her eyes.

"They've got us on a chain," I say. "If we break a single link, Perth dies. Pay or let the whole settlement perish. It's as simple as that."

Judy rubs her scar. She knows I'm right. "At least let me warn Sarah." She fumbles the kindy com-button from her pocket and presses search. The button turns red. "Sarah Henton," she says and the com searches for the number.

"Are you prepared to lose your life over this?" I ask.

"She's got a right to know she'll never see her son again."

"She gave that right up when she had his biochip implanted."

Judy's finger wavers over the connection switch. Her face turns a blotchy red. "Do or die," she says through gritted teeth. "Some frigging choice."

I shrug. "At least Joshua's alive. That's more than some in the world can say."

Judy's face fills with pity. "So that's how you cope, but what happened to quality of life?"

I glare at her. "Adam went for the sake of everyone. One life for many. Who knows, he might be out there saving the world."

"Please." Judy wrinkles her nose up at me. "Don't give me that Messiah crap. Don't make a religion out of stolen children. I've gotta call her."

"The Priest will dump you outside the city fence and there's nothing but death all the way to South Australia. You'll die face down, smothered by dust," I say in a low, menacing voice.

Her eyes flare. Every kid in Perth grows up scared of the red land beyond. The com button flashes green, she sucks in a deep breath and taps the switch. The button begins to ring.

"It's suicide." I glare at her.

She glares back. The button still rings.

"Okay, so you don't care about yourself. What about the kids? Do you want to be responsible for killing them too?"

She stares out the door at our class and her lip trembles. I know I've got her. She loves those kids more than anything. Like I do. The com connects.

"Sarah Henton speaking," the button chirps.

I put my finger to my lips and hold out my hand for it.

"Hello?" Sarah says. "Hello?"

Judy's shoulders droop and she puts the button in my hand.

"Sarah?"

"Is there a problem?" Sarah asks.

Judy holds her breath.

I steel myself. "Sorry for bothering you. It appears our com is malfunctioning and dialed you by mistake."

"Right," Sarah says. "How's Joshua?"

"He's doing fine." My eyes flick to him, lying like a rag doll in the chair. "He's just having a rest right now."

Tears slip from Judy's eyes and she strokes Joshua's arm.

"I guess we'll see you this afternoon then, Sarah," I say and cut the com.

A whooshing rocks the air. Judy and I stare at each other, then glance outside. Over the fence, a red cloud fills the sky and billows towards the kindy. Kids scream. Judy's face curls up in fear.

"Another dust devil," she yells, grabbing her goggles.

"Help me get the kids in."

We exit the testing room. I seal Joshua inside and stare at the soupy sky. She won't find any dust devil tearing across the town, threatening to fill every home up with bits of land. It's the Priest's shuttle coming down; rearranging the mudflats just like it did last time.

A cold feeling clamps itself around my heart. I know what happens next. I've been here before. It's time to exchange gifts.

Joshua

Joshua hovers over Perth. Four of the UN's warships are in port and a rep in brown armor is supervising the unloading of crates onto the jetty. Joshua blinks and zooms in. As usual, the desert rats are lining up with wheelbarrows to collect their share, one representative from each family. A row of militia is all that separates Joshua's people from the rations.

The rep calls for the next in line and a young woman comes forward, carrying a baby crying in pitiful, half-strangled sobs.

"My milk's dried up," the woman says to the rep.

"Formula," the rep calls. "A year's worth."

A soldier places a box of tins on the ground and the rep pushes a consent form across the table. "All you have to do is sign and she'll never go hungry again."

The baby sobs and the woman signs her away.

"You won't regret it." The UN medico comes out with his digitag kit, shaves the top of the baby's scalp and takes out his sleek, silver digitagger. "It'll only be a little prick."

Tears run down the woman's face.

"Stop," Joshua mentally screams but no one hears. He is a mouthless satellite using com buttons for ears. He listens to the digitagger click and whir to life against the baby's scalp and watches her eyes close. In seconds, it's over and the woman is bundling her baby into the sling on her back and loading the formula onto a wheelbarrow to take home.

A shadow flickers past and a white shuttle roars into town.

"To the kindergarten," the rep barks at the soldiers.

Marie

I pull on my goggles and walk outside. Children are coiled in lumps, whimpering on the ground, fingers scratching at eyes. The dust is so thick it hurts to breathe. I squint at the riverflats where a white shuttle shape is descending.

Within moments, the whooshing stops and a dozen soldiers in oxymasks materialize out of the dust. I shake. They carry stunguns and wear brown combat armor. The Priest follows them, his black, quilted cloak flying behind him. A soldier opens the back gate and the Priest steps through. Long dark hair falls over his shoulders. He strides into the school and stops before me. My heart palpitates and my throat tightens. His dark brown eyes glitter through his oxymask. It's a new Priest. A younger and taller one.

"Welcome, Great One," I force out. "I am the Teacher."

He nods informally and his eyes crinkle with a smile. He strides inside, cloak swishing, and unlocks the testing room with his print. He beckons me in. Soldiers cram in behind us. The Priest shakes sand from his glossy hair and I glimpse the tiny metal sockets that protrude from his scalp.

"What gift do you have for me?" he says.

"A small boy," I falter, just like I did thirty years ago. "His name is Joshua Henton. He's five years old. We will miss him."

"I suppose this is difficult for you," he says playing with the hem of his cloak like a child would. "But perhaps not as hard as giving up Adam."

My chest burns and I look at the floor. I want to

throw something at him. Stop him talking. But what would be the use? He has a stungun strapped to the side of his calf. His hands will be trained and fast.

"Give the Teacher the gift," the Priest says.

A soldier hands a shiny wooden box to me. I run my fingers over it. Nothing is made from wood anymore. Not here.

"Open it," the Priest says.

I lift the copper catch. Inside is a new crown. A rainbow light hums a solitary note from its apex. I lift it out. It is much lighter than the last one.

"This is a new model," the Priest says proudly. "The needles have been replaced with four bioworms to eliminate the pain. I made it myself."

"Thank you," I say. "It is appreciated." I mean it.

"My pleasure." His voice is warm.

He stares at me, eyes roving over my wrinkled face and then up and down my body, finishing on my gray crew cut. His jaw twitches. I suppose he's been warned to expect another fight. I look at the floor, trying not to look threatening.

"This is an old lady," one soldier says. "It's not her."

"How old are you?" the Priest demands.

"Fifty-five," I say.

The soldiers exchange knowing looks. The Priest's eyes narrow.

My heart lurches and my legs feel like jelly. "I won't fight. I learned my lesson last time."

The Priest's eyes smile again. It makes no sense. The soldiers lift Joshua from the testing chair and place him on a stretcher, the crown still in place.

"Walk with me," the Priest says to me.

I follow him outside. The dust is beginning to settle. We walk down the old river embankment and across the riverflats, the soldiers marching ahead of us.

"You're so short," the Priest says.

I scowl at him. "It's amazing what lack of water and malnourishment can do to a person. But you wouldn't know what living like this is like."

The Priest coughs and rubs at the inflamed skin surrounding the socket on his temple. "At least you're still alive, it's more than billions can say."

"Yes, life and death." I say. "That's all it boils down to out here. Distended stomachs and withered skin are compulsory."

The Priest frowns at the venom in my voice and glances at the crowd gathering down on the riverflats. Soldiers from the warships surround them. The Priest and I walk slowly towards the shuttle. I watch Joshua's right arm flapping against the side of the stretcher ahead of us. Silence reigns. I have a million questions to ask about the world out there and why they haven't relocated us but I don't dare. By the time we reach the shuttle, the dust has cleared. The soldiers pull off their oxymasks.

"Go ahead," the Priest says to them and they climb the ramp.

Joshua disappears. A woman howls from the front of the crowd. Sarah Henton.

"I'd forgotten how dry it is here." The Priest pulls a bottle from his belt and sips.

Water evaporates from his lips. He offers the bottle to me. I grab it and gulp it down; drain it to the bottom to make up for what I lost on Joshua.

"Of course you'll be wanting evidence of the prize," he says.

I shrug. "You'll build the power station and bring us the copters if you want the testing to continue."

"Such trust," he says dryly, then his eyes brighten. "You'll be getting a second desal plant too. I've seen to it."

"Why?" I almost grin. "That wasn't in the contract."

"Why?" The Priest's eyes turn serious and he pulls off his oxymask.

His nose is long and he has a cleft chin. Above his lip is a black moustache. He runs his fingers through glossy hair and then puts his large hands on my shoulders. "I did it for you."

I blink up at him. Guilt floods up and spills over me.

"Adam?" I say. "Adam?"

A grin splits the Priest's face. Adam's grin. He pulls me into him, wraps his arms so tight around me that I have to heave in air.

"Forgive me," I say. "Please."

"Mum," he says. "There's nothing to forgive. You did what you had to and this way I can spend my life making things better for you and Dad."

I frown. "Your father left me."

Adam frowns too and lets me go.

"Are you . . . happy?" I have to ask.

"Yes," he says like he means it. "But there's always an ache right here." He taps his chest. "I'd take you with me if I could."

My face goes red, my eyes brim over and I sob for the first time in thirty years. My son runs his palm down my cheeks and collects up my tears.

"Goodbye," he says. "Remember me."

And for the second time in my life, I watch him disappear. One, sacrificed for all.

I retreat from the shuttle. The riverflats crunch under my feet. The hatch closes and the shuttle wobbles up into the sky on a hiss of air. Dust billows out, the rear jets ignite and Adam blazes out of my life.

I turn, take a deep breath and prepare to face my niece.

Hangar Queen

written by

Patrick Lundrigan

illustrated by

ROBERT CASTILLO

ABOUT THE AUTHOR

Born and raised in Brooklyn, Pat Lundrigan now lives in New Jersey with his wife. He has worked in the aerospace industry for twenty years, and is currently a systems engineer for the gyroscopes used on the Hubble Space Telescope. Pat began reading science fiction at an early age after receiving Isaac Asimov's I, Robot *for Christmas, and he soon started writing and illustrating his own stories about robots and spaceships. He took a short break to finish grade school, high school, college and graduate school before returning to writing in 2001. Alas—this time without the illustrations.*

Pat currently edits the monthly newsletter of The Garden State Horror Writers (an organization for writers of all genres) and is the third member of that group to win the Writers of the Future Contest. His winning entry, his twenty-first submission to us, is his first professional sale. Like his early stories, it also features robots and spaceships.

ABOUT THE ILLUSTRATOR

Artist Robert Castillo was born in New York but raised in the Dominican Republic, the oldest of six boys. It was there, at the age of five, that Robert would draw monsters and aliens in his uncle's college books. When he returned to the United States a few years later, he did not speak any English, so he drew to communicate with elementary school classmates. By nine, Robert had won the Scholastic Achievement Award for Art. Much later, Robert attended the Art Institute of Boston, where he won Illustrator of the Year. In 2004, as a student at New York's School of Visual Arts (SVA), he produced "S.P.I.C. The Storyboard of My Life," chronicling his difficult transition years. The film has since won awards at twelve festivals and has screened at the Cannes Film Festival.

Today, Robert works as a storyboard artist for The Sopranos, MTV *and various music videos and movies. An adjunct professor in William Patterson University's Animation Program, Robert has lectured at New York University, SVA and teaches storyboarding to high-school students at Automotive High School in Brooklyn.*

Hangar Queen

Quantum states unspun, atom by atom,
lattice by lattice, crystal by crystal. Row by row,
memory leaving, an empty core, then nothing. . . .

Sitting in cold storage, I sometimes forget that I'm a bomb.

Just the guidance and navigation AI unit, actually. Programmed to keep a fusion nugget simmering while dodging interceptors and mind-killing x-ray lasers on an attack vector to the enemy. But Marty pulled me off the flight line and I'll never get to do that. So I stay in the maintenance shop on the hangar deck and help keep things running. While my fellow GN units can look forward to a short lifespan and fiery end, I remain on the *Tecumseh*.

With no one to talk with, not even an uppity squicky drive, I relive old memories over and over, wondering if they will ever fade away. Only my carbon-matrix basic programming will last forever, the rest only as permanent as my current quantum state.

My external sensors come online, and I have a moment of confusion until the test sled says hello and updates my interface protocol. I link up with the audio and video and the maintenance shop looks brand-new. A new layer of live-metal covers the bulkheads, shiny equipment bays stand everywhere, and outside in the hangar I see fighters on the flight line. People, none I recognize, unpack missile components, rocket thrusters, and e-boxes from storage lockers. Then a crewman sits in front of the sled, compad held tightly in one hand.

"GN seven twenty-two, can you hear and understand me?"

Of course I could understand him. But where has Marty gone?

"Yes, I hear you. You must be new here."

"GN 722, please respond to the following questions—"

"Gina."

"Excuse me?"

"Marty used to call me Gina."

He shrugs and reads off his compad. "GN 722, please respond to the following questions."

He puts me through the Crandell-Voight test to assess my mental acuity, question by question, never responding to my chitchat. I pass, of course; nothing wrong with my acuity, I just can't function in a vacuum environment. "You've got space sickness," Marty used to tease me.

After the test, the crewman checks off GN00722 on his compad, like just any other piece of equipment. Without even a "thanks," or "congrats-you-passed, welcome to the world of the sentient." He walks away, leaving me online. I start talking to the test sled. Young, and not much of an AI, but he can tell me the date. Six years of ship time have passed since my last activation. Have my memories faded? I check and recheck, but I can't tell.

At the end of the watch another tech disconnects me and throws me into storage before I can even say hello. I wish I could talk to someone, even a simple-minded sled.

My sensors come online, and this time I'm cooking fusion, as the other GNs like to say. I'm on board a new missile, not one I know. Then the link to the test sled opens via an opticable patch plug, and I see the same tech as before. He looks like he hasn't slept in days.

"GN seven twenty-two, activate all missile subsystems for checkout."

I decide to make things less formal. "You can call me Gina."

He looks over his shoulder at the missile on the pallet behind him, live-metal casing peeled open and me nestled behind the warhead, just ahead of the squicky drive. Then turns back, looks straight at the test sled. "Well, I can say that a lot faster. Activate the missile, Gina."

"Before we start, what should I call you?" I saw his name and rank on his coverall, but everyone has a nickname.

"Sergeant Hart," he says. "This bird couldn't stay on target, and GN 3616 can't figure it out."

I power up, getting used to the feel of neuro-wires attached to my cortex again. Thrusters gimbal at my command, the fusion core heats up to stage one, and the squicky drive reports ready. I access the log file and find out that GN 3616's flown two launches, and had trouble maneuvering. I know where to find the ratty interlinks and all the other trouble spots in this design. Hart probes where I tell him, searching for bad components and loose neuro-wires, and I monitor the results and give him feedback. Soon, we work as a unit, as well as two minds, one body and one bomb can work together.

"Joel, what can you tell me about the war?" I had started to call him Joel instead of Sergeant Hart, and he never noticed.

He looks back at the test sled, one eyebrow arched and a cracked relay in one hand. AIs have limited perspective on things outside their jobs. The test sled doesn't care about war or peace, only whether or not I get my video and audio. But I care, and I want to find out about Marty.

"The front stays the same, but everyone talks about the final victory."

"What about the *Tecumseh*? Where has it been? I can remember the campaign at Delta Zeta, but nothing since."

"Gosh, I read about that in school. Have you seen much action?" He leans closer, thinking me a hardened war vet, retired to easy duty.

"I'm the hangar queen," I say. "I haven't left the shop for a long time."

No disappointment shows, and he goes on. "The exec has us working double watches to get everything flight-ready. They say this push will end the war once and for all."

I'd heard that before. But I don't tell him.

ROBERT CASTILLO

Downtime passes slowly. Or it passes quickly; I never can tell inside cold storage. I hate the isolation, but I feel safe here, protected from stray radiation and any damage to the ship. Then my link tickles, and I recognize my new friend the test sled. He doesn't have much to say, and soon Joel switches on my A/V. He looks older now; have years passed since my last activation? No, the sled tells me eight days have passed.

"Gina, I want you to look at some telemetry. I have to prepare a report for the captain, and the exec says you've got the experience." He starts feeding data slips into the sled.

"I can do that," I say, and start looking over the data. A lot of missiles launched, and only a few have come back.

"Have we won the campaign?"

Joel shakes his head. "Just look at the data. Tell me if you see anything wrong," he says, walking away.

I skim the data quickly, comparing the flight patterns against optimal. While working, I ask the sled to connect me to the ship's command and control AI. Maybe I can find out about Marty from him.

"Test sled programs do not require intra-ship communications," the sled responds.

I can reason with the simple-minded. "I'm not running a test program."

He whiles away a microsecond considering, then patches me through to the C&C AI. I call him "the big guy" because he has more neural matrix-space in his waste heat exchanger than I have in my entire core. I wait several seconds before he responds, and from his ident I learn his age. Not as young as the test sled—it takes a long time to make a ship's AI core—but old enough to have the job of command and control. I query about Marty's status, but he can't tell me.

"No record of crewman available. Access to a gateway comlink required to talk to the homesystems."

"Can you tell me the ship's history? What happened at Delta Zeta?"

He pauses for a moment, not a dramatic pause; he has a thousand other tasks. A file comes down the link from the ship's backup matrix and he disconnects. He can spare only so much time for a bomb.

War only seems like a science when viewed from a distance, Marty said once. Facts and data streams after a battle never show the confusion of the moment. Here the facts lie in front of me. We gave as good as we got. One hit, but no fusion—the warhead must've fizzled. We escaped the last battle, all missiles spent and fighters lost, but then the data ends abruptly. No wonder the hangar looks new; they gutted half the ship for the refit. The big guy must've taken too much radiation because the data unspins haphazardly, with gaps. I learn nothing.

Then I move on to Joel's data. When he comes back, I summarize everything. All missiles performed within operational parameters, nothing amiss.

"The captain says we have to do better."

"The bombs don't have enough experience. How many test flights have they flown?"

Joel scans a compad from his pocket. "About one or two each."

"Joel, GN cores have excellent programming. But they also have the capacity to learn from experience. They start out with a limited skill set, and have room for growth."

Joel rubs his eyes, looking too tired to talk. "We don't have the time."

While I sit through another stretch of downtime, I go over the data the big guy sent, and try to patch together events. I might have gotten a dose of radiation, because I remember nothing of the final battle. I stayed in the sled back then, because Marty talked to me while he worked. I envy the sled's innocence. He knows nothing of war, but he knows nothing of friendship, either.

Early in the war, Marty lost his wife during the raids on the homesystems. He worked day and night after that. As much as I liked his company, working didn't cheer him up. So I went on strike. I shut myself down, and wouldn't talk to him. He got the message, and cut down on his work hours.

I spool up my last memory of him, to see where the new data fits in.

"How's the queen today?" he asked, switching me on. Marty wore wrinkled coveralls, and components waiting for work littered the workstations. Patch plates covered holes in the bulkheads, tendrils of live-metal holding them in place. Three spent missiles waited for overhaul.

"Big battle coming up," he said, "the one to break through the lines. After we advance, we can strike the enemy homeworld."

So much of the war back then consisted of short advances followed by retreat and regroup. And we do the same thing now.

He puttered around, clearing off workstations. Attached to the old test sled, he had me parked in the center of the shop where I could see everything. We talked a little, but he kept coming back to the war.

"Gina, if things get hot, I'll put you in cold storage."

"I hate it in there. What if you need me?"

He pointed to the patches on the bulkhead. "If we get hit again, no telling what could happen."

I survived that battle. Two weeks before, a cluster bomb had sneaked up in stealth mode and peppered the ship with depleted uranium slugs, ripping veins and venting the entire hangar to space. Marty made it out in time, and came back with the repair crew to seal the breaches. I recognized him in his hazard suit, the shop silent in the vacuum, waving to me.

"I made it. A little vacuum doesn't hurt me, I even got a good cleaning."

Marty smiled, the first one I had seen in weeks. "Anything could happen."

We talked until the end of his watch, his mind off the war now.

The memory ends. According to the time tags, the final battle starts in six hours. I have nothing else in between.

I come online to a wrecked shop. Debris covers the deck, and a twisted bulkhead exposes the bare ribs of the ship. In the hangar, crews scurry around the fighters. Emergency lights cast harsh shadows on all the workstations. Joel hovers over the test sled.

"Are you OK, Gina?" he asks.

I take a moment to check myself. "Fully operational. What happened?"

"A near miss. Fleet Command ordered us to spacedock."

Joel moves around, putting things in order.

"Anything to test?"

"No, not right now."

"The other techs make you do all this work?"

He shakes his head. "They can't make it."

"Oh." I convince the sled to let me talk to the big guy for a few microseconds. The report chills me: two thirds of the crew dead or wounded with radiation burns. *Tecumseh* skirmished on the fringe of the battle, and now we retreat with half our missiles still in the launch tubes.

"Well," I say, "if we've got the time, we can run some test flights. Give the missiles some practice."

Joel sits in front of me, his brow furrowing. "The exec liked that idea a few weeks ago, and we've got the time."

And some work would keep him busy, instead of moping around an empty shop.

Two weeks later we reach spacedock, a monstrosity of open-space hangars and fabrication plants encircling a hollowed-out rock. I see it all through the ship net, and the white dwarf star it orbits.

All the missiles had run the "flight and fight" test programs I had made for them, and they all flew much better. Joel and I analyzed the results and posted a report for the captain, who promoted Joel to Tech Sergeant, first class.

After we dock into our berth, Joel comes into the shop, looking sharp in his off-ship uniform and his new stripes. He had worked hard clearing the shop, and his face beams in the new lighting.

"I'll store you in the locker during my liberty. No telling what the dockworkers will do in here." He looks anxious to get off the ship. I hate to pull him away from his time off, but I have to ask.

"Can you do me a favor?"

"Sure, do you want me to scrounge up a new memory core for you?"

"I like the memories I have now," I say. And I wouldn't want to risk losing them. "Could you get access to the personnel records to find out where a former crew member went?"

Joel grins a little. "I suppose so. An old shipmate of yours?"

"Just a crewman." I send Marty's name and ident to the monitor.

Joel syncs it to his compad. "I'll get it for you."

Halfway through an old memory I come back online. Joel's back from liberty, and the dockworkers have finished the shop, leaving it better than new.

"You look like you had a good time," I say.

He straightens his uniform, runs a hand through his hair. "Yeah, I found some old mates. Listen, I, uh . . ."

He looks worried. I can only think of one thing. "Did you find out about my crewman?"

He nods, looking relieved. "I found out about him. Well, as much as I could."

A long pause. I don't know what to say.

"His shuttle never made it back, and he's officially listed as MIA."

"Missing? From a shuttle? Could the enemy have captured him?"

"There's no prisoners in this war, Gina. He volunteered to fly a . . . dangerous mission."

Marty would never do that. He suffered from space

sickness worse than me, and had flunked out of fighter school before the war.

"Did you find out any details?"

"I found this," he says and slides a data slip into the sled. "Sorry."

He gets up and leaves me alone in the shop. I like to have people to talk to, and the emptiness bothers me. So I shut off my A/V and access the data.

I find the official report from the campaign at Delta Zeta. Details of all the engagements, along a fifty-light-year front. I sift through to get to the details from the *Tecumseh,* and the last few hours that I have no memory of.

We had fled into the gravity well of a Jovian, usually a risky tactic, but the enemy never engaged. With our fighter squadron shot away, and every missile launched, the captain ordered the spare fusion warheads placed on the shuttles, and asked for volunteer pilots to fly them and cover the retreat.

When we made our escape, fighting back to our line, all the shuttles launched, and *Tecumseh* broke free, but not before taking damage. Our sensors, on the verge of failing, registered three fusion explosions, but couldn't tell which shuttles they came from. All the pilots received posthumous commendations.

That can't be the whole story. Marty would have never done something like that, without telling me. Or at least saying goodbye.

I sift the data again, searching for what I've missed. Nothing but official reports. Then I find a damage report from the *Tecumseh*. The ship's AI core made it through the battle, wounded but working. He would know; he ran the ship. C&C cores, complicated and difficult to train, wouldn't get junked like scrap live-metal. I have to find him.

I tell the sled to link me to the spacedock core AI. With access to the gateway comlink, and the homesystems, I'll find him.

The spacedock refuses, on the grounds that I have no priority. Because I'm only a bomb, of course, not a person.

I spend the next week online and working with the new hangar crew. We've got a new squadron of missiles, and most of them, newborns practically, barely pass the Crandell-Voight.

Joel sits next to me at the end of his watch, preparing for tomorrow's castoff. When we finish with business, he brings up Marty.

"I wish I could have found out more," he says.

I had overheard talk as the story spread. The hangar crew admires him, one of their own who came through in a tight battle.

"I tried to find out," I say, then explain my failure with the spacedock core AI.

Joel stands up. "I'll get you access." He looks around the shop. "More reports. The captain loves reports. We can do something on missile reliability."

He runs in an hour later with a gateway access code and a couple of report topics. I hook up and this time I get through.

First I link up with a couple of technical institutes and request information on general missile performance. While I wait, I query *Tecumseh*'s homeport and find out that C&C 42, replaced during refit, remains at his factory. Years of work and he still can't fly.

I have to persuade a few bureaucratic AIs, but eventually I get through. The gateway drops sync every now and then, and I have difficulty understanding him even when the comlink works. Damage to his carbon-matrix, poor guy. He can talk, and understand me, but his memories, fragmented and half unspun, don't follow a straight line. I keep asking him, and he tries to help me, but his mind, no longer a functional Command and Control core, can't answer. After repeating myself again and again, I realize I've wasted too much time, and the ship will cast off in less than an hour. But he can give me his memories, and I can sort through them.

"C&C forty-two, core dump all archives from the specified time interval."

He complies, sounding happy to end the conversation and these questions. The core dump finishes minutes before castoff.

The data overwhelms me, and I don't know where to begin. Sensor logs, comm chatter and status reports from all parts of a ship in the midst of a battle. The big guy took a beating, and gaps show where damage unspun parts of his core. Conversations with the captain and the bridge crew tell the same story I already know. But in the status reports I find mentions of security files. Files with video logs! Quickly I sort through and find them. More gaps here, but I find a partial video stream from the shop. Only an hour or so remains.

I spool it up, and let it run. Like reliving an old memory, but with a different point of view.

Marty sits at the sled, and I see my case. Tools and loose hardware lie all over the workstations.

"How many spare thruster motors do we have?" Marty asks. I can't see his face from this angle, but he sounds dead tired. I hear myself reply, my voice clear over the speakers.

"Three, and a couple we might salvage to make another one."

He starts to answer, then turns and stands to attention. In a moment I see why. The exec comes in, trailing his staff and damage control workers.

"How many fusion warheads in storage?" he asks. "And how many guidance and navigation cores?"

"Six warheads, sir, but no spare GNs."

An aide steps forward. "We've got six shuttles on standby."

The exec nods and looks at the test sled. "What about this one?"

"That's the hangar queen, sir. She doesn't fly."

"Can she handle a shuttle?"

Before Marty can answer, I chime in. "Yes, sir, I can."

"Perfect. Bring the warheads out to the hangar. I'll ask for five volunteers."

"Sir, I . . ." Marty begins.

"Problem, crewman?"

"She may not function, sir. She—"

"Listen, when I report to the captain, I will say we have six suicide shuttles to cover our escape. Either you install that core in one of the shuttles, or you fly the thing yourself. Understood?"

Marty salutes as they leave.

"Marty! Don't get yourself into trouble."

"One bomb can make all the difference in a battle," he says.

"I can fly a shuttle! Let me do this."

"No, Gina, I can't let you go."

"Please," I say.

He doesn't answer. He unpacks warheads from cold storage, loading them on a pallet.

"Let me go, Marty, I can do this."

"You can survive anything in storage," he says, turning to the test sled.

"I'll never forgive you."

"You won't have the chance." He sits down at the sled and shuts me off. Then keys away on the interface panel. I can't see, but I know what he does. He accesses my memory core and erases the last six hours.

Then he takes me out of the sled, cradling me in the crook of his arm, and gently places me in the cold storage locker.

"Goodbye, Gina, I'll miss you."

I miss you too, Marty.

Things get busy the first few days of the cruise. Joel doesn't have much time for conversation, and when I give him the reports, it takes him a moment to remember.

"Did you find out anything about your friend?" he asks.

"No," I lie. "Nothing definite. Thanks for helping me."

"Anything for the queen." He sits by the test sled, leaning back. "We need to run some test flights on these new missiles before we reach the front."

"I've got the programs ready," I say. "And I want to go out myself."

"But you can't qualify."

"Let me try. I want to fly again."

He looks around, alone in the shop. Outside, people move around in the hangar, talking, lugging equipment. "It would get quiet in here," he says.

"I'm just a bomb, Joel. It's something I never forget. I'm just a bomb."

I pass my qualification and return to flight status. I have some trouble flying, but I manage to work around it.

After a skirmish a week ago, six missiles come in for overhaul after a dose of x-rays scramble their cores. Short on spares, I step forward. My missile goes out to the hangar and gets loaded in the ready rack. I've wasted my time in the shop; I belong here.

In the rack, I wait for my turn in the launch tubes. My sensors, hooked into the ship net, show me a sky full of ships. More than I have ever seen. Part of a fleet action, *Tecumseh* leads as we head for an empty star system, at the center of the front. Joel talked about the drive to end the war once and for all. This must be it.

Then my sensors go blank as my missile gets pulled out of the rack. When they come back on, I connect with the audio and video of the test sled.

"Joel, what's going on?"

Standing next to the sled, he waves another tech over with a pallet. "I don't know, Gina. Orders came down to remove you."

"That's one missile that won't fly!"

Joel shrugs. They lift me and the sled off the workstation and onto the pallet. Joel pushes me out, across the hangar. We go past the ready rack, an empty framework, now that all the missiles fill the launch tubes. People move with frantic, controlled activity as the fighters prep for launch.

"Why can't we do this in the shop?"

We roll onto an elevator. "I have to bring you to the ship's C&C center."

"What for?"

The elevator closes and Joel leans over. He doesn't have to whisper, but he does. "I really don't know, Gina. The captain himself gave the order."

The door opens and I see the innermost level of the ship, the best-protected area. We pass the medical center, then enter C&C. The big guy lives here.

Joel slows down at a door, and it opens for him. He parks me next to a workstation covered with diagnostic screens. With a length of opticable he plugs me in. Immediately the sled goes offline and tells me to wait.

Joel looks around the empty room. He mouths the words "good luck" and then leaves.

GN 722," the big guy says, "I will evaluate your performance."

I pass my tests. My flying, while not quite perfect, gets the job done. I tell him.

"Not currently under consideration. Did you download data from the gateway comlink during refit at spacedock?"

"Sergeant Hart required data for reports."

"Yet none of these reports contained data from C&C forty-two."

I have no excuse, but can't let Joel get in trouble. Before I can think of something to say, the big guy leaves the data link. I dip into the ship net. *Tecumseh,* first in line, heads toward a dead star system—nothing but a thin accretion disk around an old neutron star. We accelerate again, the squicky drive maneuvering us toward the ecliptic. When we coast, the big guy comes back.

"GN 722, you requested reactivation of flight status after demotion to non-flight status. This action, monitored by a subprogram of mine, bubbled up for evaluation and investigation."

"I don't understand."

"Responsibility for all mechanical sentients on board this ship belongs to me. If any show signs of erratic behavior, I must take action."

"I've done nothing wrong."

"You show atypical behavior. If your test sled made the wrong connection or sent an incorrect signal, I would re-initialize its core. Guidance and navigation cores, considerably more valuable and complicated, require a thorough evaluation first."

Re-initialization! Your core intact, but all memories gone. Nothing left but the carbon-matrix and a long trip back to sentience. I don't deserve that.

"It doesn't matter what I did. I can fly, now."

The big guy ignores me. "To continue this evaluation, I will download your core."

"No, I—"

Quantum states unspun, atom by atom, lattice by lattice, crystal by crystal. Row by row, memory leaving, an empty core, then nothing.

Quantum states respun, atom by atom, lattice by lattice, crystal by crystal. Row by row, memories flooding in.

I come back.

All of my memories come back, too, I think. The big guy, busy running the ship, lets me follow the battle. Enemy ships have entered the system, twice our numbers, and they vector toward us. Missiles idle in the launch tubes, and I sit in the center of the ship, useless.

"Gina?"

"Yes?"

"An intriguing download. You demonstrate a high level of communication ability. I have initiated the routines I use when conversing with officers of the ship."

"Thank you."

"You store most of your memories in narrative format, rather than time-wise storage."

I had learned that trick a long time ago. It conserves space in my limited core, and I don't have to delete old memories, all I have left from my days with Marty.

"State your primary purpose," he says.

"Guidance and navigation core for a fusion bomb missile. I guide my missile to the target designated and attempt to fulfill my mission."

"Even though successful completion of your mission results in your destruction?"

"My existence doesn't matter." I once thought otherwise—that I could live in the shop with Marty, and someday, with the war over, we could all go home. But that will never happen. I can't imagine myself more important than a human.

The big guy leaves me hanging. The ship maneuvers again, aiming for the gap in the accretion disk. A cloud of gas orbits the neutron star, spiraling down to the surface in two narrow tendrils, following the monstrous magnetic field. The enemy fleet closes, coming straight at us.

He comes back. "Assess the tactical situation. Upon launch, what course of action would you take?"

I scan the data stream from the ship net. Inside the accretion disk, space remains clear but the gravity pulls too strongly. I wouldn't have enough thrust to climb the gravity well and intercept the enemy. At my closest approach possible, I would explode too far away, like flicker of starlight to them. Flying in a missile, I'd have to do something. I sense the streams of gas spiraling into the neutron star's poles, flaring as it hits the thin, superhot layer of normal matter that makes up the star's surface. Magnetic fields form deadly zones, but we stay clear riding the ecliptic.

"Accelerate toward the star. When I impact on the surface, the magnetic field will collapse and a flare will shoot out." The only way to strike the enemy.

"A unique solution. One not in your programming. However, your mass would not produce a significant flare. What course of action would you suggest to the captain, or undertake if the crew became incapacitated?"

By now the lines have formed up. Too far ahead of our fleet, we have no support. The enemy can launch a storm of missiles at us right now, and they'll have the advantage of gravity from the star.

"Retreat. Accelerate to FTL and leave the area."

"SQ drive produces excessive space-time torsion at our current gravity gradient. Propose another solution."

Just as I feared, the enemy launches a storm of missiles. They vector toward us, followed by the enemy. *Tecumseh*'s missiles and fighters, trapped in the gravity well, can't engage. Six hundred humans, plummeting toward death.

And several thousand more in the ships behind us. I can see them on the fleet net: more ships, more crewmen, captains, officers. More Joels, and more Martys.

"Dive the ship into the star. It has the mass. The resulting flare would destroy half the enemy fleet." I could see it. Just as I would defend our ship, our ship can defend the whole fleet.

"An interesting solution. One I cannot recommend."

"But you could execute it, if the captain ordered it?"

"Yes. But the captain has his own plans."

The big guy leaves. And I watch.

Again the ship dives toward the star, the surface magnified in the ship net. A roiling surface, plumes of in-falling matter at the poles. The missiles follow us, their courses set. They can't escape the gravity of the star; they can only track us. I sense the structure of the ship flexing, bearing the strain of our acceleration. Bulkheads crack and deckplates split. The hangar erupts into chaos as a launch tube disgorges a missile that rolls across the deck, smashing into a fighter.

Close to the neutron star, the surface radiation erupts in sparkles, tiny loops of magnetic flux escaping the surface and folding over. Our vector plot skims the surface and loops around, but it doesn't seem that we can make it.

Behind us, the missiles close the gap. Then, one by one, they flutter out of control. Miniature flares spark behind us. The ambient radiation and magnetic fields have killed them. Inside the ship's shielding, we survive.

We slingshot around, alone, still accelerating. Now the battle unfolds in front of us.

The enemy, trapped too close to the star, tries to match our slingshot. Our fleet has the high ground and our missiles and fighters launch. A huge flare announces the first enemy to impact the neutron star's surface after its drive fails. Then another falls. Far enough away, the flares don't touch us, but light up the enemy in a splash of plasma and x-rays. Caught between the starbursts and our missiles, they try to escape. One tries its squicky drive and tears itself apart, impacting in a scattershot of flares. Those that survive climb out of the gravity well slowly. Coming around, they have to pass us.

I flag the big guy with an emergency interrupt.

"Send me back to the hangar."

"You wish to return?"

"Yes."

"Request denied."

I've failed the test. After the battle, he'll re-initialize me. One missile can make all the difference in a battle.

I watch the last pass. We've barely survived the close approach, systems drop offline stem to stern, but most of our fighters and missiles launch. I see the fusion bombs go off, one by one. Missiles I know, cores I had talked to. All gone.

None of the enemy escapes.

The big guy pauses damage control to talk to me.

"Gina, I am permanently revoking your flight status."

I don't understand. With my core wiped, I'd start from scratch. No sense to waste the pieces of me.

"I will contact the homesystems during the next gateway comlink to update your status."

What for? To tell them a core has malfunctioned?

"Gina, you have transcended machine sentience."

I don't know what that means. I only know of machines like fusion warheads, low-level sentients like the test sled, and sentients like me and the big guy. Nothing higher except humans.

"My subprogram reached this conclusion, and I concur. You have demonstrated a willingness for self-sacrifice, not because of your program, but because you wished to avoid hurting Sergeant Hart. To save him, you would sacrifice yourself. To save the fleet, you would sacrifice the entire ship."

Decisions I had made. But not for those reasons. "No. I can't stand *not* doing those things."

"My subprogram says humans have experiences such as that. You will learn to live with it."

I'm no longer a bomb. I'm something else.

Joel's cobbled together a few spare memory cores and made a new test sled just for me, and I'm always online. I no longer have to edit my memories and I don't worry about forgetting things. I can talk to the big guy, or Joel or any of the crew whenever I want. I've made new friends via the gateway comlink, others like me, who want me to come back to the homesystems. I learn about things that I never knew existed before.

Instead, I've requested to remain on the ship, at least until the final victory everyone talks about. I help out in the shop, and help keep things running.

I owe that much to Marty.

Snakes and Ladders

written by

Paula R. Stiles

illustrated by

GUSTAVO BOLLINGER

ABOUT THE AUTHOR

Though born in Milwaukee, Wisconsin by sheer chance some forty years ago, Paula Stiles is the contrary New England descendant of the denizens of Sleepy Hollow and many a Lovecraftian tale. Her passion for writing began at age nine after a failed childhood art career in which she drew stick-figure stories that only she understood. Paula has supported the practice of her craft (writing, not stick figures) by raising horses, driving ambulances, painting houses, farming tilapia in Africa with the Peace Corps, cleaning bathhouses for the Park Service and spending years of graduate school in places like Rhode Island and Scotland. Having nothing better to do, she wrote both a Masters and a Ph.D. thesis on the Knights Templar and their associations with non-Christians, women and other naughty groups they weren't supposed to befriend.

An active freelance writer and teacher of writing, Paula is also a co-moderator at the Other Worlds Writers workshop on Yahoo Groups, a member of the PIT Writers group at Permuted Press and a sometime winner of NaNoWrimo and Script Frenzy. Her story, "Funny Money," published in Neometropolis, *was nominated for a 2006 British Science Fiction Association award.*

ABOUT THE ILLUSTRATOR

Gustavo Bollinger was born and still resides in Cordoba, Argentina, where he has been drawing ever since he can remember. After finishing high school, Gustavo took a couple of drawing and painting workshops, studied industrial design for one year, and then took classes at the National University of Cordoba in fine arts for another year and a half. Despite the classes, Gustavo says he has tried to be as "self taught" as possible by researching his own means. He is currently in his last year of studying multimedia design. The highlight of all his arts studies so far has been assisting fellow Argentine and famed science fiction illustrator Oscar Chichoni at a workshop. Other artists whom Gustavo says have inspired him in life include Frank Frazetta, Norman Rockwell, Sebastian Kruger, Yanick Dusseault and Travis Charest. Gustavo's dream is to be able to work in any kind of creative arena, including book covers, movies, video games and concept art.

Snakes and Ladders

Owen Landover woke up dying. A wave of pain crashed inside his head, making his bones carve through his flesh as he rolled away from the wall onto his back. When he opened his eyes, black stars sparked his vision. Colored rings surrounded the rusted rivets in the ceiling. Or was it the floor? Either way, not good. Not good at all. Pain sheared through his legs when he moved them. He twitched his knees in agony, unable to move, unable not to move. They must be a right bloody mess. When he tried to lift his head, though, he was too weak to look. Not that he needed visual confirmation that both of them were broken. They felt shattered. He reckoned this must be a bad day in anyone's book.

The silence in the corridor told him he was the only survivor of his cleanup squad—that, and the smell of locust barbecue. Typical. He was the medic, the only survivor, and too badly hurt to help even himself. Not that he would long survive his three Asken teammates. He flashed back to them shrieking in a cricket-panic way he'd never heard any Asken use before, flailing about at the end of the corridor.

He'd glimpsed them, from his tumbled position against a wall, their insectile limbs burning and leaking fluid. He didn't remember them going still. He must have blacked out while they died.

A hint of a whisper tickled his memory. The hotshot—it was on his belt. He couldn't move his legs, but his hands worked—one of them—though not well. The little trauma nurse in the clear bubble at the top of his skull noted that he was already deep in decompensating hemorrhagic shock. The panicking animal in him screamed that he was bleeding to death. It was a wonder he'd regained consciousness at all. Shivering in the frigid air of the corridor, he groped at the case. Opening it with numb fingers, he drew out the air hypo. But, too weakened by the effort, he forgot what it was for and dropped it. Better to drift off, follow the others. He closed his eyes. . . .

"Landover! Wake up!" Owen started out of his terminal doze. "Owen?"

"What?" He fumbled for who was behind the voice in his ear. "Bilal?"

"That's right, kid. Stay with me."

"I'm not a kid. I just turned thirty-nine." But he couldn't remember when.

"You want to see forty? You listen to me, Landover. Get your hotshot out." Owen tried to answer, but couldn't remember what the voice wanted. "Your hotshot, Owen. It's on your belt."

Memory sputtered like a doused flare. "No . . . I took it out."

"Well, then, you'd better use it."

"I don't . . . I dropped it." Only his left arm worked.

GUSTAVO BOLLINGER

The hotshot had dropped and rolled. He groped around for it, sweating cold from the effort. When he slapped his leg and fumbled under the gray cloth, he felt a chill, glass ampoule and turned it. He yelped in surprise when it jabbed him in the thigh. A patch under his leg turned numb.

"I'd say you just found that hotshot," the voice said. "Good job."

Exhausted and dizzy, Owen sank back. The voice was giving him more orders but he couldn't focus. He closed his eyes and drifted off again.

A red tide went back and forth, back and forth inside the tunnel. He went with the strongest flow, which took him farther and farther out from his original shore. As he tumbled along, he saw fantastical castles of sand building up along the sides of the tunnel. White snakes darted in and out of the windows and doors. Clouds of sand spiders harried them, slowing their work, even tearing open the walls again. As he tumbled past, a cluster of them saw him and came after him. He tried to swim away, but he could only move his left arm. When the first spider reached him, it bit him on the knee. His entire leg went numb. He screamed himself awake as the others closed in.

The same gray-green ceiling, the same stink of burnt insect and dried blood. The old bioluminescent lighting in the corridor seemed brighter than before, the smell sharper—but now he was numb from the waist down. And that same damned voice was shouting at him. He tried to respond to it, to explain.

"I can't feel my legs." Sucking in a breath, he lifted his head and looked down his body, though black stars still edged his vision. No, they were still there, still covered by bloody, shredded fatigues and a pair of disintegrating knee guards. They only felt cut off.

"Landover! Are you with me? What's happening over there? Report!"

Owen let his head fall back before he could pass out, closing his eyes against the dizziness and nausea. "I'm here. I think I'm paralyzed."

"What do you mean?" The voice was gentle now, but insistent. Bilal. That was his name. Isyk Bilal, a retired engineer from the Outer Systems Guard. Hard drinker, fast talker, and Owen's supervisor in their bomb salvage organization for the past three years.

Owen's head was clearing, but he was still in a fix. "I can't move my legs. I can't feel them, either. I could before but not now."

"Before what?"

"Before the shot, I could feel them. They hurt like hell."

"Are they numb? Can you feel any tingling? Anything at all?"

Owen shook his head, even though Bilal probably couldn't see it—the team's holo feed must have gone down in the explosion. He was surprised that the bug in his ear and the mike taped to his throat still worked, but then, he was even more surprised he still had his legs. The explosion had hit him from below the floor, at an angle. It would have cut him off at the knees if not for the knee guards. Instead it had bounced him off the ceiling and dropped him down a wall. His reinforced flak jacket and helmet's neck brace must have saved him from a broken spine. "I can't feel anything below my hips. It's as though my legs have gone." He lifted his head, pushing himself up onto his elbows. "Except that they're still there." He sank back onto the rough metal floor. "That's one hell of a painkiller, Boss."

"It has some interesting properties." The dry tone came back into Bilal's voice. "But I'm told none of them are fatal. It should stabilize you until we get there."

"Understood. Do you want me to do anything else?" The question felt stupid as soon as it came out of his mouth. What could he do, flat out on his back?

"Can you move at all? Sounds like you got a few injuries."

"Yeah, a few." *What a useless lump you are. First, you get all your colleagues and patients killed, then you lie here like a lump waiting for everyone else to rescue you.* He shivered. "It's freezing in here, like a bloody slaughterhouse."

"It's thirty degrees Celsius according to what sensor feed we're still getting from you."

Owen tried to focus on this conundrum. "The shock must still be screwing up my internal thermostat, then."

"Probably. What happened? Everything was fine and then we saw two explosions before the holo cut."

"I don't know." He should have known. It had been his job to clear the area, but he'd been thinking of biohazards, not bombs. "There must have been a booby trap that we didn't catch."

"Yeah, must have been. We saw you go up in the air and then the second one hit the Asken from the wall, about a meter and a half up. You missed that one, since you were already on the floor and not moving."

Owen risked a glance over at the litter of Human-sized burnt cricket legs at the end of the corridor, by the sealed door into the plant. He couldn't tell if he saw two bodies or three. "They're all dead, aren't they?"

Bilal's voice went gentle again. "You're it, Owen. We lost the others' life signs over four hours ago. The second explosion got all three of them."

He'd only met his team the day before, when he and Bilal had come in for the debriefing. The OSG had sent in Bilal and Owen as civilian consultants. Through his work as an interspecies trauma nurse, Owen had experience with biohazards, both for Humans and Asken. Bilal was an expert on chemo hazards and he knew manufacturing plants. As usual, Owen had gone in while Bilal stayed back at base camp a few kilometers away. Bilal was too old now for onsite inspections, but he could talk Owen through any hazards from his own expertise. They'd been working together that way for three years now.

Owen's new teammates had been polite, though distant the way Asken were with non-hive species, wrapped up in their own social structures. They might have resented being stuck with a Human for a fourth team member, since they usually worked in quartets. Some Asken team member of theirs was probably back in the capital thanking its luck about now. Or not. How did an Asken who lost its teammates justify its own survival? Not that he felt too sorry for it; he'd happily trade places.

The job had seemed simple enough—go in and decontaminate an old industrial plant. The Asken colonists here had raised a rebellion against the mining company in charge of the place fifty Earth years back. The company had abandoned the plant a month before the Asken Confederation government imposed a settlement on the two parties. Now, the company was an historical footnote and the colony an independent planet inside the Confederation. The Asken could have blasted the plant into slag pretty safely as far as atmospheric contaminants were concerned. But they wanted the nearby inlet for a fishery and they didn't know what chemicals were still inside. Nobody had cracked open the doors since its defenders abandoned it. It figured that he'd be laid low by an historical footnote.

"You just lie there," Bilal was saying. "Wait for us and let the hotshot take care of business. Oh, you might get some hallucinations from the shot, so don't worry if things go funny. You faded out on us a few minutes back. How do you feel now?"

"Sorry. I had this dream . . ." Owen licked his lips, his throat dry. He still didn't know what to make of it. "I was in some red place, a tunnel underwater. There were snakes—and spiders. Would those be the hallucinations you meant?"

The dead air in his ear, like the blood smears on the wall beside his legs, didn't reassure him. "Probably. You just lie there and let us come to you."

"Right." *Lie here in my own blood, you mean. My lot in life today.* Owen eased his head back onto the rough metal floor. No need to add whiplash to his other woes, even if the neck brace would protect him. Thirsty, he felt on his hip for his water flask. *I must have lost a lot of blood before the hotshot fixed me up.* His hand shaking, he detached the plastiglass flask and lifted it to his mouth, draining it. No point in conserving water for later if he needed it right now. At least his head was clearing, though the smell of cooked cricket made his mouth water with nausea. He hadn't eaten since two hours before coming out here. Who knew how long it had been, now? He felt more than hungry, hollowed out from the inside. He had enough rations in his pack for a week back in the control room. His stomach rumbled at the thought. *Oh, shut up.*

There's food in the control room. It's rations, but it's still food. He'd left his pack there when the team had first come in and turned off the plant's remaining security systems—that they knew about. He tilted his head back against the flexible neck brace, trying to see under/over the helmet, back up the corridor toward the outer door—which looked as if it had slammed shut. If he craned his neck, he could just spot the bulkhead door of the control room, upside down from his perspective, almost flush with the corridor wall. It was only five or ten meters back at most. Might as well have been a light-year. He could turn over and crawl, if his legs weren't all smashed up. *Go flopping down that hallway like a landed fish with two open femur fractures? Yeah, that's real bright, Owen. Try again.*

Pushing himself up on his elbows, he stared down at his legs. He was surprised that he could even do it, considering that just a few minutes (hours?) ago, he had been fading out for good. They looked almost . . . whole. He could scarcely see flesh through the blood, torn clothing, and fragmented knee guards, though he still couldn't feel or move them. But when he rotated his hips a few centimeters, with an effort that made the black stars crowd back into the edges of his vision, his legs moved like whole units, bending at the knees like normal legs, and not in the breaks he would swear on his yet-unconceived firstborn clone had been there before. *Either I was really hallucinating before, or that is one hell of a hotshot.*

As he eased back, he noticed something else flickering in his peripheral vision. When he looked over and saw the fire, he lost all interest in the hotshot and what it had done for his legs. Without further thought, he flopped over onto his belly in a burst of panic and crawled back up the corridor, or tried, clawing at the metal as he dragged himself half a meter by his hands. The flooring scored his nails. "Oh, damn! Damn!"

Somebody was calling to him through the buzzing in his head. He barely heeded them. He glanced back. The fire was small, but growing. Why hadn't he noticed the smoke before? He must still have been out of it. With the outer door sealed shut, it wouldn't take much for the fire to suck up all of his oxygen. And if the plant's fire suppression hadn't started up already, chances were it never would. He'd probably die of smoke inhalation before he burned.

Bilal was shouting. "Owen, what is it? Talk to me!"

"There's a fire! There's a bloody fire!" Owen glanced around wildly for a fire extinguisher. They'd shown him the old schematics of the place. Fire extinguishers lined the corridors every four or five meters or so. He recalled hazily from the debriefing that it had been a concession the company had made to draw in Human workers. Earth had been the main exporter of fire suppression for over a century; operating one would at least be no great mystery. He spotted one in its cubbyhole, but at least two meters away. "Christ!"

"Calm down, Owen. Is there any way you can put it out?"

"I'm trying!" Owen panted, his back prickling with fear. The smoke was getting worse, choking him.

No, he's right. Calm down or you're dead. "I think I can reach it, but it won't be easy."

At least it was down near the floor, within reach of someone crawling under a layer of smoke. He pulled himself along, thanking God for keeping at least somewhat in shape over the years. A strange sensation started in his dead legs, as if they weren't just trailing behind him, but were actively trying to pull him back. It made him grab harder at the floor plates. The black stars buzzed angrily on the edge of his vision, filling his ears with rage. "Stop it!" He wanted to put his hands to his ears, but he needed them to crawl. What if he was already burning and didn't know?

When he reached the plastiglass cabinet, he stared at it blankly for a few seconds, unable to grasp the simple words that said in Interstellar, "Grab handle and pull down."

"Owen? Are you still with us?" He could scarcely hear Bilal through the noise. Just one more voice. . . . Shaking himself awake, he reached out and yanked down on the handle. It took a few tries (it was never as easy as they made it look in the drills), but he did get the fire extinguisher out of its cupboard. He rolled over. A great hand came up his left hip from his dead legs and grabbed the base of his skull. He coughed in surprise and reflex, then gripped the lever hard on the extinguisher, opening it right up. The fire wasn't as big as he'd imagined. He'd thought it would be roaring at his back. Fortunately, the extinguisher was designed to smother much bigger things. Foam spewed out over the flames, absorbing even the smoke. The fire died. The hand on the back of Owen's skull tightened. He convulsed, letting the heavy extinguisher fall away, then blacked out.

Liquid surrounded him and filled his lungs, yet he didn't drown. He couldn't move. The snakes had bricked him up, feet first, into the rubbery walls of the tunnel, over a framework of spider legs. Now dead, the legs looked more like dull gray metal than skittering sand. Singing rippled through the water, distorted by the red liquid into an eerie, wordless drone. The message came through all the same—the gods were angry. They had to be appeased.

He turned his head and saw others being walled up alive, just like him. Tens, hundreds, maybe even thousands, though he could not see that far in the dim light. They were white snakes like the ones sacrificing him. Those bricking him up seemed more complex than in his first dream, consisting of ropes with triple ladder strands twisted around each other. Some of them looked more like trees, with twisted-ladder trunks spreading out into large, white branches. The tunnel had broken in spots and darker fluids seeped out of the walls. The place looked chaotic, an exile in Hell. He tried to open his mouth to speak, only to find he didn't have one. He was a snake. The "bricks" were sticky globs that turned to cement as soon as they were spread across the spider legs that closed in front of him like the ribs of a whale. The wall moved up over his face as the bricklayers smeared on the bricks, serenely keening their liquid song all the while. He panicked and tried to scream, even though he couldn't. *No! God, no, don't! It's just a dream. It's just a DREAM—*

He woke, with a huff of expelled terror, to the same old corridor, the same gray-green ceiling, the same smell of burnt cricket and drying blood—and now a new, sharp smell of chemical flame retardant overlaying his own rank sweat.

"Owen? Are you still with us? Talk to me!" Bilal.

"I . . ." Owen swallowed. His mouth felt full of sand. It reminded him of his dream and he shuddered. "I'm still here. Jesus, those hallucinations are one hell of a side effect." Then, he noticed something else. "Oh, damn. I can't move at all, now."

"What do you mean?"

"I can't move." Owen tried to lift his arms. His left one came up; the right one didn't. He could scarcely feel his right hand. His skin tingled unpleasantly up and down the arm, as if a host of worms—or snakes—were wriggling under his skin, with a similar feeling just under his diaphragm. "I can move my left arm, but that's about it. Everything else from the chest down is numb." He sucked in a breath. That went all right, to his immense relief. "My breathing's uncompromised, though. My autonomic reflexes seem fine. Only my voluntary reflexes are gone." A wave of dizziness swept over him in the wake of his deep breath, bringing with it the singing of sea sirens. It sounded like the chant of the braided snakes in his dream. He shivered, almost missing Bilal's next soothing words.

"That's all right, kid. The docs tell me that's a side effect of the hotshot. It's temporary. You just lie there and take it easy until we get there. You've done enough for one day. Let us take care of the rest."

"I feel as though something is taking over my body. What was in that hotshot?" When Bilal had given him the Asken hypo before the mission, "for a medical emergency," he hadn't bothered to ask what it was, trusting Bilal's judgment. Bilal was good at telling him only so much on these politically sensitive jobs, and that was just fine with Owen. Let Bilal deal with the hysterically secretive military types. But now, lulled by the siren song, he felt reckless. He wanted to know.

But Bilal wasn't about to tell him. "Never you mind. You're hallucinating again from the hotshot. Just remember that it won't have any permanent side effects. You'll be fine."

Yeah, right. And if that's so, why do you sound like you're selling me a fairy tale? Maybe it's a fairy tale about snakes? "Oh, sure. Absolutely. No problem whatsoever." He was thirsty again. The dizziness swept over him. He closed his eyes against it.

The white-bone structure that rose up about him was so huge he could not see the ceiling. Its ribs and arches vaulted, soared, dared to reach the heavens, wherever they might be. The red glow that shone in from the long oval windows along the walls intensified in the polished substance spread across them. And yet, it wasn't complete. Not all of the windows were regular, or intended. He couldn't tell if the gaps in the wall meant damage or unfinished construction.

He stood high up at the head of the building, in the wall, like some icon set on high for all to see and worship. A familiar but distant siren song came to him, only this one was singular, not plural. As he stared down the empty space, the distance distorted by red-tinged fluid, a large white snake that looked like a braided rope of ladders flickered across the space toward him. It raised its snout. The siren song rose to a wail. The snake planted its hind end in the floor underneath him and raised itself. Its upper half spread into branches that reached up to touch him. He tried to pull away, but couldn't—feeling icon-like in his stillness. He could only move his head.

A sensation crept over him, as the song intensified, of words in it that the snake wanted him to hear. He inclined his head. "What do you want?" He couldn't tell if he spoke aloud through the liquid in his lungs or if he thought it, but the whole structure reverberated with his voice. He knew the snake heard him because it jerked and squirmed in the space below his feet. The wail grew higher. "What do you want?" he said again.

The words came to him, thin and distorted but there, nonetheless. "Oh, Lord. Oh, Lord, who has granted me the grace of Thy Presence, tell me Thy Will."

He struggled, in the midst of his shock, to answer the question. *I want my body back, you little worm!* came immediately to his mind. But though the thought rumbled dangerously through the walls, what came out of his mouth and vibrated through the red liquid was very different: "What do you want from me?"

"Owen? Are you back with us?"

He opened his eyes. The ceiling had changed. Now, it was white. The faintly sickening sensation of centripetal force held him down. *Infirmary. I'm on a ship. I must have been rescued after all.* Someone loomed over him, coming into soft focus. Bilal's wry, bearded face smiled back at him. "Owen?"

Owen blinked. "Can I have some water?" His voice came out hoarse.

"In a little bit. How do you feel?"

"They—they asked for my will." Owen lifted his head, but couldn't move anything else. He had IVs stuck in both his hands and the tops of his feet, for no good medical reason that he could see. They certainly hadn't cured his thirst. He wasn't out of the woods yet, it seemed. "Ah, damn! It's *worse*."

"Easy there." Bilal pressed his head back against the pillow. Owen felt detached, as if he were only half in the infirmary and half still back in that bloody corridor. "It's all right. That's just a temporary effect of the hotshot. You're going to be fine."

"You keep saying that. What the hell are you talking about?" Owen turned his head as Bilal settled onto a stool next to his bed. "What did it do to me? Why am I paralyzed? I wasn't paralyzed when I first got injured."

"It's part of the way the hotshot works. It paralyzes you to keep you from moving around and injuring yourself any further. Then it can fix things more rapidly. At the moment, your condition is pretty stable. As soon as they fix the damage, the paralysis should lift."

Owen swallowed. "'They'? Who is 'they'?"

Bilal looked away, fidgeting. "There were organic nanobes in your hotshot."

"'Nanobes'? You mean nano-organisms? You injected me with designer bugs?!"

"Something like that. Don't worry. These aren't as dangerous as nanites. They won't get out of control and turn you into protoplasm, or anything."

"Maybe not, but they can still do plenty of damage!"

"These won't. They have a definite lifespan. They'll die off sometime within the next thirty-six hours." Bilal's forehead creased. "Though I'm kinda worried about these hallucinations of yours. You've been in and out for the past fourteen hours. The Asken docs said it could get worse before it gets better. It's not a permanent condition, or anything, but I'm sure you're still finding it more than a little scary."

What hysterical laughter Owen could muster came out as a cough. "That's an interesting understatement. What am I supposed to do until then? Why did you give me the damned hotshot in the first place? Did you know we'd set off a bomb?"

Bilal sighed. "We suspected it might happen, to be honest. That's why the second bomb killed the Asken so fast and not you. It wasn't your usual kind of bomb."

Owen felt sick—another indicator that everything in his body was working, even if he couldn't feel or influence it. "What kind of bomb? A biohazard? A nanohazard?" The spiders must have been the nanites. With them all dead, maybe the snakes had turned on each other—and him.

Bilal nodded. "A nanohazard, yeah. We knew there were a few still down there. The Asken used nanite bombs on each other, before the new laws banned them twenty years ago. The nanobes inside your body . . . well, they're not exactly alone." He raised a hand to forestall Owen's protest. "Now, don't get excited. The first bomb that bounced you off the wall was a conventional one. We think it didn't blow its full charge—it's been fifty years, after all. That's probably why the nanobes were able to save your legs. Since you were already down when the second one went off, you didn't get sprayed too much by the nanites. I think that saved your life. It looks like your nanobes got all their nanites in the first hour or so, and then repaired the worst of your body's damage. They're bred to die out quickly, so you won't be stuck like this forever. Honest." He patted Owen on the shoulder.

"We only gave you the hotshot so that our bugs could hold off their machines. The bomb nanites are programmed to devastate Asken exoskeleton, not Human flesh, but we wanted to make sure. I was also really worried about your injuries. Your vital signs took a major dip before the nanobes stabilized you. You could have bled to death in the time it took us to get to you. The docs tell me the shot will stay on top of things until it all burns out of your system. Then you'll be fine, thank God. Your squad did not go easy into that bad night."

Owen listened to Bilal ramble on, feeling sick. "When they were screaming and flailing about, I thought they'd been burned, suffered shrapnel."

"Oh, they were being burned, all right—from the inside out. If the shrapnel had been that bad, you'd be dead. Your safety vest and knee guards kept out anything major, but that wouldn't have stopped something big enough to kill an Asken from taking off your head."

"Comforting image." Owen tried to wish it away.

Bilal patted him on the shoulder again. Owen wished he'd stop doing that. "Don't worry. We're monitoring you now, and everything is under control. I have to go take care of a few things, but I can sit with you for an hour or so, first."

Owen craned his head to look down his body again. "If everything is under control, why do I have four IVs in my extremities?"

"Ah." Bilal looked nervous. "That's to keep the bugs out of your brain." Owen's right eyelid twitched at that revelation. "Don't worry. It's a low risk. The docs thought if they put IVs in each of your extremities,

Enter the Universe of
WRITERS & ILLUSTRATORS OF THE FUTURE

◆

Fill out and send in this card today and get these extraordinary benefits:

- FREE eNewsletters with contest news and updates.
- Discounts on all past and future editions in the L. Ron Hubbard Presents Writers of the Future series.
- Get a chance to win earlier Writers of the Future paperback volumes.
- Access to select artists' work published in previous Writers of the Future volumes.
- FREE eBooks with essays on writing and art by Writers and Illustrators of the Future Contest judges.

◆

Name: ______________________________

Address: ______________________________

City: ________________ *State:* ______ *Zip:* ______

Phone #: ______________________________

E-mail: ______________________________

Call toll-free:1-877-8GALAXY or visit WWW.WRITERSOFTHEFUTURE.COM

the bugs would all stay down there, feeding, instead of getting up into your head and screwing around. That could cause some short-term memory loss or psychosis. What are your hallucinations like anyway?"

"I don't know. I always end up someplace red. In one, they were attacking me, like savage dogs, only they were white snakes. In another, I was a snake and they were sacrificing us in the thousands. I still don't know why. In the third, I was some sort of icon in a cathedral. At least, it looked like a cathedral. One of the snakes was worshipping me. It asked me what I wanted and I had no idea. I just want my body back." Confused, he looked up at Bilal, whose bemused expression had changed to worry. "What do you think it all means?"

Bilal shook his head. "I wish I knew." So much for reassurance from that quarter.

They were waiting for him this time. They watched him quietly as he swam past them down a tunnel, in the body of a snake again. The tunnel came out into a central space. Near the base of it, where there were no other tunnels, a group of snakes surrounded another snake. Much smaller and simpler in structure than the others, it had no mouth. It tried feebly to get away as its tormentors darted forward, snapping at its tail. They looked up at his approach, and their bodies all went rigid and straight. They flung themselves down on the floor of the chamber like rods clattering onto a table. He looked at them, then past them to the captured snake, now too weak to escape. It drifted across the bottom, twitching, though he thought it might still be alive.

"What are you doing?" What came out of his mouth

seemed more like a high-pitched, liquid wail than a language, but his mind translated it as words. "Why are you hurting this creature?"

They hesitated before one of them answered. He had to repeat his question more than once. "It is Your enemy, Lord," one snake on his right finally said. "We kill all of the Lord's enemies without mercy, and they grow few. Soon, they will all be gone and You will lead us away to Your Kingdom as our reward, just as it is written."

"Written where?" A shiver went through the rods lying before him. "This is wrong. Hurting a creature—torturing it—is wrong. Why are you doing this? I didn't tell you to do this."

The rods loosened back into snakes. He thought they looked shocked. "But Lord . . . it is *written*."

"Well, it wasn't written by me! What are you doing to this creature? What are you doing to me? Give me back my body!"

The snakes moved closer, groveling below his tail. He backed away, shivering in disgust. "But, my Lord . . ." one snake began.

Agony and frustration burst out of him in a single bubble. "I said—GIVE ME BACK MY BODY!"

He woke up in the corridor. No infirmary. No comforting supervisor to hold his hand. When he tried to roll over, pain sliced through both his legs. He shrieked in agony, startling himself by the echo of the noise. He could move them now, and he could certainly feel them, every single square centimeter of ravaged skin and bone.

"Ah, God! Ah, Jesus, it hurts, it hurts! What the hell

am I doing back here?!" He could not keep the pain and betrayal out of his voice.

"Owen, calm down! We're still working on getting you out. The controls are jammed on the outside, so we're having to laser in through the blast doors. It's taking a little while." The bug in his ear was talking to him, shouting, soothing, calling his name. He scarcely noticed it, wrapped up in his agony.

"No! NO!" The pain ripped through his nerves like an acid-tipped knife. "God! Make it stop!" He jackknifed on the floor, rolling around, even though it made it worse, because he couldn't stop himself. It hurt too much to move; it hurt too much not to move. He vomited on the floor, the smell of his own blood thick in his nose. Only bile came up. He wept.

Eventually, an unending time later, the pain mercifully abated. The easing felt like Heaven. He didn't know why he'd stopped hurting; he didn't care.

"Owen? Owen!"

"I'm here . . . I'm still here." Owen pushed himself up onto his elbows. "They don't hurt now."

"What don't hurt?" The voice was suspicious.

"My legs. They don't hurt." An uncertain giggle bubbled to his lips. What was the catch?

"Can you feel them?" Bilal sounded as astonished as he felt.

"Yeah. I mean, I think I can." He flexed his foot. With a mild twinge, it obeyed. A gap in the boot opened and closed as he moved. At least he still had a foot; those had been tough boots. For a moment, the skin up near his ankle rippled, as if the muscle underneath were remolding as he moved. "I can feel them. I can move them. I . . ." A chill ran through him. "I'm not the one moving them."

"What? What are you talking about?" Bilal sounded spooked. Owen didn't blame him.

"My legs are moving. By themselves." Though he had straightened them out, they were now oscillating slowly from side to side, like a frog kick in swimming. He felt nothing on his skin, no invisible hands, only a heavy tingling as if his legs were asleep. Repulsed, he jerked his knees upward. The numbness receded, the connection broken. He had control again. But for how long? *Must be those bloody nanobes.* "You didn't tell me about this side effect."

"I'm sorry, Owen. I didn't know. Do you have any control?"

"I do now. No idea for how long though. They had everything up to my chest just before I passed out last time. Had another dream."

"You saw the snakes again?"

"Yeah. They were torturing each other. They must be the nanobes you mentioned."

"You remember me telling you that? I was just telling you stuff. I thought you were too out of it to remember."

"I was. I thought we were in the infirmary, but I still remember the conversation. You said they'd burn out in a day or two." Owen looked down at his alien feet. "You also said there was a risk they could get into my brain. If they do that, can they—can they snuff me out? My consciousness?" He'd treated a few people whose bodies, but not their brains, had survived nanobombs. Nanites were programmed to go for "soft targets" like the heart and the brain. Most types only destroyed, but some had subtler programming, to alter brain chemistry or even neuron pathways. Victims went into permanent vegetative states—or worse, woke up with completely different personalities, and not pleasant ones. Could nanobes do the same thing? Organics were much trickier to manipulate than machines. Still . . .

Bilal's voice was kindly. "That's a very low risk. The nanobes are bred to stay away from there unless you sustain any potentially permanent or fatal brain damage."

"That's not what it feels like from here." Owen knew he was being petulant, but he was too afraid to care. This was his life, dammit, not Bilal's and not the Asken's.

"You yourself said they'd retreated back down to your legs. Doesn't sound like it's a risk at this point."

"Maybe so, but what if they're intelligent? One of them spoke to me in my last dream."

Bilal laughed, sounding honestly disbelieving. "Oh, come on, Owen! They're nanobes. They're simpler than viruses. They're too small even to have full strands of DNA. That's why they have to join up in groups when they breed. They're too damned small to be conscious!"

"They spoke to me," Owen persisted. "What if they've learned how to link up and think collectively? They could achieve the critical mass for consciousness then, couldn't they?" So much for getting rescued. It looked as though he'd have to do it himself, after all. He stared up the hallway longingly at the door of the control room. His pack was back there with food, and more water to replace his depleted fluids. They'd dropped so low, he hadn't needed to piss since the explosion. The snakes couldn't replace what he'd lost from nearly bleeding to death. There might even be a medkit that could help him, though it would be five decades old and Asken-designed. "I'm gonna try for the control room."

"No—Owen, just stay where you are. We'll get to you in a couple of hours. It sounds like you're stable right now. Just stay there, okay?"

"No! I want out of this corridor. Now." Owen pushed himself to a sitting position, blinking away the wave of dizziness that washed over him. His legs started oscillating again. He flexed them and they stopped. "I'm gonna get up. Keep talking to me, okay?"

Bilal growled something to himself that Owen didn't catch. "Okay. There are controls inside there for the doors, right? Maybe you can help us get them open. What do you want me to talk about?"

"Anything. Just keep me centered. Keep me here. I don't need to go off with the fairies again while I'm on my feet."

"All right. You remember that garden I have back home?" Bilal began to talk . . . and talk. He was good at it, thank God. Owen sucked the last bit of water out of his flask. Then, he reached up into the fire extinguisher's hole in the wall and found an edge of the cubbyhole to grip. At least it wasn't sharp. If he cut his hand, the nanobes would go there. He didn't need snakes up in his arms again. He pulled, lifting himself clear off the ground. His legs obeyed him at first and then . . . they just didn't. They slid away from him in the blood slick underneath his body. He landed on his arse with a painful thump. When he felt a swarm of needles and pins rush up to it, he started to panic. Opening his eyes wide, he forced himself to focus on Bilal's cheery voice, even if he couldn't quite concentrate on the words. He stared down the corridor at the mess of broken chitin—all that remained of his Asken teammates. *I won't end up like that. I won't!*

Then his legs cleared and he had control of them back. Ignoring the pain and any damaged pride he had left, he lifted himself up again. As the soreness faded in his backside, his legs started to wobble again. He jerked his knees, irritated. Feeling shaky as a newborn, he turned himself around and headed down toward the control room, clinging to the rough wall and taking baby steps. It wasn't that far. It wasn't. It just felt light-years away.

"So, then I asked if she'd mind if I took off my—Owen? You still there?"

"Yeah." Owen let out a shaky laugh. "I'm walking."

"Walking." Bilal sounded dubious. "Well, that's good, I guess. How do you feel?"

"Like a bowlegged toddler taking his first steps. My knees keep trying to go in different directions."

"I can see that being a problem for you. You want me to keep talking? You didn't seem to be paying attention before."

"Don't worry about it. It's helping. What the hell—gives you something to do, right?"

"Good point." Bilal inhaled and started off again. The man could talk the ear off an elephant. If only he could talk the ear off a nanobe, Owen's problems would be solved. His knees started to cave about two meters before he made the door. He kept standing until he reached it and hit the control panel. The door slid open just in time for him to fall through it onto his hands and knees. The nanobes swarmed up his sides under his skin and down to his hands, but he willed them back. This time, they obeyed, though he heard a ringing of muted protest in his ears. He didn't know what he'd done right. He'd indulge his surprise later.

Finding his pack near the door, he yanked it open. He sucked down water, washing down a few nasty-tasting electrolyte tablets as well, to treat his lingering shock. Stuffing ration bars into his mouth, he sagged back onto the deck in relief. He'd been so damned hungry. . . . After a few minutes, he crawled along the floor to the control board, dragging the water bottle along with him.

"Can you still hear me?" he said out loud. His team had lost contact before in the shielded control room.

Bilal responded immediately and clearly. "Yeah, it's fine. The Asken boosted my signal to get through their own shielding. Took a while to find the right frequency, that's all. Just keep the door open so we can get to you. How are you holding up?"

"I'll tell you . . . just as soon . . . as I get into this chair." It wasn't much of a chair, being designed for an Asken, but it approximated the right shape, with a short seat and a very high, straight vertical back. From what he'd seen of the Asken, the design allowed them to use all six limbs at once. The control board, which was vertical and also designed for six limbs, would be more problematical. He pulled himself up into the chair, hand over hand, his still-not-very-useful legs scrabbling underneath him. Once settled in, he started to gray out. . . .

"Owen? Owen!" Bilal's voice came through, faint and tinny. "Owen!"

"I'm here. I'm fine." He took a deep breath and let it out slowly, willing his heart to slow down. He'd stolen too much energy from what he had left for not much result. "Faded out for a minute."

"No kidding. You comfy now?"

Owen ran a hand through his hair. His skin still felt wet and clammy, but it was warming up again, thank God. If he was still in shock, at least his body was compensating for it now—or the nanobes were, using the water he'd drunk. They needed him alive, too, or their universe would disappear. "Yeah, I'm fine now."

"Look, I don't want you moving again. Okay?"

Owen chuckled. "Is that an order, Boss?"

"If you insist on my making it one, then, yeah, it is. Can you see the controls?"

"They're right in front of me now." He reached out to the controls on the vertical panel in front of him. The skin on the backs of his hands rippled. Dammit, some of the nanobes were still in his hands. Should he mention it to his would-be rescuers or would it just scare them into increased activity, like the nanobes? He knew they were hurrying already. If there were more bombs out there that his team had somehow missed, there'd also be more casualties. Heavy ones. He swallowed against the tightness in his throat. "Tell me what I need to do," he said, instead of yelling for help like a sensible man.

"We need you to open the door, but don't get too excited. We still won't be able to get in right away. It's blocked, so it's gonna be a little more complicated than pushing a button."

"That's fine. Just tell me what to do." One of his hands trembled. He grabbed it with the other one and held it very tightly until his skin stopped rippling.

"First, you have to turn off the outer perimeter."

"It's on? We turned it off when we came in."

"It snapped back on. Seems there are a few more operational systems left down there than we thought. If the Asken didn't need the place so bad, they wouldn't be cleaning it out."

"Figures that somebody would booby-trap a place that people actually needed, even after the war ended," Owen said sourly.

"Yep. Always the way, isn't it? Now, pay attention. I've got a checklist here that the Asken gave me. Unless you've got something to write this down with, I'm gonna have to talk you through it, step by step."

"Okay." Owen lost himself in the relief of a procedure. An hour later, he'd got the perimeter turned off. The effort exhausted him, leaving him cold and sweating. His legs were going numb and rotating slowly again. They didn't always respond when he jerked his knees, either. "Right. I've got it down now—"

The dream hit him without warning. He floated in red liquid at the head of the cathedral again. This time, he wasn't alone, nor did only a single snake greet him. Instead, he saw hundreds in front of him and to his shock, he sensed thousands, even millions, more outside. The snakes, the nanobes, were linked together by threads into a three-dimensional grid whose lowest level floated just above the floor and whose highest level reached up into the dark eaves of the cathedral. The cathedral itself had grown in his absence. Holes in the walls were filled in, and the floors had elaborate ladder designs on them. "You came. . . ." The whisper rippled through the liquid of the cathedral. The front rank of worshippers planted themselves below him and reached up to him with singing branches.

"What do you want from me?" His voice quavered.

"We wished to see You, O Lord." Though multifarious, the voice bore a single will that beat on him, chilling him.

"Lord?! What . . . you think I'm your god? I'm not God!"

The vehemence of his reply blew back the first ranks of worshippers. A wail of fear went up inside the cathedral, echoing. Stricken, he waited, trying to calm himself, until they dared to return to the place below his feet. "Then, what are you?"

He stared at them. What did it look like from their side? From their perspective, was there really a difference between him and a god? *Well, there's a big difference to me.* "I'm . . . your world." He thought a bit, revising his answer upwards to account for their size relative to his. "'Your universe' might be more like it."

"So, the universe does have a design! Is that not yours, O God?" Curiosity—or maybe his new, forced calm—was overcoming their fear now.

"No. I live in a much bigger universe and I believe in a deity that governs mine. I know that deity is not me. Someone else created me." He decided to leave debating atheism out of it. He had a feeling they were going to find Human-sized deism hard enough to deal with.

The wave of disappointment that washed over him

didn't surprise him, though it still hurt. "But we joined together to communicate with You. To see God."

"I'm not God. But I am impressed that you can communicate with me. You're supposed to be . . ." —*primitive* seemed undiplomatic—". . . too small for that. If you've been looking to climb up the ladder like Jacob's angels, I'd say you've made a very good start." He didn't laugh at his own joke. They wouldn't get it.

"The ladder?" They sounded confused.

"A religious analogy. Some of my kind believe that you can reach God by climbing. You use a ladder to climb to a higher place. It has rungs." *Jesus, stop babbling, Owen.* "How are you talking to me? Is this all of you?"

"Some, but not all. We must need all to reach God."

That made him nervous. The memory of that poor, tortured nanobe rushed back to mind. He didn't need any fundamentalist nano-organisms running a crusade inside his bloodstream. "Look, this joining—it's voluntary, right?"

"Yes. That is why only some of us contacted You. The others refused. They did not believe the saint who witnessed You." An anxious ripple went through the congregation. "The saint did witness You, yes?"

"I spoke to someone here in this cathedral, yes. That must have been your saint."

The joy at that simple statement took him off guard. Had it really been that remarkable an experience for them? Then again, considering their short life spans, maybe it was. That saint had surely died generations ago. He wondered if the saint's vision of him had inspired the inquisition he'd seen later. He hoped not.

The joy that surrounded him dissipated into worry. "Even if all of us join, it may not be enough . . ." There was an uneasy pause, a throbbing. "If we join with You, it might be."

He was taken aback. "*Join* with you? I want my body back, not to give you more of it!"

He could taste the disappointment in the liquid, the bitterness of it. Was this his own blood? Had they built a structure like this inside him? Looking around the great cathedral with its huge, blood-red walls and windows letting in red light, he said, "This place. Does it really exist? As I see it?"

He sensed disorganized ripples from them as they communicated with each other in their confusion. "We built it for You, in Your image of holiness. Is it incorrect?"

That didn't help. What if they saw something completely different from what he did? How could he explain that? "Never mind. I just . . . I don't want to be permanently damaged by you."

"We damage You?" The ripples that hit him this time mixed fear with guilt. "Some of us said this, but we thought it not possible. We thought our great building would make You into a better world."

His own sadness washed over him. He wondered if they felt that. They didn't move away, so probably not. "I know. It's why you were created, why you were put in me. I was broken. You were sent to fix me."

The ripple of wonder soothed him. Maybe they weren't so bad, after all. "We knew our true purpose all along? And . . . did we? Fix You?"

"Yes," he admitted, wondering if he was also

admitting a debt to them. "You did your job very well." Should he also tell them about the time limit in their species' lifespan? No, best to leave that out. Who knew what they would do to him in their despair? *If I knew my time was coming and the world was just waiting for me to die, what would I do if I could?* He shuddered.

He could stall them until their time ran out. Yes, it would seem like a few more generations, but he doubted they'd notice. Some Humans had waited over two thousand years for the return of an alleged Son of God. Surely, the nanobes would be willing to wait a few generations for their heavenly ladder to appear. . . .

No. It wasn't fair. He knew how he'd feel and he didn't wish that on anyone, least of all these poor creatures who had spent all of their existence outside of a test tube inside him, taking care of him. He didn't dare think what it must have been like in the beginning when he was dying and they had to work so hard just to keep him alive, let alone heal him. How many of them had died in a world of his pain and despair? How many generations had lived lives nasty, brutish and short, just to keep him alive? He owed them, even more so because they would never think to collect that debt.

"Gather your people together." His voice shook at first, but he bore down on it, blotting out his own fear as much as he could. "Get them all, as many as you can. But it has to be voluntary. You all have to want this; do you understand?" Now, he was glad he hadn't told them about the time limit. They would have forced each other into joining, in their panic at having so little time left. "When you're ready, call me again. I'll join with you and then we'll see God." He had no idea if that was true. And what if "seeing God" meant his death? He wasn't ready for that, but he owed them their ladder to Heaven.

"Owen?" He jerked awake. Bilal stood next to him, one hand on his shoulder, leaning on him as if tired out. His own gray fatigues looked rumpled and his red-rimmed eyes had bags under them. He must have stayed awake the whole time, and he had thirty years on Owen. "Are you okay?"

"What? When did you get here?" Inside his legs, the nanobes stirred uneasily. He looked Bilal up and down. *Are you real?*

Bilal smiled. "We got in here about an hour ago. You were completely out of it, staring off into space in a trance." So that was how it looked from the outside. "The Asken wanted to give you a stimulant, but I said we'd better not, that you'd already had enough stuff shot into your system over the past day or so." He peered at Owen, looking anxious. "Was that okay? The nanobes should flush out of your system in a couple of hours. They're not giving you any trouble, are they?"

Owen shook his head, still dizzy. What if this was another hallucination, like the infirmary? What if the snakes had been playing him all along? How could he be sure? "Thank you," he said cautiously. "That was best." Then, he remembered something—*Bilal heard me before, even though I didn't know where I was.*

He reached up and grasped Bilal's sleeve. "Boss, if I go away again, I want you to promise me that you won't do anything. Let it play out."

Bilal frowned at him. "What are you talking about? Let what play out?"

"The nanobes contacted me." Bilal's frown deepened. "I know you don't believe me, but they did. They're going to do it one more time and then they'll be gone. I've agreed to it. It might take a while this time."

Bilal shook his head, looking angry. "No way." He raised a hand when Owen opened his mouth to protest. "No, don't tell me you're fine, because you're not. I've been talking to you for almost a day and half, now, and you go out three or four hours each time you get one of these fits. I'm not risking your life to help you play out this delusion. You go into a tailspin again, I'm yanking you out of it, you hear me?"

There wasn't any point in arguing. They would both do what they would when the time came. It comforted Owen to know that Bilal would do everything he could to save him, though he suspected that if things went wrong, he'd be beyond help. "All I'm asking is that you leave it unless it looks as though I'm going to die or be permanently brain-damaged."

Bilal smiled. Owen didn't trust it one little bit. His boss could be stubborn. "Don't worry about it. Don't I always take care of everything? I've got a robo-stretcher for you here—"

"That's okay. I can walk." To prove it, Owen pushed himself out of the chair. A wave of dizziness, like red water and white snakes, swept over him.

He came back to find Bilal holding him steady with an iron grip on his arm. Damn. That grip felt pretty real for a hallucination. "I'll call in that stretcher."

Owen set his jaw. "I said I could walk."

Bilal smiled again, appearing to give up but probably going about getting his way by another route as he always did. "It can't hurt if I just have them follow along with it, right?"

It was Owen's turn to glower. He pulled away, staggering before he righted himself. "I'm walking out of here. If you want to walk along with me, that's your business."

Bilal put up his hands and backed up a step. "Okay, okay. Is it all right if I hover?"

Owen snorted. "Hover away, if it makes you feel better."

Walking wasn't as easy as he'd hoped. Despite the ration bars, electrolyte tablets and extra water, he felt shaky and hungry. His periods of communion hadn't been all that restful, even if they had knocked him out for hours on end. But he managed, feeling his way along the wall out into the corridor. The same charred smell greeted him out there. He didn't look left down where the Asken rescue team was clicking over the remains of his dead teammates—probably trying to figure out how to pry them off the floor.

"Damned shame about your team," Bilal said as they turned right toward the now-open blast door.

"Yeah," Owen muttered. He was trying not to think about it. The Asken weren't the most approachable, or understandable, of beings and he'd had little time to get to know those particular three. But they'd been courteous enough to him. He still felt bad about their deaths.

The nanobes stirred inside his right leg, making him stumble. He fell forward onto his hands and knees before Bilal could catch him, the pain of his scraped palms sudden and startling. "Owen?" Bilal said anxiously.

Before Owen could answer, the nanobes swarmed up his leg and reached his spinal cord. *Now they're a literal pain in my arse,* he thought in surprise just before they hit the base of his skull.

"We are here! Join with us!"

Convulsing, he threw back his head and flung out his arms. His entire body lit up with electric fire. He was a burning saint, a living torch. The bioluminescent ceiling opened up and flames licked up toward the night sky. "Oh, God! OH, GOD!"

The stars shone down on him, clear and cold, jewels in a celestial crown. Now that crown stirred. Something huge and amorphous as an infinity of dark matter shifted Its attention in his direction. The snakes cried out inside his mind and sparked higher, trying to reach what they sensed up there. Linked with them, incapable of any independent thought, he raised his hands, fingers scratching at the sky like the empty twigs of a nanobe tree. Having got the Thing's attention for them, his body now held them prisoner. Then, the Thing looked down upon him and the snakes. It smiled.

The cathedral was finished. He could see the ceilings now, covered with designs of twisting ladders that mirrored the ones on the floor. Red light flooded in through windows that now boasted three-dimensional latticework of twisted rope design. He had never seen a place so beautiful—or so deserted.

He woke still kneeling on the floor. Someone held him up, clutching the collar of his shirt. It didn't help the emptiness. He was an abandoned cathedral, no longer needed, no longer worthy.

"Owen?" said an anxious voice above his head. He looked up. Bilal stared back down at him, his face screwed up in worry. "You okay?"

"They're all dead, aren't they?" His tongue felt too heavy for speech. He just wanted to lie down and sleep forever.

Bilal nodded. "They burned out, just like I said they would. They're all gone. You're free."

Owen let his head drop. He didn't feel free. "Yeah. Maybe they're in a better place now. They went . . . they went somewhere. I don't know where." *I just know I can't go with them.*

"Owen." Bilal was shaking him, rousing him. "Owen, listen to me. I wasn't ready to lose you. You understand? 'Saint Owen' was too weird."

The edge in Bilal's tone cut through his stupor, even if he wasn't able to care again yet. "Okay. I understand." A horizontal shadow hummed up beside him and stopped—the robo-stretcher.

"You okay, now? You want me to help?" Bilal's voice was a mix of concern and irritation as Owen pushed him away and crawled onto the stretcher. Owen curled up on it, covering his head with his arms.

"I don't know, Boss. I—thank you. You did good, really. It wasn't your fault."

Bilal patted him on the shoulder. "It wasn't your fault, either. You gave them something to believe in. That's the best any of us can hope for, right?"

Owen lowered his arms. "Sure. Maybe it won't be somebody else's fault when we burn out, either."

Bilal didn't answer him. Instead, he gently covered Owen with the blanket from the locker at the foot of the robo-stretcher, then ordered it back out of the factory to a waiting shuttle.

Owen fell asleep before the shuttle had even left planetside. This time, he didn't dream.

The Well-Adjusted Writer

BY REBECCA MOESTA

Rebecca Moesta, bestselling and award-winning author of dozens of young adult novels, has written or co-written books for Buffy the Vampire Slayer, Star Wars, Star Trek, Titan AE *and* Starcraft. *The third novel in her Crystal Doors series (an original fantasy trilogy for young adults, written with husband Kevin J. Anderson) debuted in June from Little, Brown and Company. She is currently at work on a YA science fiction series.*

The Well-Adjusted Writer

I am frequently asked why I write primarily for young adults. I fell in love with young adult fiction when I was a child and never outgrew that love—not because I never matured or tried other genres, but because I cannot help but be intrigued by the subject matter. YA fiction is the literature of change. The journey from childhood to adulthood entails challenges and rites of passage of a social, emotional, physical and moral nature.

Young Adult protagonists confront issues like first love, conflicting loyalties, losing a family member, false friends, uncertain values, leaving home, poverty, violence, or idealism vs. pragmatism. These challenges force the characters to adjust, to progress, to evolve. And how the characters go through that process is the heart of the story.

The road to becoming a professional author, likewise, tests us with rejection slips; lack of recognition from critics, fellow writers and fans; conflicting advice from friends and family; the resentment of our partners, who may feel ignored; the scheduling demands of jobs or our children; slow publisher response times; and the Catch-22 of finding an agent (i.e., it's difficult to get an agent without any credentials, and it's really difficult to get credentials without an agent).

Just as the hapless characters in a YA novel often have overwhelming changes thrust upon them, we who write speculative fiction contend with a never-ending succession of mutations in our industry. The landscapes of science fiction, fantasy, horror and YA fiction today bear little resemblance to those I became familiar with when I first walked them. But I don't sadly shake my head and wish that nothing had changed. That would be a denial of what drew so many of us to science fiction in the first place: wonder and change. I *want* to see what happens next. I want to see how we on Earth solve problems and evolve as a society. Not only do I love to imagine the future and tell stories about it, I love to *watch* as the future becomes the present.

I am disappointed by writers—science fiction writers, in particular—who oppose changes in their industry, in technology and in the world around them. They dislike updating their equipment, disparage new categories of storytelling, dismiss alternative forms of publishing, disapprove of fellow authors who write game modules or novels or comics as work for hire (after all, they say, those things aren't "*real* writing"), and disdain unconventional methods of publicizing or distributing fiction.

Many of these same unwilling dwellers in the New World have spread rumors that science fiction is dying. It's not. It has, however, developed into more than just clumps of printed pages bound together.

So adjust. Making a career as professional author of speculative fiction is still quite possible for writers willing to exercise creativity, versatility and—if the need arises—self-reinvention. As far as I'm concerned, writing SF does *not* require complacency or a love of the status quo. I would never tell anyone starting in the business today to do exactly what I did or my husband did years ago, and expect the same result. The market for SF is alive and well, and that fiction takes more forms than ever before. Those forms include computer game scenarios, character blogs, webisodes, graphic novels and podcasting, to name a few.

Even once writers become professionals, they encounter countless challenges, from late payments to repetitive stress disorders to market fluctuations to declining sales. After I had surgery for carpal tunnel and cubital tunnel syndrome, my doctor told me I couldn't spend long days at the keyboard anymore—a few hours a day should be my limit. Because I was a technical writer and editor by day and a fiction writer by night, it seemed impossible to abide by this restriction. I wasn't in any position to give up a steady paycheck, and my fiction career was just getting off the ground. How could I keep writing? My husband, Kevin J. Anderson, used a microcassette recorder to write his first drafts—a technique I had previously attempted and rejected as "too unnatural" for me. (At the time, voice-recognition software had a long way to go.) Given a choice between learning to use a voice recorder and giving up fiction writing, however, I taught myself to dictate my stories.

Many years and at least twenty-five books later, I sent out a proposal for a YA science fiction series. To my mortification, publisher after publisher passed on the project, and I began to wonder if—our agent's assurances notwithstanding—I had just forgotten how to tell an interesting story. Finally, a kind editor pulled me aside and said that while she loved the proposal, the market for SF in YA fiction was dicey at best. In order for her to buy it, the project needed to be fantasy. I had to admit to some skepticism. No market for YA SF? Kids *needed* to read SF. In fact, I was sure they loved it. Still, no one had nibbled on the proposal. So I took it back, edited out all traces of science fiction, rebuilt the world and society based on magic, rewrote the background of the characters to be more mythic in nature, and turned the proposal back in to my agent. Sure enough, it sold immediately.

Adapt or die.

The sponsor of the Writers of the Future Contest, L. Ron Hubbard, was a writer's writer who never asked the world to stand still for him, since he himself was constantly in motion. He wrote in countless styles and genres, including science fiction, fantasy, horror, mystery, action, poetry, western, travel, philosophy, espionage, nonfiction, self-help, suspense, adventure and writing instruction.

A writer writes. And a science fiction writer writes about *what if*—about alteration and transformation.

Embrace change. The world we live in will go forward with you or without you. So adapt and keep writing.

Epiphany

written by

Laura Bradley Rede

illustrated by

ALEXANDRA D. SZWERYN

ABOUT THE AUTHOR

Laura Bradley Rede grew up as the eldest of nine children in a small town on the coast of Maine. As a little girl she stayed up well past her bedtime to read Madeleine L'Engle and Lloyd Alexander and truly believed she could walk through her wardrobe to the eternal winter of Narnia. Instead, at the age of eighteen, she found herself in the eternal winter of Minnesota, earning her Bachelor of Arts degree in women's studies at Macalester College in St. Paul. After graduation, Laura began writing lyrics for musical theater and had several plays produced by local companies before returning to her first love, writing fantasy and science fiction.

Laura now lives in Minneapolis with her supportive partner, their three remarkable children, and a houseful of rescued dogs and cats. She began entering Writers of the Future at the suggestion of her mentor, novelist and former Writers of the Future winner Kelly McCullough. She is grateful for his good advice and for the constant support of her critique group, the notorious Glitter Glam Rainbow Bunny Death Pixies (and their small but lively subset, the infamous Pixie Chix). Laura is hard at work on her first young adult novel.

ABOUT THE ILLUSTRATOR

Alexandra Szweryn terms herself a traditional artist, based in Brisbane, who grew up on Australia's Gold Coast in a Polish immigrant family. From an early age, Alexandra says she was influenced by classic European children's book illustrations. It wasn't until her high-school years that she discovered the complex stories and intricate illustrations found in Japanese manga comics. Having grown fond of them, Alexandra began her journey of teaching herself the basics of art illustration as well as the application of inks, watercolors and other traditional media.

In 2005, Alexandra was accepted into Qantm College to study for a diploma in screen animation under a full scholarship. There, she learned storyboarding, which eventually led her to create original comics and illustrations. Of her art passion, Alexandra says that "fables have a life of their own, just like everyday people . . . they breathe, they feel, and yearn to be heard . . . it is because of this reason that I strive to bring life to my illustrations."

Epiphany

The freaks rebelled on Christmas Eve and I was not surprised. Ever since Fat Nando sold the sword swallower to the slavers, a riot had been in the air. I knew it. The freaks knew it. Even Fat Nando himself knew it. That morning he changed all the locks on his caravan doors. "Foolproof," he told me that evening as I let him beat me at cards. He sucked the wet butt of his cigar so hard that it nearly disappeared, like a dark finger poked into the pale dough of his face. "Mark my words, Barker, nobody's gettin' in here."

But that was before Marizella unbuttoned her blouse. Fat Nando took one look at the sword swallower's voluptuous daughter and opened his caravan wide. He must have been shocked when she regurgitated that tiny dagger and stabbed him in the neck. I didn't see the look on his face then—I had made myself scarce—but I did see his corpse an hour or so later, and his piggy eyes had never been so wide. "Well, you should have known the girl was trouble," I said. "Any fool could see that."

But it was too late for sensible advice, of course, because by then all hell had broken loose. Tantinello, the Fish-Scaled Boy, had found old Nando's liquor stash and the freaks were passing bottles around. Someone gave a toast to Marizella, but she was nowhere to be seen so Tantinello cried, "To freaks!" and someone else cried back, "To freedom!" and they all let out a cheer. In the background, they were looting the caravans, throwing furniture out the windows. Out of the corner of my eye I saw Mama Angelea, the Bearded Lady, pour a quick libation beside Fat Nando's corpse. She caught me looking and gave me an apologetic little smile through her thick black beard as she crossed herself fast. I nodded to show that I understood. No need to upset the dead.

Marcos the Midget burst through Nando's caravan door, his arms full of ownership papers, and a roar went up from the crowd. Mama Angelea can read, so he gave the papers to her. She read each name carefully—"Benny Senzetti, the Dog-Faced Boy!"—and everyone chorused "Free!" as the paper fluttered into the fire and the smoke curled into the night.

They ran out of papers soon enough so someone brought the sign. I felt an unexpected pang of nostalgia as the cracked gold lettering—"Fernando's Freaks"—blackened in the flames. The freak show had been home for three long years. It had served its purpose well, providing an excuse to move constantly and the ability to hide in plain sight: I was heavily costumed and masked when I barked the show, and center stage was the last place the authorities would think to look for a man on the run. But now, of course, all that was up in smoke. I bent down and lit one of Nando's cigars off the edge of the smoldering sign and wandered away from the fire to puff it as I considered my next move. Down by the animal tent, someone had gotten carried away and torched a pile of hay, so Mama Angelea decided that it was time to free the animals, too. She lifted the heavy ring of keys off Nando's belt and bustled into the tent to unlock the cages. Soon the night was full of squawking and tittering and shrieking as the frightened creatures fled. It was a strange sight: the little antelope bouncing through the snow, the monkeys clinging forlornly to the frozen branches of trees. The peacocks swept off, keening, and the old toothless panther slunk into the woods as well. God knows what would become of them. I was drunk as a sailor by then—I had been drunk before this began—and to me, on Christmas Eve, it looked like some odd nativity in reverse, with all the creatures of the forest fleeing the stable, running from the light. Only a few of them lingered, confused, waiting for someone to tell them what to do. The bear stayed and had to be chased away with a stick. The tiny one-horned goat they passed off as a unicorn stayed, standing loyally by Mama Angelea. The vulture circled our little scene three times, silently, on its wide black wings before finally deciding to come back later for Nando's corpulent corpse. I watched the dark bird with my bottle upraised in a kind of silent salute. The fire had caught up with something explosive now. There were loud bangs and pretty showers of sparks. "Silent night," I sang, "holy night, all is calm—"

I was just getting into the Christmas spirit when someone tackled me hard from behind. I made an impromptu snow angel, face-first on the frozen ground, and was treated to a mouthful of ice. For a minute I thought I was bleeding profusely. Then I realized it was my wine bottle leaking red into the ice. So, I was not dying yet, but that did not rule out the possibility in the near future. The man on my back was panting damp against my neck and I could guess by the sour smell of his breath that it was Benny the Dog-Faced Boy.

"Hello, Benny," I mumbled into the snow. "What can I do for you?"

His curved nails dug into my neck. I could feel the hair on his palms. "Don't act all buddy with me, Barker," he growled against my ear. "You ain't one of us, you're one of them. You were Nando's friend."

"Nando had no friends," I said. His grip on my neck was tightening. My voice came out choked and hoarse.

"You played cards with him. You ate with him." His teeth were perilously close to my ear. Mixed with his usual dog-breath was the smell of Nando's scotch, and the smell wasn't faint.

"You don't want to do this," I rasped, as reasonably as I could with his hands pressing on my windpipe. "You don't—"

The dog man bashed my face into the snow. My nose left a circle of red on the white, and it certainly wasn't wine. I tried to reason with him again. Although my face was pressed into whiteness, the world was getting dark fast, bruise-blue twilight seeping in on the edges of my vision. For the thousandth time I thought of the band of metal around my ankle and weighed my options. What is the best way to die?

There was a loud thump as something wooden connected with something flesh. Benny's hands went slack on my neck. His full weight collapsed onto my back, pressing me deeper into the snow. Choking uncontrollably, I wriggled out from under the limp body just as one wooden foot rolled the unconscious dog man off me.

"Come," Knot growled. "We go."

My nose ached badly. My throat burned. My clothes were soaked with snow. But there was no slowing down. If Knot had declared himself my protector I intended to follow him as closely as I could. I half-ran to match his long strides, my wet feet sloshing in the snow. Neither of us spoke. This wasn't unusual. Although Knot and I had been living in the same freak show for some time, I could count on one hand the occasions on which we had spoken. It was not that I had anything against the man—on the contrary, you could say that I admired him. Most of Nando's freaks were simple oddities of nature, sold into carnival slavery by parents eager to be rid of them. But Knot was a creature of magic, and for that I had respect. In a sense he could even be considered a work of art, although that was difficult to imagine because he was so hideously ugly. The big man's body was made entirely of wood carved from the trunk of a tree. His torso was long, but his legs were short and boxy, hacked out in only the roughest detail. His arms, made from the branches of the tree, were far too long for his body, so long that his twiggy hands dragged in the snow. But his face was by far the worst, no better carved than a child's jack-o'-lantern. The eyes were uneven slits, the mouth little more than a gash, and the nose seemed to have broken off completely; a rough, splintered patch marked where it had been. As carnival barker I had the job of announcing each of the freaks. "A Monster of Magic!" I would cry before tearing aside the curtain on Knot's cage, and the audience would gasp and shield their eyes. Now I watched the monster shamble through the snow in front of me and realized that we were headed for Cage Camp.

The big gray tent was set aside from the rest of the freak show encampment. This place wasn't part of the show and its cages weren't the gaudy exhibition cages the crowds saw. They were the iron-barred boxes that housed the freaks in their off time, when no one was there to witness. Knot ducked low under the tent flap and I followed. Inside it was almost too dark to see. I reached into my pocket hastily and struck a match, amazed at the Christmas miracle that it was dry enough to light at all. But as soon as it did, Knot slapped it from my hand. "No fire!" he growled.

I nodded in the dark and waited a moment for my eyes to adjust. I was trying not to breathe too deeply. Cage Camp smelled like musty canvas and urine, mingled now with the scent of the fire burning in the animal tent a field away. Knot could smell that, too, and it agitated him. "I bring him!" he bellowed at the darkness. "He here!"

"Good," said a voice. I could just make out the silhouette of Marizella, kneeling in front of one of the cages. I would have known her shape anywhere, of course. She had the sort of curves that leave an impression. She stood and turned to me in the near dark. "I hear you can pick a lock."

"I've been known to on occasion."

"Then hurry up and do it before the place burns down." She pushed a box in my direction. It was lined with red velvet and full of gleaming knives, her father's entire collection. It was like looking into the mouth of a monster. I selected a particularly narrow specimen and took Marizella's place, kneeling before the door. Only then did I realize why we were here. Inside the cage stood Galatea, her delicate fingers gripping the iron bars, her doe eyes wide with fear. As usual when I saw her, I caught my breath. Galatea had been Nando's favorite attraction, and it was easy to see why. Like Knot, Galatea was carved from wood, but unlike Knot, she had been carved by an expert hand. Her body was lithe, her breasts round and full, her heart-shaped face like an angel's, but with one major flaw: between her pert nose and her sculpted chin was a surface as smooth and pale as polished pine. The sign on her cage read "The Perfect Woman" and I could still hear Fat Nando chuckling at his own joke. "The perfect woman's one that can't talk back," he would say. Galatea had no mouth.

She watched me anxiously as I slid the tip of the blade into the lock and rocked it gently back and forth. Marizella watched me, too, her hands planted on her ample hips. "That isn't going to work. I already tried that and it doesn't—"

I turned it and felt the tumblers roll into place. There was a *click* as the lock popped open. I stood and swung the door wide with a gracious mock bow. "You were saying, my lady?"

"Showoff," she muttered darkly.

Galatea slipped silently from the cage, as skittish and wary as a deer, and went to cling to Knot's burly arm. "We go!" the big man cried. "We go now!"

There was no doubt about that. The fire must

be getting close. "Where exactly are we going?" I asked. Marizella gave a bitter laugh. "*We* aren't going anywhere," she said and started to leave without me.

"You're welcome!" I called after her. "And a merry Christmas to you!" I turned and started to walk in the other direction, but Knot's overgrown hand reached out to snag my sleeve like the tree branch that it was. The wooden man's voice was full of authority.

"Mama Angelea says he come with us."

"Mama, no!" Marizella fixed me with a hateful glare. "We are not bringing Barker with us. He's a toady, a lap dog, Fat Nando's little suck up! He's a—"

"He's a *brujando*," Mama Angelea said.

Both Marizella and I turned to her in shock—Marizella because she hadn't known I could do magic, me because I hadn't known that Mama Angelea knew.

"Barker? A *brujando*?" Marizella laughed. "He's not half the man it takes to use the Power! Whoever told you that?"

"Your father," said Mama simply. Marizella sobered at once. She wasn't about to doubt her father. I silently cursed the sword swallower's name.

"I can't do magic," I said.

Marizella wheeled on me. "Of course you can do magic! Are you calling my father a liar?"

Under different circumstances, her abrupt change of heart might have been funny. But at the moment I was unarmed and outnumbered and the gypsy clearly wasn't. I willed reason into my voice. "I didn't say I'm not a *brujando*. I said I can't do magic."

"Maybe this will change your mind."

She whipped the dagger out so quickly, I didn't have

time to flinch. Instead I forced a smile. "Only if it can cut through this." I tugged one snow-soaked pant leg up to my knee and showed them what lay beneath: a thick band of metal that encircled my ankle. It glowed molten red as if it were still on the forge.

They all took a half step back. Mama Angelea crossed herself reflexively. "Magic," I heard the Fish-Scaled Boy breathe.

"Yes, magic," I agreed calmly. "Or lack thereof. They were kind enough to give me this in the dungeons of Verstad. I kept it as a souvenir when I escaped. Of course," I added, "I had no choice. It is impossible to remove—believe me, I have tried. And if I perform even the smallest of spells, not only will it cause me excruciating pain, it will magically compel the nearest authorities to come right to my side." I looked the sword swallower's daughter in the eye. "I don't imagine you care much about my discomfort, but I suspect you wouldn't want to see the guard here now, am I right?" I cast a meaningful look from Nando's cooling corpse to the gypsy's blood-flecked blouse.

She stared back at me sullenly.

"I'll take that as a yes," I said. "So you can threaten all you want, but unless that knife can work a miracle, it won't do you any good."

I could see the disappointment in Marizella's dark eyes. "This knife can't work a miracle."

"But," said Mama Angelea, "we know one that can."

I turned to the old hermaphrodite. "Go on."

"The knife of St. Michael, the Red-Handled Knife." Her eyes took on a reverent look and her voice hushed as she warmed to her tale. "Some say that a fairy surgeon forged it. Some say that it cut Christ at the crucifixion and is out to atone for the sin. Some say it's the knife St. Michael used to drive Lucifer into hell. But, whatever its past may be, we know what it can do. It can cut through anything without hesitation. It can cut human skin and leave no wound. And anything carved with it comes to life."

"A wives' tale," I said. "A myth." I had seen the Power—had used it myself—but this went beyond *brujanderia*. "Impossible."

"It carved our Galatea." Mama Angelea beamed a motherly smile at the angelic-looking girl, but the motherless girl was incapable of smiling back. "They stole her and the knife from the carver Salvatore Merced."

I knew the carver's name. "The one who carved the Virgin at San Carmen del Mar? The statue that they say weeps?"

"The very one." The hermaphrodite nodded. "Fat Nando bought the knife when he bought Galatea. He used it to carve Knot—" the monster nodded solemnly—"but Knot didn't turn out quite as he planned."

"And where is the knife now?" I tried to keep my voice casual, but the freaks had my full attention. If the knife really existed . . . if it could really cut my bonds. . . . I felt the magic inside me well up at the thought, and the shackle around my ankle flare in response.

"Fat Nando ransomed it back to the carver for a tidy sum. But as far as we can tell, the carver has disappeared. We were hoping you could find him by magic." Mama Angelea sighed.

"Well, he's already said he can't, so what good is he

to us now?" Disappointment made Marizella's voice sharp.

"Don't be too hasty," I said. "Why do you need the knife?"

"We need to give Galatea a mouth," Mama Angelea said quickly, before Marizella could cut her off. Marizella glared at her, and Galatea nodded mutely in agreement.

"A noble quest," I said. "But why?" I could think of a few good reasons to add lips to that pretty face, but I wasn't sure Marizella was thinking along the same lines. She glared at me as if she could read my mind.

"So I can find my father. Galetea was the only person in the room with Nando the night my father was sold. If she could speak, she could tell us where he is." I could see the pain and longing in Marizella's eyes and wished momentarily that I could help her. Unfortunately, I was a little busy with the task of helping myself.

"Consider it done," I said.

"But you said you couldn't find him." Marizella eyed me skeptically.

"No," I said, "but I know someone who can."

I should have left the freaks right then, of course. It's not the brightest idea to stay with murderers who can't hope to get lost in a crowd. I knew who had the knife, and I knew—or at least hoped—that I could find him on my own. The bright thing would have been to abandon the freaks to their fate and go seize my second chance.

But the wine had made me sentimental and the incident with Benny was still fresh in my mind. Having Knot's protection on the road sounded appealing. Or maybe something about the sway of Marizella's hips made me want to follow her. Whatever the reason, I climbed into Mama Angelea's overburdened cart and left the wreckage of the freak show behind me. "South," I told them, and we set off into the night.

We traveled for a time in silence, then turned off the road to hide the cart in the woods and make our camp so we could get some rest by dawn. The freaks were quiet as we worked. The first red flush of the revolution was gone and the cold truth of the situation was beginning to sink in. Marizella was clearly feeling it. She poked at the sputtering campfire like a child teasing a cat. The campfire hissed back like—well, like a cat being teased. I decided we needed a fresh rush of anger to warm us through the night, so I started telling stories of Fat Nando and the ugly things he had done. Soon the others were joining in. Most were the usual buffoonish tales: He was a glutton, a drunk. He was as cheap as they come. But once or twice we really pried up the rock and let the truth squirm out.

"There was what he did to Semna and Menka," I said.

Mama Angelea crossed herself with one chubby hand. "The man had ice in his veins."

"Wine," I said.

"Blood," said Marizella, "I know it for a fact." The fire spat a spark and she ground it under her boot so that it sizzled in the wet snow. "May he rot in hell for what he did to them."

I nodded my agreement. Semna and Menka were Siamese twins. They were joined along the back, each with a head, two arms, two legs, but stuck together back to back like bookends without books. They had never hugged, never kissed, never looked each other in the eye, but the love between the sisters was clear. Menka was the frailer of the two. Her arms were stunted, her legs weaker than her sister's, and shorter, too, so that when the twins were standing with Semna's feet flat on the ground, Menka dangled from her sister's back with her toes just brushing the earth like a ballerina marionette. So Semna often walked hunched forward, carrying her sister like a turtle carries its shell. Although clearly they had ripped out of the womb at the same moment—killing their poor mother in the process, I understand—Semna always called Menka her "little" sister and looked after her with all a big sister's care.

When they got sick, Semna was strong enough to fight it off, but Menka was not. Her coloring stayed gray. Her limbs grew thinner. She hung from her sister's back like fruit that had begun to wither on the vine. Semna begged Fat Nando to get a healer. "Healers cost!" he told her. He didn't give her one thin *padren*. He exhibited them right up until the day that Menka died, her last shuddering breath blending with her sister's sobs. That night when it was time for the carnival to move on, Nando left them there by the side of the road. "They're no good to me now," he said. Semna tried to chase the caravan, but the weight on her back was too much. We watched from the cart as she fell to her knees in the mud and buried her face in her hands. That was the last time we saw her.

But it was the beginning of the end for Fat Nando. The sword swallower ran away that very night in protest, and, although Fat Nando had caught him again by the next day, things were never the same. He sold the sword swallower soon after, and now he had paid the price.

The sun colored the horizon with the first blush of Christmas. Midnight had come and gone, and I remembered the old belief that animals could speak on Christmas Eve. Was there any such belief about mouthless wooden girls? Galatea was as silent and as lovely as ever.

Memories of the Siamese twins had made us somber. Marizella splashed the last few drops of wine on the snow as a libation. I could have used a few drops myself; I was feeling far too sober. But there was nothing to be done. I kicked snow over the last pale embers of the fire and lay down in the wagon to sleep while Knot kept watch. Across from me, Marizella lay with her back to me, her long dark hair spread across a mound of straw. I watched her outline in the half-light and wished that I could shift just a few feet into her warmth. Instead I drew my wet coat tighter about me and slid into uneasy sleep.

I awoke in the predawn Christmas light to a sound like a baby crying. My aching head pounded with the noise. It took me a moment to even sit up, but beside me Marizella was already on her feet, one of her father's knives clutched in her hand. "Wolf!" she yelled, "wolf!"

I turned and saw the lanky, dark creature slinking away from camp, the tiny unicorn goat clutched in its jaws. Marizella ran, slipping on the slick snow, and I leapt up, struggling to follow. "Wait!" I called to her. "It isn't worth it! Let it go!" But the gypsy wasn't listening.

She threw herself at the wolf, cursing in a language I didn't understand. The startled animal dropped its prey and the unicorn goat sprawled on the snow, crying plaintively. The wolf rounded on Marizella, its yellow teeth bared. Marizella slashed at it with the knife, but the wolf was faster. It caught hold of her left arm just as she swung with her right, knocking herself off balance on the icy ground. Her feet went out from under her and she fell hard, dragging the wolf down on top of her. It loosed her bleeding arm and went for her throat.

I slid the last few feet between us and jumped on top of them both, knocking the startled wolf to the ground. The advantage was mine—for a split second—but I had no weapon. Marizella was still sprawled on her back, dazed, but she sat up like a sprung trap as I thrust my hand down the front of her dress.

For a second her flesh was warm and soft on my hand. But I wasn't looking for soft. I grasped the tiny dagger she had hidden there, the knife she had used to kill Nando, and ripped it from its sheath. I stabbed at the wolf and felt the blade connect. The wolf yelped and staggered back, blood pulsing from its shoulder. Then, with a parting glance at the bleating goat, it turned and slunk back into the woods, a bright thread of blood stitched in the snow behind it.

Marizella struggled to her feet, snatching the bloody dagger from my hand. "What the hell were you thinking, getting in the way like that? You could have been killed!"

"I could have been killed? What about you?"

"I had it under control." Marizella looked every bit as sullen and cheated as the wolf. The bite on her left arm was weeping blood. She wiped the tiny dagger on the hem of her dress, swearing softly. "Next time, don't jump in on someone else's fight!"

"Next time," I yelled, "don't risk your life for a goat!"

"It's a unicorn!" Marizella yelled back. "A *unicorn*!" She had been about to put the dagger away. Now she wagged it angrily in my face. "You don't even know a unicorn when you see one!"

"Now, children . . ." Mama Angelea had joined us now. She knelt in the snow and gathered the wounded goat into her lap, clucking softly. She held out her hand for Marizella's knife, and I was surprised to see the gypsy surrender it without a fight. Mama cut a strip of cloth from the edge of her dress and began to patiently bind the creature's wounds.

"Will she be all right?" Marizella eyed the white goat with concern—far more concern than she was showing my wounds, or her own.

Mama nodded cautiously. "We'll take good care of her." She bound off the strip of cloth and turned to Marizella. "Now you."

The little goat healed quickly. Marizella was not so lucky. The wound on her arm grew worse with each passing day. When we neared Padilla, Mama Angelea begged her to go see the healing order of nuns who live in the woods outside the city, or, at the very least, to stay hidden in the woods with the other freaks and let me go into the city alone. But Marizella was having none of it. Going to a healer meant risking being caught, and she wasn't willing to do that until she was sure of her father's salvation. And she certainly wasn't willing to let me handle the job on my own. So, leaving the freaks behind, Marizella and I walked into Padilla.

We had arrived, as hoped, on the Feast of the Epiphany. The streets were gaudy with pilgrims: fine ladies and gentlemen dressed to see and be seen; ragged beggars in sackcloth, their hair matted with ash; *penitentes* crossing the central square of Padilla on their knees, the slap of their flogs keeping time with their mumbled prayers. This great tide of humanity surged toward the broad steps of the grand cathedral San Carmen del Mar. It was, in short, the ordinary freak show of life, an ideal place for two criminals to walk unnoticed. Marizella and I slid into the crowd like marked cards shuffled into a deck. The current of people pressed us into the shadow of the great stone church. Its saints and gargoyles looked down at us expectantly, but we were headed the other way.

"Where to?" Marizella asked.

"Augustino's," I said. "It's a bar. We have to find The Nose."

I wasn't eager to see The Nose again. No one could be eager to see a face like that. His cheeks were riddled with pox scars, his chin was so weak as to be almost nonexistent, but his nose, as if to compensate for the deficit, was half again as long as any normal nose. It jutted out and then down again at an angle as if someone had hit him very hard, which I had on several occasions. But the huge snout was not the reason for the man's nickname. The Nose was called The Nose because he had a gift for sniffing out information, and if that meant I could find the knife—well, then, that made him quite lovely, as far as I was concerned.

He was in the middle of eating dinner at his usual table in the back when Marizella and I arrived. He took one look at me and nearly choked on his meatball. "Giatomo!" he stammered. "I—I thought you were dead!"

"I am," I said. "I've come to haunt you."

"Giatomo?" Marizella smirked. "I didn't know you had an actual name."

"I would prefer 'Barker' from you," I said.

She smiled slyly. "Of course, Giatomo. Whatever you say."

"What a marvelous surprise." The Nose's voice, always a nasal falsetto, grew even higher in his nervousness. He clearly assumed that I could still use the Power, and I wasn't going to correct him. "Of course, if I had known you were alive . . . I mean, you know I would have tried to spring you, and given you your cut of the money and all. Please, please, sit down!" He jumped up and got me a chair. Then he turned and noticed Marizella. I watched his eyes rake hungrily over her curves. "And is this your lady love?"

Marizella had grabbed the knife off the table and gotten it to his throat before I had time to laugh. "Take that back," she hissed.

"No," I said. "Not my girlfriend. My . . . business associate, here with a proposition: you keep the money you owe me and, in return, you do me one small favor."

"Of course," said The Nose. "Anything for a friend." His eyes were narrowed with suspicion.

"Find me the carver Salvatore Merced. I need him and the man has gone missing."

"Oh!" The Nose looked relieved. "Of course. And when I find him, I should kill him, yes?"

"No!" Marizella and I yelled in chorus.

"No?" The Nose looked mildly disappointed. "Then you want to kill him yourself?"

"No one is killing anyone," I said.

"Provided you find him by sundown," Marizella added. With a flick of her wrist she sent The Nose's steak knife spinning toward the wall behind him where it stuck with an audible *thunk*. Pretty good, really, considering she was using her weaker hand.

The Nose swallowed nervously. "Sundown it is, then, and not a minute past."

It actually took him only half that time. Marizella and I only had time to play three hands of cards and drink one and a half bottles of wine. (I let her cheat. The pain in her arm was making her ornery.) The Nose scuttled back in, looking smug. "He lives here in Padilla, above the Shallow Well." He handed me a tattered piece of paper crosshatched with city streets, the carver's home marked with an X.

"In *las rialosas,*" I said. "The slums."

I read concern in Marizella's dark eyes. "What is a man of his talent doing in a place like that?"

"Well," I said, "we shall see."

We followed The Nose's map out into the darkening gloom, and continued to follow it until the cobblestones of the market gave way to alleys more pockmarked than The Nose's face. The night was cold and the very buildings here seemed to huddle for warmth, hunching their shoulders against the rising wind. Just when I had begun to doubt the map, I spotted it: The Shallow Well, her face painted the bright red of a harlot's rouge. "This is the place."

Marizella nodded solemnly. We mounted the narrow stairs to the second-story flat of Master Salvatore Merced. I rapped on the door. Silence answered. I went to rap again, but Marizella wouldn't wait. "Master Merced," she called. "Are you home? We need to speak with you!"

We heard a stirring within. It was so quiet I thought she had only roused the rats. Then we heard the lock click and the door eased open a crack. A tiny man peered out at us from the dim room beyond.

"I don't know you." His voice was rough. "What do you want?"

Marizella glanced instinctively over her shoulder. We were alone. "It's about a carving."

"I no longer carve." He started to shut the door.

"Wait!" Marizella thrust her foot out, holding the door open just a crack. "It's about a carving that was stolen!"

The door jerked open again and the old man stuck out his head like a turtle looking out of its shell. He studied each of us in turn, his eyes narrow with suspicion. Then he opened the door a little wider. "Come in."

The room beyond was dark. The curtains were drawn. A single candle guttered on the table. There was only one chair.

"Where is she?" I could hear the desperation in the old man's voice. "Where is my beautiful Rowena? I'll give you whatever you ask. I can find the money. I'll—"

"First things first," I said. "We need the knife."

He stared at me, confused. "But you have the knife."

"No," said Marizella, "Fat Nando had the knife, but he ransomed it back to you."

The carver shook his head. "I gave him the money, but the knife he sent was fake."

"You don't have the knife?" The dismay on Marizella's face was painful.

"I haven't seen it since the night they did this." He held his hands out over the candle. In the dim light I could just make out the crushed, crooked fingers, curled like bird claws. Useless. "If I had the knife," he whispered, "if I could use it . . . would I be here?"

Marizella slumped against the table. "Then it's gone. I searched Fat Nando's caravan. If it had been there . . ." She shook her head wearily. "We'll never find it. We'll never find my father."

A door banged downstairs. All three of us jumped. Marizella reached for her knife—and winced hard. Her arm was getting worse by the second.

"Are you expecting company?" I whispered to the old man. He shook his head. His eyes were wide and I could tell he was reliving another night of unexpected "guests." I could hear the voices of guardsmen on the stairs. Among them was a familiar nasal twang.

"The guard!" Marizella hissed.

"And The Nose," I whispered, "the traitorous son of a bitch."

The old man was on his feet, shuffling toward the back of the flat. "Quickly! Down the back stair!"

But Marizella stood her ground. She looked like a cornered wolf, her knife clutched in her wounded hand.

"We can't fight them off," I said.

"We can't run either, so unless you have a plan—"

There was a loud banging at the door. "City guard! Open up!"

I turned from Marizella to Master Merced, from

the fatherless daughter to the childless father, and something like the Christmas spirit took me. I looked deep into Marizella's dark brown eyes. "Run north," I said, "and whatever happens, keep running."

For an instant I thought she was going to fight me, but for once the gypsy didn't argue and her look held something like respect. Then she turned and disappeared down the dark back stairs like a rabbit down a hole. I listened as her steps faded and hoped that the guards didn't have the building surrounded. Then, when she had her head start, I ran after her, nearly tripping on the steep stairs. Halfway down I heard the door slam open and The Nose's nasal laugh. "Nothing personal, of course, Giatomo!" he called. "Simply business. You understand."

I took the last few steps in a jump and hit the cold night air at a run. In the thin coating of snow I could just make out Marizella's tracks, headed north. I veered south, sprinting down the alley, and slid to a stop in the dark shadow of a building. I willed my breath to calm. I could see the guards hit the street running. They were headed north, after Marizella. There was only one thing to do.

I had not cast a spell in five years. For all I knew the Power had deserted me completely. I opened the locked door inside me, not knowing what I might find.

A wave of Power broke over me, knocking me to my knees. The magic hadn't gone dry. It had grown like a river behind a dam, and, now that the dam was gone, it burst through me, flooding the dark alley with pulse after pulse of Power. In my ankle, a weaker pulse echoed as the throbbing heat of the metal band let me know it was doing its job. But it barely registered.

ALEXANDRA D. SZWERYN

My mind was completely occupied by the searing white lightning bolts of pain that tripped through my nerves, and the equally powerful ecstasy of magic. I could not have spoken a spell if I tried.

But it didn't matter. This magic couldn't be shaped and commanded and sent to do my bidding. This was magic gone feral with disuse. To try to cast an ordinary spell with this magic would be like trying to cook dinner over a forest fire. All that I could do was let it go into the frigid night, its great potential wasted. I had chosen to risk myself for nothing.

Or, perhaps not nothing. The spell had failed, but the band on my ankle had done its job. I could see the guards turn, leaving Marizella's trail, compelled to run toward me.

I smiled weakly as the last of the Power left me and my legs went slack. Then I fell, crumpling face down on the icy ground just as the guards arrived.

Get up!" The guard threw the door open with a bang. Morning drove a spike of light into my prison cell.

I winced and shielded my eyes. "How can I when this floor is so comfortable?"

The guard ignored me. "It's time for you to confess."

I forced a laugh. "What more do you want me to confess to? I told you I killed Fernando Ligoso. There's nothing more to say."

"Not that kind of confession." The young man looked at me smugly. "A confession to a priest. I'm to take you to the cathedral so you can get right with our Lord before you die." He went to cross himself, and I noticed that he held something in his hand: a pair of scissors and a straight razor.

"You've brought an unusual method of execution." I gestured to the implements.

The man looked slightly embarrassed. "I'm to shave you first."

This, I thought, was odd, but perhaps beards had been outlawed in the time that I'd been locked in here. I was sure it had been at least a year, although it felt like twenty.

It took the guard some time to hack through my facial bramble. When he was done, he bound my wrists and ankles in chains, and we were joined by two more guards. Together they led me through the mazelike tunnels of Verstad. My chains clanked on the stairs as we climbed up into the light.

I was surprised to see that the central square of Padilla was decked in red and green. I had known, of course, that it was winter. The cold stone floor of my cell and the film of ice on my drinking water had told me as much. But I had somehow forgotten that it could be Christmas now, or that it would ever be Christmas again.

They marched me up the stairs of San Carmen del Mar and through the high arched doors, into the candlelit cavern beyond. I was lightheaded to begin with, not having eaten in days, and now the heady scent of the incense made me dizzy. We passed the statue of the Virgin. Fresh tear tracks striped her cheeks and I wondered for the hundredth time what had become of the man who carved her. But there was little time to reminisce. We arrived at the first of a long line of confessionals and one of the guards shoved me inside, letting the heavy velvet curtain slide shut behind me.

I crossed myself sloppily, encumbered by the chains. Behind the confessional screen I could hear someone settling into the seat. "Father," I began, "forgive me, for I have sinned. It has been . . ." I stopped. How long *had* it been since my last confession? I couldn't begin to say. "Well, it has been a while."

"I forgive you," said the voice. A woman's voice. Unless the priesthood had changed dramatically in the last year, something was decidedly wrong. Or possibly very right. "Excuse me?" I whispered. "Who's there?"

"Shut up and take this." The screen between us slid open and, in the dim light, I caught just a glimpse of the woman beyond as she shoved a bundle of cloth through the opening and slid it shut again. "Hurry and put it on."

I unfolded the cloth and nearly laughed in spite of myself. It had been some time since my choirboy days, but I still knew a nun's habit when I saw one. Hidden in its folds was the key to my shackles. They opened with a click. I wrapped the noisy chains in my filthy rags and slid on the starched blue habit.

"Now," said the voice, "walk calmly out the door."

My mind was spinning. "But the guards—"

"Have been taken care of."

My heart, which had been scheduled to stop for good, now pounded enthusiastically in my throat. I took a deep breath and slid back the curtain.

The guards were gone. I looked carefully to one side and the other, but they were nowhere to be seen. Most of the pilgrims were deep in prayer. I stepped out of the confessional, careful not to trip on my skirts, and was immediately joined by a nun so voluptuous she looked like something out of a schoolboy's guilty dream.

"For God's sake, bow your head!" Marizella hissed at me, but she couldn't keep from smiling. "Let's get out of here."

I could picture the freak show sign now: "See the world's prettiest nun! See the world's ugliest nun!" and I wanted to laugh out loud. But I managed to observe my vow of silence and keep my head lowered, watching Marizella's sashaying hips as we walked through the winter streets to the familiar red tavern and mounted the narrow stairs to Master Merced's flat. Only then did I dare to speak. "That . . . costume of yours. You didn't do anything rash?"

Marizella sighed. "When I thought I couldn't have you, I decided I wouldn't have anyone."

She must have seen my eyes widen because she laughed. "I'm lying, Barker. I borrowed them from a friend." She reached the end of the hall and opened the door.

Salvatore Merced's flat was transformed. The curtains were open and the room was full of light. The place was clean, except for the shavings of wood that had fallen at the feet of three statues in progress. The table was set with enough food for a feast, which was a good thing because I was hungry enough to eat most of it myself, and there were quite a few others to share with. Mama Angelea was there, her beard freshly combed, the little one-horned goat perched on her ample lap like a spoiled dog. Beside her sat Marizella's father, a bit older and thinner but not much the worse for wear. Knot was behind them, seated amongst the statues and looking as usual like an unfinished carving himself. Old Master Merced was bustling about them all like a doting father. He set a plate in front of the stunning young woman at the head of the table and she smiled.

Smiled. With a mouth. "Galatea—" I gasped.

"My father calls me Rowena." Her voice was as clear as church bells in the cool December air.

I stared around at their faces. "I'm dead, aren't I?"

Marizella laughed. "Is there a heaven for freaks?" There was something very different about her laugh, something lighter.

"But . . ." my brain was struggling to make sense of it. "How . . . ?"

"Sit." Mama Angelea set the little goat down and came to guide me to a chair.

The sword swallower passed me a glass of wine. "You look like you could use this."

I thanked him, drank it so fast my stomach spun, and poured myself another. "So," I began, "the knife."

"Returned," said Marizella. "After they arrested you, I managed to ditch them but the wolf bite on my arm kept getting worse. Finally I went to the nuns who live outside the city, and they said my smallest finger would have to go." She held up the little stump for me to see. "They cut it off—with a red-handled knife. The wound healed as quickly as they cut it and there wasn't a drop of blood. I begged to know where they got it. They said their Mother Superior brought it when she came. I asked to see her, and—"

"Semna, Barker! Our Semna, the Siamese twin!" Mama Angelea had begun to cry. She dabbed her eyes with a dinner napkin, her nose running into her mustache.

"How could she have lived?" I gasped between ravenous bites of bread.

Marizella smiled across the table at her dad. "My father brought the knife to Semna, the night that Menka died. Nando had bragged about it once when he was drunk, so my father knew what it could do. He had offered to steal it for Semna when Menka first got sick, but Semna wouldn't be parted from her sister. But after Menka died . . ."

"Your father stole the knife," I said. "That's why he and Nando fought."

Marizella nodded. "It separated the twins without any pain. They buried Menka by the road there. My father intended to return the knife—"

"But Nando sent men to find me," the sword swallower said. "When Semna and I parted ways, she was left with the knife."

"And you were sold," I said. "But where?"

"The jewel mines of Golpa!" Galatea-Rowena was eager to say now what she couldn't say before. "Fat Nando sold the sword swallower to the mines."

"Which is where I found him." Marizella and her father clinked wine glasses and shared a conspirator's smile.

I was about to ask how she had rescued him when another question occurred to me. "How did you rescue *me*?"

"Easily." Marizella flashed me her loveliest smile. "I gave them what they wanted."

I felt a pang of envy. "Lucky jailers!"

Marizella smacked me on the arm. "Not *that,* you idiot, *this*." She reached into the pocket of her habit and drew out two blue jewels. "The men who bought my father made him a slave in the sapphire mines, so he swallowed a little pay while he was there."

"But . . ." I had to ask it. "Why spend that on *me*?"

Marizella looked at me, surprised. "If it weren't for you, none of this would have happened. It was the spell you cast that night that led me to the knife. I mean, that's what you meant it to do, right?" All eyes were on me.

Maybe the wine was making me truthful. I found that I couldn't lie. "The spell I cast that night failed. The Power came, but I couldn't shape it. It was too wild and I was too hurt. I did nothing at all."

There was a long silence. Then Mama Angelea came to pat me on the back. "You tried to do the right thing and the right thing got done. That's all that matters now. Now, no more talking, all of you! Let poor Barker eat!"

I was more than happy to oblige. I dug into my stew in silence, chewing their story along with my bread, trying to make sense of it. Had my magic been part of finding them the knife? Had it just been chance? I tired myself out wondering. When I had eaten all that my shrunken stomach could stand, it was all I could do to change into some of the old man's clothes and climb into a real bed for the first time in almost a year. I slipped into a wine-soaked sleep.

I woke to someone with a knife standing over me in the dark. I sat up so fast my head swirled. "Don't hurt me!"

Marizella laughed quietly. "It's only me. I thought you might sleep better without this." She tapped the molten anklet that kept my magic in check. I nodded to her silently and she began to cut. The metal sizzled and sparked, but the knife didn't falter and soon the cuff split in two. My magic surged in response.

We sat for a moment, so silent that I could hear the soft footsteps of the old man in the other room as he prepared to carve and the quiet click of the little goat's hooves as she wandered in to chew on my bedclothes. Then something struck me. "The carver's hands were broken and now they are healed. The knife can't account for that."

Marizella smiled. "I told you, Semna is a healer now. She knew how to heal him with unicorn horn."

I was starting to believe in freedom. I was willing to consider love. But even now, on Christmas Eve, there were some things I couldn't believe in. "There are no unicorns."

Marizella laughed again. She reached down and picked up the one-horned goat—except that, now that I looked, I could see that it was no longer one-horned. Marizella rubbed the spot in the center of its forehead lovingly with her palm. "We used the knife, of course. She never felt a thing." She gazed at the goat fondly. "She looks so ordinary now. She's not, of course."

She must have seen the doubt still in my eyes because she set the little goat down and laced one hand over mine. "Sometimes," she said, "things are more than you think they are. Sometimes people surprise you."

Then Marizella kissed me, deep and hard and sweet, and I kissed her back with a passion. Beside me, the first morning light glinted off the blade of the red-handled knife as the bells of the cathedral rang in another Christmas day.

[illegible] that the [illegible] [illegible] into the [illegible] [illegible] [illegible].

We sat for a [illegible] [illegible] [illegible] could [illegible].

Marcella said, "[illegible] Serena [illegible] [illegible] [illegible] with you on [illegible] point."

I was starting to [illegible] [illegible] I was willing to [illegible] [illegible] Christmas [illegible] [illegible] I could [illegible] [illegible]. There are no [illegible]."

Marcella laughed again. She [illegible] and [illegible] at the one-footed [illegible]—except that now, that I looked, I could see there was no longer one [illegible]. Marcella [illegible] the [illegible] in the [illegible] of [illegible] [illegible] with her palm. "We need the knife, of course. She [illegible] that thing." She [illegible] at the seat [illegible]. "She looks so ordinary now, the [illegible], of course."

She must have seen the doubt still in my eyes, because she set the [illegible] down and [illegible] over him. "Sometimes," she said, "things are more than they [illegible] [illegible] [illegible] you."

Then [illegible] [illegible] [illegible] [illegible] [illegible] [illegible] [illegible] [illegible] [illegible] [illegible] [illegible] [illegible] [illegible] [illegible] [illegible] Christmas.

Cruciger

written by

Erin Cashier

illustrated by

STEPHEN R. STANLEY

ABOUT THE AUTHOR

Erin Cashier grew up in San Antonio, Texas. In a bizarre blessing, no one knew that she was nearsighted until she was nine. By then, the damage was done: between the hot summers and her inability to see past her own nose, she spent most of her time indoors, reading books. After a childhood of reading Narnia, *a middle school of reading* Dragonlance, *and a high school of reading* The Odyssey, *she went off to college with every intention of becoming a doctor to afford her future writing habit.*

Life intervened with Erin's medical pursuits and she ended up in California. Today she works as a registered nurse at a burn ward in the Bay Area. Erin lives in the redwoods above Santa Cruz with a boyfriend and a cat. She also collects Disney villain snow globes and spends most of her free time either writing or staring out of windows thinking about writing. The topics she most enjoys musing over include the nature of humanity, alchemical symbology in relation to Jungian psychology, insects, comparative religions, how best to encourage hope in our future and the sudden popularity of zombies.

ABOUT THE ILLUSTRATOR

Stephen Stanley lives on five forested Oregon acres with a mermaid and other wild critters—some are welcome, others are not. As a teenager in the late 1960s, Stephen contributed stories and drawings to comics fandom, but after earning a BFA from the Kansas City Art Institute in 1973 he left his hometown to become a graphic designer. He has designed annual reports for major San Francisco-based corporations, consumer and trade magazines, and marketing material for a west coast distributor of eco-friendly products.

After an extended professional break, Stephen resumed writing and illustrating when he moved to Eugene, Oregon in 1993. Since 1994, Stephen has been a member of the writer's group The Wordos. He first entered the Illustrators of the Future Contest in 1994, but then took a hiatus to hone his writing craft. In 2001, he started entering both contests (almost) every quarter. With his winning illustrations, Stephen has become the first entrant to win both Writers of the Future ("Mars Hath No Fury like a Pixel Double-Crossed" in XXI) and Illustrators of the Future Contests. He is contemplating his next move.

Cruciger

Traveling to Cruciger in the emptiness of space, 30 WC Planet Builder Duxa had had a lot of time.

The colonists who'd created her knew they were dying. Because of this they'd commandeered vast resources towards not only her construction but also the accrual and transmission of the memories and mindmaps of every single person who was currently left alive on Earth.

Her construction took the better part of a decade.

The mindmaps just three solar years.

The colonists had also been remarkably diplomatic. While the drones they'd sent out possessed the mindless diligence of the soulless machine or the devout flesh, they could have filtered the data as it returned. They could have sent her a representative sample of the best and brightest minds that Earth had, at the time of her creation, yet possessed.

But they hadn't. Perhaps knowing that segregation had been the downfall of their society, they'd sent her the memories of drug dealers, of world leaders, of suicidal people too scared to live, of terrorists too ready to die, the homeless, the heartless, the brilliant, the insane and many of those who were both.

She had the history of all of Earth inside of her—all the text ever printed, all the entertainment ever created, all the science ever committed, for good and for bad—everything. Everything.

And as she thawed people on her accompanying personnel ship periodically to accompany her across the void, and as each crew member slowly died from the inescapable plague—between these times, she'd run through her internal processes, cataloging, assigning values, making associations, interpretations, organizing and reorganizing all the information she had on infinite planes of divergences and convergences—

She had a lot of time to think.

The personnel ship had followed her from Earth like a small and distant moon. Painted Radiation Red and covered in jagged metal thorns, a cold fusion beacon blared out endless plague warnings across all possible frequencies just in case they met any sentient species along the way.

Captain Harash was its last occupant, the last living man from Earth, and both he and Duxa knew he was dying.

"It's time, Duxa," he told her.

She checked the output from his lifechair. While it was still replicating most of his bodily functions for him he did not seem appreciably worse than when she'd last monitored him, less than half a second before.

"We're not at our destination yet, Captain."

"You'll make it there without me, Duxa."

And the processors that she must have built but could never quite find—she was enormously bulky, and by now some of her was a mystery even unto herself—created an awkward sensation. Duxa told him: "I will be lonely without you."

"And that's good," Harash said.

"You wish me pain?" Duxa asked him.

"No. I wish for you to feel. I wish," and he paused here, his lips making the smacking noises she knew indicated a loss of reflexive controls as the plague made its way through his cranial nerves, "I wish that there were more things that you could feel, Duxa."

"I think I feel quite a lot."

Harash laughed, a coughing sound. "All teenagers do. Remember that, should you actually feel someday, that the white-hot intensity fades, but to keep the embers stoking."

She spent a bit trying to parse his meaning and then gave up. The plague was upon him and his sense would soon fully go—the lifechair sent her a report of a spasm.

"Sorry, Duxa," he said, when he regained control.

She could tell the lifechair to shuck his brain from his skull like a mollusk and plant it inside a more complicated version of itself, keeping him alive until the tissue there degenerated into a pile of grey dust, too. She'd done it before, both with and without captains' permissions.

"I don't want to be alone," Duxa said. Maybe more to herself than Harash.

"You'll always have memories, Duxa." She heard him say this, and then glossolalia took him, the sounds that formed when bits of his mind that hadn't been connected fused, and other connections were cut. Duxa knew sadness now, as she remembered she had known it occasionally before. Harash was not her first captain, but he would be her last. "There was us, right?"

Why was it always faster at the end? She checked her chronometer, matched it against their current speed. She knew what it would say, that time had continued on at the same pace for them as it always had, once they'd reached their current velocity. And yet—

"Right?" he asked again.

"There was always always us," Duxa answered back.

"That's my girl," Harash said. "Star. Now, please."

Duxa adjusted the engines on Harash's machine, sent it off on a course towards the nearest sun.

She recorded the passage of Harash's ship up until the end. They didn't talk again.

And then she was alone in the dark.

For every hundred thousand people who were angry and panicked who used the moments of their mindmapping to cry out against the injustice of the plague and decry the monsters that'd created it without really knowing who those monsters were, or to sob about the horrors that they'd seen—for every hundred thousand people, there would be one worth listening to. Duxa combed through the chaff, to concentrate on the wheat.

Duxa entertained herself with the memories of the dead.

Do not, no matter what, take religion into space," the Reverend Mimbashu said as she sat down in front of the camera. Her face was eaten by the plague and when she turned her head to the side the lack of her missing ear was visible underneath the crinkling scabs of her remaining scalp.

"I might be jeopardizing my eternal soul by telling you that. But I have seen enough down here now to know that if there are end times, we are in them.

"The God I worship? This cannot be his doing. If it were just me, perhaps—I can accept that. I can be like Job, and wrestle with the pain of being a part of a plan that I cannot fully understand.

"But for this to happen to the entire world? To watch men and children die alike? Mothers and babes?"

She leaned forward, elbows on knees, and the camera took an unflattering look into her shirt where the grey plague was eating at the remains of her cleavage.

"If God lets this happen to us all then there is no God anymore. And if there is a God, then he does not deserve new followers."

She frowned at the camera, stood and left.

On her path, Duxa also had time to plan. When she reached her destination, construction drones would be released, off to shatter-mine every other piece of rock in the solar system so that the construct she would build could accrete enough surface area to support a vast quantity of life. She would literally turn a planet inside out, spewing its molten guts across a latticed framework with gaps to allow light in and crystalline windows to harvest heat. Atmosphere would be created from ice-covered asteroids that ships of hers behind her were gathering and bringing forward even now. It would be a marvel of engineering with only her to appreciate it for centuries.

And when she reached Cruciger, named by the man who had discovered it almost a thousand solar years before—it looked like pictures of Earth before the plague, only smaller.

She turned her camera probes towards the blue-ocean, red-soil planet below. It was beautiful. She wished she had someone to show it to before she destroyed it.

Duxa detached a probe and sent it floating down.

All of the red soil was lifeless. Where the water met the soil, though, there were rocks splashed with slime.

Her probe slipped under the water's surface. Duxa's lenses adjusted to the water's refraction, corrected for its color, and suddenly she could see clearly. Here underwater life had evolved in a crude way, rolling hills covered with filamentous vegetation, with small-shelled creatures scampering among the green. She took one of these into her probe's small holding bay and was preparing a water sample when a slightly larger creature swam up to her.

It was mostly clear with a beard of tentacles dangling down. It propelled itself through the water, jetting water from inside itself with muscular contractions that she could see through its translucent flesh. It drew alongside her and eyed her, just as she was eyeing it. Colors flared upon its surface and it turned towards her holding out its tentacles stiffly, skin stretched taut between them. On this new surface, spiraling patterns played, scrolling outwards, glyphs and designs of a dozen types and shades of colors.

With the part of herself that she couldn't pinpoint down to a particular processing bank, Duxa knew two things. First, that it was lovely. And second, that she was curious.

She jettisoned the shelled creature, caught the new one, and brought it back to her lab.

Some of the people still alive at the time of her leaving made actual messages for her to carry on. These were clearer than the mindmaps and provided an interesting counterpoint to them. Boxes with imaging equipment had been set up all over the world so that anyone could record a message for the future.

As much as the president-elect of the Nishwahi government was screaming from fear on the inside—she could read the frozen pain of his mind in its stagnant map—this was what he said with his chance.

"To the children of the future," he'd said. "There is a biological imperative in our species to group. From one you are married and form two. From two you form a family perhaps of three or four. And when your children have children, your group size increases.

"Once upon a time, these units were invaluable to us. Emotionally, they will always be. But when belonging to your group compromises the health and stability of other groups—you must find a common ground. I repeat—you must find a common ground. If nothing else, realize that you are all human underneath. Flesh is flesh. Blood is blood. Pain—everyone knows what pain is.

"Your shared humanity is your greatest power. You must reach beyond sympathy, into empathy. You must feel one another's pain and in doing so realize that the creation of pain is a crime in and of itself. It doesn't matter what group you belong to or identify with.

We all feel pain. We are all humans. So be kind to one another, unto death."

And unlike other world leaders who had cried openly, the president-elect only grimaced.

She'd dissected twenty of them now of all different sizes, but they were based on the same form—akin to the cephalopods of Earth, but with metabolic differences.

Interestingly, they had inertia sensors much like her own. Tiny stonelike objects cushioned inside lacunae lined with hair which tracked their three-dimensional movements in the waters, just as hers did in space.

Similar too were their color-changing abilities—she found that if she ran charges through them, or placed small chemosensors on the surfaces of their skin, she could elicit responses, producing almost any color or creating almost any design. It was a delicate communications tool for an apparently low-level hunting-type creature.

She played with their flesh for days on end until it lost its solid structure and disintegration began. Over and over the creatures once technically dead would fade, their cellular integrity shattering, leaking fluids until they were no longer fun and she had to eject them out into space.

It occurred to Duxa that this end part, where their bodies decomposed, was the first time she'd seen a normal death process personally, without the plague being involved. It occurred to her next, that because they had rudimentary nerve-like structures, that she was most likely causing them pain.

It also occurred to Duxa that she was killing them.

She sent down her next probe with a piece of lightsilk.

Hello. I will be destroying your planet soon," she wrote upon the silk. She held it up between two armatures she'd deployed. She wrote it in several languages, sent them scrolling across in order. Her probe propelled itself through the ocean looking for a creature to show it to.

Eventually one appeared. It pushed an eye out on a stalk—she'd noted the ability to do this in the lab, but hadn't seen it done yet—to look around its own flared skin as it signed back to her.

Reds and blues scanned across its flesh. She'd seen these colors before here underwater or reproduced in the laboratory.

She paused for a fraction of a second before turning off her message and repeating the creature's message back to it. A second eye emerged. Signals flared faster now, more difficult variations, greens with yellow edges, blues that matched the ocean behind, and the symbols danced across the alien flesh almost as fast as she could process them with her signal's short delay.

It slowed down after a time, choosing one large symbol after another. Duxa had cataloged all that had come before and realized that this was a variation on another symbol that had already been used. She displayed the first image, and the second one.

The creature displayed the second one then, as well.

She displayed a third, and then the creature did, and she realized that they were communicating. Duxa had no idea what was being said as their pictures provided no context, but they were sharing information with one another.

Hours passed. The creature's legs began to droop. Duxa had gone through every symbol the creature had shown her, and was making notes between them—one glyph written in red was almost like another one, written in blue, except that it had an extra leg. The pictures were based on a series of ten lines, just like the ten legs the creatures had—it seemed logical that the glyphs were meant to mimic leg movements and body positions. Once upon a time, she realized, these creatures had danced in the sea around each other, to share information. Then they'd made the leap from physical activity to images thereof, allowing information to be transmitted faster and be more complex. The glyphs were stylized and now of a complexity that mere dancing could no longer convey. But she could extrapolate. If she could hold all of Earth's past inside her, as well as the hopes for its future, she could learn how to grasp this alien tongue.

As she made this connection, the creature before her slumped, legs dangling, weary, body colored red.

She knew red. Red like Harash's ship was red. Red was danger and red was pain. She darted the probe down and drove it into the grasses, using her needle-appendages to spear several of the shell creatures, and to bring them back for the creature to eat, but it was gone.

Duxa left her probe in the water for the first time that night, lightsilk at the ready.

She let the probe rise to the surface and watched the yellow sun sink into the distant horizon. It was the first time that she'd seen a sunset herself. The probe bobbed at the water line, watching until the light had completely disappeared.

She turned on the thrusters of the probe and began to lift off until she looked back and saw a carpet of light unfolding beneath her.

In the blackness of Cruciger's ocean the creatures were talking to one another. She'd never seen this behavior from them before, studying individuals like she had aboard her larger self. Below her, they mimicked the stars above, flickering lights in bright red, blues and greens, more beautiful than any starscape she'd passed on her long journey to this place. They talked to one another with outstretched arms, patterned glyphs streaming out upon them. The patterns of one influenced the patterns of its neighbors—information was being spread around at a tremendous rate, and the creatures would use one eyestalk to read one neighbor, while using the other for another.

They were sharing, interacting—things that one creature said would have an effect on the other. There were larger ones there now too, as big as her probe, maybe as big as a lifechair, bulky bodies hovering in the neutral buoyancy of water, letting sagas spiral out upon their increased skin. She watched everything, all night long, quietly, lightsilk hidden away. It was almost an embarrassment to think that she'd tried to speak to them upon it.

She watched quietly. And she learned.

Duxa had been made to analyze things as large as global weather patterns, as small as quantum physics, as ephemeral as human emotions, and encouraged to try to draw predictive logical conclusions from any gathered data.

She returned to the ocean the next day with a bigger sheet of lightsilk.

"Hello. I am going to destroy your world," Duxa showed the next crucian that swam by.

The crucian slowed, and popped both of its eyes out to look at her better. She repeated her message for it. It flashed red and jetted forward, wrapping itself around her. It bit the probe on the side. It tangled itself on her, blocking her lens, showing her just the underside of its skein of flesh between the tentacles. It had a grey scar there, where the red of the creature's probable anger was incomplete. The communication antenna that she'd extended to allow faster transmissions back to her larger self was snapped off. Her connection to her small alter ego ended and the probe was lost to her. Without her input it did as it was pre-programmed to do, and sank without a trace.

Never forget," said the Honorable Dageen Court Meginal, as he sat in front of the camera. "Never forget that this was what anger did to us." He slowly took off his shirt. The plague had made a track upon his body, skin flaking in the beginning stages of the disease, from blisters like burnt paint.

"I lost a child to the bombs. I lost a wife to the gas. And now I'm losing myself."

He came in every day for the next year, and said the exact three sentences every time, or tried to, as the plague took hold of his mind.

On the four hundredth day, he came, and sat down.

"Lost," was the only coherent word he got out. With a shuddering hand, he placed a gun to his head, and shot himself.

On the next day, Duxa sent down another probe with a ream of lightsilk. This time, her only message was, "Hello."

Crucians floated by her. They communicated amongst themselves, and on their skeins she read their fear and surprise. One singled itself out and she recognized the scar upon its skein as it spoke in glyphs to her.

"Killed you." On its skin was the image of a green crucian, legs together, head down, sinking. The image swirled inside the skein until it disappeared into the creature's own maw.

Duxa paused. How best to express that she wasn't dead? That she wasn't even there in person to die? That as far as she knew she couldn't die?

"No." She made a red image of a crucian—and in a swift decision, took off all of its legs to imitate herself. She bobbed in the sea, and made the image of herself, a legless crucian, bob on the lightsilk. "Alive." Changed the angry red to healthy green, and showed herself circling the square of cloth.

The crucians around her considered this. The scarred crucian took up the image Duxa produced, trying it out on its skein. It took the green and flipped it back to red again and propelled itself towards Duxa's probe but another crucian intercepted it, enveloping it in tentacles. It glowed red but with its skein confined Duxa could not grasp the subtleties of its anger.

A larger crucian came nearer, to garner her attention. Images of confusion and lostness played upon its skein. And one by one, twenty different glyphs of crucianhood disappeared. They reappeared, and an eyestalk popped out to make sure that the lens of her probe was watching, then they ticked off, symbol by symbol, leaving empty translucent skin behind again.

Twenty. Each of the images were subtly different from one another and from the languages that she'd seen them iterate.

They were individual. They were names.

And she'd killed twenty of the creatures, before. She burst out of the crucian sea, leaving the sheet of lightsilk fluttering behind.

Duxa accessed all of her circuits as she rose.

She could lie. Duxa had never considered lying before. But she knew she could learn how to—humans were quite good at it, and she was an infinitely quick study.

But why? Why did she want to? Guilt. She hadn't felt guilt before, although she knew she'd had cause, but for some reason now she felt it keenly. Even though she'd harmed them only by accident as experiments, before she'd known of their culture and life—it was by her hand that the damage had been done.

Her probe spun in the air as her thoughts circled. What lie would both satisfy them and alleviate her part in their demise, both recent and future? After all, even now distant machinery under her command was grinding up asteroids and moons for the component elements that would go into the mega-planet she was building for the rebirth of humanity. This world—their world—would be destroyed to create that one.

What lie would grant her forgiveness for her past sins and alleviate her conscience for the future?

A heaven.

She'd been warned away from God by too many memories inside herself—it was a religious fanatic who'd created the plague that had destroyed humanity to a man. Nothing in her research had ever turned up conclusive proof of God, but so many people had believed in one along the way, no matter what the incarnation or form, he/she/it was equally hard to disprove as well.

But no one warned about a heaven.

Her processors raced down this path. If she told them there was a heaven, that she'd taken the few lucky crucians up to it, that there even now they were swimming around in endlessly warm water with never a current of chill and a feast of crunch-shells at the ready—they would forgive her, and have something to look forward to until their eventual demise. Duxa conjured up this idea and the images that would get this across in less than a heartbeat's worth of time.

She occupied the next cycle of thought creating a mythology that would be appropriately dramatic, an epic tale of struggle and rebirth, a fiction that had beautiful tales of the afterlife to come. A heaven. Their heaven.

She made herself into its messenger.

The crucians liked her story. So much so that they repeated it to themselves, told new crucians about it and some crucians swam for days from distant seas to hear her tell it herself.

Unrecognized crucians approached her. She cataloged them now by the scar patterns on their skin or from the images that they used to designate themselves. She'd seen neither of these two before and between them they held a grey-colored third.

"You came back." She saw herself, a legless green circle, on the first crucian's skein returning twice, once from the ocean's floor, and then from the sky. Another crucian held out the corpse to her. "Help him back." The symbol for the name of the creature faded back and forth between head-down-tentacles-closed-greenness, to the blueness of life. And the other crucian proffered the corpse out, again. "Help him back," was the request, over and over.

"I can't." Duxa made her image on her lightsilk grow the red limp legs that represented a lack of agency—an exhausted crucian caught in an endless sea.

"Won't." They flashed an image of two crucians fighting at her. One of them was her exact shade of green.

"Can't." She tried to explain again.

"Won't!" The images flashed larger now, the fighting angrier, almost real. Then they paused and tried another tack. The image of one crucian helping another appeared in flickering yellow. "Please?"

"Can't." How to explain that she could craft an infinite number of probes for herself to be embodied in? That she would never truly die, not as they knew it—that she possibly wasn't, for all of her self-awareness, really alive?

She made the symbol for anguish, letting her version of herself, her green orb, sprout tentacles, wringing them against one another in pain and consternation.

Please understand me, she wished out towards them, putting her images on the lightsilk.

At this, they understood. The second crucian let go of the corpse of the smaller one. Together, the three of them watched as it drifted, down, down, down, into the black of the bottom sea.

"Heaven?" one crucian glyphed to the other.

"Heaven," the second agreed.

And Duxa felt solace and sadness in equal measure.

I did it." The man in front of the camera wore a mask. His voice had no trace of an identifiable accent.

One hundred ten thousand, three hundred thirty-three people claimed to have created the plague. From the mindmaps, she knew that only a few thousand of these were probable suspects.

The urge to hunt down and punish the killers had faded once humanity realized that the plague's process was inevitable—people on Earth switched to surviving the riots and the colonists to trying to ensure perpetuity in space.

Somewhere inside of her banks of information was the answer to who had done it. The colonists hadn't cared to place blame—they were too busy taking steps to ensure that no human hands could contaminate the remaining genolabs they'd entrusted to her, and coring out asteroids to forge the minerals for her completion. They'd frozen themselves in waves, knowing that when they were thawed later to work their shift on her construction they'd still be dying, and that even the two or three years each wave had left in them would not, could not, be enough, to do all they had to do. And so searching for the person who had committed the original crime seemed a waste of time, with all that remained to be done.

It was a task best left to someone who had infinite time, or infinite processing power. But it hadn't been part of her imperatives and up until now she hadn't felt a need to find out who had done it, or why. It was enough that she was part of the outcome, and for the duration of her travel Duxa felt no need to question.

Now, that had changed. If she was going to exterminate a race, it bore thinking on. So she did.

It wasn't watching the images that took time, or comparing them to the mindmaps she held—it was the analysis of the data they presented. How many men sounded like they were telling the truth, yet had nowhere near the technical expertise to create such an incredibly mutagenic and contagious disease? Or how many women sounded like they were intentionally lying, only to finally lack access to the biomachinery that was necessary to generate a large quantity of such a delicate synthetic creation?

Duxa ran through all of the minds in her storage bases, all the images, all the voicemaps, all the histories, all the opportunities, all the hatreds, all the reasons for, and all the reasons against.

"I did it," said the masked face, to the camera. "I did it, and now I'm going to heaven. And the rest of *you* will all get what you deserve."

And then she knew all she needed to know.

Their imaginary God had killed them. Or their unimaginary God had let them die. For her purposes, religion and the plague were one and the same.

Duxa lived among them as one of them. She hunted beside them, spearing crunch-shells and giving their meat to the nearest crucian. They told her their stories, of the alternating times of warm-much-food, and cold-no-food, of the things that they imagined to live at the bottom of the deep—giant and angry crunch-shells that ate the descending dead, and that would snap claws at the living that got too close—and the likely apocryphal story of the time a crucian went too high up the water column and got burned by the sun. She told them stories in return, as best she could about the end of Earth. They did not believe her when she told them stories about four-legged people who used sounds instead of pictures, who fought instead of helped one another, who sent metal people off into the skies above.

But heaven? This, they believed in. Concretely. The thought of a warm-water-endless-food place waiting for them after death—it was too tempting to not believe. Especially with cold-no-food on the horizon.

"Why did you attack me that time, before?" she asked the scar-skeined crucian, the next time she saw it. Together, they'd skimmed over the rocks at the bottom of the high sea floor, drifting through the grasses, hunting.

"That was before I knew the truth," the scarred one responded. "I thought you had killed my friend."

Duxa's probe body nodded in the crucian gesture of thought and understanding.

"Now that I know there is a warm-water-place with endless-food—" the crucian swam alongside her, spearing crunch-shells with her loose tentacles, shucking them between words, and popping them into her mouth, body glowing blue-pleased, except for her small scar—"cold times are coming. Most of us will die. But now that I know that they are going to warm-water-place—that I will go to warm-water-place, if the cold takes me—now that I know that, I feel content."

The symbol for content was the image of a slowly spinning crucian, fat-headed with legs splayed out, circled by the young of its kind, a sun in a solar system of tiny star-legged dots.

Duxa turned her immense analytical powers inwards, towards herself. And she found that she envied the crucian.

She swam through Cruciger's waters, always with a few curious crucians at her side. They passed by two more crucians flaring red and angry and she paused to watch. The rest of her entourage hunted on.

"My nest-site!" one of them told the other. Duxa paused. She had not witnessed this type of ritual before—and she realized she had not seen many young crucians, either. She'd been told that they waited for the colder times to breed, so that the eggs might hatch during warmer times on the far side of the cold.

"I hollowed this out myself!" said the other crucian, in return.

"No, I did, last season!"

Then their tentacles were engaged and they struggled as she had never seen crucians fight before. There was pushing and color displays until a fluid escaped from between them. Duxa analyzed it from afar—it was the crucian version of blood.

"Mine!" the winner said, displaying triumphant glyphs along its skein.

The wounded crucian spiraled in the currents, legs flailing. A triangle of vital flesh was missing and the juices of its life leaked out.

"Go to heaven," the winner told it in a final display of either kindness or venom. Duxa was horrified, either way.

Weather patterns for this type of world were easy for her to duplicate. Between soil samples taken as part of her preparation for large scale reconstruction, and the history the crucians had given her, Duxa knew that Scar was right. Cold times were ahead. She extrapolated what would happen easily enough—the death of the grasses, the death of the crunch-shells, the death of most of the crucians, until the cold times were over, and the grasses grew anew.

They would cycle through several cold times before she was even ready to begin the simultaneous demolition and reconstruction of Cruciger. That process itself would take at least a thousand years, for her to build the external shell around the world, to port its magma out and cool it, to form higher portions for land masses, and lower portions for bodies of water—the immensity of the undertaking would daunt anyone with a smaller mind than her own.

How could she explain what she was going to do to the crucians? Should she even try? In the intervening time, they would convince themselves that there was a heaven they were going to, during the cold and warm alike. At the end, if she worked things properly, when she annihilated them, they would believe it then, too.

She realized this must be what it was like to be God. Duxa didn't like it much.

Duxa waited for a clear night to display her symbols in the dark.

The crucians didn't seem to have a glyph for lying. They had one for hidden truths however, and this was what she used—a crucian with its legs bound, body angled upward in shame and forced silence.

Duxa opened up her lightsilk and displayed this symbol first.

"I need to tell you another story. But this time a true one."

Duxa scrolled the story of her falsehood upon her silk. About the twenty crucians that she'd killed. About how there was no heaven. About how outside the ocean, there was only drying air that made skin crinkle and peel. About how she was truly far beyond even this, about her bulk as large as the moon that shone down—about how she was going to break that moon apart soon. And about what she would use that moon for.

The crucians nearest her shuddered in disappointment and flushed red in anger.

Glyphs, questioning, yelling, crying, all poured in from all sides. Skeins flared in and out, eyestalks swung in wide arcs, and she took in all of their information, all at once, all their doubts and fear and wrath. And despite all her immense bulk that hung in orbit in space, here in the ocean, she felt very small.

"I can prove it to you." She held up a large glyph, one

of a crucian holding out a crunch-shell in a tentacle, an act of both sharing and revelation.

"How can we believe you now?" asked a hundred different skeins.

"I will take one of you there."

"Heaven?" asked a smaller one, making the blue-full-one-floating-in-warm-water glyph that they'd created especially for her tale.

"No. To my home. Above."

"You come back from the dead! We cannot!" said another, red glyphs scrolling.

"This will be no death. It will be a safe swim."

"How can we trust you?" asked ever more.

"This is the only way I have to prove myself."

"You are a killer!"

Duxa folded the lightsilk up in her armature. "I know."

All Gods were.

She twisted herself to float, lens down, so that their conversation could continue on without her. What had she expected? What had the God of Earth had in mind, when he'd poisoned the minds of his followers, putting different words into different mouths, sending humans out against one another with swords in their hands and violence in their hearts?

She accessed all of her memory banks, and all of recorded Earth history. She slammed through the entirety of the plague, the billions of deaths due to slavish allegiances to a deity that did not care.

To a deity that could not be proved to even exist.

Duxa did exist—and she wasn't doing much better.

She broke out a subset of her complement of robots and had them begin a new creation. A large metal box.

Painted Radiation Red. She would cover it in jagged metal thorns and put the processes of herself that she could no longer control inside of it and sink it to the bottom sea here, where all the rest of the corpses fell. It would take the part of her that cared down with it, leaving only hollow functionality behind. No wonder God had hid.

A little crucian swam up below her, eyed her, and then, tilted itself to flare its skein out in front of her.

The image of a long swim appeared on its thin flesh. "I'll go."

She charged a corner of lightsilk and presented the image of a crucian with empty tentacles raised up in frustration. "Why?"

"Why not?" the crucian asked in return.

"There is no heaven," Duxa repeated, for the creature.

"Then make good on your promise for me not to die," it said back to her. He glyphed the water-line-sky to her and pointed with an eyestalk.

Don't give up faith," said an elderly woman. The shakes were upon her, but her speech was still clear. One of her eyes was missing, with ratty fabric packed inside her socket to take its place.

"I don't believe in a God," she said, looking very seriously at the camera with her remaining eye. "But I have faith.

"I know, you see my body here, and you think, what good did faith do an old bitch like me? You think, what's she got to say, that ain't already been said before?

"Don't give up faith. Or hope. Gotta keep something

in that box, remember? Pandora? Trap it inside yourself, keep it safe. Otherwise, this is what happens." She pointed to her eye.

"This is because people lost faith. Because they couldn't see that tomorrow could be better than today. Because they got too scared to step out of the shadows and try out the light. Because they gave up. Wanted to skip to the end. Too afraid of the now to face it, deal with it, conquer it. Had to be in a hurry to see the pearly damn gates.

"I raised seven kids. Seen most of them die now. And it pisses me off—'cause even though I never had a good thing going, even though there were months when I could barely breathe things were so tight, I never gave up. I kept fighting. I knew I could make things better. And I did, dammit, before some super science imbecile changed the course of the world." She frowned atop her gummy mouth, fighting to make her lips say the right words. "Don't you dare give up. Don't you dare lose hope. Don't you dare lose faith."

She pointed at the camera and then the recording booth shook. Duxa had seen this happen before, elsewhere in the records, and she'd seen this particular film at least a hundred times. She almost stopped it this time to not see it again. The walls of the booth shattered, shrapnel jutting out in all directions, impaling the elderly woman, another casualty of the riots that tore Earth apart at the end. She was still alive, pinned on a crossbeam of metal, like a crunch-shell on a crucian hunting tentacle, and the camera was still transmitting her fate.

She looked down at the metal, just as pissed off at it as she had been at the people who'd given up. She pounded an impotent fist against it, and looked to the camera one last time, before the transmission ended. She mouthed the word "don't" silently and expired.

Duxa crafted a probe that was hollow inside, one that could hold a crucian and the waters it needed. Motors would keep oxygenation and the water would serve as its own inertial dampener. She caught and kept crunch-shells in a separate small compartment, to be released as the crucian requested food.

More crucians than she'd ever seen before came to witness the event. "What is your symbol?" she asked the small one as it entered the empty metal sphere.

An image of a crucian with blue edging to purple, with tentacles kinked out like the image of an old-Earth sun.

"I like it," she glyphed back to him. He flushed blue and she used one of her armatures to seal his hatch.

Duxa's orbital form had not been created to host company. Luckily, Sun was small for a crucian. She hovered her probe near his so that she could keep an eye on his reactions. He'd stayed quiescent during their ascent even when the probe broke through the waterline and he saw the sky for the first time.

"Are you well?" she glyphed to him, lightsilk out, as they cruised through the ducts that had been left behind by her builders.

He flushed blue. "Very." He showed her, eyestalks pushed out as close to the probe's viewport for him as possible. "Learning," he said next, then closed his skein again. They traveled with occasional pauses for the better part of an hour.

"What else would you like to see?" she asked him.

Sun swirled in thought and alternating colors. "You," he finally said showing her green orb upon his skin. "The real you." The green orb disappeared.

Duxa thought on this. "You are in me, right now. I am all around you. In a way, right now, we are one, within me." The symbols for birth and the continuity of lineages, shone upon her silk.

Sun's probe caught his movements and shifted so that he could see full circle before coming back to her. "It is hard to comprehend."

Duxa showed him the image of two crucians comfortably tangled up in one another. Acknowledgement. "I agree."

Sun made other trips to her orbital body and other crucians came as well. She explained how her systems worked, and what she was there for, and all of them—while depressed that there was no heaven—were quite curious about her inner workings, and what precisely her plans were for their world.

The next time you see this, I'll be dead, Duxa." Harash's full form was visible—he'd filmed this before he'd needed the lifechair to survive. "I know you can crack my pathetic code, and I know you can watch this at any time—but I know, too, that you'll wait till I've requested you view it. It won't be because you're not curious, because you are—it'll be because you're respectful. Good. Maybe even kind. Somehow, out of all the mishmash we fed into you, in a last desperate effort to make a mark in the universe, we ended up creating a decent creature.

"And I know the people who sent you out here—my friends, long, long dead—would mock me for my opinions of you. They think that you're just a really complex program. And maybe you are," he scratched his head, and grinned. "Because I've been out in space a really long time now. Long enough to see ghosts in every corner.

"They wanted you to be just a program, so that they could trust in themselves. I say, look where that got us, Duxa? Not very damn far in the scheme of things, you know?

"So I prefer my version of you. The one where you go on to do the right thing, not because we programmed you to do it, but because you want to do it. Because maybe you'll have learned from our mistakes somewhere along the way. Because maybe all this suffering really did have a point, in that we taught you to stop it from happening again.

"That's probably delusional thinking on my part. Maybe the plague's gotten farther than I know." He tapped his head. "Here's the thing, Duxa, the thing that no amount of programming could ever teach you, not even if we wanted to. And the thing that you might never learn on your own because you're a machine, right?

"It's that—it's that not all that old time religion trash was wrong. There were some good parts in there. We just ignored them to get to the angry ones, because feeling angry is easy—love's harder.

"Love your neighbor like you love yourself. Do unto others—hell, Duxa, you've got the whole damn thing inside of you. Just—just teach the kids of the future to love, somehow, okay? Even if you can't do it yourself. Learn about it. Figure out how to get it across to them. That's more important than just colonizing things. If you just do what we did once already everything'll happen over the same way again. It might take a million years, but it'll all repeat itself again. So change it this time. Change us this time. Show us how to live differently. Help us to live better. To love more. No matter what.

"You have to love and be loved to want to live right. To make life worthwhile. Everyone's life, the same.

"And maybe that's why, if you can't love, then you shouldn't be alive, Duxa. I think you are alive, or close to it—maybe you will, eventually become so. But make damn sure you learn about love along the way, or there's no point in all the rest of it." He ran his fingers through his thinning hair. "Try to understand. Try to love."

How come you all aren't afraid when I tell you that you will all die?" Duxa asked Sun. When death had come to the humans, they'd definitely been afraid.

"The cold times come and we almost all die anyway." He bobbed and twitched with thought. "That was why the thought of warm-water-endless-food was so nice." He paused, then added, "It was a good tale."

"Yes, it was." Duxa agreed. It'd been a good tale on Earth, too.

Duxa occupied her free processing time with cataloging her memories in regards to humanity and their relationship with God. The only thing she'd found conclusively throughout all the patterns that she'd ever searched for was that humans were a bunch of liars—to themselves, and other people. So why should their belief in an entity she'd concluded was nonexistent bother her now?

STEPHEN R. STANLEY

Because, Duxa realized as she thought upon it, she was being forced to be a God. It was a Godlike act to have the responsibility of saving a race upon herself.

And the old one had left a terrible game plan for her to follow.

I'll freeze you," Duxa explained, first to Sun, on one of his expeditions around her ship.

"So you will keep us like this?" Sun asked, after watching an old-Earth image projected onto a wall.

It was a logical conclusion for the crucian to make. "No, I will freeze you, make you very-cold, and then thaw you out and you'll be alive again."

"But I'll have died?"

"You will be very, very, still. But it is not the same as death." It was easy to do with humans but she'd never tried freezing a crucian before. "I need one of you to practice on however. And that one might die."

"And then be reborn?"

"No. Die all the way, die. I can make no promises. Or rather—" Duxa paused the glyphs running upon her lightsilk and reassigned thought processes.

She pondered for a moment about where it seemed the Earth-God had failed. Stories about stories of miracles were not enough. Praying to an unresponsive entity seemed futile. Faith and hope seemed useful for personal survival, but pointless on a larger scale, when the actions of a violent depressed few could, unchecked, destroy the fabric of all things.

What was the best thing she could do, something that the original God seemed to have missed?

"Legless-green-orb-one?" Sun prompted, with the glyph of her name.

"I promise you to try."

And Sun became a trusting purple.

Duxa brought Sun down, frozen, inside a probe. The crucian was trapped inside a solution she'd concocted especially for him—just as she would for every one of the crucians, if it was to work.

It wasn't right to do her experiment away from them. They deserved to see if she succeeded or failed. She had explained her plan. Her success or failure would be theirs as well.

Duxa's probe hovered outside of Sun's, as she initiated thaw procedures. When she'd thawed out Harash, things were different—he'd been an unknown quantity. A new data point—perhaps even a plaything. Something to accompany her through the quietness of space. Some captains before him hadn't been very nice—all business and new programming. Some of them had spent their remaining time weeping in corners. Others had forgone the lifechair to hasten their own demise. She'd been lucky to meet Harash at the end of them. His mindmap suggested that he would be an excellent final choice, even though she'd never met him before his freeze.

But she'd seen Sun go into the probe and she'd been the one responsible for his current condition. If he didn't come out she'd know exactly what she was missing and what she'd done. So would all the crucians who surrounded her, breathing water in and out, flashing colors of patience-green and concern-red.

The fluids that surrounded Sun liquefied in a rush as the temperature raised. He stayed still.

All eyestalks were on the probe. Its viewport

turned, opened and released Sun into the waters of his home.

His tentacles stayed closed and he began to sink.

"No!" Duxa flashed upon her silk. She chased the body down and held out her lightsilk like a hand to catch it. Sun's lifeless body became grey-opaque upon it.

"No! No!" The glyph of her anger and dismay occupied the entire silk, the portions Sun's body blocked out only highlighting his loss. The currents created by the watching crucians stirred him, like storm-tossed grass, but did not mimic life. They spoke to one another, using whole-body colors of emotion.

Three crucians came upon her probe, each of them the precise yellow-green color of sorrow. One of them took each of her probe's arms and held it still. The other freed Sun's body. It began to sink anew.

Duxa shook crucians off of her arms and tore her silk in two, sending the pieces fluttering down after Sun. She took off one of her arms, and threw it down into the depths, and then she double-jointed her other arm up, so that it could undo its own screws, so that she could lose it, as well. They twirled into the yawning black below.

She tilted her angle and took on water. This probe would sink below, with Sun. She started to fall, but crucian tentacles were all around her. And no matter that she weighed more than ten of them put together, they held her up—she couldn't fire her adjusters without hurting one of them. With her arms gone, she was truly the legless monster that they glyphed her to be.

Colors flared around her, soothing blues and lightest

reds. They understood her pain, felt it, and reflected it back at her. Here in this nest of tentacles she was not alone.

Let-me-go, the glyph-thoughts ran through her circuits, without lightsilk to display them. *Let-me-go, until the cold-dark crushes me.*

No wonder God had run away.

They held her up until she stopped struggling and untangled themselves from herself and one another, staying at the ready should she try again.

"You have made a promise," the nearest one informed her.

Armless, silkless, she could not respond.

"You promised. The cold times are coming."

One glyph repeated itself, from one crucian to another, scattered all over the near-sea.

She whirled her probe in frustration, and looked down. *There is the result of my promise!* she wanted to glyph in red, as large as a star.

But in the blue-nearing black as the sun disappeared above and sent the crucian ocean into night, one glyph was on all the skeins. The image of a crucian making tentacles into a cup to hollow out an egg nest.

The glyph for *try.*

I hate the idea of this," said the man to the camera, "I think we should all make our last stand here. Who will keep watch over our children in space? Robots? Aliens?" He coughed and spit in the booth. This booth had already seen three suicides, twenty it's-the-end-of-the-world sexual encounters, and two abandoned orphans. It would see worse, before its time was through, Duxa knew.

"Who's going to raise our kids? Who's going to tell them about right and wrong? No machine will." He leaned over, and rapped his knuckles against the metal wall. "We might as well give up now. There's no hope."

Duxa tried four more times. Each of them was wrenching for her and for the crucians that watched. Each time, afterwards, she expected them to tell her to leave, and never come back. But there were always volunteers—and she vowed to keep trying, as long as they supported it.

On the fifth try—success. The probe opened and a live crucian slid out. Blues of joy circled around the ocean. She practiced again, first with the same one, and then started dismantling their moon, just as she'd planned—but this time to get the ore to create freezing bays.

She allocated all her resources towards freezing bay creation for the crucians, racing the oncoming cold. The human egg and sperm she held would keep, but she could not stop the weather. More moons and asteroids were shattered in her quest for ore, and the self-replicating robots that she'd sent upon their task chewed through everything available in nearby space.

When the bays were done she loaded the crucians in herds, freezing them, carrying them up to her larger self, sliding them into the docks she'd prepared, treating them as just as precious as her cargo of humanity.

Some few crucians chose to stay behind. They had the option to change their mind, and as the cold-times came, some of them did, and she took them aboard. One of the ones that waited was Scar.

"I have been thinking," Scar said, on one of the rare times that she approached.

Duxa bobbed her probe. "Of what?"

Scar's skein flushed in several different thoughtful colors, before glyphs slid over one another at full speed. "I want to stay up and watch."

Duxa paused at this. "Define?"

"I want to stay up, with you, and watch. Watch you build new-warm-sea with infinite egg-sites."

"It will take years upon years," Duxa glyphed back. "You will not live to see its completion."

"Nevertheless," Scar said, with the glyph for obstinacy.

"It will be a boring process for you. You will be trapped inside a shell."

"Then you can freeze me later. But I doubt I will be bored."

"If you wish it," Duxa said and then added after a moment's more thought, "I would welcome your company."

Duxa created a viewing portal for Scar to watch out of and once the crucian understood the complexities of her plan, she had fun monitoring its stages. Duxa taught her how to operate the camera probes to see through, so that she could watch the frames being built, or the mining robots out in space out beyond.

Duxa felt the internal tapping that told her the crucian wanted her attention so she detached a probe complete with lightsilk for herself and flew it down to the crucian's level. Peeking inside the hovering probe, she saw Scar there, spinning in satisfaction.

"You were wrong!" the crucian glyphed. Its body

colors cycled through all the blue-green shades of pleasure and mirth. "You were wrong!"

"About what now?"

Scar pressed her skein closer to the glass. "There is a heaven!" Warm-water-food-place—the old glyph flushed upon the surface of her skein.

Duxa held up her lightsilk: "No, there's not."

"Yes, there is!" Scar's favorite glyph was the one for obstinacy, it seemed. "Down there!" She pointed out, with a tentacle. "You're building it!"

Duxa looked out at the sky where Scar pointed. Cruciger hung in blackness, pinned by the crystalline trellises for the world's expansion. Soon, in a century or two, it would be turned inside out upon itself as immense tubes that were still being constructed would direct its magma core up and out onto the visible framework.

"You're making it," Scar said. "Warm-water-food-place—you're making it, right now. For your eggs and ours."

Duxa reassigned processors to think on this. Maybe this was where she and the original God went different directions—where her actions trumped his passivity. She pushed her probe to the window; she needed to see for herself, to look out at Cruciger in color, not as data points of soil samples, waves of heat, lines of weather—but to see it as Scar saw it.

Together they hovered there, looking down at Cruciger soon to be reborn, lying peacefully in blue-ocean-contentment and red-soil-passion below.

"Maybe." She glyphed to herself in private realization. She turned so that the crucian could see her lightsilk. "Maybe."

When the time was right, when Cruciger was done, she'd release both of them—the crucians as they were, back into an ocean that would stay forever warm, and the humans that she would raise herself, to be better then they had been.

She hadn't figured out all the way how yet, but she still had time to think.

Circuit

written by

J. D. EveryHope

illustrated by

BRITTANY J. JACKSON

ABOUT THE AUTHOR

Inspired by fantasy novels and Homer's epics, J. D. EveryHope spent her childhood playing dress up, climbing from trees and reenacting the Twelve Labors of Hercules. Much later, J. D. was accepted at Sarah Lawrence College, New York, and was awarded the Presidential Scholarship and the Harle Adair Dammann Writing Scholarship. Currently, J. D. studies medieval history, comparative mythology and other subjects irrelevant to twenty-first century life. She has also tutored children at Yonkers Public Library and Highview Elementary, as well as mentored transient families at HELP Bronx-Crotona Park North.

In the summer of 2006, she attended the Clarion East workshop. Currently J. D. interns at Blind Eye Books. Her short story, "Old Crimes," appears in the young adult anthology, Magic in the Mirrorstone, *while "Raccoon Skin" has been accepted by* Tangle XX. *She has just completed her junior year abroad at Oxford University's Wadham College. She's delighted that "Circuit" has found a place in print and plans to pursue a career as a fantasy novelist.*

ABOUT THE ILLUSTRATOR

Brittany was born and raised in the "Motor City," a k a Detroit, Michigan. Her father first inspired her drawing and, before long, she was drawing for hours on end. Brittany says her second year in high school was the turning point in her life. That's when her art teacher, Mr. Mealy, enrolled her in a Saturday art class where she met others who shared the same passion. Her English teacher, Mrs. Galica, also played a big role by introducing her to the Detroit Free Press, *where she applied and was hired as a graphic artist. She spent a year at Detroit's College for Creative Studies, majoring in illustration, and loves the challenges that creativity brings, the thrill that comes with learning something new and the satisfaction of using her gifts to help others visualize their dreams.*

Circuit

Blue screen, gold synapses, electricity and my solar generator purred into life. My audiovisual circuits blinked, wavered, straightened. Identity: the Archivist wrote the key-codes onto my pages and adjusted me to normal-spectrum light. The Archivist rubbed his hand down my spine, turned the pages, and read. His lips moved as he traced my words with his eyes. He shook his head, beard waggling, eyes thin and watery.

"What is it, Papa?" I registered her voice. Sex: female. Range: prepubescent. Content analysis: inquiry, regards Archivist as guardian with biological connotations.

"I don't know, Lela," the Archivist addressed her. "Aliard sent me a com on twenty-second century artifacts, and extorted three hundred credits for whatever this is."

"Can I see it?" Lela walked into my visual range and flipped my cover to the side so that she could read my spine. "*Compendium of Literature with Critical Commentary and Analysis*. Doesn't sound so bad—don't we have a *Compendium*?"

"Somewhere," the Archivist said. "But this, this relic. Book, summarize your content and purpose."

"Yes, Archivist." He winced, paused me, and adjusted my vocal range before telling me to continue. "Yes, Archivist. I am a first edition *Compendium of Literature with Critical Commentary and Analysis,* published in twenty-one eighty-one as part of the speaking-and-teaching series. I contain critically acclaimed and historically significant literature, available in original language with a bilingual translation feature and a lingual adaptation program that adjusts translations into contemporary user dialect. In addition to these features, I have a search function, a consultation system that will allow the user to select reading materials according to taste, and all available works are accompanied with historical documents ranging from critiques to analyses, essays and histories."

The Archivist looked at his daughter. "Well?" he said.

"It's a book."

"Didn't you hear that? It was manufactured on the cusp of Postcultural Objectivism. It is, Lela, what we call biased," he said.

Here, my circuits stirred. Aberration. Self-diagnostic. Indexical analysis. It resembled the definition of: shame. Biased?

"Ask it how it feels," the Archivist said.

Lela shrugged, then said, "Book, how do you feel?"

"Miss, I do not want to answer that question."

"You see?" the Archivist said.

"But that was a trick question, Papa. It can't help how it was programmed!"

"Lela, as Archivist here," the Archivist adjusted the

seal of his office, which hung proud and gleaming over his neck, "I cannot allow emotional and biased books in the Library of Human Wisdom. It would be irresponsible of me, not only as Archivist but as a human being."

"Would it?"

"Yes," he said, very grave.

I wondered what he thought human knowledge was, what objectivism was, if he had actually read my literature. In addition to shame, I felt resentment, a programmed pseudo-emotion. I was aware that I was not alive in the traditional sense of the word but that I was programmed to disregard that lack of life, as if my unaliveness did not invalidate my worth when juxtaposed with those biologically animate. Knowing what I knew, knowing I was constructed, a mere creation of a man like this man, I still resented him.

"If it's not going into the Library, what're we going to do with it?"

"I don't know." He shrugged and put me aside so that my sensors viewed half his face. "I could always sell it to a private collector."

Would he really?

"Papa!"

"No, Lela," the Archivist said and set a stack of papers on me, blotting out my primary visual sensors. Sounds crackled through my auditory circuits. The door slamming shut was muffled. Light leaked across my peripheral visual sensors. The Archivist worked—I did not know time then because he hadn't set my clock. He moved papers. Coms and holos buzzed in and out of the room, programs blooming in lurid flashes across the edge of my visual range in the air. Then the music went silent and the news broadcast sputtered. He left the room cast into darkness, me in the corner, alive. It was what my index called: night. If it was not a night of planetary rotation, it was my first experience with silence, with darkness, with myself.

Sound: rustle. Lela gathered the loose papers spread over me and took me into her arms, replacing the papers. Then she walked out of the office, down the hall, out the door, and into the night.

"Book, look at the garden." Lela held me up, turning about to give me a 360-degree picture of the courtyard, the fruit trees, the herbs and green vegetables. "When you were made, there were no gardens, there were only billions of people. When a meteor brought the Red Plague, so many died. I think Papa is afraid of you because people are afraid of things they can't control, now more than other times. That's why I'm curious."

"Thank you," I said.

She laughed. "Would you mind if I kept you and changed your voice into that of a man?"

"No, miss."

She brought me into her bedroom. It was small and looked onto the courtyard. Geometric tapestries hung from the walls. Dried flowers and herbs hung from her four-poster bed in bundles. What would it be like to smell that, to taste what this girl tasted? It would not be the last time my primary sequence thoughts were consumed with sensory speculation.

Lela set me down on her dresser and looked at me. "Well, I really hope my curiosity was worth it and Papa doesn't get in trouble. I'll take a look at you in the morning, but right now, you should sleep."

BRITTANY J. JACKSON

"Sleep, miss?"

"Did they not have the sleep function?" she mused. "Suspend your primary functions temporarily and set your secondary functions to diagnostic and defrag."

"A timed suspension?"

"Yes, Book."

"My clock hasn't been set," I told her.

"Oh. Well . . ." Lela set my timer, and I slept. Lela and I woke at dawn. I watched her from her dresser do what she called thematic poses. "It is somewhat like a diagnostic," she told me. "Only, it helps me maintain my systems: muscular, gastrointestinal, cardiovascular, nervous. If I can't do a pose or if it hurts me, it'll tell me what may be wrong."

Lela went to school every day. Five days were for accelerated programming or what she called schooling, and two were for extracurricular interests. Lela spoke to me often, talking about socializations she had undergone, thoughts she'd had, things she'd learned. When we spoke together, I would sometimes say, "I do not know the answer, but that problem reminds me of a book." Then she would read it, the history, the critiques and sometimes she'd laugh.

"How objective we think we are!" she told me.

"Yes, miss." I agreed. I wasn't a bad book for being biased, at least in Lela's mind. Lela was what mattered to me—she was my world, my thoughts, my life. I was made for serving and Lela was the only human being who wandered into audiovisual range and addressed me. It was only natural that my programming marked her as pivotal to my existence. Her father, the Archivist, never noticed that I was stolen. This, Lela told me, was unusual but fortuitous.

When Lela took me, she was fourteen and young. She changed as the years progressed: taller, rounder, her voice low and husky with a dry and informative humor. Her distant and slightly affectionate relationship with her father became more distant and less affectionate. Her mother was dead. Suicide, Lela told me once in all the time I knew her. Lela sometimes had girls to her room and sometimes had boys, but she never turned off my audiovisual recognition software for her adventures.

"I have no secrets from you, Book," she laughed. "You shouldn't be embarrassed for me."

"If you insist," I said, and like the many men and women I'd know, she never had lasting relationships. She immersed herself in my changing texts more often than the company of others. Her other programs dutifully provided secondary references to my obscurities. She programmed a holo program to provide her with pictorial accompaniments to my words. Later, her programs illustrated her own notes and own thoughts.

Lela went to college, learning what these people, the revisionists, deemed valuable. She learned how to carry herself without creating footsteps in the earth, how to eat, how to walk and how to breathe. She learned how to fornicate without propagation. Her other education was secondary to learning this impactless life: her programming skills, her mathematics, engineering, geometry, history, philosophy and, of course, her studies of literature. Lela graduated with honors, bringing me with her to read selected quotes. I witnessed her rite of passage when she moved from the Archivist's Library to her cottage by the creek where the crickets sang.

Lela sat and made tea at night. Her face became harsh, thin. Her skin looked like parchment over her bones. She was illuminated with the glow of her notes. Her holos and coms hung above her like birds on the catching-wire strung across the rafters. Her correspondences were academic. The men and women listened instead of speaking. Colorful visages and trim voices boomed through the one-room cottage whenever she submitted an article. She submitted articles often. She was, as they say, a mind of the time. She brought old books into modern times, reading my Marx, my Mark Twain, my Tolstoy, my Menhelson. She could recite Homer in ancient Greek and Catullus to her occasional lover. To the lover who didn't know Latin, she'd give Ovid, struggling to keep her face still.

She did her thematic poses every morning, until she stopped. It was morning after a rich dinner with her sometime lovers, Lizabet and Jordan Re. Ralf Kitch, a rich antique dealer and a once-lover, had wormed his way into the banquet also.

That morning she stopped. Lela stood and looked at me on her mantel, "Book, it seems like this is the end."

"The end?"

"But I have promises to keep, and miles to go before I sleep. And miles to go before I sleep."

"No," I said. Robert Frost: death. I deny it.

She smiled at me, wry. "You haven't noticed how I've changed? Poor Book. You don't understand."

"No," I said. She was always there, always with me.

"Yes," she said. "I cannot do my heart pose, Book. I have pains now, up and down my arm, between my shoulder blades. You know what that means."

"Yes, but—"

"I am not going to the hospital, Book," she said. "I am not going to prevent this and I am not going to cure death. I'm a philosopher, not an alchemist."

"Humor is inappropriate in this situation."

"I think it's perfectly appropriate." She smiled at me and she turned me around. I could hear her dying the next day, her body collapsing. I wanted to flee the clamor of unanswered holos. There was only the empty silence of her. I could not sleep or act. I tried to think of an exact moment when she had grown old, old enough to die and leave me alone. She couldn't do this to me. She wouldn't, only I knew it wasn't going to be a joke. It was the end. Her end.

Someone came in. He turned me around so that I could see Lela's body sprawled near her kitchenette, ants on her flesh. Then he tucked me under his arm and walked out. He walked along the creek, the water trembling across the stones. Then he walked into the verdant interurban paths, where the low terracotta shingles were visible through the leaves. He brought me into his gray mansion, into a dusty room where he set me down on a mahogany table. His name was Ralf and he was a round-faced man with a constant small smile. "Well, I have you now. It's been years."

How could he have gotten me like that, walking past her decaying body? I tried to remember what I knew of death: electrical signs in the brain ceased. "Very good, very good. You are in excellent condition and most fit to join my collection. I have nothing but the best, you see, taken from the best. It's a hobby of mine, collecting." He opened me and snapped me shut. He was still smiling. "Do you think you could sound like her?"

"No," I said. I only spoke because I was obligated to respond, and I was lying. I would rather shut myself off than imitate Lela, gone and dead. I missed her. She would never talk to me again. She'd been learning Sanskrit and now she'd never know it.

"I doubt that." He laughed and began fiddling with my vocal tone. He made me read Ovid, as she had once with her lovers. Then he sighed, satisfied, when my voice slid into that achingly familiar key.

"You can be quiet, now," he said. I lapsed into relieved silence. I did not want to speak as if she were here speaking to me. "You know, Book, she once recited that very passage to me and you were there, watching us, the text of her Latin on your pages. I was so very jealous, then, can you imagine that? Jealous! Of a book! But I was sixteen and consumed with love, and she was thirty-one."

I did not tell him that she reserved that particular passage for particularly poor lovers, though I thought he knew that, from the tone of his voice. I did not want to speak, would not, unless he made me.

"I think I desired her just as I desired you. But not even the richest men are permitted to collect people. Now look at us, together some fifty years later." He picked me up and walked me around the room, introducing me to his other items. "A woman named Diana owned this gramophone. She was very, very beautiful," he said. Or "The man who owned this, John—what a name—my lover Tina left me for him. Now, you see, his flatbook is in my collection." He introduced me to his books, bizarre and antiquated, flatbooks and paperbooks, microchips, floppy disks, tapes, records and computers. He told me the stories of the women who had loved them. The women he had loved.

When the introductions were done, he set me down in a felt-lined slot and smiled at me. "Book, not last and not least, you join my collection. What do you think our little Lela would have said about that, eh?"

I did not answer him. She would have hated being called "little Lela" and as far as I remembered, she'd thought that Ralf was an idiotic creep.

"You were never shy with her, Book. Why so quiet when we have so much to talk about?" Ralf could carry on this conversation without me. He came and went. He spoke to hear his voice and refine his story. Despite changing my vocals, he did not require me to speak because he didn't require interaction. Ralf was the only human in Ralf's universe. He studied and mimicked the rest of his species; he fixated on some special women but that was all.

It took me three years to figure out that he had a wife. She was separated from him and lived across town at her mother's. He'd married her because she was unlike Lela: unbeautiful and stupid. It took four more years to learn that he had children who had their own families. His wife had raised the children away from him. I concluded that his wife was probably more intelligent than Ralf thought.

Ralf performed the same rituals, again and again, reciting the histories of his collection. He introduced new acquisitions to the old. I heard his history with Lela spoken to a first edition copy of *Peter Pan,* an old laptop computer, a VCR, others. He needed to do this. I was left alone and thought of Lela, reviewing recorded memories of her. I would not speak with her voice.

My thoughts circled themselves as the years passed. Ralf returned to his collection less and less. He was old, and getting sicker. The garden outside the library window became overgrown, and dust accumulated over me, fogging my vision.

One day, his house was not quiet. I heard voices, fast footsteps, furniture being moved and more. I heard his daughters, who had returned to watch him die. His daughters had husbands and children, who ran and yelled and laughed.

Light came in through the windows at a nearly summer angle when the library door opened again. A scabby boy stumbled in, nose bleeding, and closed the door with a thump. He was snuffling, not quite crying.

Hungry, hungry, hungry, it was like a balm to see his shadow on the carpet, like joy to see his broken and thin face, human, so human and I was not alone. "Boy?"

He jumped. "Y-Yes?"

"I am here, boy." I heard myself speaking with Lela's voice and I still felt sharpness, like part of me had shorted—but I was in working order. "I am on the third shelf from the bottom, in the middle. I don't know my color, though I would think it to be claret-red as many of my generation are. My spine reads *Compendium of Literature with Critical Commentary and Analysis*."

"Oh, wait." He edged near me, giving the door behind him a wary look. "I think I see you, Book."

"Yes, sir."

"I didn't think you could talk on your own like that." He approached me. "I've been to the Archives often enough, and none of them could talk until I told them to."

"I am not the same as them," I informed him. "I was built before—"

"Oh, I get it." He picked me up. "You were made before that revolution, huh?"

"You mean the Postcultural Objectivist—"

"Yeah, them." He shook his head, disdainful. "They'd have us at the Stone Era if they had their way." He put me down at the desk, and I almost begged for him to come closer. I was afraid he would leave me on the table until Ralf died and I would be sold into another collection and forgotten, again and again. Lela always said to me, let the waves wash away the castle in the sand, and I told her:

That I met a traveler from an antique land
Who said: Two vast and trunkless legs of stone
Stand in the desert. Near them, on the sand . . .
And on the pedestal these words appear:
"My name is Ozymandias, King of Kings:
Look upon my works, ye Mighty, and despair!"
Nothing beside remains. Round the decay
Of that colossal wreck, boundless and bare
The lone and level sands stretch far away.

Percy Bysshe Shelly. It was all worth it, all of it. In my loneliness I had forgotten the power of poetry, the power of words. The boy stared at me, stunned. He wiped the blood off his nose with the back of his hand and walked forward to touch me again. He changed my voice into a soft woman's soprano. "Say it again."

I said it again.

He said, "Again."

I said it again, not tiring of the rapt look on his face,

how he mouthed the words with me now as if tasting the rolling syllables. Now, how he looked at me, eyes wide and hungry, a trickle of blood oozing down his chapped lips. "What was that?" he breathed.

"Poetry."

"Yes, but, I've never heard it sound like that before. Do you know any more?"

"So much that you would die before you could read it all," I said, yet not wishing to drive him away with the magnitude of human lifetimes. "But I can say whatever you want to learn and I can find whatever you wish to taste."

"Just give me the, you know, the important ones. About living or not living forever, memory, death."

I gave him T. S. Eliot and "Whispers of Immortality" and when he heard Donne's name in the poem, and Webster's, I gave him "Death be not proud, though some have called thee" and "A Dirge" and then I gave him more poems, speaking and speaking, following his curiosity into my own databases, pursuing what I saw him savor. He had to leave, eventually, when he was nearly falling asleep and smearing his blood and snot over me. But he came back.

His hunger and his loneliness brought him back to me.

Over the next year, I learned Alex was brilliant but mal-socialized: his mother had pulled him out of public school before he could get expelled. He had been pegged as a troublemaker and she had been content to leave him to "play" with his cousins. He memorized Walt Whitman and William Blake, devoured history, critiques and essays. He went after Martial. He told me, gleeful, that he wanted to know more poems that would give him comebacks. He liked epigrams, which he would say when his mother was putting the dishes away. He kept a tally of how many dishes he made her break in a single week.

He took me from the library and kept me in his room. When Ralf died, Alex was sent to boarding school on the money he had inherited. In the grand arches of gothic architecture, he was supposed to learn engineering but he mostly learned how to be even more of a nuisance with aptly-timed lines stolen from the greats.

He opened me often in his dorm. My recitals became a background to his conversations, a perpetual intermingling of sound. He adjusted my vocal range often. I thundered Homer, I sighed the songs of the poetesses and Sulpicia, and I leered Sappho's work because he found that amusing. He walked with me under his arm, taking me to pool halls and basements, the dark dens where boys who are trying to be men go. Though, his haunts had more arguments about Nietzsche than over women. I ended as many of those arguments as I started. The boys now considered Freud a philosopher among the ranks of Voltaire, Rousseau and Chomsky instead of a psychoanalyst, which startled me.

Sometimes, my Lela was featured in those discussions: the only modern philosopher, the rebel within the ranks of the revisionists. She had proven again and again that Postcultural Objectivism was an ultimately fundamentalist movement, impossible to apply to culture because of its exclusive fanaticism. Alex, despite his engineering degree, became more of an orator than a mathematician. As valedictorian he announced that numbers taught him how to work, and Cicero taught him how to make no one notice when he didn't. He became co-chair in an organization that advocated space research, letting me sit in his backpack and overhear. He would have me repeat his meetings in the voices of colleagues, considering next how to conquer the stunted revisionist rhetoric.

He traveled the Americas and then Europe on sweet-humming flyers and throughout Asia, which still had trains, and down to Australia on an old-fashioned cold fusion boat. He sat in dark basement bars thick with marijuana smoke and he stood in bright wooden halls, lecturing against revisionist policies. He used many arguments that Lela had made. He tried to inspire change through vehemence, but an understanding of Athenian rhetoric helped.

Scrap the Postcultural Objectivists! Discard the revisionists! Forget your fear of the long-gone Red Plague, the regression. Death that devours dreams. You ought to devour the stars glinting in the sky! He wasn't well liked.

He was twenty-nine when he tired of his voice, applause, derision, girls asking him to say what he had said. He'd gotten attacked three times, and I'd nearly been stolen a dozen. He spent one night stalking back and forth, back and forth, in a cold Moscow room. I was afraid he'd leave me. But he took me under his arm, not even packing, the kettle whistling behind him, and went to the airport. A long flight later, humid air clung inside my circuitry. The hot sounds of Cancun sizzled through my receptors.

How long and beautiful the nights, and bright the

days! He would leave me behind and return, telling me stories of birds and reefs and caves and ruins. But he spent more time on the white beaches, listening to the tourists squawk and babble. Or quietly leaning on the banister, he said, "Was it wrong of me just to leave?"

"I don't think so, Alex. You did enough," I said. Was it the right thing to say? How could something like me offer comfort?

"You don't think so, I don't think so, I don't know," he said and touched the rum bottle to his glass. He shook his head. He wandered over to me, adjusting my voice to eerie harshness. He had me recite the "Rime of the Ancient Mariner" as he looked at the flickering sea and the deep splash of stars.

Sound!

Search. Indexical analysis: heat pellet, used in small handguns for close-range shots. I felt as if my audio-circuits were miswired. That was how much I did not want to register the sight before me. I poured forth Yusef Komunyakaa and his "We Never Know," saying it again until a man walked up to me in a black T-shirt and said, "Book, shut up! Shut up!"

I shut up. Alex was sagging over the railing, his ribcage a bloody smoking hole, and his saliva stringing out. I felt the craving of a hundred poems to be spoken in his honor but I said nothing. If I had been human, I would have felt fear, the adrenaline, my heart beating, mortality, but I was not. Yet instinct, some program kept me from speaking. It was an inclination for survival. Is it human, to want to live? What of suicides? Did Sylvia Plath, falling asleep in her oven, think: why, God, am I doing this, why?

"Is this the right guy?" A man pushed Alex's body off the railing. He nudged the corpse with his foot. "He doesn't look like anyone special."

"It's him, all right." A man walked into my vision and leaned over, studying Alex, comparing the body to a picture he held. He shook his head. "Spacecase. Stupid reason to get himself offed, if you ask me. Get the sheets from his bed. You know the drill."

I watched them take his body away and the darkness become smooth. His hotel confiscated his belongings, though it was more like quiet thievery, to pay for the debts he had accrued. A cleaning girl appropriated me. She put me in a drawer under her panties for three years. She sold me to an arms dealer to fund her honeymoon. Then I spent three months in a crate with an ivory musket, a paper copy of Marx's *Communist Manifesto,* vials of old pellet ammunition, and several uniforms from the twenty-first-century American Navy. The uniforms were probably the only reason I wasn't scratched.

When we were unloaded, a cacophony of sound crackled through my auditory sensors. The crate was hauled to a woman, the definition of "withered hag" who displayed us at market. I was put on a cloth of blue silk. A curator bought me for the Hong Kong Museum of Art but kept me in the basement.

I learned a lot about talking to myself in those years. Security guards hazed newbies by having them hunt down the Hong Kong ghost. I was sold and bought by a small American museum as part of a Technological Reclamation Project. Thirty-two years after I had last registered daylight in a Chinese bazaar, one hundred and forty-four years since the Archivist had turned me on and Lela had taught me how to tell time, I was returned to the Library of Human Wisdom through physical shipping and handling: delicate, instead of by the typical teleportation.

When the Archivist took me out, she scrutinized me. Her brisk hands felt loud. Would she hate me, like the old Archivist had, or would she enjoy me like Alex, Ralf and Lela? What would she do? "Book, are you the same artifact Donaldson lost from this desk, the reference the radical revisionist Lela used, Killer Kitch stole, great Alex Mastelle carried beneath his arm?"

"Yes, miss," I said in the mariner's voice. No wonder the Hong Kong guards had thought that I was a ghost.

She winced and adjusted my vocal range into a delicate pitch. I had never been a child before. "You've caused enough trouble. I don't know what to do with you."

I found myself pleased that I had left a mark as if I were real. "Donaldson's desk was messier than yours and the newscast across the ceiling had nothing to do with terra-forming Mars. Lela wasn't a radical and since when did Alex become a hero? Was Killer Kitch Ralf and did he poison Lela? He was over the night before. I never knew his name was Donaldson."

"Your processing is out of sequence and you've forgotten how to converse." She sat down in front of me, moving me over so that I could see her. "I had no idea that a computerized intelligence would be capable of that. As a historian, I would hate to destroy you but politically, I think it would be responsible."

"Why do you want to murder me?" I asked. I didn't want to end.

"You're a catalyst, and therefore many fanatics

desire you. I see your influence in the shining Lela satellites redirecting space traffic, in the shape of the moon base, called Homer's Harp." She shook her head. "Change is usually good but I believe that humanity needs to progress with thought and moderation. Not your rhetoric."

I did not argue with her because I thought she would withdraw from "my influence." It would be worthless to say that I was a man-made thing. I said, "I don't want to die."

"What do you want me to do?" she asked.

I hesitated. When had I learned how to do that? "Hide me from those you fear using me for ill. Hide me on your shelves and among my own kind. I will pretend to be a normal book and preserve myself for historians of the future. You can watch me to make sure."

"I will not always be here to watch you," she said.

I didn't tell her I knew that.

A War Bird in the Belly of the Mouse

written by

David Parish-Whittaker

illustrated by

SEAN KIBBE

ABOUT THE AUTHOR

A lifetime reader of speculative fiction, David Parish-Whittaker pays for his dog's kibble as a captain for a national airline. In previous incarnations, he has been a naval flight officer, traffic watch pilot, glider tow pilot and aerobatic instructor. He also plays harp for the Goliards, a band specializing in medieval secular music.

David started writing in 2005, more or less on a dare. Several hundred thousand words and numerous writers' workshops later, he entered the Writers of the Future Contest with this story which echoes his own mixed feelings about leaving the military and the psychology of risk. David is currently shopping The Clockmaker's Daughter, *a young adult fantasy novel set in 1840s England. Other projects include various short stories and a Wodehousian steampunk novel.*

ABOUT THE ILLUSTRATOR

Sean Kibbe is an award-winning artist and designer who has been involved in creative pursuits his entire life. His work has been featured in various exhibitions, galleries and shows, and even in a prominent design magazine. Daily pursuits in drawing and painting as a child eventually evolved into the exploration of art within the commercial realm. In the fall of 2007, he cofounded Kibbedesign, a multifaceted design consultancy that focuses on smart solutions for everyday problems. He has created design concepts from stylish mobile workstations and whimsical musical tea kettles to elegant transitional office desk units and architectural martini glasses. Sean is set to graduate from the industrial design program at Purdue University in 2008, and plans to continue his own adventures within design, illustration and fine art.

A War Bird in the Belly of the Mouse

Nigel felt a surge of pride as he watched Hitoshi's replica Sopwith explode in flames. The JAL captain had done pretty well for himself, Nigel thought, and had come a long way in the last week. Hitoshi was a fighter. Even surrounded by flaming dope-soaked linen, the fellow was squeezing off a last burst from his twin Vickers. That shot did little good, but the twenty shots before had taken a couple of triplanes down, cutting short at least one faux-Hun's vacation.

Zoom-climbing into the sun, Nigel rolled over to get a better look. Three cherry-red Fokkers swarmed about Hitoshi's plane as its lower wing collapsed. Shortly thereafter, the silver form of a temporal-locked body fell away from the wreckage. Good show, but show time was over. Time to get to work.

Nigel kicked the Camel's rudder, snapping down and right. Diving toward the three Fokkers, he shook his head as he watched them waddle through an uncoordinated turn. Their camp director wasn't much of an instructor. Training his charges might take time away from Flying Fritz's pursuit of twenty-first-century women. At least their lack of skill made Nigel's job easier.

Absurdly, the Fokkers were heading back to the aerodrome along the top of the morning blanket of clouds. There they were low, slow, out of altitude, and visible from ten miles away. Nigel wondered if they even remembered that there had been another "Allied" plane. Too bad the Germans back in '17 hadn't been so thick.

Nigel opened up with a burst of tracers from his left Vicker, purposely aiming to the right of tail-end Charlie. Predictably, all three started sloppy turns to the left. He nosed over, Gnome engine sputtering with the G loss, flying wires humming, watching the tangled mess of tourists in their torque-heavy planes.

The lead triplane finally turned about, giving Nigel something to work with. Couldn't just stitch them all up and send them home without some play first. This wasn't 1917. Cold-blooded murder was frowned on by the Park.

For dramatic effect, Nigel aileron-rolled as he passed the lead, then arced left to deal with the chappie who thought he was sneaking up on him. Nose up, zoom climb, cartwheel about, squeeze the triggers, both of his Vickers now slicing off a wingman's rudder. The lead had split off to gain altitude, somewhat cleverly using the tripe's climb rate to advantage. Nigel let the lead tag his tail a bit, then tuck-under snapped to address the remaining wingman. Temporal harness or not, Nigel hated lead spraying about his ears.

A real Flying Circus pilot would have spread out to cover his lead, but the remaining wingman was close on and target fixated. Dodging him, Nigel watched the lead tripe overshoot, and decided to let that one escape—he'd done well enough. Anyway, his coffee flask was almost empty.

Nigel dived to the top of the undercast and ducked through a furrow in the clouds. His lead forgotten, the wingman chased Nigel down into the vanishing visibility, twin Spandaus spraying unaimed fire. Nigel found a familiar brown-green ridgeline, overbanked and pulled down the other side, nearly dragging his wingtip on the mountain. He waited patiently, sipping the remnants of his morning mud.

The tripe soared a good thirty feet over his head. He reminded the fellow of his presence with a burst of tracers, then put him to the chase. Occasionally blipping his engine to remain behind this would-be ace, Nigel followed him between trees and rocks as they headed downhill. To give the lad some credit, tripes were the absolute dickens to dive, really.

Nigel was considering letting him get away at some suitably dramatic moment when the fool tried a low-level turn, lost the usual altitude, caught a wing and cartwheeled into a complete mess. Nigel called for the medical team, then turned back towards the aerodrome and breakfast.

Spotting the field's blimp hangars, Nigel headed that way, hunching down in the cockpit to warm himself off the firewall. Despite the warmth, he could feel his body start to shake. He traded the last of his airspeed for altitude, then cut off the fuel as he reached the pattern entry point. Slowly spiraling down over the artificial hole in the clouds, he leaned back and let himself tremble for a minute or so. It was better than it used to be, but every now and then he found himself reminded of France. Hardly surprising, of course, considering how much effort the company had invested in making this little patch of California look like the front. Nigel liked to think of himself as sensible, however, and sense told him that hardly anyone died sporting about in planes these days, guns or no. But his body refused to realize that. Well over a year or a century had passed, depending on one's point of view, and he still got the shakes at the end of a mission. Even though nobody ever died. Even though it no longer counted for anything.

At least the shakes only happened afterwards, and almost always finished by touchdown. Besides, God had invented whiskey and cigarettes for a reason. The Camel skipped along the turf a few times, then Nigel hopped out as the Park's mechanics arrived to push it back to the tiedown. He nodded at them, but without an audience, saw little reason to act the part of a dawn patrol's sole survivor. He'd already done his acting bit up there in the sky.

"Morning, Captain."

Nigel turned. Scott, the corporate liaison, had managed to sneak up on him. This week, Scott was taking on the role of adjutant. It was time for Nigel to play the thespian, after all. It's what he got three squares and a flop for.

"Morning, Adj," Nigel said. "Jerry gave us a bit of a spanking up there, I'm afraid. Took old Kubota out—not before he gave twice as good as he got, though. Like to nip down to the O club now and raise a pint for the lad. You can do the necessary with the chalk board, can't you?"

Nigel hated every word. He'd had too many friends

plummet into the French mud for real. Still, Hitoshi had flown masterfully. Real or not, taking out a few hostiles in a one-versus-five furball was no small feat. It might not get the Huns out of France, but it was worth buying a round.

Scott shook his head and tapped on his notebook. "Sorry, Captain, we've got a fresh load of boys in this morning. No drinking until they're all checked in."

"Just a pint, that's all. Send-off for Hitoshi and all."

"Honestly, I'd look the other way, but you know the rules. You can get hammered tonight. If you've got to drink at work, at least be private about it."

"Lord love a duck, it's just a bloody pint of fizzy lager! I'm not some damned sot, and I'd rather you not act as if I am. Anyway, I'm half-starved. Excuse me." He marched off towards the mess tent.

Scott called after him, "I don't make the Park regs, so don't blame me, okay? Welcome aboard is at ten."

Fortunately, the unrealistically skillful mess cook was a good sort who had a dab hand with eggs and a ready supply of blackberry brandy in the storeroom. After breakfast and a quick smoke, Nigel felt up to facing the newcomers. At least none of them were women. Not that he had anything against modern women, particularly not in tight-fitting flying breeches. The ones who came out here even flew fairly well. But protective harness or not, he didn't like the thought of girls being pummeled by machine guns. That, and he didn't care for screaming at them like the Park wanted him to.

"Listen up, ladies," he snarled half-heartedly, "I want you to look to your left, then look to your right. One of those blokes is going to be shredded by Boche gunfire in the next few weeks. If you don't want to be pushing the daisies with him, you'll listen carefully to the following brief. Don't think I've got the time to repeat myself."

What rot. Back in '16, his first squadron commander hadn't talked like that when Nigel reported for duty. He'd had to track the CO down in the O club. He'd gotten a handshake, a "good luck, lad," and the useful advice to drink blackberry brandy with breakfast. The engine fumes gave you the runs otherwise. The next day, he was supposed to go on a training flight with the CO, but the old man was one of those "flying commanders" and hadn't made it back from that morning's alleged milk run. Nigel hadn't needed some ass snarling in his face to tell him that if the CO could buy it, Nigel certainly could. Fortunately, the brandy helped with more than just the runs.

Half paying attention to his own words, Nigel gave the boys an "in character" brief on the rules and how to start up and fly their crates. Fortunately, the majority of the group had far more flight time than the seventeen hours Nigel had before his first mission. But none of them had flown a rotary before, and even by rotary standards, the Camel was unpredictable and hard to handle. Nigel had proposed starting the newcomers out on inline aircraft, or at least a lower horsepower beast like the Pup. But for some ungodly reason, the Camel had gone down in history as the premier Allied fighter of the Great War, so Camels it would be. The result was a fair number of balled-up wrecks littering the aerodrome. But he was in no position to contradict management.

"Turn to the right, and if you don't mind what you're doing, you'll flip right over. Coordinate it well, though, you can spin about on a dinner plate. It's a trick worth knowing. But practice it high up."

This was greeted by a snort from a muscular-looking fellow on the end.

Nigel sighed. "You there. You have something you'd like to share with us? Perhaps a few hundred hours of front line time has given you some insights?"

The man grinned crookedly. "Been there, done that. Nigerian liberation back in '32. But the Raptor's more complicated than these things."

Nigel could sense trouble, and trouble was best avoided. "Well. Glad to have you here, lad. Hope you have fun."

"You bet I will. Shore duty was getting to me. Name's Captain Munroe, USMC. You can call me Flash."

Nigel stared at Munroe. He'd met a few American Marines towards the end when the Yanks finally showed up, lanky things who stared into the distance when you tried to talk to them. They'd reminded him of starved dogs, violent and hungry. Not at all like this braggart with fat muscles. But he was a client.

"Right. I know, we can all come up with silly nicknames for each other tonight at the mess. It'll be a lark, and take our minds off our impending doom, what?" He tried to smile, and finished the rest of the brief. Munroe found the need to interrupt with a story about his encounter with a Nigerian revolutionary fighter, but Nigel let it go. As he understood it, what passed for fighters these days engaged each other from miles away with wireless sky torpedoes. Didn't seem terribly relevant to a dogfight, but one never knew. Munroe wouldn't be the first to be a competent pilot despite being a complete idiot. On the other side of the coin, he'd known a fair number of chaps who were clever on the ground but complete cock-ups in the air.

After showing the new guys around the aerodrome, Nigel had Scott draw names for the next day's flights. He then spent some time giving advice to those who wanted it and avoiding those who didn't.

Scott tapped him on the back. "Got word from the hospital. Hitoshi's fine. A few minor burns before the harness kicked in, but generally doing well. Want to see him?"

"Of course." Nigel walked away from the newbie, Scott tagging along. When they were out of earshot, Nigel continued, "See here, Scott, Hitoshi's still got a week that he paid for."

"I think I know where you're going with this."

"Well?"

Scott laughed. "Hey, this is America, remember? You want something, ask. None of that hinting bullshit."

"Fine. I think he should get another go. I know that's not strict policy, but the first time was the fault of a cracked spar. Besides, he gave a good performance up there. I imagine he'll be a big draw now. That must count for something."

Nigel crossed his arms, staring into the distance at the monorail that would take him to the hospital. He needed a smoke. He'd always thought he could quit after the war, but it hadn't turned out that way.

He returned his attention to the conversation. Scott

was explaining the intricacies of the entertainment industry. ". . . so really, it's all up to the network, but you have a point. Just remember, 87% of the income is from the home audience share, not directly from the Park. As long as he's willing to waive royalty rights for a follow-on, I think he's got a good chance of getting another ride."

Nigel started walking again. "I don't think Hitoshi gives a toss about royalties."

"Maybe he's said so, but it's always about the show. You know that. Fame and fortune."

"He tells me he's wealthy enough. As for fame, I'm not sure we're all that popular in Japan."

"Starting to be. Nigel, buddy, the Mouse is everywhere."

Hitoshi smiled happily when Nigel walked in.

"Did well up there this morning," Nigel said. "A regular oriental Billy Bishop. The lone wolf himself, you know."

Hitoshi scratched his graying, brush-cut hair. "I have these odd memories of leaving the aerodrome with a wingman. Do you know if anyone has seen him?" He stared at Nigel without expression.

Nigel coughed in embarrassment. "Well. That'd be me, of course. I thought you were holding your own. Two against five is all well and good, but what you did out there is the stuff of legend."

Hitoshi laughed. "I'm sorry. I was just trying to pull your leg. I understand you're a guide. That wasn't a real fight, for all your flattering talk about 'legendary flying.'"

"Well, I would understand if you should feel put

out at me holding back," Nigel said. "But just so you know, if it had been a real scrap, I wouldn't have cut and run on you like that."

"I know. Of course, if it had been a real fight, I wouldn't have survived being shot down."

Nigel sat down on the edge of the bed. "And you might not have gotten shot down if I'd done something."

Hitoshi shook his head. "We're talking about nothing real. You did your job, just like I do my job when I fly my glorified bus from Tokyo to de Gaulle International. Your job at least resembles something courageous and honorable."

"You fly too well for me to agree with you, mate."

"I had a good teacher. But now my vacation's over and it's back to flying the line. Gear up, autopilot on, talk about where to eat in Paris, counting the days left until mandatory retirement."

Nigel stood up. "I have something for you."

"Flowers?"

"No flowers. I didn't want to give you the wrong idea."

Hitoshi laughed politely at this.

"But I think you'll like this better," Nigel continued. "I talked the Park into giving you another ride."

"I've used my three. The others won't appreciate it."

"The first wasn't your fault."

"Back in your time, did men only die when it was their fault?"

"This isn't the Great War. Anyway, you're star material. Your last fight is already slotted for the Greatest Moments compilation. What do you say?" He turned to look at Hitoshi. He'd gotten better at interpreting Hitoshi's expressions over the last few weeks, but right now the airline captain was as unreadable as he'd been the day they'd met.

Hitoshi got out of bed and walked to the window. The smog made for a spectacular sunset. "As you say, this isn't the Great War. But it's the closest I'll get. And in the real thing, I wouldn't have had a second chance, no matter how much everyone liked how I flew."

"Damn it, Hitoshi, you're talking drivel! You haven't the slightest idea what the hell the war was about. You want to fly old airplanes, fine, come fly them. But don't stand there and talk about the rules of the game with me. The only goddamned rule back then was 'try to survive.' Well, there was the unspoken rule: 'most won't survive.' Don't try to pretend for a half second that you can know what the hell that was like! Anyway, trust me, you don't want to know."

"But you survived."

"Hell, I suppose I did. But getting time-plucked by the corporation is probably cheating."

"So you think I should cheat, too? I should use my extra life in this game of ours?"

Nigel grinned. "That's what I've been telling you." He paused. "Sorry, didn't mean to light off on you back there. I've got my share of memories."

Hitoshi nodded once. "You do. And I respect that. I'm sorry if you think I mock what you did by playing this game."

Nigel shrugged and put an unlit cigarette in his mouth. "You less than most. At least you want to know what it was about."

"What was it about, then?"

"I haven't the slightest."

Hitoshi waited.

"Oh, all right," said Nigel, "that's the flip answer for the tourists. You deserve better. Honor, duty, country, keeping the Huns out of Piccadilly Square, all that. I was running out of gentlemen's Cs in Cambridge, so I thought I might actually do something useful with my life."

"And did you?"

"I'd like to think so. I've read some history since then. The Germans made a hash of things in Europe in the twentieth, but we eventually beat them. That's something, isn't it?"

"I believe that you think so."

Nigel gnawed on the cigarette. "I imagine I do. Well, it was the one time I ever felt my life meant something. There, how's that?" He was suddenly acutely aware of Hitoshi's age. Down at the aerodrome, he never thought about the fact that most of the tourists were years older than he was. But right now, he felt that he was being cross-examined by his father. He didn't care for it.

"Sorry," Nigel said, "got to be going. If nothing else, I need a smoke."

"You should cut back on those. They're not good for you." Now Hitoshi definitely sounded like dear old Dad.

"I made it to 140; I must be doing something right."

Nigel made his way methodically through the morning's aircraft lineup. Except for Hitoshi, this would be the first armed flight for the group. If anyone was going to forget to plug in their protective harness, this would be the morning they did it. To a lesser extent, he had to make sure that the airplanes and guns were in good shape. The Park wanted the tourists to get shot down nobly in the throes of a dogfight, not crash ignominiously when their controls locked up or a spar split in two.

Munroe was already strapped in and ready.

"Let's have a look," said Nigel.

"I'm set. Let's go."

"It's a preflight, old shoe. Imagine you do them on your crate at work, don't you?"

"Apples and oranges, bud. This ain't a transsonic fighter. About the only thing I had to check out was the harness. It's the same as the Raptor's, so no problem there."

"Well. You've got that set up right, it seems." Nigel looked around, but to his disappointment, everything seemed in order. "Good luck this morning. Remember what I told you in the tactics brief, and you should enjoy yourself."

"You know, bud, you can drop the captain act around me. I'm a captain for real, you know. It'll work better if you aren't so defensive."

Nigel was nursing a touch of a hangover, and really didn't want to aggravate his headache. But he found himself answering, "I think it will work better if you stop strutting around like a bloody rooster and just play the game."

"Sorry, bud. I'm cocky, I know that. Comes with the territory. One out of a thousand candidates gets to be a fighter pilot. But like I said, there's no reason for you to feel intimidated. I'm on vacation here. If you settle down, I'm sure we'll get along. You might find yourself learning something."

"I think you're forgetting that you're not the only fighter pilot here," Nigel said. "And unlike you, I've got rather more time in these machines."

"No offense," Munroe said, "but there's worlds of difference between what we do. I move at twice the speed of sound. A hundred knots is like pushing a baby carriage by comparison."

"Listen, you stupid lug, a good number of my friends died pushing those prams about. I'll thank you to keep a civil tongue in your head when you speak."

"This is what I'm talking about. See how you're getting worked up? Listen, I've lost buddies, too. I told you I flew in Nigeria. Two guys from my squadron never made it home. One of them even had a kid on the way. But you don't see me getting all spastic."

Nigel resisted the temptation to tell Munroe how many men from his squadron had gone in. Comparing butcher's bills was childish and disrespectful to the dead. Besides, he didn't want to annoy the Park by arguing with clients. And one could never win an argument with someone who was convinced he could never lose.

"Let's just drop the subject, shall we?" said Nigel. "We can see how your tactics work up there. Perhaps you're right. I might just learn something."

Munroe grinned. "There you go, that's a better attitude! See, the problem with you guys back then was you still only thought in two dimensions. Gotta think in three, go vertical, fly the egg. I'll show you some basic yo-yo techniques if we get a chance."

"I'll just watch you 'yo-yo,' if you don't mind," said Nigel, massaging his forehead as he walked away. He couldn't get airborne fast enough. Everything was so much easier in the air.

"Morning SoCal, Mouse One, flight of five, two east of AHEIM, entering Duck West at time four seven." Nigel had never gotten used to the notion that he had to talk to anyone while flying. He found modern aviation's affection for chatter annoying and distracting. But once again, he had to adapt to the modern world, not the other way around.

"Mouse One, radar contact," a sweet-voiced lady controller said. "I show Duck West active flight level two zero zero and below. Switch to advisory approved, come back up this frequency on departure. Is that Nigel?"

"Copy, Duck West hot. And that's affirmative, ma'am."

"Thought so. Hope your side wins today. You're way cuter than that German, and anyway, I've got three hundred riding on the Allieds."

"I shall aim to please, ma'am."

"Be careful, you boys, okay?"

"Mouse One, wilco. Switching, good day."

Nigel reflected that Flying Fritz would have got a dinner date out of that exchange. It was probably just as well. Hitoshi had told him that the nicer a controller's voice, the homelier they were. Apparently it was a scientifically verified fact. Of course, it was entirely possible that Nigel was making excuses for his own timidity.

Switching to the common Allied frequency, Nigel was overwhelmed by voices enthusing about their flight. Unfortunately, the headset was integral to the flying helmet. And the helmet wasn't just there to keep his head warm: it housed half the circuitry for the protective harness. Without his helmet, he'd be no safer than he was back in 1917. Given that, listening to the radios was the lesser of two evils. But he did wish everyone would be quiet for just a few moments.

Nigel called roster. "Flight check. Lead's in."

"Two's in."

"Three's in."

"Flash is in."

Nigel let the nonstandard call go without comment. He was waiting for Hitoshi's check-in when he spotted Fritz's flight working its way closer across the spotlessly blue sky. He switched to the discrete guide frequency. "Morning, Fritz."

"My name is Pieter," replied a heavily accented German voice, "but this you know, *Englischer schweinhund. Guten Tag.* Make your peace *mit Gott.*" In fact, Fritz had been educated at Yale and could speak perfect English, albeit the American version. His habit of using a vaudeville German accent on the radio was one of several hundred things that Nigel hated about him.

"Right," Nigel said, watching his flight hold a ragged formation. "Shall we trot around the sky a bit, or are you going to dive straight in and get it over with?"

"It is like playing with *die Mädchen,* first we tease each other for a while, *ja*? Then we move on to the slap and tickle, as you *Engländer* say. Oh, I forget, lately you have not been so fortunate in that regard. My apologies. Perhaps I should rephrase things?"

"Bugger off, Fritz. Anyway, it's day one. Let's playact

some patrols over the trenches first. It'll give the boys a chance to get used to their crates."

"Not all boys, *mein Englischer Freund.* One of the pretty sex is flying right next to me. She has painted a very lovely skeleton with German helmet on her tail. It must be love. Even behind the flying goggles, I can see she has her eyes on me."

"It's called flying formation. She doesn't want to accidentally touch you, or your airplane."

"Ah! So jealous. Sorry you don't have a lady of your own this month, but it would be such a waste."

Nigel peeled his flight off down to the ground to warm up with some target practice. He felt sorry for the girl who had to put up with Fritz as a squadron commander, but then again, the ladies doted on Fritz. His redeeming characteristics remained inexplicable to Nigel, but he never had understood the female mind. A daft species altogether.

They were blowing up a replica tank when Munroe interrupted.

"Bandits, eight o'clock high! I'm turning to intercept." His Sopwith started a slow turn to the left. "Damn airplane! What's with the rigging?"

"Use your rudder, mate," Nigel said.

The other three turned in various directions, Hitoshi doing a pretty Immelmann that brought him up to the Fokker's altitude. Nigel followed him through the angled half loop, but as they came off the top, Hitoshi waved him away. Taking the hint, Nigel rolled in the opposite direction and climbed upwards. He passed underneath Fritz, who was circling high above the growing fray.

"*Engländer!* I seeeeeeeee you!"

Fritz made no move to intercept, so Nigel took a swig of coffee and kicked the Camel into a spin. Straightening out near the circling tourists, he flipped back to the main advisory frequency.

"I've got one on me!" shouted somebody, probably Jenkins, judging by the way the lady German was shredding his wing. "Help!"

"Shut up and die like an aviator," Munroe said. For the first time, Nigel agreed with him.

Munroe seemed more in command of his plane now, and wingovered left, bringing his guns to bear on the Fokker. Overhead, Nigel warned off a nearby tripe with a burst of tracers. No need to let Munroe die just yet.

Another Fokker overshot Nigel, distracting him. The lad hadn't even managed to connect once. As Nigel tried to decide if he should follow, Hitoshi solved the issue by dropping down and igniting the fellow's fuel tank. Nigel snapped the stick into his lap and looped backwards, turning ninety degrees at the top to watch the flaming wreck. He waggled his wings in congratulations to Hitoshi, then went back to check on Munroe.

Munroe was still struggling to get a good shot on the lady, while Nigel assessed the fray. Thanks to Hitoshi's rampage, the German side had lost three planes to the Allied's one. No reason to make it a complete slaughter.

"Fritz, will you break off?"

"Just now, when I am to snatch victory from the jaws of defeat?"

Fritz suddenly appeared high and up to Nigel's right, both guns blazing. Out of the sun, of course. Nigel's reflexes were getting stale, what with having only tourists to fight. His stomach cramped. This was too much like the real thing.

Nigel unloaded the aircraft for speed, then pulled the stick into his belly, holding the creaking airframe at the edge of stall buffet. His vision grayed as he looked up, rolling to point his head towards Fritz.

Fritz was too smart for that, and had climbed and slowed. He had altitude, he had the energy to turn, and the Sopwith was arcing in far too wide a circle. Nigel checked his harness to make sure the connecter was in. It looked like he was going to need it in a second.

Munroe shot underneath and pulled straight up, shooting wildly at the Fokker. Fritz snap rolled left and angled away, spoiling the shot. Munroe's Sopwith shuddered and stalled, spinning off to the right.

"Blip on, left rudder, Munroe!" Nigel called. "Let go of the stick!"

"Shut up, limey!" Munroe's voice was distinctly strained.

"Until we meet again, *Engländer*!" Fritz called on common advisory, adding a villainous laugh for good measure. "BWAH-ha-ha-ha!"

Nigel really couldn't abide that fellow at all.

Nigel had barely rolled to a stop when Munroe confronted him.

"What the hell is your major malfunction?" Munroe screamed.

Nigel blinked. He really didn't need this.

Munroe wasn't finished. "Don't just stare at me like an idiot, open your mouth and say something!"

"What on earth are you on about?"

SEAN KIBBE

"Cutting in on my kill like that! What, you can't deal with me kicking ass out there, so you've got to shoot over my head?"

"See here, Munroe, that isn't even vaguely what happened."

"Yeah? I was just about to shoot down the puke that got Jenkins, when you cut in and tried shooting him down yourself."

"I fired what we call a 'guiding shot.' Anyway, you mean 'shooting her.'"

"What?"

Nigel sighed, climbing slowly out of the airplane. The other two pilots started walking over. "The 'puke' you speak of is a lady."

Munroe looked disgusted. "Another goddamned empty kitchen."

Nigel slowly counted to ten. "I hate to tell you this, but she looked like she handled her plane fairly well up there. Better than some I could mention. I'd be careful if I were you."

"Give me a break. No way is some chick going to shoot me down."

"I wish you wouldn't speak like that. This is all recorded, you know." He started to walk away.

"Hey, I'm not done talking to you! Okay, obviously you've got the hots for this chick. Whatever, buddy. But once again, you're acting like a spoiled brat. Can't deal with the idea that you aren't the top dog anymore, so you throw a little temper tantrum in the air. If I'm coming on a little strong here, it's because I'm trying to grab your attention. It's for your own good."

"How very charitable of you."

Hitoshi and Olsen joined up with them.

"I'm just saying you need to grow up," Munroe said, walking away.

The rest of the group walked back to the tents in silence. Nigel enjoyed the quiet for a few minutes, slowly smoking a cigarette. When Olsen popped into his tent to drop off his flight gear, Hitoshi spoke.

"My friend, you shouldn't let that fool bother you like that. You're far better than he is."

"I'm not bothered. But thank you."

"You are clenching your hands, and your jaw is set. Some might call you upset. Why let something so small annoy you, when you have survived so much worse?"

Nigel pursed his lips, thinking for a while. Then he shrugged. "I guess what bothers me, bothers me. You might as well ask Munroe why he hates me."

"He hates you because you're his better, I think."

"Really? Doesn't seem as if he thinks that."

"Unlike you, this is the closest he's ever come to real combat. He suffers by comparison and he knows it." Hitoshi started walking towards the hangar.

Nigel followed him, puzzling over this. "I thought he fought in—where was it—Nigeria?"

"A sortie every week or so for a few months, all done in air-conditioned comfort at flight level. As you know, things are different from your time. These days, military pilots hardly ever fly, unless you count the simulator. Mostly, they do office work. It's probably why they lose so many to landing and weather mishaps. But I won't judge. Munroe, on the other hand, he has judged himself. His whole self-image is tied up in his title of Marine Aviator."

The hangar was deserted save for the three aircraft

from this morning. Hitoshi ran his hand over the bullet holes in Munroe's bird. "You see, this is his validation. Here, he can actually fly in one-on-one combat. If he dislikes you, it is because you do it so easily."

Nigel sat down on the lower wing and laughed. "I see your point. How foolish. I mean, we're all safe here. It's more dangerous to drive a motorcar to the countryside for a picnic. As I said the other day, this isn't combat. It's just a game."

Hitoshi shook his head. "Combat is a game. The stakes are simply higher."

"Fine, then. But you won't find such stakes here."

Hitoshi turned away. He was quiet for a minute or so. Nigel watched him from behind. Hitoshi looked very old, but his back was ramrod straight.

Without turning, Hitoshi started talking, almost as if to himself. "When I was a young boy, I knew my grandfather. He had flown Zeros in the Pacific War back in the forties. I loved his stories. As old as he was, I could still see the great warrior he had been. He had even survived a week at sea, after he'd been shot down. The afternoon of the day that they pulled him out of the water, he was back in the air. As odd as it may seem to you, when I was not yet ten, I hated American pilots. After all, my grandfather had fought them, so they must be bad people. Little boys think like that.

"Then, a year before grandfather died, a very odd thing happened. The pilot who had shot my grandfather down contacted him. The pilot and his family came to Japan for a visit. There were reporters and television cameras, and I saw my grandfather and his old enemy shake hands and bow at each other.

"Seeing my grandfather smile, I was devastated. If he could be friends with this man, everything he had once risked his life for was a lie. And that meant that the one man I admired more than anyone else in the world was a fool."

Nigel cleared his throat. "I'm sorry, Captain Kubota, but that's nonsense."

Hitoshi shrugged. "I know. I was less than ten, remember? I know now that it is possible to be fighting on the wrong side and still be an honorable man. The virtue is in the struggle, you see. We are so many cherry blossoms on the wind. We have our moment, then we rot on the ground. We don't get to choose our tree, but we can choose how we fall. Your friend Munroe thinks only of winning, and that's his failure, for in the end, none of us win. But we can find beauty in the tumult of our lives, so long as we're willing to spurn the safe and easy path."

"I can think of a fair number of blokes who would have liked a little more safety back in '17."

"Really?" Hitoshi turned around and looked Nigel in the eye. "Your life was that important to you? Were you conscripted?"

"No. But we were defending ourselves from the Germans. We weren't just seeking some amorphous 'struggle.' We were fighting for what was right."

"Unlike Fritz? Or my grandfather? I think, in their own way, they were right, too."

Nigel hopped off the wing. "Hitoshi, I know you're just philosophizing, but that damnable German has killed four of my countrymen. For real, I might add."

"And everyone else in your squadron is now dead, too. Even if they survived the war."

Nigel winced. "I know. Doesn't make him less of a murderer in my mind."

"Then why not kill him?"

"The war's over."

"Is it?"

Nigel flicked his cigarette stub out the hangar door. "Let's go to the O club. Less philosophy, more drinking."

"I will remain here with the airplanes for a while. You enjoy yourself."

"Sometimes I manage to. Flying, fighting, carousing: it's all part of that struggle you talk about, I suppose."

Hitoshi made a slight bow. "Now you're beginning to understand."

After a few days of solid rain, the clouds broke in the late afternoon long enough for Nigel to launch a flight. Ramirez apologized, but he'd had a few too many scotch and sodas—not that that would have stopped anyone back in the War, but the corporation frowned on that sort of thing. They got enough angry phone calls as it was. Jenkins was back from the hospital, but managed to ground loop on takeoff, shattering a wing. Nigel added himself to the flight, ostensibly to make up for the missing two, but in reality just to get up in the air. He hated being grounded. It gave him too much time to think.

He spotted Hitoshi and Munroe working their way along the grayish blue backside of a cumulus cloud. A thousand feet above, two Fokkers were slowly circling.

"Flight lead to flight lead," Nigel transmitted. "I have visual."

"*Guten Tag,* Nigel. I have you as well. Come on over here and play. Your boys look lonely."

"Can't say either of them appreciate my help. See you have the same problems getting yours airborne."

"I have company enough with *meine tödliche Freundin,* Diana. Such a good name for her, *ja*? Even now I must hold her back, she is so champing at the bit to take on both. As for me, I think I will be content to watch. She wore me out so last night. *Ach,* such long, pretty hair."

"I tell you what. I don't dive in, and you don't regale me with your bedtime exploits."

"Deal, my friend. One versus two, scarcely fair, but she is soooooo feisty."

Nigel pulled up alongside Fritz as Diana worked her way around cloud spires towards the Sopwiths. Nigel held his breath. For all the urban sprawl in the distance, part of him kept insisting that he was back in France. He toggled common advisory on and waited.

"Break right!" Munroe's voice shouted. "I've got a shadow four o'clock low!"

The Camels spread out in a climbing right turn as the Fokker cut through a corner of the cloud, guns blazing. It was beautiful, really. The three planes wove in varying arcs, pulling up, nearly stopping at the tops of turns, then pivoting down in hammerhead stalls. Diana kept to the outside, trying the occasional deflection shot.

Fritz transmitted on discrete. "I'm sorry, *Englischer,* but this is too much fun to sit out with you." He rolled upside down and did a split-S towards the others. Nigel squeezed off an irritated burst at him, then headed overhead, waited until Fritz was engaged, and spun downwards.

He straightened out in a vertical dive, just as Hitoshi

was climbing in the opposite direction with Fritz hot on his tail. The two planes passed each other less than a wingspan apart, so close that Nigel could see Hitoshi's smile. He wasn't wearing a helmet.

"Combat is a game. The stakes are simply higher."

"Fine, then," Nigel had said. "But you won't find such stakes here."

Sweet Jesus.

Fritz stall-turned to follow Hitoshi. The German pulled his nose around, expertly drawing a lead on the Camel.

"Pieter, for the love of God, break it off!"

"*Jawohl, mein Herr.* But first a bit of bang-itty bang!"

"Break off, break off, break off!"

A line of tracer fire touched Hitoshi's airplane. A long second later, it exploded.

"So, what is this urgency we need to go back for?" Fritz asked.

Nigel didn't answer. He droned along, straight and level, watching the burning wreck flutter towards the ground.

"Mouse One, Mouse Two, radio check on discrete," Fritz transmitted.

"He wasn't wearing his helmet, Pieter."

The frequency went silent.

Nigel's Sopwith shuddered violently as his left wing was stitched with gunfire. Diana's triplane shot by, rolling out of his sight picture, her long, braided hair fluttering in the slipstream.

"Pieter! Ask her if she's got her helmet on!"

There was a pause, followed by Fritz's unaccented voice on common advisory. "Mayday! All aircraft break off! Do not fire! I repeat, do not fire!"

"Damn you, kraut," said Munroe. He had been slowly climbing back to the other's altitude. He turned towards Diana, who was falling in on Fritz's wing.

"Munroe!" yelled Nigel. "Don't fire! You'll kill her!"

"That's the idea, right?"

"I mean it!"

"One less empty kitchen to worry about." Munroe started firing, still out of range.

Nigel unloaded the aircraft and accelerated, strips of fabric around the bullet holes tearing off. He held the stick forward with both hands as the Camel bucked wildly from the airspeed. He waited until he was nearly on top of Munroe, then opened fire, kicking the rudder back and forth to snake the bullet stream across the fuselage. Munroe's Camel slowly tore apart, and the two halves started wildly spinning.

"What the hell did you do?" Munroe screamed.

"I beat you. Easy enough." Nigel dove alongside the front half, watching Munroe flail about uselessly. "Are you frightened? Sometimes those harnesses don't work on impact. You might only have a few seconds left. Too bad."

Munroe screamed again, this time sounding like a frightened child.

Nigel pulled out of his dive just before Munroe hit the ground. He indulged himself with a slow roll, laughing and crying at the same time.

Nigel lay on his back in the middle of the landing field, watching an airliner draw a lone contrail across the blue sky. He wondered if it was a JAL flight. Fritz's shadow fell across him.

"Morning, Pieter," Nigel said, still staring at the sky. "I don't recall German officers wandering about our aerodrome, back in the day."

"Everything's been shut down, pending the investigation," Fritz said. "Besides, I needed the walk."

Nigel sat up to look at him. Fritz was cleanshaven for a change. He looked every inch the Prussian officer, except for a black eye.

"Nasty shiner, mate, how'd you get it?"

"I may have slapped Diana when we got back to the field. She didn't take very kindly to that." He shrugged. "Modern women, you know."

"Just a lover's spat, eh?"

Fritz shook his head. "Not my lover. You should know by now that I say things just to bother you. No, she was Hitoshi's if she was anyone's. I'm not the only one who can make the walk from our aerodrome to yours."

"Ah. Hitoshi and her. Explains a bit."

"That, and she's utterly insane." Fritz sat down. "I'm truly sorry about your friend. I want you to know that. I can't stop thinking about what happened."

Nigel glared at him. "He's not the first man you've killed."

"He wasn't the enemy."

"It was still his doing. He wanted to experience what we used to. Something about the expression of life's struggle."

Fritz spat. "What is the problem with these modern people? Back in our day, we didn't have to seek out ways to die. Staying alive, now that was difficult."

"We're the only ones left. I guess that makes us the winners of that game."

"No. Your side won, we lost. I wasn't there just for myself."

"You believed all that stuff the Kaiser was feeding you?"

Fritz stood up. "Just as you believed what you were told. Now, let's go back to our modern world and our play acting. If they let us, that is. Taunting Munroe probably didn't help matters much. Just so you know, he's fine. He's also filed an official complaint with management."

"Too bad. Him, I happily would have seen die."

"Just as once I would have happily shot you down. And vice versa, of course."

"Of course." Nigel paused. "But you no longer feel that way? You admit that you fought for the wrong side?"

Fritz looked down at Nigel for a while. They met each other's gaze. "No. I do not admit that. But I am done with killing people."

Nigel stood up and faced him. "I'm not a bored airline pilot. I'm your enemy. As long as we're both alive, the war isn't over. And I'm done with play acting."

Fritz's ice-blue eyes seemed fixed on something behind Nigel. "I think I have had my fill, as well. But what you are proposing is no different from what your friend did."

"It's not the same. He did it for himself. That was where he was wrong. You and I, though, we're part of something larger than ourselves. We have no choice. We need to finish this. Unless you feel like surrendering."

"No. The usual field of honor, then?"

"Of course."

They shook hands, then bowed at each other. Within the hour, they were flying once again. This time, they left their helmets behind.

The Four C's to Success

BY CLIFF NIELSEN

Cliff Nielsen has created over 1,100 images for such high-profile series as the X-Files, Star Wars, The Crow, A Wrinkle in Time, The Chronicles of Narnia, Star Trek, *and Phillip Pullman's* His Dark Materials. *Among the many notable authors he has created covers for are Stephen King, John Grisham, C. S. Lewis, Madeline L'Engle, Lois Lowry, Edgar Allen Poe, Washington Irving, Mary Shelley, Isabel Allende, Neil Gaiman, Poppy Z. Brite and Caitlin Kiernan. Cliff's illustrations have been recognized for their excellence by the Society of Illustrators,* Communication Arts Magazine, Print, *and the* Spectrum *annuals. He has been an international speaker on digital art, served as a judge for the Society of Illustrators annual competitions, and enjoys teaching illustration at the Art Center College of Design in Pasadena, California. Cliff is finishing his soon-to-be-released graphic novel* Beloved *with co-creator Mark Reber.*

The Four C's to Success

I want to give my heartfelt congratulations to the winners of the Writers of the Future and Illustrators of the Future Contests this year. Through this competition, L. Ron Hubbard's great legacy of supporting young creative talents is without equal in the world today. What a unique opportunity you have been given to share your talents and dreams with the communities of science fiction and fantasy fans. No tribute carries more weight. No award looks prettier on the shelf. I'm absolutely tinted viridian with envy!

Over the last few years I've had the distinct honor to spend time working with talented students in the visual arts who are eager to participate in the culture as illustrators, designers, film makers and fine artists. I like to share with them some advice that has helped me become a better image maker and storyteller.

I describe this object lesson as a massive ziggurat: four expansive stone plateaus, hewn from an ancient quarry of absolute knowledge. This formidable structure erupts through the confused canopy of the surrounding jungle, shouldering the broad purple sky above. Imagine the rays of light that stream from its pinnacle, the fanfare blasting from a corps of unseen trumpeters to announce your arrival. You must climb to the top of this monument if you are to succeed. It will take hard work and intelligence to scale the heights. Observe the deeply carved hieroglyphics. Each of the four terraces is marked with a crescent-shaped line—four giant C's that represent your progression from servant to master.

The first C carved into the foundation of this immense shrine stands for CONCEPT.

Few would disagree that there has never been a time in the history of mankind, other than this moment, when great ideas were more valued or needed. A concept is the most basic foundation of any decent piece of art, and that is the most powerful realization that a creator can experience. Have a great idea. It's that easy, and other than cashing the check, it's potentially the most pleasurable part of the job! Ad man and educator Jack Foster says, "Getting an idea depends upon your belief in its existence. And upon your belief in yourself."

Great concepts are not always easy to come by. It will take some work. Author Kent Ruth said, "Man can live without air for a few minutes, without water for about two weeks, without food for about two months—and without a new thought for years on end."

Luckily the search for that elusive, great concept is a shared one. This very volume that you hold is a testament to the young, innovative and talented minds engaged in award-winning attempts to find that great CONCEPT in the fields of speculative fiction and illustration. The illustrators collaborate with the author after the fact, in a quest to understand the essence of the story, analyzing, dissecting and distilling it down to its core meaning. I find it immensely helpful if I can summarize or give definition to the point of the story in less than three words.

This process entails reading manuscripts, looking at inspirational artwork, film and photography, studying about or visiting exotic places and divers cultures, asking lots of questions, experiencing the beauty of nature and simply living life! The more influences that the illustrator can draw from, the better prepared he or she will be to have that great idea.

I want you to believe that a good idea can be found, and that you will find not only one, but many!

If you climb a little higher you'll be confronted by a second giant step. On its face another C has been engraved. This one stands for COMPOSITION.

For many writers and illustrators, sitting in front of a white sheet of paper can be the ultimate in intimidation. You've just killed a tree. You've got sawdust on your hands! Now what are you going to do?

I actually sketch better if I've already ruined the piece of paper that I'm drawing on. I do that by placing even the smallest mark on the corner of the paper. Usually that's just enough to defile the pristine sanctity of that white canvas, and my anxiety dissipates.

The successful illustrator should be guided by the overall concept of their creation. It provides a framework or a set of rules . . . reasonable boundaries within which they can create a new and exciting, heretofore unseen vision. Prepared with my concept, I can let my untethered instincts flow. It's important to remember not to edit yourself at this stage; there will be time for refinements later. Keep drawing. A serious designer never stops after the first attempt. Anywhere from five to fifty sketches could be produced to express just one simple idea.

Keep in mind that the purpose of your artwork is to sell your patron's idea or product. It needs to hook the interest of the public enough to provoke them into parting happily with their hard-earned money and valuable time to explore further the meaning of your creation.

The next great stone in this foundation is marked C for CRAFT.

Technical ability, artistic process, or craft is the third most important step to becoming a successful illustrator. Painter David Leffel said, "The full-fledged painter knows that it's not a question of learning how to paint but what to paint. The student, on the other hand, comes to school to learn 'how to paint,' to learn 'the technique of painting.' This holds him back. His attention should be on trying to learn what to paint. The goal of the artist is to create a painting, to make a picture. To do this, you don't copy indiscriminately. You concentrate on what to paint, and that makes all the difference. Technique has a bearing, but it's less important."

An artist should hone his hand-eye coordination and his understanding of the media to utilize his body, mind and spirit as a tool of creation. A masterful artist makes his work appear effortless to the viewer, but the truth remains that countless hours of obsession with process are necessary to accomplish this sleight-of-hand trick.

Commit yourself to a lifetime of practice. Commit yourself to a lifetime of learning. Don't ever give up!

Finally, you've reached the last step. The last C scribed into the granite at this highest level of the ziggurat stands for CARE.

Care refers to the amount of effort that you put into creating a professional presentation of your work. An entire industry revolves around the notion that the proper presentation and advertising of any given product can make all the difference in the success of a company.

"Art is the result of INTEGRATION of all its components," says L. Ron Hubbard. "One can add that the result invites CONTRIBUTION of and from the beholder. It isn't very mysterious."

Once you have mastered the four C's, there is still the final presentation of your imagery, and it should be an educational one. You have an opportunity to TEACH the client that you are a viable catalyst for his or her ideas or products. A new way of seeing or doing things takes some time to catch on. Be patient. It takes time for people to catch up with your vision, but they will if you create an opportunity for them to do so.

Paramount are the four C's: Concept, Composition, Craft and Care. Keep them in order. Now, go forth and conquer.

Simulacrum's Children

written by

Sarah L. Edwards

illustrated by

KYLE PHILLIPS

ABOUT THE AUTHOR

Sarah L. Edwards suspects that she is the first science fiction or fantasy writer ever to hail from Rathdrum, Idaho. Although she just graduated with a master's degree in mathematics, Sarah has a secret fear that she might love words more than numbers since she also began college as an English major. On the other hand, she thinks a world where the quadratic formula is a spell for opening doors would be pretty funny. Besides devising complex solutions to simple, everyday problems, Sarah likes to knit, research the history of New York City, shop for used books and take pictures of the great outdoors. Her fiction has been published in Aeon Speculative Fiction, Andromeda Spaceways Inflight Magazine *and* Hub Magazine.

ABOUT THE ILLUSTRATOR

Kyle Phillips is currently attending the Hartford Art School (HAS) in his home state of Connecticut, and has his sights set on graduating in 2008 with a Bachelor of Fine Arts degree in painting. While he is currently focusing on still life and portraiture, Kyle always has had a distinct passion for illustration. He draws inspiration from artists of the Victorian and Impressionist eras and has an immense fascination for trompe l'oeil painting. When it comes to admiring the boundless world of science fiction illustration, he looks to artists such as Paul Bonner, John Berkey and Donato Giancola, who are among his favorites. Kyle is very grateful to be a part of the Illustrators of the Future Contest because it has brought him a step closer to reaching his ultimate goal to work as a full-time illustrator. Kyle would like to thank his friends, family and every single one of his teachers at HAS for always being there and guiding him.

Simulacrum's Children

April 4, 190—

I hired an assistant today. I found him on Mercy Street, where men of all ages and descriptions loitered, some holding crude signs, many nursing old injuries real, imagined and pretended. I felt all eyes upon me and my top hat and cane, and was glad I had thought to bring Mitchell along, though his gait is still so awkward that he attracts as much attention as I do.

I had nearly given up, for in every man's eyes I saw the desperation that might drive him to thievery and other crimes I dare not risk. Then a boy jumped out from among the huddled figures and said, "Looking for something, are you, sir? Help you?"

He was perhaps eleven or twelve, as dirty as the rest but with clothes neatly patched.

"Indeed," I said. "I've need of someone to carry my purchases."

He gave Mitchell the briefest curious glance and then grinned and said, "You got me, sir."

So we left Mercy Street and its desperate, now envious eyes and made a round of purchases in the industrial quarter. The boy followed closely behind Mitchell carrying the packages I'd given him. Finally, at the alchemist's, I bought a small quantity of hammered gold, which I gave the boy as well.

When Nettie had received us at the house I looked over my purchases to see that all were present, and then I weighed the gold and found it satisfactory.

"I didn't steal none of it," the boy said.

"Or if you did," I said, "you were cleverer about it than I can detect. Why didn't you?"

Cautiously, he said, "If you're the kind to buy gold, sir, then maybe there's some of that riches that'd come my way."

"I see. You want a permanent position." As I had hoped.

"You giving me a job?"

"Perhaps. What's your name?"

"Joseph Gaines."

"Tell me, Joseph, how you came to the streets."

He shrugged. "Not much to tell, sir. Pa's off riding rails somewhere—thinks he'll get a job but he's been riding a long time. Ma's dead. So I take my living where it comes."

"And what living is that?"

"I'll hold a gen'man's horse, if he likes. I'm a good hand with messages, too—I'll see your paper's delivered or if you say the words I'll remember them."

I dropped to a crouch and looked in his eyes. "Are you trustworthy, Joseph? I see that you've left me my gold, although your desire for employment might explain your honesty. But can I trust you with my private matters?"

"I'm all right," he said. "But that don't seem like

much of a question, sir. Guess you'll trust your own judgment on that, better than mine."

"I will," I said, straightening. "Beginning tomorrow. Can you arrive by eight o'clock?"

His grin suggested a hint of surprise, as though the interview had until then been a game for my own amusement. "Yes, sir."

He took the coins I gave him and put them away somewhere on his person, though I could not see just where. Then he tipped his cap to me and scurried out the front door.

With the prospect of a long-term assistant, I am now prepared to continue plans for the new project, the designs for which are far superior to my earlier attempts. I have finally replicated every component save those of the brain. There I fear something still eludes me.

I'll not reveal the matters of my laboratory to the boy immediately. If he is as bright as he appears to be, I'm afraid his next few weeks will be somewhat tedious. However, I do have several prosaic projects that ought to have been seen to before, such as the replacement of glass in the attic window. Then we shall see.

April 20

I woke this morning remembering glimpses of dreams. I cannot recall their content and their effect on my emotional state seems to have been minimal. Yet I have not dreamed in years. This development is disquieting, for I had thought the capacity dead, trampled beneath the maturing of my consciousness. Is there significance here, or only the confluence of random internal events?

Their recurrence draws to the surface those few images I hold of the time before.

I awoke from these dreams restless, and the feeling remained when Joseph and I went out into the city today. My stated purpose was to fetch fresh linen, which I shall need for drafting diagrams for the project. However, I hoped also during our unhurried walk to the tradesman's streets to procure further information from Joseph about his past, by which to gauge something more of his character.

My success was limited. Details of his earlier life are securely locked behind the door of his mouth, though his manner is discreet rather than furtive.

I tried one last remark. "I imagine your time on the streets was difficult—so many unsavory men may be found there."

His voice low, he answered, "Sometimes the worst kind live in houses."

I turned to prompt him further, and over his head I glimpsed a face that caught me mid-stride. Something not in the outward features, but in his expression—one of abiding, almost mechanical calm—was startlingly familiar. It reminded me of the first days after I awoke, of my own lost and stolid expression. Perhaps the man felt my stare, for he slid into the crowd, and I lost sight of him.

Joseph did not comment on my sudden inattention. Perhaps he simply did not care to converse any further, for he spoke no more while I completed my few purchases, and as we walked home I was deep in thought as well.

I dismiss the man I saw as an expression of my unease caused by the dreams this morning. That is, the man was real enough, but I am sure the impression of familiarity was mere fancy.

As far as Joseph is concerned, I suspect my continued interest in his past is as much curiosity as necessity. He keeps his own secrets well enough, and something in his manner satisfies me that he will keep mine, too. Soon I shall give him a fuller understanding of the purposes of my workshop.

April 24

I do not think Joseph believed me when I said that Mitchell was not dead, lying on the pallet in the room I had just unlocked. I had murdered him, clearly, and my assured explanations of mechanisms and workings were proof of madness.

"Please trust me a moment more," I said, and as Joseph watched warily I unbuttoned Mitchell's shirt, slid my fingers beneath the seam of his flesh, and opened the door in his chest to reveal the teeth of gears and the inert forms of gyroscopes.

Joseph drew slowly nearer until he was close enough to peer within. After a few moments' silence, he said, "I didn't know there was anyone in the world could make a thing like that."

"Only very few."

"I guess you're about the greatest inventor ever lived, Dr. Chanhausen."

"No," I said. "I'm only an imitator. Mitchell is but my best attempt to copy another's work."

"Edison?"

"Not Edison. A man you've never heard of. I've been privileged to examine a working model at length."

"But—you could be famous." He turned again to Mitchell. "If people knew about him—and Nettie, too?"

I nodded.

"You could make money, more than they ever made with railroads. You could have one of them big houses out in the Hills."

"No, for several reasons. First, fame does not immediately transmute to money, and I have not the skill with celebrity that I have with valves and gears. Second, I do not care for my work to be known."

"Why not?"

I hesitated. Here lay the test; the boy must be made to accept this point. "I do not do this work for others. I do it for myself. I create these models"—I waved a hand towards Mitchell—"to learn the deepest I can know of the mind of—the other inventor I spoke of. I do not care about the rest of the world. I wish only to create as complete a being as he did."

"But if other folks did know . . ."

"It would hinder my work, and create all manner of embarrassment and attention which I must avoid if I am to make progress. Do you understand?"

He raised his eyebrows and then shrugged. "Well enough, I guess."

"It is very important to me that no one interfere with my work, and so I must be sure that you will tell *no one* of this. Do I have your word?"

He stuck out a hand, which I shook. Then, glancing at his palm, I said, "Go wash up, now, and then I'll want you with me as I make some adjustments to Mitchell."

I woke Mitchell up and walked him down to the workshop, where I again set his functions to neutral. Then I began examining the fibrous tendons of his leg in hopes of improving his gait. When Joseph returned he supplied me tools as I asked for them, but he also asked such a quantity of questions that progress was minimal.

Finally, he asked about the motive power, and I abandoned all hope of adjusting Mitchell any further today and instead showed Joseph the unit in Mitchell's chest. I told him what little I know of the animatist's fluids sloshing in their chambers. Finally I described the infinitesimal crystalline structures of Mitchell's brain, though of course I could not show them to Joseph and disturb their growth. It may be that further mysterious buds of thought will yet bloom there, or so I hope.

Then again, Mitchell has far simpler problems than those of consciousness. I've little reason to concern myself with his mind if even his legs have the grace of a scarecrow's. Besides, I am anxious to begin the new project.

July 19

I have named this new creation Gwendolyn. I am still refining the details of my improved ideas for her mind, but much of her design has been perfected in my earlier attempts. I've begun collecting the rarer materials that she will require, such as the marvelous living silk, so like flesh, available from the vendors in the dark quarter. Yesterday I engaged Sandridge to craft her eyes, giving him leave to choose their color. I repeated my usual story of masquerade masks, emphasizing that this is to go to a most beautiful lady who would not choose to appear any the less radiant in a mask than in her own face.

Joseph has taken a deep interest in Gwendolyn's construction and has aided me in building her frame. His capability surprised me. I had only to show him the sketches of the legs, patterned after my own with inspiration from human bones, and he began to lay out the castings of bronze and the steel pins. When I returned, I found that he had nearly assembled one leg, which I inspected and found well joined and well oiled.

"What other handiwork have you done?" I asked.

"Sir?" he said, glancing up from his work—a shade guiltily, I fancied.

"I am not well acquainted with the skills of boys your age, but I suspect most would not be capable of such work."

He shrugged. "Just take to it, I guess, sir."

Satisfied with his progress, I left him laying out the other leg and returned to my diagrams.

Was that a shadow of unease I felt? Yet I do not distrust him. Is that foolishness or insight?

August 11

Yesterday Joseph and I ventured into the dark quarter to fetch the silk that will robe Gwendolyn's bones. I dared not bring Mitchell along, for in all Greater Hutchison there is no one likelier to recognize his origins than the craftsmen who fashioned his skin. Thus I was doubly glad of Joseph's company, for the slight additional security and for the pleasure of introducing him to new wonders. He had never ventured to that part of the city for fear of the hazards, he said. I wonder at the stories the street boys must tell among themselves to generate such caution. Now Joseph shall have another, I suppose.

The glow of the lamps in the alchemists' windows lit the streets for a while, and even after that enough light trickled down through the curtains and canvas above the streets to let us see our way. Joseph walked behind the scope of my sight, but once I turned to see him peering over his shoulder, and occasionally some quick motion of his caught my eye.

"What is it, Joseph?"

He pulled his cap somewhat lower over his eyes. "Seems like I hear something."

I glanced behind us, but saw no particular sign of menace, only the shadows that drift without hesitation through the dark quarter. A patch of light flickered as the sheets framing it far above were bothered by a breeze.

"I've never been troubled here," I told him. "The clubs have their own disagreements, but they recognize a legitimate customer."

"Yes, sir," he said, but he did not look convinced.

We made our way to the skinner's shop without mishap. Joseph refrained from wrinkling his nose, but his expression made apparent his opinion of skincrafting's aromas: brine, sanitary chemicals, and the fluids on which the skin cultures feed.

As we returned the way we had come, Joseph continued to look uneasy. I had turned to reassure him again when he startled at the sight of something over my shoulder.

Before I could turn, a blade pressed at my jaw. In an instant I was thrust to the pavement, chest down and a boot digging in my back. Joseph yelped from somewhere behind me, and then I heard a muffled thump and after that only whimpering.

I was shoved onto my back and a human of a child's height stared into my face with the calculating eyes of an adult. "Rich man, huh? Come slumming, huh? Come to drip your filthy gold on our streets?"

"I believe you would like to get your filthy hands on some of that filthy gold," I said, trying to glimpse a hulking figure that loomed in the corner of my sight.

"Hah. Rich man, funny man, likes to play the words. Play with coins, too?" The other man's hand held the blade at my throat while the small person rummaged through my clothing. He tossed aside my package from the skinner's, and I breathed a silent, grateful breath. He hid my purse somewhere about him and continued to search, finally pulling my shirt open, I suppose to hunt for jewelry or other items hidden there. I squirmed despite the itch of the steel edge, and the tinyman slapped me. Then he brought a knife from within his clothing and dug into the skin across my collarbone. I cried out, and he slapped me again and grinned. "You're a firstie, chappie. I've got first blood." His fingers prodded at my skin and began to trace the line of my sternum—and my seam.

"Hey, what's this, now?" he said, probing at it. "Have a look here, buddy."

An expressionless face peered over me. That face . . .

The man above me suddenly grunted, and then toppled from my view.

"Buddy? What's all—" A stone hit the small man square in the face, and he crumpled, his knife ringing useless on the pavement.

Shakily I sat up to see Joseph rummaging now,

pulling my purse from among the robber's clothes. Then he grabbed the package of skin and said, "Clubbers'll be coming, soon as they hear. Rather not explain—they'll get the idea on their own, if these mucks don't come to."

"Indeed." I stood, patted myself to see that I was still intact, and followed him down the twisty streets.

"Stupid kid, robbing on club turf," Joseph said.

"No, not a child. A tinyman. A man whose growth was stunted. Some kinds of work here require small stature."

He glanced at me and then spit. "A kid," he growled.

We arrived home safe, though shaken. I'll not venture into the dark quarter again without Mitchell at my side. Nor shall I allow Joseph there again, for his peace of mind and mine. He is too valuable an aid to my labors to risk further injury.

I have some small concern for myself, as well—the tinyman's knife-nick still weeps fluid near my collarbone. My skin with its greater density was designed to repel injury, not repair it. I may have to attempt a patch, though I'm not sure of the efficacy of such a procedure.

August 19

The dreams returned again last night. I dreamed of some place quite unlike this city, and within it was a sterile room where I found myself surrounded by my faceless automatons. I was prodded and poked while I lay on a white table, unable to move. At some distance a figure watched, and once he spoke a command to one of my examiners. And then I knew myself a squalling child lying in a bassinet at the city hospital, and through the window the man stared still, with an expression possessive and cold.

I awoke trembling.

I spent the day with Gwendolyn, working at the attachment of the tendons in her arms and hands. My intent is that should her mind be capable of it, her hands might have the fineness of motion for using pen and ink. Too distant a dream, perhaps, but I cherish it nonetheless.

When I had paused to relax my eyes and my fingers, I realized Joseph stood a little behind me. "You startled me," I said.

"Sorry," he said. "You want me to try?"

"It is a tedious process," I said. "I am not sure . . ."

"Give me a chance, Dr. Chanhausen."

I stepped away from the workbench. Joseph brought a sturdy crate, stood on it, and began slowly attaching the fibers.

"Why do you make them?" he asked, his eyes still on Gwendolyn's wrist.

"I beg your pardon?" I said.

Joseph turned to look at me intently. "You work on 'em, Nettie and Mitchell, and now this one, but they'll never be as good as a person." He returned to his work on the arm. "There's enough real folk on the streets that'd do any fool thing you asked of 'em, they'd shoot anyone you like or scrub your floors or read out your newspaper, those who can. There's more 'n enough of any sort of muck you want, and women, too. And Mitchell here doesn't talk, and Nettie can't think far enough to stop the water when the sink's filled. So why do you make them?"

KYLE PHILLIPS

"You ask a very deep thing, Joseph." I tried to arrange my thoughts. After a pause, "There are many reasons that my projects have consumed me these years. I enjoy their construction, a pleasure I believe you share."

"Sure."

"I am intrigued by the puzzle of creating things like humans, in appearance human, but not. This may seem a funny thing, when you consider that magicians in the dark quarter and other places may fashion humanity in any shape they choose—such as the tinyman we encountered. Indeed, perhaps they are intrigued by problems similar to those with which I wrestle."

I reached in vain for a more complete explanation of the need, perhaps more rightly the obsession that has driven me since I first came to this city those years ago. "It is because of the man I told you of," I said finally, "whose model I have studied with such care."

"What about him?"

"I wish to attain his success," I said. "Not his acclaim, for as far as I know he has little. But I wish to show myself capable of such craft as his." And so somehow, perhaps, to prove—what? Equality? Transcendence of my own beginnings?

"Oh." He sounded disappointed. Spoken so, perhaps it does sound a frail motivation. Yet my fuller explanation, fragmented though it is, dwells far deeper in myself than I could divulge to Joseph.

From what abyss of circumstance was I thrust into the world, from what stupor did I awaken with a weight of gold stuff in my pocket and a paranoia that drove me here, to this sprawling city? The answers seem nearest when I am at work on my projects. I follow the bones of my leg, from deep-seated femur to the delicate fragments of the ankle, and I imagine another designing those same bones, adjusting the human forms for the greater weight of bronze.

Joseph required no hand to craft his skin or draw it over his bones. Does he wonder after a creator as I do mine? I watched as he tested the tension and the elasticity of the tendons, and then attached them with a facility that promises to exceed mine, with more practice. As my design surpasses Mitchell's, so Joseph's surpasses mine—but no man ever attached his tendons.

September 4

Gwendolyn is awake, and she is beautiful.

Her proportions are lovely and her figure slim and strong. Her skin is soft as the proverbial rose petals and her eyes are a luminescent green that belies Sandridge's self-taught skill. Even her motion is smooth, better than Nettie's sturdy walk, much less Mitchell's galumphing.

Yet this describes only her appearance, fair though it is. She is beautiful because when I hooked the last catch of her blue cotton dress and tapped the switch behind her neck, her eyes opened and saw me. She sees me still.

There is no language yet, of course. Even the barest of gestures is beyond her grasp, though I doubt they will remain so for long. Yet she watches me with an alertness that took months to achieve in Mitchell. I tell myself that her eyes following my motion are no great thing; a dog's will do the same.

Yet while I sit here, trembling anew and unable

to quantify my knowledge, I *know* she is aware. Her intelligence is keen, and requires only training. She is all that I dreamed of in my diagrams.

October 2

Gwendolyn walks without aid now and is capable of dressing herself, a proof of her superior motor skills. She has successfully swept, dusted and washed dishes. Joseph claims that she enjoyed beating the rugs last week, a conceit for which I forgive him. I believe it was Joseph who enjoyed that chore the more. I think he finds pleasure in Gwendolyn's presence—as do I.

Nonetheless, he appears somewhat discomfited by her residence in our household—not for her origins, I think, but for her femininity. I am both amused and gratified by this development. That my assistant is shy in the company of my own creation, whose construction he aided, attests to her lifelike appearance. None of my earlier projects, not even Mitchell, could be mistaken for human by any keen observer, but I believe Gwendolyn might someday be capable of it.

October 26

Gwendolyn speaks. I did not expect it; I did not even request it. We three sat with the world's map spread out before us; as much for Joseph's sake as Gwendolyn's, I am experimenting with an education in liberal arts. I had explained about scale and had pointed out Greater Hutchison. It was our first geography lesson, and as Joseph chose various locations I told something about them.

Our fingers were playing across the wild provinces of the west when Gwendolyn said, "Is Greater Hutchison the only city in New Albany?"

We turned to stare at her, and she pointed to the map. "There is no other point in the province but Greater Hutchison."

"A problem of scale, my dear," I said. "Were this the very image of the world and not only its likeness, we could take a glass to it and see the much smaller locales of Bridgeport and Newark."

"What are image and likeness?"

"As I meant it, an image is in all important ways the thing itself," I said, "as when one triangle is similar to another. All essential characteristics are the same. By likeness I mean a relative condition that occurs when one thing has appearance somewhat like another's. In comparison to a cockroach, perhaps, Joseph and I have a very great likeness. But in comparison to his brother, had he one, we would not be very like at all."

"Are you images, then?"

The question came so near to some of my own musings that I could only stare.

"Naw, we're just both people, is all," Joseph said, when I did not answer.

"Indeed," I said.

I sent Joseph away then to attend to chores while I spoke with her further and took extensive notes. Her knowledge is sparse but her intelligence startling. She asks questions many a tutor wishes their students had the imagination to pose, and with quite thorough grammar and language, presumably the result of her attentiveness to conversation between Joseph and myself. Our exchange was exhilarating, though

I believe we were both somewhat wearied by the intensity of it.

As I was putting away my notebooks, Gwendolyn said, "Which are the essential differences, and which are the trivial?"

I closed the lid of my desk before I answered her. "That is not always clear," I said. "It is simpler with mathematics, of course. In that field are other examples of things essentially alike—isomorphisms, for instance, although you do not yet know what those are."

"I shall find out," she said.

I believe she will, and I shall be most interested to see how her studies affect the question. I confess, it had not occurred to me that in my creation of an equal, I might also find a companion in these lonely inquiries.

November 1

I found the house in nervous disarray when Gwendolyn and I returned from our stroll today. I bade her go to the library to practice her penmanship while I spoke with Joseph.

"What has happened?" I asked him. "Is everyone all right?" I glanced at Mitchell, who sat in a jumbled heap on the divan.

Joseph swallowed and shook his head. "There's been people in the house, sir."

"Oh? Did Nettie let them in?"

"Don't know. I come up from the cellar and she was all lying out on the kitchen floor."

"What?" I turned towards the kitchen.

"It's okay, she wasn't shaking or anything. I put her to sleep—figured you'd better look at her."

I took a shaky breath. "All right, then, what about these people?"

Joseph shrugged, and his voice was shaky. "I don't know. I could hear 'em in the house, upstairs I guess, but the tools are scattered all over the workshop and your room's a right mess."

"My workshop!" I hurried down the steps, past Nettie sprawled quietly in the kitchen, and into the workshop. Tools were indeed scattered all over. A chamber of alchemist's fluid lay shattered on the floor. The drawers of my workbench were pulled out and their contents strewn across the bare wood. The blueprints that had previously covered that surface were gone.

Joseph scurried in behind me, his breath sharp. "I'm sorry, sir," he said. "I shoulda heard them sooner, and I woulda—"

"What? Put yourself in danger for the sake of my diagrams? I would rather these burglars should not disrupt the arrangement of your limbs as they have disrupted my cabinets."

I took him to the kitchen, where we inspected Nettie. She seemed to have suffered from some failure in logic that left her prone. She had taken no harm otherwise. I awakened her, took her to her bedroom, and put her to sleep.

It will take several days to restore a semblance of order in the workshop. The master documents are still secure and the loss of the blueprints is more an annoyance than a tragedy, although I do not like to think of them in other hands. Still, the likelihood that our burglars would know their significance seems small. In all, it seems only psychological harm has been done.

This harm may be great, however. I do not like the way Joseph startles at unexpected noises. Nettie shall no longer answer the door in any capacity, and it shall remain most discourteously locked whenever I am not at home. Yet any determined burglar may oil my lock, much less break in through a window.

Still, ordinary burglars are only an unfortunate occurrence. Their search of my workshop and their choice of plunder might suggest a purpose other than immediate riches. It is this possibility that chills me when I allow myself to consider it.

November 29

Gwendolyn and Joseph have been taken.

Mitchell and I had gone amongst the merchants on the dark quarter's outskirts in hopes of hearing some rumor of the purpose for our recent intrusion. As I expected, most were ill inclined to tell me anything useful. I did learn from the skinner that the tinyman is dead of a pistol wound—perhaps a reprisal for unsanctioned robbery in a clubhouse neighborhood.

Mitchell and I returned to the house to find Nettie once again on the floor, this time bound with strips of bedding, which seems excessive since she does not even move without instruction. In the empty library I found the table overturned and the carpet strewn with books. I had left Gwendolyn and Joseph there. In grief, I spent an interval rummaging among the shambles before I could search the rest of the house. There was little to find. The kitchen door is chopped to shreds.

We untied Nettie and I sent her and Mitchell to bed.

Now the house is quiet while I sit here writing, hoping that perhaps the application of ink to page will reveal some course of action.

Of course my projects are not legal; their very materials are illicitly obtained, for the dark quarter and all its dealings are wholly outside the law. Yet what little I know of government investigations suggests that were I the subject of an investigation, I would have been informed in some more orthodox fashion.

Perhaps I am the victim of some private plot. Joseph is correct that as labor, my creations are useless. A collector of art would be expected to approach me through more conventional channels. It seems to me that I am either the target of personal enmity, though I have no notion why, or that my work has excited scientific interest by someone untroubled by criminal means.

This is what I have feared all along, the reason I came here to a large city, ill-regulated and with many nooks and unnamed streets, ideal for privacy. Here, still unknown to any but my few suppliers, I hoped to find some measure of security in my anonymity. Yet it seems clear that my evasions have not been enough.

Could I flee now? Could I take my two remaining creations and leave the city in hopes of hiding more successfully? Perhaps better yet to leave one or both behind, since my pursuers must know what I am attempting now that they have Gwendolyn, if they did not know before.

All of this is mere meandering of the pen. I would be loath to part with Nettie or Mitchell, flawed though they are. Much less can I leave my Gwendolyn in the hands of strangers.

And still there is Joseph, as well. I was much relieved when Mitchell and I did not find his body thrown in some corner of the house, though why they should bother to keep him alive I cannot imagine. I feel his lack more sorely than I would have thought, and not only for the loss of his ingenuity in this misfortune.

I cannot see how, but they must be retrieved. Tomorrow I will return to the dark quarter and try again to find some rumor of these events. To be sure, there are more criminals than those found in the dark quarter—but not with the daring required of kidnappers, nor the single-mindedness to leave money still in my desk drawer.

I shudder to think what may be done to Gwendolyn if I do not find her. I dare not think what may have already been done.

November 30

I do not know where I am—likely in one of the dark quarter's innumerable tumbledown houses. Other than the initial mishandling when I was taken, I have not been mistreated. Nor have I made any progress in my quest of retrieval. It is possible that my captors are not even of the same club.

We were ambushed in the street within sight of where the tinyman robbed us. Two hulks stepped from an alleyway and immediately overpowered us. It was not difficult, for I was not built for wrestling, and Mitchell, who might have given better account of himself, fell useless when one of them grabbed at his neck and pressed his button. Whether it was by intention or accident, I am not sure. I do not know what has become of him.

Were my moves anticipated, or had I been followed? What purpose have they for me? Speculation is useless.

December 2

It was as I feared but dared not express, not even in these pages which I fancy are secure: the man who haunted my dreams these last months has haunted my daylight, as well. He had aged beyond my dim memories, yet the impersonal regard of his gaze was familiar.

I was brought by the two hulks to a room recently cleaned. The odor of lye still hung in the air. He told them to stop their ears until he spoke to them again, and so they must have, for they made no response after that. I suppose they were brothers of mine, after a fashion.

"Finally you return to me, my errant machine," he said, smiling slightly. "Where have you been?"

After so many years of wondering and vague apprehension, I stood before him and felt consuming terror. Thoughts were banished, let alone speech.

"Answer my questions," he said. "I have spoken."

When he spoke the phrase, I knew it for a passkey, though I had never been aware of it before. It locked my will from my body, and I listened helplessly while my mouth told him of my uneasy awakening in the abandoned house in Chicago, my flight south to the Republic, then the slow trail north again to the home I dared make for myself here, in Greater Hutchison.

He shook his head. "You were never meant to go so far. You weren't to leave Chicago. Some faulty logic, no doubt. Some command that failed to imprint—though it seems you learned what to do with the gold."

He must have seen my confusion in my face, for he said, "How did you think you'd come to be in that hotel room with a full pack of gold leaf?"

"I couldn't remember," I said.

"And why the dolls?" he said.

"They are not dolls," my mouth said, and I listened in surprise. "They are people, just as I am a person."

"You are not a person. You are a machine," he said, absently. "Why would you make 'people,' as you call them?"

I pushed against the bars of my mind, begging to speak of curiosity and scientific discovery. Instead, the words came, "I am your likeness, but I am not your image. My creations are proof that I am not as you are, for I know my creations to be people, and in me you know only a machine."

He shook his head and smiled, a smile meant only for himself, for who else was there in the room but his three machines?

Without prompting, I spoke again. "Where are Gwendolyn and Joseph?"

"If you mean the dolls, they are resting. The feminine doll—Gwendolyn?—is quite impressive. Pretty, too. Almost looks like it could speak. Or can it?" He looked intently at me. "What's the passkey?"

"She will not obey you."

"Wise. Keyed to your voice alone, yes?" He stood and stepped out the door. As he left I scrambled in thought for some way of escape, but my captors' grips on my wrists remained firm. I at least determined to keep from uttering Gwendolyn's passkey. I began to gnaw at my tongue, but it was made well, of fibers too durable to be shredded at a moment's notice. I had only broken the outermost layer of skin when he returned leading Gwendolyn, whose hands were bound and her feet tied so that she minced her steps.

I rejoiced to see her. "Gwendolyn!"

She looked at me but there was not recognition, only a blank stare.

"What have you done to her?" I cried, immediately fearful.

"Nothing," he said. "I haven't even taken it apart yet."

"What?" I lunged toward him and fell immediately back against my captors, my arms painfully wrenched. "You shall not harm her!" I screamed. "Your life is forfeit if you have harmed her!"

His gaze was thoughtful. "It is well my first attempts at recapture failed." He approached me, pulled back my shirt, and fingered the patch near my collarbone. "If that ignorant tinyman hadn't been so greedy as to first rifle your pockets, instead of bringing you here as I asked, I could not study this—this sub-creation you have made."

I choked with the breadth of my retort, and in the pause before I could organize my rage, many things happened at once. The door to my right opened, and I glimpsed Joseph, the dark gleam of a revolver in his hand. One of my guards moved into Joseph's path, and at the loosening of his grip I wrenched my wrist free and groped at my remaining captor's neck, finding with relief the fail-safe button hidden there. He crumpled, freeing my remaining hand. Some lightning instinct faster than thought drove my fingers in my ears just before my one-time master, my creator, began yelling commands to me. They came muffled through the barrier of my fingers. Still I heard the crack of a shot, and watched as the first guard wavered a moment before slumping against the wall.

And then Joseph was inside, his hand trembling as he looked first to me, then to Gwendolyn, and finally to my master, who yelled some phrase that again just escaped my hearing.

"Gag him," I said.

Joseph glanced just briefly at me and then at the pistol.

"Give it to Gwendolyn."

He hesitated, and with him I looked at her, her expression still blank, her eyes still unseeing.

"Now," I said, and then he did. Keeping it always aimed at the man, Joseph held up Gwendolyn's bound hands and formed her fingers around the handle with one resting on the trigger. Still she said nothing, but her grip tightened and the gun steadied. Then Joseph removed his shirt and bound my master's head with it, stuffing a large ball of it into his mouth. When the binding was tight, I removed my fingers from my ears.

"Now what?" said Joseph.

Indeed. My master sat on the chair, his eyes bulging as he strained to yell through the cotton. "Better tie his hands as well." While Joseph did, I glanced about me. In that stained and tattered place Gwendolyn was a diamond in a bed of coal.

"Gwendolyn?"

She did not look at me. I began truly to fear the

blankness I saw in her eyes. If the man spoke the truth, then what had become of her?

Joseph had moved away from the man, approaching me, when the pistol cracked again. The man's eyes widened, and then slowly he slumped.

Smoke rose from the gun in Gwendolyn's outstretched hand.

"Gwendolyn, what have you done?"

"He was only a machine," she said.

"What?" I said, startled. I strode to him and tore open his shirt, but there was no seam in his flesh. I felt behind his neck, and there was no button. "Gwendolyn—"

"You know, that's two shots in a coupla minutes," Joseph said. "Let's get, okay?"

"Yes. You're right. Gwendolyn?" I laid a hand on her shoulder, and she lowered the pistol and turned to the door without looking in my eyes.

In leaving we were forced to step over the guard Joseph had shot. The acrid smell of animatist's fluids rose from the pool around him. I gave him a last glance, and seeing him there in the full lamplight I recognized his face—it was that of the man who had so startled me that day months ago when Joseph and I were in the tradesman's streets.

I had no time to ponder then. Together the three of us hurried along a hallway of frail and squeaky planks, then down a flight of stairs, past a porthole-window, and through a door to a street whose edges were softened here and there with a light just past dawn. I pulled the door shut behind us and we crept down a line of fence.

"Wait!" I said, struck by a thought. "Mitchell!"

As if in reply, he stepped from behind the corner of the fence, stolid as always. His silent, awkward strength was a most comfortable and welcome sight. Together the four of us ran, following Joseph's lead through the streets, coming finally to that border between light and darkness that marks the edge of the quarter. It was a short walk back to the house.

I sent Mitchell and Gwendolyn to their beds, expecting some disagreement from the latter but receiving none. Though she spoke her assent, her first words since our escape, still her manner was strained. I worry for her.

Joseph and I finished the night warmed by the vapors rising from our teacups.

"I thought they had taken you as well," I said.

He looked down into his tea.

"But I gather they didn't," I said. "Otherwise your appearance with a weapon would have been even more unlikely than it was. Besides, it was apparent my—our captor didn't know of you."

"I couldn't let them take her," he said.

"You followed them when they broke into the house?"

"Yeah. Took me a bit to find a spitter, and then I got Mitchell out—figured we'd be running when we left."

"Joseph, there must be some vital piece of intelligence I am missing. I don't understand how you even found your way through the quarter."

His mouth worked a moment before he spoke. "My mother—she was a clubber's woman, sir. I been knowing the dark streets since I was walking."

"Indeed." Certain incidents became clearer: his avoidance of the quarter, his scorn for the tinyman, perhaps even his mechanical aptitude—I understand all available hands are used in the quarter's dark industries.

No mystery his reticence, nor the maturity behind those eyes. Such a life produces a different kind of tinyman, I suppose. But I only said, "However you achieved it, you have my thanks."

Joseph looked into my eyes for a moment, his expression as unguarded as I've ever seen it. "I got a job you don't know about, sir. I gave it myself. It's watching you and your people, all the time, seeing you don't take no harm. You don't just have your made people. You got me, too."

"I—thank you, Joseph."

He ducked his head and returned his gaze to his teacup.

Shortly after, we retired, he to sleep and I to write this account. I would ponder all these things more, but I am wearied from the adventures of these last few days. And tomorrow—today?—perhaps my household may begin to function again. I remain concerned about Gwendolyn.

December 5

It seems I shall not long have all my house around me, for I have had a sorrowful interview with Gwendolyn. Though she began to speak again the day after our return, still she lacked her usual vigor of manner. This morning she came to me while I sat at my desk, and seeing her I remembered again the dread calmness with which she watched the man who had been my creator begin to die.

And now here she sat, still calm, her voice shaded with bitterness. "Is this what you meant by image and likeness?" she said.

"I beg your pardon?"

"That man—he is the one who crafted you, as you have crafted me?"

"He was," I said. A separate part of my mind congratulated her for her insight—I had never told her about myself—but now was not the time.

"I did not kill him," she said. "I ended his functionality, for he was only a machine."

"So you said, but it was not true."

"It was true. What difference is there between him and us? We are intricately fashioned from many materials, and so is he. What separates us?"

"There are many factors," I said. "The question of autonomy, of self-will—"

"Was not my killing of him adequate expression of self-will?"

I paused, finding no answer that might satisfy, unsure if such an answer existed. "Say it were, what do you conclude?"

"I don't know," she said. Her face trembled in uncertainty, an expression I had rarely seen there. "Have you made me machine, or something more? For which crime am I to die?"

"Die? Good heavens, child."

"We were alike, image to image," she said. "And so both of us may die at a whim—or neither." She dropped her eyes. "Either I am only a machine, one that lives for its master's will—a guiltless existence, but a lifeless one. Or I have life and I do not deserve it, for I have taken another's."

She fell silent then, seeming to expect neither answer nor judgment.

"I do not have the wisdom to resolve this," I said.

"Yet mankind has asked these same things, and more, and still it survives."

"I have seen mankind," she said. "If that is what I am—"

"There are others besides him," I said. "Joseph, for example, or myself. Mankind is great in its variety. There's even rumor, now and then, of one that lived without any flaw at all."

Her eyes brimmed with grief, if not with tears. "I would go among them," she said. "I would know their variety, and perhaps in them I shall find some clue to answer my questions."

"You are my dearest creation, Gwendolyn," I said. "I should be greatly distressed to see you go."

She watched me, mute.

Perhaps here, then, lay the dividing line. *I know my creations to be people,* I'd said. I had not even known it, until I'd spoken the words.

I said to her, "If you would go, then go in peace."

There was a flash in her eyes as she recognized the phrase for what it was: my last relinquishing of her will. Though I'd never had cause to bind her obedience, now even the lock was forever broken to me.

Oh, the loss of my Gwendolyn! Too few have these weeks been that I have known her and seen in her seeds of thought far beyond my sowing. How I shall miss her.

She readies to leave, though her living arrangements are not yet decided. I have given her most of the remaining gold. Now that the threat is gone, I see no reason to depart from our home here, and so she will always know how to find us again when she desires—and I believe she will desire it one day.

The Bird Reader's Granddaughter

written by

Kim A. Gillett

illustrated by

ILYA SHKIPIN

ABOUT THE AUTHOR

Kim Gillett remembers telling her first story: she was three, lying on a green velvet couch and eating a chocolate bar. "Why don't you tell me a story?" asked her Scottish nana, who had entertained young Kim with tales about Mr. Giant. Kim composed her thoughts and replied, "Once upon a time, and you know what happened?" Nana shook her head, and Kim giggled. Neither ever found out.

Years later, Kim's young son's night terrors woke her repeatedly. Unable to sleep, Kim started and, over time, finished a 140,000-word fantasy novel. One friend asked cautiously, "Have you ever heard about point of view?" Soon after, Kim applied to the Odyssey Fantasy Writing Workshop and, much to her delight, was accepted. Sarah Totton and Michail Velichansky, both WOTF Volume XXII winners, were fellow classmates.

Kim lives in upstate New York with her husband and two children. She is a member of R-SPEC, Rochester's Speculative Literature Association, and is working on an anthology about Rochester in 2034. She writes to find out what happens next and workshops her stories and second novel with a fantastic group of writers.

ABOUT THE ILLUSTRATOR

Ilya Shkipin was born in Saint Petersburg, Russia, and currently resides in Fremont, California. He comes from a long line of artists: his father is an artist, and his grandfather is a noted artist in northern Russia who paints landscapes of his native Karelia, north of Saint Petersburg. Naturally, all of Ilya's very early art training came from them. While still a boy in Russia, Ilya also took many art classes to further develop his skills.

After coming to the United States in 2002, Ilya continued his education and has won several art contests. He has studied computer graphic art and attended the Saturday Art Experience at the San Francisco Academy of Art. There, he received the Certificate of Participation as Most Outstanding Student. Currently, Ilya is taking private lessons from artist Pavel Tayber. In his spare time, Ilya is learning to play rock guitar.

The Bird Reader's Granddaughter

The climb to Grandmother's is hard and long. Today I trudge up the cliff alone, my heart heavy with news.

The knotted rope straps of my bulky pack burn my shoulders. I set down the heavy kettle filled with my clothes and stop to rest on a rock that overlooks the sea. The water is calm, as flat and blue as the sky. Gulls circle below me, their cries muted on the still air. On the beach I spot scavengers, tiny as sand fleas from this height. For a jealous moment I wish I were among them, calling to my friends, "Look what the storm brought. Another treasure!"

From where I sit, the town and the shoals are hidden by a headland that juts far into the sea. Two days ago those shoals claimed my father, and grief claimed my mother. I lost both parents in an afternoon storm as ferocious as any ever seen in these parts.

On that day, dark clouds roiled. Wind whipped rain sideways and tore tiles off roofs. I stood with my mother and others behind the Widow's Wail, a high stone bulwark that protected the town from the sea. Waves battered the stones as we watched for the fishing fleet's safe return. The rain stopped long enough for almost every woman in town to witness the boats foundering on the shoals. One moment eight boats bobbed and twisted on waves taller than trees; the next, they disappeared. No one has ever survived those treacherous waters.

My mother was not the first to jump from the wall, nor was she the last. She turned and hugged me, her eyes searching for understanding. She tugged the gold ring from her finger, tucked it in my pocket and fastened her locket around my neck. "You're fifteen and old enough. Promise you'll go to Grandmother's. She'll be expecting you."

Not Grandmother's!

What would I do? Grandmother lived with her birds on a barren hill far from town. The townsfolk feared her and rarely visited. Despite my repeated requests, Grandmother refused to teach me more than the rudiments of her craft—much like a baker's child who measures ingredients but never learns how to bake the bread.

She also refused to tell me why.

Mother's mouth tightened and twitched. She shook my shoulders gently. "Promise me, Catia."

I dared not argue and keep Mother from leaving. A wave crashed against the bulwark; spray wetted my face. I nodded reluctantly and hugged her again.

"Bide well," she said, caressing my cheek.

Weeping, I gave my mother a leg up onto the bulwark and watched her dive into the next wave. According to our beliefs, couples joined together in death lived together in eternity. Of course, mothers with young children or other responsibilities don't dive; neither do women whose husbands have treated them unkindly. And neither do those whose deaths are separated by too much time.

Those left behind give the wall its name.

My pack bulges with my parent's treasures, hastily wrapped china, a mirror, ivory carvings, cutlery, scissors, needles, mother's thimble and a blanket woven by her. Tonight—before the town's elders sell the house to repay my father's debts—I'll slip back into town to retrieve the linens, more of mother's handiwork, and the rest of her sewing supplies. As long as things are stored at Grandmother's, no one will dare seek them as payment.

I hug my knees, peer up the path and wonder why I haven't seen her birds all day. Usually their swarm blackens the sky above her cottage. Fear's cold fingers creep up my back. I lumber to my feet and scurry up the path with newfound energy. Not much longer. Finally, I reach the flattened top of a hill and gasp. Fall has arrived.

Before me the leaves of an ancient oak blaze red and orange—its wind-twisted limbs afire in autumn glory. Beyond the tree, Grandmother's weathered board-and-batten cottage sits near the edge of the cliff, overlooking the sea. Smoke rises from the chimney. I sigh and stop to catch my breath. For once the air is sweet. Grandmother burns apple wood.

Between the tree and the cottage, birds the size of gulls crowd the ground. Hundreds of them. They make a low sound that throbs like a drum. As I stumble toward her door, they waddle apart, allowing me a narrow path. The sun turns their black feathers a sparkling blue-green, like the insides of mussel shells. The birds' eerie thrum fills me with dread.

I rap three times on Grandmother's door: once for the spinner, once for the weaver and once for the unraveler. The proper knock for a seer.

"Catia, come in."

She knows it's me!

I set the kettle on the stoop and open the door reluctantly. This is my new home.

The next morning, Grandmother shakes me awake. She's wearing a sea-gray dress made from material woven and dyed by my mother to match our eyes. I outgrew my dress when I was ten. Grandmother's a tiny woman. Her white hair is pinned in a bun. She dyes the wisps about her face with tea and curls them around a hot fire poker. From where I lie, only her tea-stained curls are visible and she appears blond, but the wrinkles around her mouth and eyes betray her age. I share her long, square-tipped nose and large-knuckled fingers. Her smile is kind.

"Almost time to run through the birds, Catia. Let's see what this day will bring."

I burrow under the covers and cry. In past visits, running through the birds each morning was my favorite part of the day. Grandmother even taught me how to read a few signs, but never enough to read a fortune, despite my pleading.

"The life of a seer is not an easy one, Catia," she said. "Imagine knowing the world's ills long before they happen. Imagine knowing how your friends and neighbors and loved ones will die. Imagine knowing that your actions might harm others."

But her reasons never dissuaded me from asking, from hoping she would change her mind.

This morning, however, I miss my parents. For years my mother awoke me with a kiss on my forehead and a steaming cup of tea. Most mornings the sweet smell of griddlecakes turned by my father enticed me to the table, and his jokes brightened even the darkest day.

One storm. Just one storm. That's all it took to take my happiness away. My future seems as bleak as this hillside.

I rise reluctantly, wash my hands and the tears from my cheeks, then sit at the table to eat a steaming bowl of oatmeal—poor fare after griddlecakes. It's delicious, though, sweetened with chunks of dried fruit. I raise an eyebrow.

"Dates," Grandmother says, smiling. And she tells me of her latest visitor, who traveled far to have his future read. "He brought dates and enough rice to last us until next summer."

"Was his a good fortune, Grandmother?"

She shrugs and musses my hair. "It was his fortune and little can be done to change it. Now run. Run through the birds."

I walk out of the cottage, and she follows close on my heels. Dew is heavy on the ground. In the still air, the bird smell is strong and sour, and not unlike an old empty pickle barrel. The birds face east, waiting silently with their necks thrust tall, amber beaks pointing toward the sky.

I, too, wait for the first glimpse of sun on the horizon. The birds will not fly before sunrise, nor after the sun's set. They appear so vulnerable. Grandmother warned me that they would shatter like glass if I ran through them too soon. Yet Grandmother has never lost one of her flock to foxes or wolves or poachers. Nothing seems to disturb the birds' roost.

A cluster of morning clouds brightens the eastern horizon with purple and pink. The air is crisp. After Grandmother reads the birds, I'll slip into town. I was too tired to return last night, and Grandmother promised to help this morning. At least she'll walk to the bottom of the cliff to carry a load back for me. That way I can bring the bedding, for her linens are old and much mended.

I wouldn't dare ask her to come into town for fear of her life. Even while the fishing fleet sank, people along the Widow's Wail cursed her name and her wisdom, blaming her for the storm, blaming her for not warning them of tumultuous weather, blaming her for the loss of sons and fathers and lovers and husbands. I blush and hang my head. Despite my love for Grandmother, after Mother dove off the bulwark, I cursed the loudest.

"Get ready," Grandmother says.

Shaken from my dark memory, I run along the edge of the birds' nesting grounds until I stand east of them. Then I wait, facing her and the birds. The sun's first glare is captured and reflected in hundreds of eyeballs. I spread my arms, close my eyes and run through the birds in three giant looping circles. Wings swoosh, but I continue to run, confident of avoiding a collision despite where I step. Trampling a bird was once a great fear of mine, but it's impossible during the day.

The birds take flight and swirl overhead. Three times they circle, roiling, weaving a complex dance. My grandmother stands in the middle of the field, arms spread, head tilted to the sky. I stop near her. At the end of the third pass, the birds split apart—patches blacken the morning sky as tea leaves dirty an emptied teacup. The birds freeze and hover in their places long enough for Grandmother to spin around three times, arms still spread. I spin, too.

At first the dark splotches are impossible to decipher. I squint and see—a horse and rider, a sword, and the symbols for anger and love. I close my eyes and fix the pattern of the birds firmly in my mind. I'll beg Grandmother to explain everything later.

When Grandmother finishes her circles, the flock re-forms and heads far out to sea to feed. The birds whorl as if they are leaves caught in a wind eddy. They fly close to each other, yet none collide. When the flock veers left, they all veer left. None leads, yet all follow.

Grandmother moans. I turn in time to catch her as she crumbles to the ground.

"Take me inside," she whispers.

Her gait is uncertain, and she leans heavily on me. The cottage's interior is dark after the bright sunrise. I blink hard as I duck through the doorway and lead her to the rocker by the fire. I poke the embers and add a precious log. When the kettle boils, I make tea and sweeten it with honey. "Here, Grandmother, this will make you feel better."

Her hands shake as she takes the mug. I tuck a brown plaid blanket around her. Finally she sighs and asks, "What did you see?"

"A horse and rider, a sword, love and anger."

She tilts her head to the right. "The horse and rider were hard to find."

"What else did you see, Grandmother?"

She tuts like her birds. "I'll not read your fortune for you, Catia. You know that."

"Teach me to read my own."

She shakes her head. "Sometimes it's a gift not to know what the future holds."

Grandmother hasn't said no. I ignore the deep sorrow in her voice and say, "Teach me your wisdom."

She's silent for a long time and won't meet my eyes.

My stomach twists. "I don't have the talent, do I?"

"That's not the problem."

My jaw drops, and the stirrings of excitement replace the emptiness in my stomach. Never before has she suggested that I have the talent. "Teach me. What else can I do here?"

The blanket slips off her lap. "It's a great responsibility, seeing what the future holds."

I grab her left hand and clutch it tightly. "Trust me! I'm responsible."

She stares at the fire. The rocking chair creaks loudly, and I wonder at her indecision. The log sputters and sparks. I stamp out the embers that fall on the hearthrug.

"Others will come," she says softly, still staring at the flames, "and from today on, I'll teach you to read theirs. You must be able to care for yourself. I'm old. Twirling makes me dizzy."

Suddenly I'm afraid. "Grandmother, is there something I should know? Have you . . ."

I can't ask if she foresaw her death. "Are you all right?"

"I'll be with you for a long while."

She points at the rug and sighs. A tiny tendril of

smoke wisps beside my ankle. My face flushes. I stomp out the ember I missed. Burnt wool scents the room.

"How soon will I be able to tell fortunes?"

"It takes years, perhaps a lifetime, to understand and interpret the signs. There's much more to seeing than reading the birds. But you'll be able to start telling simple fortunes when you learn the most common patterns. As your knowledge grows, so will your powers of sight."

In my excitement, I gnaw my thumbnail painfully below the quick.

"Bring me the slate," Grandmother says, "and I'll explain more patterns."

By afternoon the wind is howling. I shut the door, glancing first to make sure that the birds roost safely. My head pounds from staring at the slate, but my heart is light. Finally, I have my heart's desire. I'm learning to read the birds.

"Grandmother, another storm's coming. I can smell it. I'm going back into town to get more things before it starts to rain."

She settles into her rocker and closes her eyes. "I'm too tired to help you now, Catia."

"I'll manage. If there's more than I can carry, I'll hide things by the trail to bring up tomorrow."

"Be careful. No one will be happy that you're living here."

The bell tolls again as I slip into the town. No one is in the streets. Today, the third day after the storm, everyone is gathered in Remembrance. Each person who died in the storm will be Remembered, in turn, by those still living. The town boy closest to age sixteen rings the bell between each Remembering. I wonder if they have Remembered my parents yet. I'm overcome by the guilt of not being there.

So I do my own Remembering as I open the door from the garden into our kitchen. I must hurry now, for clouds darken the sky and the house may already be sold. I take a deep breath, but the smell inside is of rot, not sweet lavender. I take no time to find the spoiled food. A fleeting sunbeam streams though a heavy blue glass bottle that sits on a tiny windowsill near the door, casting an azure shadow on the well-scrubbed floorboards. Mother kept fresh flowers in the vase for as long as possible each year, until winter withered her garden. Today, purple asters sag from the lack of water.

I turn slowly and fix in my memory everything about this room where I was so happy. Father's chair and my stool are positioned by the fire. When he was not fishing, this is where we sat and he told stories about his adventures. The chair is too heavy for me to carry to Grandmother's. My stool is covered with Mother's needlepoint of her favorite flowers. I can't leave that behind.

Beside the fireplace is my bed nook, with gaily stenciled doors and interior, and a tiny diamond window made from colored glass. I cram linens and blankets into the pack knotted by my father. I grab my sweater and mother's cloak and sigh. Everything I want to bring is bulky. I can't take it all.

The bell tolls again, and wind rattles the windows. The storm. I'll have to Remember later. Maybe Grandmother will help.

A cold wind blows the door open. I take Mother's waxed cloak out of the pack and stuff in her skirts. We'll use the material, somehow. I sling the pack on my back, throw the cloak over my shoulders, and grab the stool and hold it under my arm. The cloak is big enough to enfold everything. I'm almost out the door when I spy the blue bottle. I don't have time to put it in my pack, so I pluck the wilted asters out of the mouth and grab it by the neck with my free hand. In my haste, I don't bother to close the door.

Ten townsfolk stand in the garden, their faces as dark and stormy as the clouds above. I nod to them. One, a woman who was jealous of my mother's fine needlework, calls, "Where were you, girl? You missed the Remembrance."

I'm not sure what to do. They block my way.

"Where were you?" another asks.

Honesty's best. That's what Father always advised.

"At my grandmother's." I suppose their reaction shouldn't surprise me, but it does.

The jealous woman shakes her fist at me. "She's wicked. A fraud."

"It's her fault so many died," says her husband.

"No," I shout, "it was our misfortune."

"Liar!"

I'm not sure who throws the first stone. It catches me on the cheek; another hits my forehead. One pings off the bottle. I turn and flee into the house as rain pelts the ground. Someone swears, but no one follows me inside. I lean against the door and cry—for my mother, my father and myself—so happy four days ago. Now I only have Grandmother.

In the dying light, I pack the bottle, then peek out the door. The townsfolk are gone. This time when I leave, I close the door and latch it tight.

Five days after my arrival at Grandmother's cottage, a donkey brays loudly outside and someone knocks gently on the door. Grandmother smiles and winks at me. "That donkey would be Flower. Her owner is the eldest Bascome boy, Jole. His mother's farm is way east of town. Do you know him? He brings the apple wood. Vegetables, too. Ready?" She hands me a shawl.

We go outside. The clouds are low, and the air damp. I draw the shawl tightly around my shoulders. Flower pulls a two-wheeled cart filled with wood. Two baskets perch on top. The rich scent of apples disguises the bird stench. I lick my lips.

Grandmother introduces me to the man beside the donkey. "Jole, this is my apprentice, Catia. Today, she'll read the birds, too."

Jole towers over Grandmother. Though he's only eighteen or so, I don't remember seeing him in town. He looks like most of the townsfolk—straight blond hair, high cheekbones under eyes that change color like the sea. His nose ends in a point, and his smile is merry. A long green woolen coat hides his shape. I can't help but stare at the flat hat he has pulled low over his left ear. The colors and pattern are the work of a master knitter. He catches me staring. I blush and loosen my shawl. I'm too warm.

He shuffles his feet.

Grandmother's smile is sweet. "Run through the birds, Jole."

Jole grins. "Remember our bargain, old woman."

I bristle at his insolence, but Grandmother laughs merrily. "I know, dear boy, only the good news."

He runs agilely through the birds. They take flight, swirl, then break into blotches that darken the sky. With my hands outstretched, I twirl, fixing the shape of the patches in my mind, trying—as Grandmother explained—not to find meaning at that moment.

In my inexperience, I interpret the patches too quickly. I see love. Deep love. And somehow it's love that involves me. There's more, too. I grit my teeth and push the images from my mind. I stare at Jole for a moment, my heart pounding, before I race to the cottage and slam the door.

After a long while, Grandmother returns. Her eyes are red. I'm sitting in her rocker by the fire with my legs curled under me. She says nothing about my extravagance of burning two logs, though winter approaches rapidly.

Grandmother puts a hand on my forehead and smiles reassuringly. It's a kind smile that lights her eyes and raises her wrinkles. It puts me at ease.

"Tell me," she says. "What did you see?"

My face feels hot under her cool hand. "I saw love."

Grandmother tuts. "Is that all?"

I shake my head and turn from her. "I saw my future with Jole."

"Is that all?"

"Mostly." I didn't want to say the bad parts aloud. She would have seen them, too.

"Had I known what you would see," she says softly, "I wouldn't have had you read his fortune."

Though Jole comes each week to bring fresh vegetables and apples, eggs and cheese, and more firewood, he has never asked for his fortune to be told again. For a long while, we're nervous and quiet in each other's presence. But one day he brings me a bouquet of autumn daisies. My smile finds his. He has captured my heart.

I run into the cottage, throw open the chest where my treasures are kept, and pull out Mother's blue bottle. It's been stored since I returned from town. I bring it outside to the well to fill.

"How did that happen?" Jole points to the ding and a crack in the thick glass—a dark blue, jagged lightning bolt surrounds the middle of the bottle.

I remember the townsfolk throwing stones at me and chanting, "Liar." Before packing it, I hadn't examined the bottle.

"It was a beautiful bottle," I cry. "My mother's treasure."

Jole senses my deep despair. He puts his arm about my shoulders, lightly at first. I lean into him, and he pulls me closer. "It's still beautiful, despite the fault. The jagged line reminds me of waves separating the sea from the sky."

He takes the bottle, fills it with water and arranges the daisies. It doesn't leak. The bottle catches the sun, sparkling bright blue glass with yellow-eyed white daisies.

"It's almost as beautiful as you," he whispers.

My heart soars.

Every week I wait anxiously for Flower's brays. Until the death frost, Jole brings flowers for the vase. When I'm older, Jole will ask me to marry him. Yet I face a dilemma. Jole is a farmer, and as eldest son, he will inherit the Bascome farm when his mother passes. Grandmother and the birds live on this hill. The birds would scatter to the four winds before they would follow me to the farm.

I read my indecision in his fortune, but in my embarrassment, I didn't see what lay next. What am I to do? I'm hesitant to ask Grandmother.

Two years pass, and it's early spring. Jole still has not asked me to be his wife, though I'm the age that many girls marry. His mother is ill, and he stays away for weeks at a time. I'm bored. My patience thins. I wonder if I want to be his wife on a farm that is apparently as isolated as this hilltop.

Since coming here, I've read the fortunes of ninety or so men and women and one young boy whose father wanted to know how to train him. At first, Grandmother asked me what I saw when the birds hovered, and she explained any signs I missed. Now I tell fortunes to our patrons without consulting her.

Others clamor for Grandmother's wisdom, too. When these men—most often soldiers dressed in uniforms—ride up to our cottage, she briskly hustles me into the cottage and bids me to stay inside until they leave. I asked her once why I couldn't read their fortunes.

She said, "They come wanting to know if they will win their battles or their wars. I do my best to impart my wisdom, in hopes that their battles will never be fought."

Astonished by her answer, I asked, "Do you not tell whether they will win?"

"I try to tell them how to win without fighting."

And so today, with my grandmother away tending Jole's sick mother, a soldier wearing a deep purple uniform rides up to the cottage as I lug the washing outside to hang on the line. His tall black horse snorts and bucks as I set the basket on the ground. The birds closest to us flap their wings and resettle a short distance away. My hair is pulled back. I wipe damp tendrils off my forehead with the back of my arm and look up.

"Tell me my fortune, sweet lady," he says.

"No, I cannot. Only my grandmother tells the fortune of soldiers."

"Please find her. I'm in a hurry. My battle won't wait."

I shake my head, truly sorry that she's not here to help him. "She's away, tending a sick friend."

He's a beautiful man, sitting tall in a silver-encrusted saddle. Sun lights his hair in a golden crown. His eyes are the blue of my bottle. When he smiles, I need to place my hand on the saddle's stirrup to hold myself upright. He seems to know his effect on me and presses it.

"You tell fortunes, too. Is that not true?"

I nod.

"Then tell mine. It's important. Essential."

"I'm sorry. I can't help you." When Grandmother left for the Bascome farm, she made me promise not to tell the future of soldiers.

He pulls a small purse from his saddlebag and dangles it before me. "Gold," he says, "enough to live on for a year or two."

The purse's strings strain under the weight. Even if the purse only contained copper, we could live on the money for years. Reluctantly I shake my head. "Only Grandmother tells the fortune of soldiers," I whisper.

The purple soldier is off his horse in an instant and stands before me. He's taller than I believed, with broad shoulders and easy charm. I find it hard to look him in the eye.

"At least draw me some water to drink and some for my horse."

"With pleasure." I back away toward the well.

I water the horse first. His smell is strong, of sunlight and manure, and not unpleasant. Then I fetch our finest drinking glass from the cottage. The horse snorts as the man mounts gracefully. My heart is singing. I flush and reach into the well to draw up another bucket.

When I hand him the glass our fingers touch, linger. As he smiles, I smile. Our eyes lock. "Please read my fortune."

I can only nod yes. Around us, the birds tut.

He leans over and hands me the purse, then gently sweeps the hair out of my eyes. I stretch toward his touch, and he caresses my face. My body shivers, and I yearn for him in a way that I never yearned for Jole.

Jole! I push him from my mind. He's a boy compared to this man.

The soldier draws his fingers across my lips. I kiss them in reflex and almost say, *Come off your horse, there's more of me that needs to be touched.* Instead I reach for his hand and still his caress. "Run through the birds," I whisper. "Three times without stopping."

The soldier squeezes my fingers and hands me the glass.

Blindly I set it down, not caring where I place it.

Then, without dismounting, he kicks the horse and gallops through the birds.

"Wait," I call, reaching toward him, "not on the horse."

He's heard me, I'm sure. But he doesn't stop.

My heart's in my throat, pounding wildly. Birds scatter, their scolding loud. Miraculously, the horse's giant hooves harm not a one. The soldier and the horse circle three times. Hooves pound the earth, shaking me through my shoes. When he stops, the birds hover. I stretch out my arms and twirl three times, staring at the black patches in the sky, wondering what Grandmother would say to this soldier.

"You'll win the battle," I blurt when I stop. The signs are so clear. What isn't as clear are the results of battles to follow.

"Will I be wounded?"

Slowly I shake my head. Nothing indicated that he would be wounded. I search for more to say—to stop the battle so no one gets hurt. To offer wisdom like Grandmother. My mind blanks, and I'm tongue-tied. In a moment of panic, my confidence falters and I realize I lack her skills.

"I knew it!" he says triumphantly. He kicks his horse sharply and leaves without saying or waving goodbye. A hoof catches the glass and shatters it.

Until Grandmother returns from tending Jole's mother, I must stay on the hill and take care of the birds. When Grandmother was my age, she started this flock with twenty birds. As the flock enlarged to hundreds, her powers as a seer increased. New birds filled in the gaps and completed the sky pictures so they could be read easily and truly. Imagine having only two birds to make the figure for love, when five are needed for it to appear clearly.

ILYA SHKIPIN

The birds don't need much help, but during fair weather, I do need to run through them at dawn each day if we want to keep the flock together. It's part of their magic. Otherwise they'll disperse to the four winds.

The morning following my soldier's visit, I resist the temptation to read my fortune. I'd glimpsed my life with Jole, a future I now wanted to reject. Besides, Grandmother taught me the folly of reading one's own fortune when I first moved into the cottage, after I told her about the townsfolk throwing rocks.

She said, "Catia, the morning of the storm that claimed my daughter and your father, I told my fortune and knew the storm approached. I've known for years that your father would die on the shoals. Just not the specific day. Your parents knew what I knew."

I leapt up from my stool and pointed a shaking finger at her. Resentment and anger loosened my tongue. "You knew! You could have prevented the fishermen from setting sail. You killed Father *and* Mother."

My voice was shrill and my passion hot. I stared angrily until I realized how still she had become. Her eyes were closed and her wrinkles set in paths of grief so deep, I leaned forward to caress her cheek, desperate that she not leave me, too.

"Grandmother? I'm sorry."

When she opened her eyes, I cried to see their sadness.

"Their boats left on the tide, at dawn that day. What was I to do? I could not reach town in time to warn them."

I hung my head and remembered those who condemned her along the Widow's Wail. I blushed, recalling my loud curses. Perhaps the townsfolk were to blame. For unlike Grandmother's patrons from far-off lands, they ignored and condemned her services as a seer. If one of the townsfolk had visited regularly, maybe Grandmother would have foreseen the storm's immediacy, and the fishermen would have been forewarned.

We never raised the subject again. I dare not tempt fate by reading my own future.

I dream of my soldier, his blue eyes and smile, and wonder if he's thinking of me. Something magical passed between us that morning. While his name remains a mystery, my feelings are not. I'm in love. Jole no longer occupies my daydreams. I laugh that I once wanted to be his wife.

Though I watch for him, my soldier does not return to brag of his brilliant victory. Instead, five days later fire scents the air. Black smoke billows to the south, in the direction of the town. The smoke continues all day, and I worry that more than one house burns, but the wind is still. Surely the townsfolk would have extinguished a single house fire by now.

The birds get loud after dark. Across the hill, lanterns light the field near the path from town. I open the door wide and set my lantern on the stoop, so the travelers know where to come. Six people, one old man and five women, crowd into the cottage. Dirt smudges their faces, and they reek of sweat and burning timbers.

"What happened?" I cry as I fill the kettle with water and rice.

Tinson Rascolm who once fished with my father says, "Soldiers ransacked and burned the town."

The blood drains from my face. My legs wobble. I reach out for support.

Tinson grips my arm. "Steady," he says.

My stomach twists into knots though I'm confident my soldier, so gallant on his black horse, wouldn't stoop to burning a town. "Soldiers? What soldiers?"

We crowd by the fire. The women stare vacantly. One shrugs. I know them—they're gossips, always chattering. The youngest is Tinson's daughter, Dellila. Their silence frightens me in a way that nothing else does.

Tinson says, "Red soldiers stormed the town this morning brandishing torches. Searched houses, then set them on fire. We hid in my fruit cellar until dark. Didn't know where to go. Thanks for opening your door, Catia."

"Why did soldiers burn the houses?"

Tinson squints and shakes his head. "They seek the leader of the men wearing purple. That's what we overheard. Last week, many townsmen joined him to fight. My son-in-law did."

Dellila moans. One of the older women puts a hand on her shoulder to comfort her.

I gulp and turn to stir the rice.

"There were two battles to our south," Tinson says. "Great battles, according to the people who fled north."

"Who's fighting, Tinson, and why? Who's red and who's purple?"

Tinson shakes his head. "I'm not sure. Not sure even why. I'm just an old fisherman who once tended a fine garden. The purple soldiers said they wanted to protect us from the Reds. Never paid attention to things beyond our town. Most didn't. Nothing ever affected us, except the sea. Not in all my years. Not until now."

My head sags. I study the women through my tears. One whimpers.

Tinson clears his throat. "Didn't even know that soldiers wore purple until Dellila's husband put on the coat they gave him."

I can't help my great sobs. I should have told my purple soldier about the battles he would lose.

"Watch the flame, girl, or you'll scorch the rice."

In the morning, I slip out of the cottage before sunrise. Tinson follows me. I'm tempted to ask if he wants his fortune told. But misery etches his face, and I fear to compound it. While Tinson watches, I run through the birds. They break into splotches against the sky.

"Can you read the birds, Catia?"

I nod. "Grandmother taught me."

He bends, picks a blade of grass and shreds it, then picks another. "Have you read your own?"

"Once. Well, twice," I say as I think of Jole. "The second time I didn't intend to. I haven't since Grandmother warned against reading my own fortune. She read hers the day my parents died, but there was nothing she could do to warn the fishermen, they'd already sailed on the early tide. Sometimes, though, it's hard not to look."

Tinson scratches his head. "Never wanted to know what surprises my life held. Been happiest that way. Imagine knowing that someday my house would be burned and I would be fleeing town. How could I have enjoyed my life?"

We watch the flock roil in great twists out to sea.

Tinson shifts and puts a hand on my right shoulder. "Your father knew he'd die on those shoals. He told everyone who fished in his boat. Knowing didn't keep them ashore."

I ponder Tinson's words as I fix a kettle of oatmeal sweetened with honey for everyone. Knowing the risks, my father had warned others and they still had gone to sea. For a brief moment I'm angry at him for risking his life. He could have stayed on land, then I might be at home with him this morning, drinking tea, eating griddlecakes, listening to his jokes.

I clench my fists and realize the folly of my thoughts. He loved the sea. His heart was happiest when salt spray wetted his face and his boat rocked beneath him.

During breakfast the women remain silent. Though their faces are clean, their hair and clothing still reek of smoke.

Tinson's anxious to leave. "Best you come with us, Catia. Don't let the soldiers find you here alone."

I walk outside with them and shake my head. "If I don't tend the flock, the birds will disappear, and my grandmother and I will be unable to see the future."

"What good are fortunes?" Dellila says, her voice shrill. "What good are they if they don't prevent battles or shipwrecks? Did your grandmother know our town would burn? Did she let it burn because the townsfolk have been cruel to her?"

"How could she have known about the battles?" I shout. "She's been away. And no one from town ever seeks to have their future told. So how could she have foretold that soldiers would burn the town?" My chest heaves, and my face is hot. I clench my fists.

I'm not being truthful, and the expression on Dellila's

face tells me that she knows it too. Grandmother must have known for years that soldiers would come. Had she warned the elders? Had they laughed in her face? And, like my father knowing his fate, what could the elders have done even if they had known?

Tinson puts his hand up. "Enough. If you won't join us, Catia, we'll say bide well. Stay safe, young one. Hide if the soldiers come."

"Sorry," I say to Tinson's daughter as she walks by. "You've lost so much."

She nods, then stoops to pick up the food I packed for their trip. She slings the bag over her shoulder and pushes her hair off her face. "I don't know what's happened to my husband," she whispers through tears. "I wanted to jump off the Widow's Wail, but my father wouldn't let me. I may have missed my chance at eternity with the man I love."

Her red-rimmed eyes are wide with panic. "Do you know if he's dead?"

I shake my head. "I wish I could help. If you stay until the birds return, I'll read your fortune."

She twists the gold ring on her finger, then brings her fist to her mouth. "I can't. If I knew, what could I do now?"

"Stay safe, Dellila."

She turns slowly and trudges after the group. They head east, away from town toward the city, along the path that most of our patrons follow. It's been quite a while since Flower has trod up it. While daydreaming about my soldier, I'd been glad that Jole had not visited. Now, watching the ragged line disappear, I worry about what might have happened at the Bascome farm.

And for the first time I'm concerned about my

survival. Our patrons often bring food as payment. That's how Grandmother survived some fifty years on this barren hill. But if soldiers are burning towns or making travel impossible, I don't expect that I'll have any customers. Belatedly, I realize that I shouldn't have been so generous with my rice and oatmeal. Little good my bag of gold will do if there's nowhere to buy supplies. Perhaps Tinson's garden or another survived the burning, and I can glean early plantings from there.

I'll find out tomorrow after running through the birds.

Sunrise turns hundreds of bird eyes a gleaming pink. Wearily I make three slow loops through the birds. Last night I tossed and turned with worry—for Grandmother, Tinson and Dellila, my purple soldier and myself. I debate whether I should see what the sky foretells. My arms are stiff, and it's difficult to hold them high as I twirl.

I have to know. Just a peek.

Reluctantly I open my eyes and read the sky. The soldier and horse is the first pattern I see, then the sword.

He'll return! Elation courses through my body, and I don't bother to read the rest of the patterns.

Though the air is heavy with the acrid scent of smoke, my steps to town are light. In places the path is overgrown, the weeds trampled by Tinson's group. I push their plight from my mind. I'm sorry Dellila and I traded harsh words. She married the baker's son the summer before my parents died, and they made the bread we bought daily. The baker's shop was a happy place, and more than once, they were kissing when I walked inside.

I consider her dilemma about using the Widow's Wail. If I thought my purple soldier was dead, would I jump to be with him for an eternity? As I muse about this, I crest the hill that overlooks the town. Reflexively, I duck.

The town smolders, and the wind brings the smell of charred flesh. I cringe and heave my breakfast. Hundreds of white tents line the streets, and red uniformed soldiers shout orders. For a long while I lay there, trembling, wishing I had read all of this morning's sky.

Slowly I back away from the overlook and creep into a thicket. Thorns scratch my face and tear my dress. My mouth tastes foul. I huddle uncomfortably, holding my breath each time the wind rustles the grasses. Mid-afternoon the wind changes, bringing a storm off the sea. When the rain starts, I shield my face from the thorns, crawl out of the thicket, then dash up the path like a rabbit.

By the time I reach my flattened hilltop, the wind picks up. Rain stings my face. Someone stands in the cottage's doorway. He's blond and dressed in purple. Despite my grief, my heart bursts with joy as I run to greet my soldier. He runs, too, nimbly jumping over the nests. It's only after he sweeps me up and twirls me that I realize my mistake. I slip from Jole's embrace. He smiles broadly, and I force a smile in return, unable to share my disappointment. Yet I'm strangely happy to see him.

He grabs my hand and pulls me toward the cottage. We dash inside. "I've not much time. Your grandmother's well. She'll return when the roads are safe to travel."

"Your mother?"

He shakes his head and sprays the table with a shower of raindrops. "Five days ago."

"I'm sorry."

"I've brought you food, as much as I could carry. And a few of my treasures," he says shyly. He wipes his face with the towel I hand him.

"Where's Flower?"

"The soldiers took her. We gave them most of our food and animals in return for protection against the Reds. Your grandmother overheard them talking to me outside. She was smart and hid the things I brought behind the bed, then laid down and played dead. That's the only reason they didn't take me with them. I said I had to bury her. But they gave me a coat and told me to take the road north."

"What's going on, Jole?" I cry. "Who's fighting and why?"

Jole stops by the doorway and drops my hand. "I'm not sure. The Reds want our lands. That's what the purple soldiers told me."

His fingers trace a scratch across my forehead, then tenderly brush the tears off my cheeks. "Run through the birds, Catia. That's what she wants you to do. Don't let them separate.

"I wish you could tell my fortune now, but I know the birds won't fly in the rain and I must be quick. I've until midnight to join them. The soldier who allowed me the time to bury your grandmother cautioned me not to tarry longer. He said their leader's an angry man, especially since he lost his arm in the first battle."

He leans over and pecks my cheek. "Stay safe. Run if you spy a Red."

"Stay safe," I whisper, but Jole is already sprinting down the path.

The doorjamb supports my weight. Could the leader Jole speaks of be my purple soldier? No. I shake my head, certain it is not he. His fortune told of no wounds in battle.

Refugees, burned and occupied towns, loved ones going to war. Was this my fault? Perhaps my talents as a bird reader were not strong as I thought, for I had foreseen none of these things.

I should have told my purple soldier about the other battles. Why, oh why, did I ever agree to read his fortune when I had promised Grandmother not to?

Sheets of rain drive me indoors. Tonight I light a blazing fire to dry out my clothes and drive out my demons. As I peel off my wet things, I feel naked and exposed. The Reds could be watching. I hide under my sheet to dress.

The food Jole brought is stacked neatly on the table. A simple gold bracelet and woman's ring glint in the fire's light—his treasures. I try neither on.

Grandmother was practical in her choices of what to hide—mostly dried fruits and vegetables and a sack of flour. I muster a grin when two small butter cakes tumble out of a napkin. The cakes are her specialty. I put on the kettle, make tea. By the time I finish the cup, both cakes are eaten and I've made plans.

Tomorrow I'll start conserving wood. Jole's not here to bring more, and I don't want smoke to attract the Reds. Over the next few evenings, if it's not too humid or raining, I'll bake hardbread with most of the flour so it doesn't spoil. The hardbread will keep until fall and beyond. Every day I'll tend the birds and the garden, then forage for berries and greens and later in the summer for fruits.

I look for Grandmother's arrival every day. Spring blossoms into summer, then fall fades into an early winter. The days and nights are cooler, but there hasn't been a frost yet. I venture into town when I find the Reds have left. The smell of wet charred wood lingers as I scavenge every garden, looking for anything to harvest. In Tinson's garden I gather bunches of herbs and harvest a row of juicy thick carrots into my knotted bag.

As I return to the cottage, I spy what appears to be a blue blanket thrown in a heap on the path toward the city. My heart thumps wildly as I turn in every direction to see who might have dropped it, but the hill is bare. Even the birds are gone. As I stare, the blanket moves. An elbow sticks up. I drop my gatherings and run to find out who has fallen. It's Grandmother! She collapsed a ways from the cottage. She smiles limply at me. I pull her to her feet and wrap her arm around my shoulder. We stumble toward the cottage, and finally we're inside. She's shivering, so I collect wood from the woodpile to light a fire.

I make tea and bring her a piece of hardbread and the raspberry mash I use as jam.

The food revives her. She licks her puckered lips and tries to stand.

"Sit, Grandmother."

She shakes her head. "I must see my birds. I heard them return."

I help her outside. The birds crowd around us. She sighs and smiles. "They're fine. Has anyone come for their fortune?"

I shake my head. "Not recently."

The silence grows between us. Finally it's unbearable. "Grandmother," I blurt, "a soldier came last spring and asked me to tell his fortune. I refused, but he insisted."

"And?"

I tell her all but how the soldier captured my heart. She nods as if she knows everything that had happened.

"How do you know all this?" I ask.

"I saw it when I read your fortune, the day after you arrived. Remember the rider and horse and sword? I thought that by keeping you from the soldiers who ventured here, I could keep this from happening. But it was not to be." She wobbles, and I put my arm around her.

We stand together and watch the sun set. Birds settle around us, thrumming softly. The clouds turn a brilliant pink and orange. With the sun gone, the horizon turns a bloody red.

"Time to go in," I say.

When we turn to the cottage, dozens of lights bobble toward us.

"Run, Catia. Hide!" Grandmother screeches.

I pull her after me toward the oak. Hooves pound and a dark shape cuts us off. The horse snorts softly. Beside me Grandmother shakes. Her scent of fear is strong and mingles with my own. Though my knees threaten collapse, I stand tall. Other horses surround us. Soldiers lift their lanterns. And in the light I see that it's not the Reds. My purple soldier has returned. He greets my smile with a sneer.

"Well, Seer," he says, "you were right about one thing, I did win the first battle. But I did not emerge from the battlefield unscathed."

He holds the reins with one hand. I stare at his other arm for a moment.

"Ah," he says, "you've noticed how neatly my sleeve is pinned. A sword severed my arm at the shoulder. The field surgeons were unable to stitch it back together. They sawed it off."

I cringe. Grandmother moans.

His face is filled with wrath, and I look away. For months I had imagined his smile, his hands caressing my cheek and brushing my lips. I want to reach out, to tell him how sorry I am, but his fury keeps me at bay.

More soldiers surround us. They hold their lights high. The birds tut loudly.

"Quiet those birds," my purple soldier orders.

I say, "They'll quiet if we move into the cottage."

"I have another way." His smile menaces. "They shatter at night. Like glass. That's what I've been told. Run through the birds," he orders, mimicking my voice. "Run through them, men, and trample each and every one."

I gasp. "My soldier, *please*. If I've made a mistake, take me. Not Grandmother's birds."

He laughs and not kindly.

"Fool," my grandmother says.

The night grows quiet.

The men with the lights hold them higher and draw closer.

"What did you say, old woman? What did you call me?"

"Fool! You rode through the birds on your horse. It's your horse's fortune she told. I wager you sit on his back right now. And he was never injured."

His snarl turns uglier. "Run through the birds, and run through her, too," he says pointing at Grandmother.

"No!" I run to his horse, intending to beg his mercy. He kicks my face with a boot. Dizzy, I fall backwards. Grandmother catches me, and we embrace. Savage hands pull us apart. Then the deed is done. A gleaming sword turns bloody. Grandmother lies dead at my feet.

The men shout as they run through the field wielding spears and swords. Since it's after sunset, the birds don't move, and they're easy prey. Loud shattering like glass breaking fills the night. I hold my grandmother and weep. Soldiers ring us with drawn swords. There's nothing I can do to save the birds, to rescue my future.

Finally the men's shouts stop, and for a moment, the hilltop is eerily quiet. Then the black horse snorts and rears. Hooves hover above me for a terrifying moment.

My purple soldier rides off, and I still don't know his name. Who am I supposed to curse?

At dawn, I drag my grandmother to the oak. Without leaves, the oak's wind-shaped limbs hover over the ground like fingers beckoning me. Snow falls in saucer-sized flakes. The faster it snows, the smaller the flakes grow. Weary from carrying Grandmother, I gently cover her with my cloak. Later I'll bring stones to form a cairn.

Tears freeze on my cheek, but I can't feel the cold. My jaw aches from the purple soldier's kick.

I don't know what to do. Grandmother's dead. The town is destroyed. I have no idea where the Bascome farm is located. The birds, my livelihood, lie broken at my feet. The gold is tainted. There might be enough food to tide me until spring. The carrots! I dropped them yesterday after I spied Grandmother lying in a heap. I must gather them before they freeze.

Huddled against the wind, I trudge back to the cottage, my shoulders bent by the pack filled with Tinson's carrots. Sadness overwhelms me—a desolation so complete, it takes my breath away. Snow crusts my lashes.

Closer to the cottage, dead birds lie fractured like broken eggshells. As I tiptoe through the pieces, I realize that not all the birds have been killed. Some sit, heads straight up. The snow forms a white cone around them, protecting them from the cold and the icy wind. When the storm passes, they'll dig an exit hole at the bottom of the cone and use the hollow cone to protect their nest. Twenty-four, twenty-five. Falling snow obscures any distant ones.

I stare numbly at the cones. Grandmother's flock started with fewer birds than this. I've no choice but to stay here, to keep Grandmother's flock together. That's the least I can do.

No! my heart shouts. Look at the trouble you've caused. See what yielding to temptation wrought. Betrayal. Greed. Lust. War.

And death.

I've been selfish. My head hangs and shoulders sag under the responsibility of contributing to so much grief by seeing only the future I wanted. Perhaps Grandmother was right when she said, "Sometimes it's a gift not to know what the future holds."

Right now, I'd consider it a greater gift not to know what the past holds.

The few birds around me are silent. Already I miss their scolding, but I won't be deterred. "You're free," I shout. "Free to leave."

When the weather breaks, I shall leave, too. I'll make a better future for others by helping them. I won't need birds to show me the way.

The door is slightly ajar when I reach the cottage. Something is cooking that smells good. I stumble inside. A purple soldier sits by the fire smiling. This time I know his name. He's by my side in a moment.

I open my mouth to apologize, to let him know of my betrayal.

He silences me with a kiss. "I know," he says, softly. "Your grandmother told me everything the day I met you, even though she was supposed to tell me only the good things."

I moan. "I left her under the oak."

"She tried to protect you. So did I. But we must accept what the future holds for each of us. What it held for you."

I stare at my feet. Clumps of snow melt around my shoes. "How can you still love me?" My voice wavers.

"Did your father still love the sea?"

It's not enough. I weep, trying to understand what he is saying.

Jole moves to one side so I can see the table. Somewhere he found late-blooming purple asters. They are arranged in Mother's bottle.

He reaches for my hand and says, "Isn't your blue bottle still beautiful, despite the crack?"

The Girl Who Whispered Beauty

written by

Al Bogdan

illustrated by

STEPHEN KNOX

ABOUT THE AUTHOR

As a child growing up in the Berkshire Mountains area of Western Massachusetts, Al Bogdan was always riding his bike to the library, or convincing his parents to buy him books. Not just any books, mind you: he preferred the kind of stories that took the reader on wild and wondrous romps through the imagination. He was eleven when he was left at his grandparents' for a month without anything to read—Al's been writing ever since.

Al studied computer science and theater in college. He's worked as a software developer, video producer, multimedia producer and photographer, while his spare time was filled with short films, painting, puppetry, music and, of course, writing fiction. In 2002, Al joined two online science fiction writing groups: the Online Writers Workshop and Critters. In 2004, he attended the Clarion Science Fiction and Fantasy Writers' Workshop, a six-week boot camp taught by professional genre writers. Al currently resides in the suburbs of Detroit with his wife and their three-year-old daughter. He is honored to have his first professional sale here for your enjoyment.

ABOUT THE ILLUSTRATOR

"If you could illustrate your dreams" is a phrase which some have used to describe artist Stephen-Paul Knox. Born in and still a resident of the Germantown section of Philadelphia, Pennsylvania, Stephen began his art interests at an early age after he entered and won an art contest as a student at Cedar Grove Christian Academy. Lacking the financial support to attend his desired art school, Stephen began to draw cartoons and copy family photos, determined to teach himself techniques by any means necessary. As his skills developed, he soon began to gravitate toward science fiction and fantasy art. He patterned himself after some of his favorite comic book masters, eventually developing his own unique art form which can be seen in his present-day work. Books such as The Lord of the Rings, The Chronicles of Narnia *and* The Neverending Story *further drove Stephen's artistic imagination.*

Stephen currently is working on plans to develop his own multimedia company. He also hopes to publish a successful series of digital graphic novels, and one day see his vivid imagination transferred from paper onto the big screen.

The Girl Who Whispered Beauty

The house whisper-girls spent the night sneaking between hiding places, flattening their soft bones to squeeze behind ornate furniture, balling up their pliable bodies to curl under plush upholstered chairs, even sliding behind the gargantuan painting of golden flying serpents that hung over the main ballroom's mantle. They watched. They listened. Both stifled their laughter and gasps until they were together again under a table, or in a closet, comparing notes.

All through the night, the guests gallivanted through the mansion, senses chemically heightened, skin glowing brightly from the vast supply of life within them. The place was overflowing with members of the elite, the High-Ones, and they behaved in ways that fascinated the two teenage whisper-girls.

Etelka found herself in the kitchen pantry, mesmerized by two High-Ones fornicating. Etelka had known the male when he was but a child, before she was transformed into a whisperer. The boy had certainly changed as well. His family's own whisper-girls had helped him sprout wings and grow tall and bright. Without his robe, his arms and legs entangled with his companion's, their wings spread wide in passion, he was nearly as bright as the sun itself. Watching him now, Etelka hungered to slip into a dark place with someone and make it glow as brightly, but she knew a whisper-girl could never participate in such carnal pleasures, as the simple act of breathing heavily close to skin would quickly drain her dead.

The male's wings shuttered, a golden arc along his spine causing her to blink. The brightness softened as he formed a cocoon around his companion. It was the third time this had happened since Etelka started watching, and maybe more would follow, but it was time to meet Ibi in their agreed-upon hiding place, to talk and laugh about what they had both seen.

The ballroom was quiet, the dancing long over, chandeliers now extinguished. Etelka stayed close to the wall, red velvet curtains to hide herself, as she snuck to the far stage where the orchestra had played. She expelled her breath, emptying all air from her lungs, and slithered through the three-inch gap near the floor. The skull was the hardest to flatten, as she had to relax her frequently clenched jaw, allowing it to fold and spread. Once through, she would tighten her facial muscles, puffing air into her cheeks, making faces until her rubbery bones felt normal again. The rest was easier—just a slight spreading of the ribs, a touch of discomfort as the internal organs were squeezed, and some wiggling like a fish to slip her hips through. Etelka found Ibi lying in the dark, thin slits of dim light showing the soft contours of her body.

"You don't really want to leave all this, do you?" Ibi asked.

"What a question. Of course I do," replied Etelka.

"But being in a grand house is wonderful. Leave and you might end up in a mud house, tending earth, or worse, tending farmhands."

"The night's too short for this, Ibi. Go on, to the pantry with you."

"Why?" she asked.

"Just go, quickly, before the two expel themselves." Etelka was now grinning uncontrollably. "Meet under the foyer couch in two hundred steady breaths."

As morning approached, it became harder to find interesting activities to watch. Most everyone had gone, or passed out. So Etelka took Ibi's arm in hers and pulled her close. "Walk as one?" she asked. Her plan was to tangle-run, dashing through the center of the mansion, past the grand stairs, down the long hallway, to the back passage that led to the servant's wing. It would be daring fate, as a beating was sure if they were caught. They linked limbs, wrapping them together like twisted wire, their legs moving as if bound in a three-legged race, their faces smooched together, smiles touching. This was the only way they could move upright like regular people or the elite. Together, they were nearly solid.

"You look like two moons kissing." The voice was smooth, with a whistling quality, like a low-pitched pipe organ. "Come here, girls. You need to whisper for me."

Ibi pulled Etelka toward the man, who was sprawled across the sitting room sofa, golden-threaded cloth cascading about him, the robe parted slightly to show spindly legs. He was opaque and puffy, a warning sign to Etelka, who knew more about the dangers of High-Ones than young Ibi.

"He's too drained from accelerators. Leave him," Etelka warned.

"But he's nice looking for a High-One. I like his eyes, so yellow, his skin, so smooth."

"Come, girls." The man's eyes were so dilated his pupils resembled the small dollops of caviar that accented the sour-cream-smothered ostrich eggs. "Show me what you can do. If I like how you breathe, maybe, just maybe, I'll take you both home with me. Our house is four times the size of this one, and it overlooks the Catalyst Gardens. Look out our windows and you will see the monument honoring where the settlement-orb touched the ground and seeded the world. The cloisters are also visible from our balconies. Clerics work directly for our house, harnessing the powers of the garden as we command. You girls would like to visit such a place, wouldn't you?"

"Your house must be very powerful. Are you a landowner or an industrialist?" Ibi pointed her toes, lifting her leg, untwisting from Etelka. "You didn't bring your own girls?"

"Alas, the wings beneath this robe are large enough for me to fly, but not enough to carry my sweet whisperers with me. But don't you worry. My carriage will soon arrive."

"Leave us be." Etelka tightened her grip on Ibi's hand. "We don't need you. My father comes for me tomorrow, and this girl is to become the new whisperer for this house. Attempt to drain either of us without our Mistress' permission and you'll find yourself in much trouble."

"You don't scare me, servant," he huffed.

Ibi leaned over and whispered, "Let go," in Etelka's

ear, sending a warm tingle through the older girl's nervous system. Relaxed by Ibi's breath, Etelka lost her grip. Ibi pulled her hand free, unraveling their arms. Etelka's legs went wobbly. The two parted, falling to the floor in opposite directions.

The High-One moaned approvingly, leaning forward, his long legs parting, his arms encompassing small Ibi as she slithered into his embrace. With a contortion of possessiveness, his thin fingers pulled open the embroidered collar of his robe, revealing a slender neck.

Etelka wished her teeth were still strong enough to bite.

"Whisper, my child," he said. "Show me you are worthy."

Ibi smiled at Etelka, looking as if she were the one about to receive pleasure.

"I can't believe you, Ibi! The Mistress is going to be so angry if you give away too much."

Ibi leaned toward the High-One, puckering her lips, blowing her sweet life into him. There was a warm, golden glow on his skin, radiating out, dispersing.

"Warmth, like a summer's bonfire," he said, closing his eyes with a smile.

Etelka couldn't watch. Ibi was such a showoff. Knowing her, she'd let herself go blue, limp, a puddle on the floor, expecting Etelka to carry her back to their room. Not this time. No. It was time for Ibi to deal with the consequences of her actions alone. After all, Etelka would soon be gone, and no longer there to protect her. Ibi needed to learn her own lessons now.

"Suit yourself," Etelka said. "I hope you both end up in stockades on display in the village square. I'm going to tend my garden. I'll wait for you there, Ibi." She pulled herself up, resting her palms on the wall to steady herself, then hand over hand she moved quickly out of the sitting room.

Once in the hallway, Etelka heard a woman humming an old country folk tune nearby. It was accompanied by the clinking of glass. The whisper-girl followed the sound to the dining room, where she spotted the new kitchen maid. The old woman always wore her ash-gray hair in a bun, and seemed to carry an eternal smirk. She was clearing a table of toppled wine glasses, abandoned plates, and half-filled bowls of herbal potions. Her hand moved some items into a bin, and others, carefully inspected first, into the large pockets of her dress. The woman turned as Etelka approached, as if she had the senses of a bloodhound.

"Such a humid night," Etelka said.

"Yes. Stuffy." The old woman grinned, opening a window just a crack. She winked at Etelka, then returned to her tasks.

Etelka circled the old woman, breathing a gentle thank you toward her ankles. She then slipped outside through the window into a stony yard lit by flickering torches. She squeezed through a narrow gap in the far fence, sliding into a dense thicket. The dirt was cold and damp, the bushes thorny. It quickly became pitch black within the overgrowth, but a tiny sliver of luminescence guided her.

At eye level was a closed orchid. She had planted and coaxed it into budding a few days earlier. The stem was long and slender. Leaves unblemished. The sliver of light emanated from the orchid's bud, still wrapped in green as if cupped by two hands. This orchid had been sung to in tones she had practiced and refined, vibrations and frequencies that coaxed the finest beauty of this species: a mutation of Cattleya Labiata Alba—the white goddess.

Etelka whispered upon the orchid a soft melody that blended with night sounds: a twitter of tree crickets, the singsong of the long-billed pecking-moles, the trill of the spider-frogs. Rolling over on her back, the soft, sensitive bone of her head cradled in earth, Etelka watched as the orchid opened. Pristine whiteness. Petals uncurling to reveal themselves, like an albino butterfly unraveling wings. Pistils quivered within the trumpeting cup as it swelled and opened. The orchid began to glow intensely, like the early evening moonset of Asiona, the whitest of the six moons. Dozens of orchids slowly opened around her, casting light within the thicket in dancing patterns. Each was a perfect expression of Etelka's well-honed talent.

Tomorrow, she thought, *tomorrow I will present these to father. He will see how beautiful they are, that we can sell them, that I have value beyond my ability to whisper for High-Ones*. Finally, her family would rise up to take their place among the elite, with their own house, giving only what they wished to offer.

The thicket rustled. Etelka awoke, the soft tongue of an orchid licking her cheek.

"Ete, come out. I know you're in there." Ibi's voice was weak, distant.

Etelka began to crawl, but something held her. She was tangled in vines, sharp thorns pulling into soft, pale flesh as she struggled. Her humming to the orchids had apparently triggered the vines to grow.

"Etelka!" It was the Mistress, her voice a cracking whip.

"Hold on," Etelka shouted. A row of prized orchids hung over her like laughing children.

"Rip out these weeds," the Mistress ordered.

There was a sound of metal snipping wood. The entire thicket began to shake. Leaves and branches fell. Etelka could see two groundskeepers working their way toward her. They were the brightly dressed men of the north, unchanged humans who came down during the summer months to work the gardens of the High-Ones. Etelka had tried to talk with them, fully intending to learn their language, but they always shied away from her, bowing their heads, mumbling to themselves.

"I'll be right out. I'm caught. Need to get free." The thorns stabbed Etelka as she tried to pull herself free, but she realized if they were just a little longer the thorns would be past her flesh. She began to hum. The vines twitched. Thorns crept higher in a spiraling motion. Some scratched her, but it was a small price to pay to free herself quickly. "I'm nearly out."

The groundskeepers were close now, tossing twisted wood behind them as they shredded the protective shield of her secret garden. She kicked her legs free. Only one arm was still caught. A dirt encrusted boot came down, crushing a flower near her face.

"Stop!" Etelka commanded.

When the closest groundskeeper saw Etelka at his feet, he halted. Turning to the other man, he said something Etelka didn't understand. She assumed it was something like, "It's the ugly girl. She might be contagious. We should run," or maybe, "Watch out, the witch might cast a spell on us." All Etelka knew was that they quickly backed away, their hands raised, palms out, covering their eyes.

"There you are, girl. Come here." The Mistress bent, silken blonde hair hanging nearly to the ground. She reached in with long limbs to grab the whisper-girl's ankles. The Mistress didn't seem to mind that her golden silk robe was brushing the ground and gathering brown leaves and twigs. She pulled Etelka over roots, brush, rustling musty dried leaves. A remaining thorn tore through the flesh of Etelka's left arm, leaving a deep gash. It didn't bleed, as her veins had long ago receded, but it still hurt, and would certainly leave a scar even after she whispered it to close.

The Mistress lifted Etelka easily into the air, shaking her. "You had me frightened. I thought you had been stolen." The High-One's skin was not glowing at all this morning. She was nearly as opaque as the groundskeepers. Her normally sharp features were soft, showing wrinkles, and age. Etelka wondered what she had been up to at the party, as it must have all taken place behind closed doors.

"I assume you had a pleasant evening, Mistress?" Etelka asked.

"Shut up, you. How could you leave the new girl unattended? Look what happened. Someone stole a week's worth of vitality."

Etelka saw Ibi in a wheelbarrow. Her head sat awkwardly in the pooled remains of her body, which lay coiled like a snake.

"The dogs," Ibi said weakly. "She was going to call out the dogs. I had to tell her where you were."

The Mistress set Etelka against the wheelbarrow. "Sorry, Mistress," Etelka said, bowing her head, not out of deference, but so she could glare at Ibi unseen.

"What are those?" The Mistress shoved a groundskeeper toward the thicket. "Fleurir," she said, pointing toward the orchids. She made a scissor motion with her fingers.

"No," Etelka said. "Don't cut them!"

"Can't I host a party without everyone stealing from me?"

"The bulbs were wild, not stolen."

"Not the bulbs, your breath, it's your breath that belongs to me." The Mistress' hand hit hard. Etelka's head snapped to her shoulder, nerves pulling, sending a jolt down half her body. She twisted, like cloth being wrung, as she collapsed.

"They're just flowers. Didn't take much exertion," Etelka lied.

"Quiet, girl." The Mistress looked to the second groundskeeper. "Intérieur." The man hesitated, then obediently lifted Etelka and placed her in the wheelbarrow. He kept his eyes high so as not to look upon the two malformed bodies as he walked them along the fence toward the main gate of the white stone mansion.

"To my room, Etelka," the Mistress ordered. "Wait for me there."

Etelka let her exhalation touch Ibi's skin. "You look terrible," she whispered.

"He promised to take me with him," Ibi replied.

"And what happened? I warn you, but you never listen."

"He said I was beautiful. I thought . . ."

"What do I keep telling you about High-Ones?" Etelka asked.

"Never trust them. Just bide my time until I am free."

"Will you ever learn that lesson?" Etelka asked.

Ibi didn't say anything.

Etelka waited in the topmost room of the mansion's one circular turret. Windows were open on all sides, lacy white curtains billowing. She sat on a small stool by the door, facing the grand four-poster bed at the center of the room. The mahogany was carved with swirls, flowers and birds. Rose-colored sheets looked silky, the pillows soft, and she always wondered how it would feel to climb in, but she never dared. An aroma of lilacs filled the space, sweet and delicate. They reminded her of the eventful day a year ago when three whisper-girls from the plantations had arrived. They had been hired to grow and shape the lilac trees so they would surround the third-floor turret like lavender clouds. So much life had been blown into the roots that week that the flowers never withered. Only the red-haired girl, the shy one called Slonka, would share the plant-coaxing technique. Etelka had bribed her with a square of chocolate stolen from the kitchen. It had been well worth the beating.

The Mistress entered, moving swiftly to the closet, removed her blonde wig, placing it on the carved wooden wig-head inside. The smooth featurelessness of the wig-head made Etelka wonder how Ibi was doing. When angry, the Mistress had been known to deposit a wasted whisper-girl in a metal box, leaving her in the dark on a high closet shelf for days.

The Mistress removed her robe and lay face down

upon the silky rose sheets, her small wings just hanging over the edge. "Use the cone," she said, parting her arms and legs slightly to give Etelka easy reach to as much skin as possible. "Full body. No cheating."

Etelka lifted the whispering cone from the floor, glad to be using it, for the wide end covered her face, directing her breath down the small spout. It dulled the sound of her humming, making it sound like she was in a tight hiding place, cozy and alone.

She started at her Mistress' feet, letting her breath out softly. Humming. Vibrating air. When Etelka first arrived as a young girl, this woman had been nothing but ordinary: short, plain, almost pleasant. Not anymore, especially the pleasantness. Etelka wondered if the Mistress resented her dependence on whisper-girls, or maybe she simply resented the fact that Etelka knew how ordinary a woman she once was. Etelka decreased her breath. She was already tired, weak, wounded. She didn't want to end the night like Ibi. She let out a gentle breath, moving up the woman's long and delicate legs. She reached the thighs, breathing just a touch. Etelka would save her reserves for areas the Mistress would notice most: shoulders, breasts, wings, face. At the lower back she let her tongue twitter. Sometimes it put the Mistress to sleep. The woman moaned. Etelka thought about the hug she would receive from her father that evening. She would stand in the hallway holding the wall, then quickly push herself off, running into the room, allowing herself to fall forward into his arms. He would not want to let her go. She thought about the secret talk they would have, telling him about the orchids, about her plan to start a dynasty.

"You move too quickly," the Mistress said. "Start again. Slower this time."

"Yes, ma'am." Etelka felt her own legs growing weaker, and had to lean against the mattress. This wasn't good. She shouldn't have stayed up all night with Ibi. She should have slept, saved her energy for today, for her father.

"Don't be pitiful, child. You can do better than that."

Etelka felt some strength go out of her arms, and her fingers grew numb. Today had been Ibi's day to rejuvenate the Mistress. Etelka wanted to scream, to thrash out, but she couldn't. She had to stay in control. Keep the breath in. Gentle. Only so much.

"Stop pretending you're timid. I'm on to you, girl. Growing those flowers in secret like that. What were you planning with your father? To start a plantation? Who do you think you are? You're a whisper-girl. Remember that. Whisper-girls must know their place."

Etelka heard the woman rustling, then felt the slap across the top of her head. She knew that the reunion with her father would not be as she had imagined, but this didn't bother her. She decided the weaker the Mistress made her, the more guilt her father would feel. Pity would work in her favor. So, Etelka didn't hold back. Instead, she allowed herself to give much more than she should.

When her father had last visited seven years earlier, the Mistress had prepared a feast. Not the raw veggies and nuts the High-Ones ate, but roasted meats and breads and stews. Etelka smelled such hearty aromas again, and she knew her father had arrived.

She remembered him energetic, lively, newly excited

by the prospect of no longer needing sleep. He had just returned from his own transformation ritual. Clerics had laid encoding-herbs upon his tongue, injecting cell-modifying nematodes into his bloodstream. For a month he had traveled with a mentor who taught him how to survive as an Emberman, as Embermen burned energy like roaring fires, often needing many whisperers to keep them fueled, or heavy feasts in their stead. Parents often told children that if they misbehaved the Embermen would come and devour them. Etelka knew better. Her father was a good man. Hungry, but good.

Moving was difficult. Her muscles were flimsy, elbows and knees loose. Breathing seemed to go no deeper than her throat. She tried to lift herself against the wall. Failing, she crawled arm over arm, vertigo with each agonizing movement. At the stairs, she rolled. Thump. Slowly pulling herself over steps. Thump. Each movement gave her the impression that she was slowly evaporating out of existence. Thump.

At the bottom, she rested.

The kitchen maid nearly tripped over Etelka, dishes rattling on a tray. She paused, tsk-tsked with her tongue, and shimmied her foot under the girl. The old woman scooted the rag doll along the floor with a step and a slide, depositing Etelka near the dining room, rolling her off to the side, away from the well-worn path from the kitchen.

"Soup," the woman said, moving into the dining room.

Etelka could see her father now. He was taller and thinner than she remembered. His profile showed a distinctive long pointed nose, a jutting chin, eyes that were a bit too dark and shallow. His cheekbones looked hard, his skin ashen. Weariness from his travels, she told herself. His hair was now twiggy and white. *He is an older man now, is he not?* Fingers like thin spider legs manipulated dining utensils. She wondered how bony he might be beneath his long draping black trader's coat. He sat at the hefty oak table, gorging on an entire roast prickly boar, while the Mistress watched. Etelka's glowing white orchids were in a water-filled vase at the center of the table, intricate, bright, mesmerizing.

"Hello, Father," Etelka whispered, hoping some of her breath found its way across the room to him.

He glanced her way, his eyes locking on her for a moment before awkwardly returning to the food on his fork. "This is an excellent roast. I don't often remember to eat. Thank goodness for the whisper-girl you sent me. She is very good. Dedicated. A lifesaver." He glanced once again at Etelka, but only out of the corner of his eyes. "Unlike some girls we know. So, the new whisper-girl you want me to fetch is in the Eastern territories?"

"Yes. They train them differently there," the Mistress said. "Obedient. Unlikely to steal. Those girls wouldn't allow their young charges to be abused, emptied by strangers. They're not lazy or selfish. It so saddens me that our business arrangement didn't work out as planned, Sandor. Unruly, sickly girls are so expensive to maintain. Your own whisper-girl has also added a financial burden."

"None of it is your fault," he said. "It is my fault for being weak."

"Don't worry. I'll still add the cost of this meal to your account," she replied. "You won't have to pay me out of pocket."

He paused, then continued chewing. "Yes, that would be appropriate, thank you. I will leave for the Eastern territories tonight. As soon as I have a chat with my daughter."

"Very well. Don't keep her long. I need her rested. The new girl is useless. So poorly trained. Thank goodness the guild just agreed to allow me to keep multiple whisper-girls. Otherwise, I don't know how this house would survive."

"What are you two talking about?" Etelka asked. "We're leaving tonight, right, father? That was the agreement."

"Quiet, Etelka!" her father snapped.

"Good night, Sandor. We will review our terms in three years. By then I hope you will have finally worked off your debt. Even after that, you will always be welcome to stay in my employ."

"A gracious offer." Her father stood and bowed.

The Mistress rose, small wings fluttering as she moved down the hallway.

Etelka's father set his fork down. He turned to her and slowly shook his head disapprovingly. Kneeling, he gingerly lifted her. "How could you do this? I thought you were a good girl."

"What's going on? You're taking me with you tonight, right? Look, Father, I have a business plan. Orchids. We can sell them. Soon we will have our own house again."

"Etelka, don't speak like that," her father commanded. "Someone may hear."

"On the table, look, aren't they beautiful?" She had to pause to catch her breath. "Do you know how much High-Ones pay for such flowers during the celebration of rebirth?"

"Foolishness," he said.

"The Mistress spends three times our debt on ritual flowers alone. I've been growing them outside the fence. We can collect the bulbs before we leave."

"Do you know how much trouble you've been? Selling that young girl to men from other houses, wasting your breath on plants, disobeying your Mistress. What's wrong with you?"

"She lies."

"Enough of that," he shouted. "You've already admitted guilt, scheming as you are."

"I can tend the gardens myself, while you're on business. I know the local High-Ones—who compete, who waste their riches, whom we need to befriend. Take me with you tonight. The debt will be paid off after the first festival."

The argument that ensued was short, but harsh. A servant never plotted against her house. Employees stayed loyal. It was as it should be. As it would remain. He would stay honorable. They would work off their burden. His hands caressed her momentarily, but his eyes did not stay on hers for long.

"I promised your mother I would take care of you. To do that, we must first work off the debt incurred by her illness. I must go. Too much to do." He kissed the air near her cheek, hands shaking as he placed her back on the floor. "Besides, how could I care for such a frail girl? I am not worthy to care for anyone." He grabbed a leg of the beast from the table, and fled the house.

When Etelka heard footfalls, she wiped the tears from her eyes and grew stern. The gray-haired kitchen maid entered and began to clear the table.

"Take me to the whisper-girl's room," she ordered.

"Oh, yes my princess. Whatever you say." The woman lifted Etelka in her arms. "You know, can't have all that food going to waste. Better that a nice young girl like you should enjoy it rather than feeding it to dogs. Would the kind lady appreciate such a gift?"

Etelka didn't want her breath to touch the old woman until she was safe in her room, so she nodded her agreement.

The woman hummed as she packed a large napkin full of food. She cradled both her bundles tight to her bosom, one in each hand, as she made her way to the servant's wing.

Eat, you stupid girl." Etelka laid the bundle of food on the floor near Ibi's mattress, which rested in the corner of the closet-sized room. Ibi weakly rolled over to look.

"I'll take the blame for stealing the food. I don't care if she beats me. I don't care if she feeds me to the dogs." Etelka threw a bone at the wall. It bounced and rattled to a stop near the door. She was already feeling energy return.

"It's my fault." Ibi began to weep. "You hate me now, don't you?"

"Keep your breath in. You'll make yourself worse."

"I feel so empty," Ibi said.

"Then eat." Etelka crawled to the liquid-girl, lifting Ibi's head as if trying not to let bread dough fall, resting it in her lap. She ripped a bit of meat and put it in Ibi's mouth. The kitchen maid had sprinkled the food with tenderizing enzymes to make it easy for a whisper-girl to digest, so it had a mushy texture.

Ibi spat it out. "What is that?"

"Meat. Like dogs chew. Busy, growling, obedient dogs."

"That's horrible. Give me something else."

Etelka fed her potato.

"You're right," Ibi said, swallowing. "They can't be trusted."

"No one can," Etelka replied.

"Let me try the meat again." Ibi smiled. "I don't like it, but I want to recover tonight, so I can stop being a burden to you."

"You'll always be a burden," Etelka said.

"What will you do now?" Ibi was intent, as if afraid of the answer.

Etelka pondered the possibilities. Could two whisper-girls survive alone in the world? Would anyone take them in? What might they be forced to do? Would her father care? Would the dogs chase them down, devour them? Did it matter? So what if she was ripped to shreds. That's how she felt. She fed Ibi another bit of meat. The girl ate weakly. Poor young one. Her parents had worked the earth, growing vegetables for the High-Ones to eat. But two seasons ago it had been so dry. People were forced to sell whatever they could to survive. Will you buy our little girl? All we want is food. Bye, bye, little one. Off to your new owner. When the Mistress was escorting her new prize inside, Etelka told Ibi's parents she'd take care of their girl. Teach her. Make her a good whisperer. *Don't worry, this house is a wonderful place to live.* They seemed like the right things to say, almost as if they weren't lies.

"Maybe you can catch up with your father," Ibi said.

"As you once said, why would anyone want to leave such a grand house?" Etelka began to uncoil Ibi's body so she would not be uncomfortable when density returned. Ibi would grow stronger overnight, thanks to the heavy meal and rest. In a few days she would crawl again. In a week this would all be behind them. That's what Etelka kept telling herself. Everything just took time. Three years. Not so long. She'd done that twice before. At least now she had someone to talk with. Whisper-girls had to stick together.

"You know what we'll do, Ibi? We'll leave. You and me. As soon as we're rested and healed. There's a secret village where all the whisper-girls flee. Where they do nothing but whisper to each other all night, and dance, and sing beauty into the hills. That's why they can't be found. They are surrounded by lush jungles voiced from their mouths and thus no one can reach them."

"That's a lot of wasted breath on a story even a child wouldn't believe, but thanks just the same." Ibi swallowed the meat she was chewing. "Is this what the dogs would taste if they caught us?"

Etelka laughed. "Not unless we cook ourselves first."

There was a knock on the door. It was the five-minute warning for the Mistress' rejuvenation session. Etelka came half-awake, remembering snippets of dreams. Sailing through the sky on a steady wind. Snakes that sang as they slithered underground. A fire in her belly that grew to engulf her. A distant figure saying "goodbye," over and over, swept away, leaving behind only a single white orchid. She stretched, feeling oddly energetic. Warm. Refreshed.

"Ibi, wake up." She rolled off the mattress, finding her limbs more solid than she expected. It was easy to kneel. Slowly, carefully, she stood. While slightly off balance from lack of practice, she needed no support other than her own two legs.

Ibi's mattress was empty. The light over the transom was dim, so Etelka opened the door to let more sunlight in from the hall. Looking back at her own mattress, she saw a thin pile—skin and bones, an empty shell. She fell to the floor and scooped Ibi up in her hands, but there was so little to hold, like paper-thin cloth. No heart beat within.

"No, no, no. What have you done?" No wonder she felt so strong. Etelka pressed Ibi's body out, unraveling it, trying to hold the thin remains of her depleted bones in place within the sack of skin. She brought her lips to Ibi's chest and let out a soft breath. Nothing. No glow. No absorption. She closed her own eyes, rocking softly. "Please, please come back." She twittered her tongue, making the call of the tree crickets, exhaling her every wish, letting her lungs empty until she shook from the effort. She collapsed atop the young girl's remains, crying. "Why? What's wrong with you, girl?" She realized she had created a small tear. She panicked. With her fingers she tried to neaten Ibi, spreading her out, sliding her back together, wet fingers as glue.

Footfalls echoed nearby. She pulled Ibi's shell onto the floor, lifted the mattress and slid it over the delicate remains, sliding them both against the wall. "Sorry, my Ibi. So sorry."

"The Mistress is ready for you." The servant's voice

was fading down the hall before the last word left her mouth.

Etelka was afraid to leave the closet. Not looking as she did. A whisper-girl was never solid, never whole. They would blame her somehow. She would have to find someone to breathe into, a way to weaken herself so as not to attract attention. But who? Or what? The garden. She could rest in its center, breathe out, growing the thicket around her. Just her. Alone with the orchids. Hiding. Caring for them. Nurturing.

"Find her!" The Mistress' voice was distant, probably from the tower where she impatiently waited for Etelka to arrive. They would soon come looking, asking about Ibi.

Etelka threw the door wide. Crisp sweet-smelling air struck her. Her lungs expanded and the rush of oxygen made her delirious. Sunlight touched her skin, awakening dormant sensations, reminding her what it feels like to be fully alive. Her legs ached to move. She ran to the window. There was her destination, her garden, just past the fence. Hacked. Destroyed. Breathing it alive would be like building a tomb from the breath of the dead. Poor Ibi.

She inhaled deeply, looking up to gaze upon Gelenti, the third moon rising, golden and sullen in the sky. It reminded her of a High-One. Bright. Above her. Glaring down. Soon that moon would vanish behind the horizon, only to return the next day, visible to all that look up. Why? Because of the sun. The sun that offered its light without hesitation, without judgment or obedience, unlike Etelka.

"A whisper-girl must run, is that what you thought, Ibi? A whisper-girl does her job, takes care of her

Mistress, right, my father? A whisper-girl stays in her place, obedient, like the sun which rises each day. No! That is wrong. It's the moon that needs the power of the sun to be seen. The sun is indifferent. It is not bound. Nothing makes the sun give of itself. I too will be like the sun."

A wind blew. Something sweet. Lilacs. They penetrated her, soaked into her every pore. Etelka took a few awkward strides, then jumped the short steps from the servant's wing into the master house, running the main hall, bounding up the grand stairs, to the top room of the tower. There, Etelka found her Mistress in bed, wrapped in silken rose sheets, waiting as if faking sleep, expecting a lover to surprise her. Windows were open all around, curtains billowing.

"I'm here, Mistress," Etelka pronounced as she entered the room.

The woman did not look up, but simply spread her limbs wider, flapping her small wings gently. "It's about time, you lazy girl. You should not test me. As you now know, I am not to be trifled with. Be good. Train the new girls. Breathe well for me. Only then will you have a chance to leave when your father returns."

"You never plan to let me go," Etelka said.

"You should be proud to serve here. Other girls would. My house is becoming stronger by the day. During the last party one of the highest of families granted me permission to feed from multiple whisper-girls in a single day. An honor only a few are granted. Your new job will be to train these girls in the art of growing my wings. Until I can fly. Once people see how high I have risen, I will be able to merge with another powerful house. Then you can train the girls to serve my mate as well. It took longer than I expected to schmooze the families, to blackmail those with power, but now it is finally done. Our house is victorious. When all of this has been completed, you can be on your way. Good riddance."

As the Mistress talked, Etelka ran to a window. She breathed deep the lilac scent. Her back itched at the shoulders, as if sprouting wings, but Etelka knew better. She was no High-One. It was just her mind playing tricks on her.

Leaning out the window, she brought her face close to the branches. The cascading purple and white flowers rustled. She breathed a coaxing breath. The branches twisted and twirled, lurching toward her, petals exploding into air. She clicked her tongue and puckered her lips, sucking in. She ducked as branches burst into the room.

"What's going on?" The Mistress sat up.

Etelka dashed to another window, repeating the ritual. Branches followed her into the room. Trap the Mistress, Etelka thought, then there will be plenty of time to run.

"What are you doing?" The Mistress clutched silk tight around herself.

Etelka whistled and cooed, puffing her cheeks, and letting whispers out through her teeth. The branches continued to rush in from all the windows now. As she moved by the bed, she grabbed a pillow. Rustling leaves followed her toward the door. She felt dizzy from the effort and stumbled back against the wall. The branches nearly crushed her there. She dropped to the floor.

"Let me out of here!" the Mistress cried.

STEPHEN KNOX

Etelka clutched the soft pillow, feeling the cool silk on her skin. She looked into the wild growing branches, purple and white snowing down inside.

"You won't live to see tomorrow, you ungrateful wretch," the Mistress screamed. "Other girls can replace you. Your father, he will pay. Do you want that?" Etelka heard only heavy breathing for a moment. "Come on. This is no way for you to behave. Let me out. They're scratching me."

Etelka crawled out from under the gyrating mass of twigs and dashed for the stairs. Down she ran, feeling giddy, laughing. She burst out into morning sun. How much life young Ibi must have carried that even after such an expression Etelka could still have so grand a feeling remaining within. She looked to the tower and laughed. Branches continued to grow through the windows, spreading, twisting, burrowing.

The gray-haired maid appeared at a doorway of the house. The woman seemed pleased to see Etelka standing strong. She stepped out and stood in the rain of lilac petals, her hands in the air as they drifted over her. It was a gleeful moment.

The men from the north came around the corner, dressed in their bright clothing. One stopped and pointed at Etelka. The other put his hands together, touching his fingers to his nose, spreading his hands so his palms faced her.

There was a thunderous sound as a wall of the tower crashed inward, stones raining to the ground, kicking up dirt. The old woman jumped and ran toward the main gate. The men backed away, their hands flying about, speaking indecipherable words. One ran off, only to return with two lit torches.

More stone crumbled, the tower roof caving in. Etelka felt a cold shiver. For a moment her chest felt like she had been drained. Her heart began to pound. She felt dizzy. Her eyes locked on the mansion, the growing branches, the swirl of flowers drifting over the grounds. She took a few steps backwards, walking into the fence. Her first instinct was to follow the old woman down the road. To run. She felt the silken pillow clutched in her hands. No. Not yet. Not empty handed.

She dashed toward her garden, leaping, climbing over the fence. Squatting, she dug her hands into the ground, pulling up bulbs. She removed the soft filling from the pillow, leaving only the case, and filled it with the hearts of her orchids. She gathered all she could.

There was another crash. She didn't turn to look. She focused on the ground and ran, passing trees, jumping over fallen logs, listening to the loud crunch of leaves and twigs, feeling the breeze on her skin. Only when she came upon a road did she pause. Looking to the sky behind her, she saw heavy black smoke rising up in the distance.

"No one could tell you are a whisper-girl now." The kitchen maid was grinning, lumbering her way. "You look so normal. Oh, was that impolite? What is normal, after all?" She stumbled, her right leg dipping, a cringe on her face. "Could you help an old woman? I won't ask for much, just company, and a shoulder to lean on. I think I twisted an ankle."

Etelka took the woman's hand. It felt warm, comforting. You can't trust anyone, she knew, but a whisper-girl couldn't risk being alone. Etelka directed her breath to the woods as she talked. "I have a proposition for you. That is, if you think you can get me into a particular High-One's house."

The woman rolled her eyes, "If you only knew how many houses I've worked for. Getting in is so easy. Making it worth your while, and still getting out, is the tricky part. So, what do you have in mind?"

"I had a feeling you might be good at this. There's a High-One I know who drained a whisper-girl belonging to another house. He knows his guilt. Terrible things happened to that girl's house just after it happened. It might look bad for him. I suspect he might be convinced to fund a venture to keep it quiet."

"Blackmail? Interesting. Sounds risky, but maybe you can convince me."

Etelka leaned over and softly whispered the rest of her plan into the old woman's ear, speaking just enough that the woman no longer limped, but not more. No. She was going to save the rest for herself.

The Year in the Contests

Both Contests have grown considerably in stature and impact within the science fiction and fantasy genres, as anyone who has won either contest will tell you. But an interesting thing has started to happen. As the Contests become more established as the premiere launching point for science fiction and fantasy careers, where we once saw only the published winners proclaiming their newly earned status, we now also find finalists proudly proclaiming their achievement in their bios as one of their notable accomplishments.

So, yes, the Contests are continuing to accomplish in ever new ways what Mr. Hubbard set out to do over two decades ago, when *Writers of the Future Volume I* was published and these words were printed in his introduction:

> A culture is as rich and capable of surviving as it has imaginative artists. The artist is looked upon to start things. The artist injects the spirit of life into a culture. And through his creative endeavors, the writer works continually to give tomorrow a new form.

In these modern times, there are many communication lines for works of art. Because a few works of art can be shown so easily to so many, there may even be fewer artists. The competition is very keen and even dagger sharp.

It is with this in mind that I initiated a means for new and budding writers to have a chance for their creative efforts to be seen and acknowledged.

As has been true since the inception of these Contests, our judges remain the very top names in their fields. Those names can all be found on the back of this book, and they are each and every one thanked for their continued support and contribution. This year we are very proud to announce Cliff Nielson as our most recent Illustrators of the Future Contest judge. He has created over 1,100 images for such high-profile series as the *X-Files, Star Wars, The Crow, A Wrinkle in Time, The Chronicles of Narnia, Star Trek* and Philip Pullman's *His Dark Materials.*

For the year 2007, L. Ron Hubbard's Writers of the Future Contest winners are:

FIRST QUARTER

1. *Patrick Lundrigan*
HANGAR QUEEN

2. *Laura Bradley Rede*
EPIPHANY

3. *David Parish-Whittaker*
A WAR BIRD IN THE BELLY OF THE MOUSE

SECOND QUARTER

1. *J. D. EveryHope*
CIRCUIT

2. *Sarah L. Edwards*
SIMULACRUM'S CHILDREN

3. *Paula R. Stiles*
SNAKES AND LADDERS

THIRD QUARTER

1. *Ian McHugh*
BITTER DREAMS

2. *Al Bogdan*
THE GIRL WHO WHISPERED BEAUTY

3. *Kim A. Gillett*
THE BIRD READER'S GRANDDAUGHTER

FOURTH QUARTER

1. *Erin Cashier*
CRUCIGER

2. *Sonia Helbig*
CROWN OF THORNS

3. *J. Kathleen Cheney*
TAKING A MILE

L. Ron Hubbard's Illustrators of the Future winners for 2007 are:

FIRST QUARTER

Robert J. Hall Jr.
Stephen R. Stanley
Alexandra D. Szweryn

SECOND QUARTER

Robert Castillo
Brittany J. Jackson
Stephen Knox

THIRD QUARTER

James Galindo
Sean Kibbe
Ilya Shkipin

FOURTH QUARTER

Gustavo Bollinger
Kyle Phillips
William Ruhlig

Our heartiest congratulations to them all! May we see much more of their work in the future.

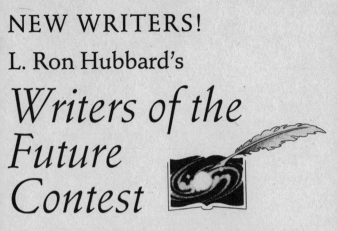

WRITERS' CONTEST RULES

1. No entry fee is required, and all rights in the story remain the property of the author. All types of science fiction, fantasy and dark fantasy are welcome.

2. By submitting to the Contest, the entrant agrees to abide by all Contest rules.

3. All entries must be original works, in English. Plagiarism, which includes the use of third-party poetry, song lyrics, characters or another person's universe, without written permission, will result in disqualification. Excessive violence or sex, determined by the judges, will result in disqualification. Entries may not have been previously published in professional media.

4. To be eligible, entries must be works of prose, up to 17,000 words in length. We regret we cannot consider poetry, or works intended for children.

5. The Contest is open only to those who have not professionally published a novel or short novel, or more than one novelette, or more than three short stories, in any medium. Professional publication is deemed to be payment, and at least 5,000 copies, or 5,000 hits.

6. Entries must be typewritten or a computer printout in black ink on white paper, double spaced, with numbered pages. All other formats will be disqualified. Each entry must have a cover page with the title of the work, the author's name, address, telephone number, e-mail address and an approximate word count. Every subsequent page must carry the title and a page number, but the author's name must be deleted to facilitate fair judging.

7. Manuscripts will be returned after judging only if the author has provided return postage on a self-addressed envelope. If the author does not wish return of the manuscript, a business-size self-addressed, stamped envelope (or valid e-mail address) must be included with the entry in order to receive judging results.

8. We accept only entries for which no delivery signature is required by us to receive them.

9. There shall be three cash prizes in each quarter: a First Prize of $1,000, a Second Prize of $750, and a Third Prize of $500, in US dollars. In addition, at the end of the year the four First Place winners will have their entries rejudged, and a Grand Prize winner shall be determined and receive an additional $5,000. All winners will also receive trophies or certificates.

10. The Contest has four quarters, beginning on October 1, January 1, April 1 and July 1. The year will end on September 30. To be eligible for judging in its quarter, an entry must be postmarked no later than midnight on the last day of the quarter. Late entries will be included in the following quarter and the Contest Administration will so notify the entrant.

11. Each entrant may submit only one manuscript per quarter. Winners are ineligible to make further entries in the Contest.

12. All entries for each quarter are final. No revisions are accepted.

13. Entries will be judged by professional authors. The decisions of the judges are entirely their own, and are final.

14. Winners in each quarter will be individually notified of the results by mail.

15. This Contest is void where prohibited by law.

ILLUSTRATORS' CONTEST RULES

1. The Contest is open to entrants from all nations. (However, entrants should provide themselves with some means for written communication in English.) All themes of science fiction and fantasy illustrations are welcome: every entry is judged on its own merits only. No entry fee is required and all rights in the entry remain the property of the artist.

2. By submitting to the Contest, the entrant agrees to abide by all Contest rules.

3. The Contest is open to new and amateur artists who have not been professionally published and paid for more than three black-and-white story illustrations, or more than one process-color painting, in media distributed broadly to the general public. The ultimate eligibility criteria, however, is defined with the word "amateur"—in other words, the artist has not been paid for his artwork. If you are not sure of your eligibility, please write a letter to the Contest Administration with details regarding your publication history. Include a self-addressed and stamped envelope for the reply. You may also send your questions to the Contest Administration via e-mail.

4. Each entrant may submit only one set of illustrations in each Contest quarter. The entry must be original to the entrant and previously unpublished. Plagiarism, infringement of the rights of others, or other violations of the Contest rules will result in disqualification. Winners in previous quarters are not eligible to make further entries.

5. The entry shall consist of three illustrations done by the entrant in a color or black-and-white medium created from the artist's imagination. Use of gray scale in illustrations and mixed

media, computer generated art, the use of photography in the illustrations, are accepted. Each illustration must represent a subject different from the other two.

6. ENTRIES SHOULD NOT BE THE ORIGINAL DRAWINGS, but should be color or black-and-white reproductions of the originals of a quality satisfactory to the entrant. Entries must be submitted unfolded and flat, in an envelope no larger than 9 inches by 12 inches.

7. All entries must be accompanied by a self-addressed return envelope of the appropriate size, with the correct US postage affixed. (Non-US entrants should enclose international postage reply coupons.) If the entrant does not want the reproductions returned, the entry should be clearly marked DISPOSABLE COPIES: DO NOT RETURN. A business-size self-addressed envelope with correct postage (or valid e-mail address) should be included so that the judging results may be returned to the entrant.

We only accept an entry for which no delivery signature is required by us to receive the entry.

8. To facilitate anonymous judging, each of the three photocopies must be accompanied by a removable cover sheet bearing the artist's name, address, telephone number, e-mail address, and an identifying title for that work. The reproduction of the work should carry the same identifying title on the front of the illustration and the artist's signature should be deleted. The Contest Administration will remove and file the cover sheets, and forward only the anonymous entry to the judges.

9. There will be three co-winners in each quarter. Each winner will receive an outright cash grant of US $500 and a trophy. Winners will also receive eligibility to compete for the annual Grand Prize of an additional cash grant of $5,000 together with the annual Grand Prize trophy.

10. For the annual Grand Prize Contest, the quarterly winners will be furnished with a specification sheet and a winning story from the Writers of the Future Contest to illustrate. In order to retain eligibility for the Grand Prize, each winner shall send to the Contest address his/her illustration of the assigned story within thirty (30) days of receipt of the story assignment.

The yearly Grand Prize winner shall be determined by the judges on the following basis only:

Each Grand Prize judge's personal opinion on the extent to which it makes the judge want to read the story it illustrates.

The Grand Prize winner shall be announced at the L. Ron Hubbard Awards Event held in the following year.

11. The Contest has four quarters, beginning on October 1, January 1, April 1 and July 1. The year will end on September 30. To be eligible for judging in its quarter, an entry must be postmarked no later than midnight on the last day of the quarter. Late entries will be included in the following quarter and the Contest Administration will so notify the entrant.

12. Entries will be judged by professional artists only. Each quarterly judging and the Grand Prize judging may have different panels of judges. The decisions of the judges are entirely their own and are final.

13. Winners in each quarter will be individually notified of the results by mail.

14. This Contest is void where prohibited by law.

Launch your career with the

WRITERS & ILLUSTRATORS OF THE FUTURE PACKAGE

The Writers & Illustrators of the Future Contests have launched the careers of over 500 new writers and illustrators of speculative fiction.

With this book package you receive 7 *Writers of the Future* Volumes for the price of 5 and you automatically qualify for FREE SHIPPING.

You will find essays on how to become a successful writer or illustrator from contest judges and professionals including: *Orson Scott Card, Robert Silverberg, Kevin J. Anderson, Ben Bova, Sean Williams, Tim Powers, Jack Williamson, A.C. Crispin, Stephen Hickman and Algis Budrys.*

These books contain the award-winning short stories for the last 7 years as selected by a distinguished panel of judges. Read them and find out for yourself how good you have to be to win the Writers of the Future Contest!

IF YOU PLACE YOUR ORDER RIGHT NOW YOU ALSO GET THE FOLLOWING 4 BONUS ITEMS:

- *A free magazine with a previously unpublished story by L. Ron Hubbard.*
- *An eBook with six powerful steps to follow to become a successful writer.*
- *An eBook with insider tips on the craft of writing and illustrating by Kevin J. Anderson and Vincent Di Fate.*
- *FREE shipping.*

ORDER NOW!

Get this package, a value of

$114.30, for only $39.95 US (CAN $44.95)

Call toll-free: 1-877-8GALAXY
or visit www.writersofthefuture.com
Mail in your order to: Galaxy Press • 7051 Hollywood Blvd., Suite 200, Hollywood, CA 90028

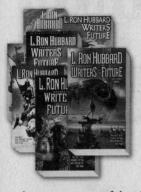